MAKE IT
OUT
ALIVE

Also by Allison Brennan

Beach Reads and Deadly Deeds

Quinn & Costa Thrillers

The Third to Die
Tell No Lies
The Wrong Victim
Seven Girls Gone
The Missing Witness
See How They Hide

Angelhart Investigations

You'll Never Find Me
Don't Say a Word

Regan Merritt Series

The Sorority Murder
Don't Open the Door

MAKE IT
OUT
ALIVE

ALLISON BRENNAN

HANOVER
SQUARE
PRESS

HANOVER
SQUARE
PRESS™

Recycling programs
for this product may
not exist in your area.

ISBN-13: 978-1-335-00141-2

Make It Out Alive

Hanover Square Press
22 Adelaide St. West, 41st Floor
Toronto, Ontario M5H 4E3, Canada
HanoverSqPress.com

HarperCollins Publishers
Macken House, 39/40 Mayor Street Upper,
Dublin 1, D01 C9W8, Ireland
www.HarperCollins.com

Printed in U.S.A.

This book marks my twentieth anniversary as a published author. I dedicate it to everyone who helped me get to this point:

To my first agent, Kim Whalen, who took me on as an unpublished author. To Linda Marrow at Ballantine, who bought my first book. To Charlotte Herscher, who helped make me a better storyteller. To Dana Isaacson, who helped make me a better writer.

To Dan Conaway at Writers House, who agreed to represent me fifteen years ago in the middle of turmoil and continues to guide my ship. To Kelley Ragland, who is truly an editor who edits in all the best ways. To Kathy Sagan, who loved Quinn & Costa as much as I do and helped me breathe life into the first book, and to April Osborn and Dina Davis, who are keeping this series going strong with their skillful editorial guidance.

To the publishers I've had, the marketing and publicity teams, the sales force, the cover artists, the ebook designers, the book printers, buyers, and sellers. To the book reviewers and bloggers and podcasters and librarians and booksellers who spread the word and help me find readers.

To my writing buddies who have encouraged me from the very beginning and are always there to listen when I need it, especially Toni Causey and J.T. Ellison. To Anna Stewart and Karin Tabke, who told me I would be published before I believed it myself. To my first critique group (Karin, Sharon, Edie, Amy, Jan, Michelle, Liz). To my very first reader, Trisha McKay. And to the first author who gave me a quote, Mariah Stewart.

To all my readers—I honestly would not be here with fifty-one published books and countless short stories to my name without you.

And to my family, who have given me the love, support, and space to write for the last twenty years. Especially to my mom, who always told me I could.

Never underestimate the power of jealousy and the power of envy to destroy.

—Oliver Stone

FRIDAY

FRIDAY

1

Matt Costa stood rigid in the cramped observation room of the Flagler County Sheriff's Department, the air thick with sweat and adrenaline. Beside him, District Attorney John Anson buzzed with barely contained triumph—nearly two hours in, and he was still riding high. Garrett Reid had walked straight into a felony: the attempted abduction of two undercover agents. No resistance, no fighting back. Just a quiet, eerie surrender, like a man who already knew the outcome.

Now, behind the glass, Reid sat pale and dazed under the harsh fluorescent lights, looking from Detective Bianca Fuentes to FBI Agent Michael Harris. His confusion had to be an act. Why didn't he ask for a lawyer from the beginning? Reid couldn't be this clueless. Yet all he had done for one hour, forty minutes was listen, answer simple questions, repeat that there was a misunderstanding, and shake his head in disbelief. Eventually, he would clam up. Eventually, he would ask to make a call.

Matt, though pleased Reid had been captured without anyone on his team injured, was not as excited about the arrest as the

DA. There was something scratching at the back of his mind, an itch that it had all happened too easily, too smoothly. They needed physical evidence or a confession to prove he was the murderer they'd been looking for; if they got the confession, they needed information to lead them to physical evidence. Until Matt had tangible proof in which to wrap up this case with an unimpeachable bow, he wouldn't be satisfied.

Reid checked all the boxes of Dr. Catherine Jones's profile. Single, white, male. He was thirty, right in the sweet spot of her twenty-five to forty age range. Above average IQ, and had worked at the resort where the newlyweds went missing, in a position that was below his skill set—Reid was a college graduate who worked in Maintenance at Sapphire Shoals. Attractive, fit, personable, lived alone. Check, check, check, and check.

Flagler County law enforcement had called the FBI for assistance shortly after the abduction of the third pair of newlyweds one month ago. At first, they treated the case as missing persons, but when the bodies of Mitch and Sheila Avila washed up on shore a week later, it became a double homicide—the fifth and sixth murders of what they now knew was a serial killer targeting honeymooning couples at the large, popular resort.

The idea for Matt and Kara to pose as newlyweds had been Catherine's—and it was a good one. Kara matched the profile of the three murdered women: in their thirties, blonde, petite. She and Catherine crafted a convincing backstory, similar enough to the victims to draw attention but not so exact as to raise suspicion. Kara slipped easily into the undercover role; Matt didn't. Every quiet moment felt like a countdown. He couldn't shake the feeling that someone was watching, waiting to strike. But he trusted his team.

Five days into their staged "honeymoon," Garrett Reid made his move. He drugged their breakfast. Knowing the victims had been drugged, Matt and Kara had tested each meal for ketamine—when this time the coffee and juice tested positive, they pretended to pass out. Reid crept into their cottage. As soon as he entered with a laundry cart—perfect for transporting two bodies—Matt's team swooped in and made the arrest.

In the interview room, Detective Fuentes, a seasoned detective who had been spearheading the investigation locally, had already gone through preliminary questions. Name, address, place of employment, a timeline of Reid's morning. Softball questions, almost friendly. She offered water and soda, tried to make him comfortable, but he maintained that look of confusion.

"I really don't understand why I'm here," Reid said, not for the first time.

"We arrested you for assault and kidnapping, do you understand the charges?"

"I understand *what* you think, but I don't understand *why* you think I did anything wrong," Reid said. "It's clearly a misunderstanding." He nodded, as if to emphasize his theory. "Just a misunderstanding."

Reid didn't look like a killer, but after nearly fifteen years in the Bureau, Matt had learned never to judge by appearances. Not every killer looked the part. Reid was attractive in an unremarkable way—dark, neatly cut hair; suntanned skin from working outdoors; clear blue eyes; a strong jawline. Fit but not imposing, he looked harmless.

Fuentes said, "At 9:15 this morning, you delivered room service to cottage 14, one of the private beachside suites at the Sapphire Shoals Resort and Spa, registered to Mathias and Kara Costa. Correct?"

"Yes, ma'am," Reid said. His demeanor remained polite and confused. That he wasn't agitated bothered Matt. He should be nervous by now.

"And you delivered the food through the main door, correct?"

"Yes, of course."

"And then, fifty minutes later, you entered the cottage from the private beachside entrance."

He hesitated, then nodded. "Yeah."

"You had a laundry cart with you."

"Uh-huh," he said.

"Why?"

"Why what?"

"Why did you enter the cottage with a laundry cart?"

He frowned, as if thinking. "I saw them, the Costas? I saw them on the floor. I thought they were hurt."

"Why didn't you call security? Or your manager?" Michael interjected. He played the part of the stern, disapproving cop. It wasn't an act.

"I wanted to confirm. You know, it was weird, and I was just walking by—"

"You were walking by with a laundry cart on the beach," Fuentes said.

"Not the beach—I was on the path," he said. "The cart was there, but the housekeeping staff wasn't around, and it was a hazard, so I was taking it back to the storage room, and that path is faster. Like I said, just a misunderstanding. I'm sorry. Can I go now?"

"No," Michael said. "Why did you take the cart into the cottage?"

Reid shrugged. "I don't really know. I didn't think about it."

"Do you make it a habit to walk into guest rooms without being invited?" Michael said.

"I told you," Reid said, showing the first sign of exaspera-tion, "I thought they were in distress. I didn't—I guess I didn't really think much, I wanted to help, so I went in."

Fuentes changed the subject. A good way to throw him off, Matt knew. He used the tactic himself at times.

"Do you know Josh and Emily Henderson?"

"No."

"They were guests at the resort last fall, two months after you started working there."

"I don't remember most of the guests."

"What about Kevin and Jenny Blair?"

"No," he said in a polite but firm tone. "I *said* I don't remember most of the guests, and I don't even handle room service. I only took room service to that cottage because Ginger—she works the kitchen—was busy. I was going on my break in that direction and offered to take it for her."

Reid had strong evaluations from his supervisor. Staff liked him because he was always willing to help out, thus his excuse that he was helping Ginger was believable.

They'd already confirmed with Ginger that this was true; however, it *was* unusual.

Matt believed Garrett on this point, because it would give him a partial alibi. It wasn't his job, he didn't know what was under the domes, he just delivered the food, he had no idea who could have added the ketamine to the orange juice and coffee. A plausible excuse.

"Mitch and Sheila Avila. They stayed in the cottage next door to the Costa suite one month ago. You repaired their leaky shower."

Reid shrugged. "I do a lot of repairs, so I probably did. But I don't remember them."

"You're telling me that you—as an employee—don't remember the six guests who were murdered over the course of the last seven months? No one on staff talked about it? Management didn't have a staff meeting to discuss how *six people* went missing from the resort and were later found dead?"

Reid hesitated. This was a mistake. Matt could practically see him quickly calculating the situation.

At that moment, Matt had no doubt of Garrett Reid's guilt. He was almost positive when they arrested him in their cottage,

7

but this hesitation, the shrewdness behind his eyes, and Matt was certain.

But everything they had was circumstantial. A good lawyer would get this guy off. They needed physical evidence that tied Garrett Reid to at least one of the victims.

"Of course I heard about the people who disappeared from the resort, but I don't remember their names. It didn't have anything to do with me. Alena—Alena Porter, the manager—she said that if we saw anything unusual, or anyone hanging around where they shouldn't be, to call security. And, um, they added a couple security officers I heard?" He shrugged. "I just fix stuff. I do good work, ask my boss."

Michael asked, "Take us through today. When you clocked in, what you did, when Ginger asked you to take the tray to cottage 14, and go from there."

"I already told you," Reid whined.

"Tell us again. We need to document every minute of your day from when you arrived at work until you were arrested."

"And then I can go?"

Fuentes said, "You are under arrest, Mr. Reid. You're not going anywhere. You'll be arraigned on Monday and the judge will decide whether you are released on bail or remanded into custody."

Matt winced. That was exactly the wrong thing to say. She should have just repeated Michael's question, not answered his.

Reid stared at her. "I, uh, well, I think—dammit. I didn't do anything. I'm innocent. But you think I'm guilty."

"Convince me that you're not," Fuentes said.

"I didn't do anything!" He now sounded like any criminal proclaiming his innocence. "I swear, it's a misunderstanding, and I didn't mean harm to anyone." He took a deep breath. "I think I need a lawyer now."

Well, shit.

Anson scowled and tapped on the window. Interview over.

"We'll contact the public defender's office," Fuentes began.

"No, I'd like to make a call," he said. "I know a lawyer who'll help me."

"If that's what you'd prefer," she said, her voice calm but her body tense. The lawyer was inevitable, but Matt wished they had gotten more out of him first.

Matt and John Anson walked down the hall. "We have enough to keep him over the weekend," John said. "Once the search is complete, we'll have more."

"I don't like that he's not worried," Matt said. "As if he knows we won't find anything in his car or apartment. We need to find the secondary location."

Catherine had determined from the beginning that there was a remote, secondary location where the victims had been detained for several days before they were killed. That was based partly on forensics, and partly on logistics. So Reid likely had good reason to believe they wouldn't find evidence in his apartment. Fortunately, now that he'd been arrested, the FBI and sheriff's department were going to learn every detail of his life: friends and family, if he had access to a vacant building, if he had a second vehicle.

"We have a good team here," John said. "We'll find a thread and pull. No one is going to rest until we have what we need to keep Garrett Reid behind bars for the rest of his life."

Matt hoped that was true, but hoping wasn't one of the pillars of law enforcement. His confidence was shaken, and he wished they had found at least ketamine on Reid's person, which would have been far more damning.

John opened the door to the small conference room that they'd been using for their task force meetings after Matt and his team came down from Quantico. Matt walked over to the credenza and grabbed a lukewarm bottle of water. Kara hadn't checked in yet; she was part of the team searching Reid's apartment.

"Have you heard anything from the search?" he asked John.

"Not yet," he said, unconcerned, glancing through messages next to where he had a small workstation. "I need to work on getting the warrant expanded to cover Reid's finances, credit reports, phone records. I want to get to the judge before he leaves for the night. If I interrupt his weekend, he'll be in a dour mood. You can use this conference room if you need it. I'll check in once I have more."

John tossed half the notes, and put the rest under a notepad, on which he wrote a quick note. "If you need me, text."

John left and Matt pulled out his phone to text Tony a status report.

Garrett Reid was only one of fourteen men with access to the resort who fit Catherine's profile. When they took race out of the profile, there were forty-two possibilities. Of those, two-thirds were vendors or part-time employees. But they had prioritized the initial fourteen men because most serial killers rarely deviated from their own race. So they'd run basic background and criminal searches on the forty-two, but deeper backgrounds on the fourteen.

And none of them had any serious bumps.

In addition, Catherine was adamant that the first victim would connect to the killer, even if only in passing. The first victims were Emily and Josh Henderson. And while Emily was originally from California, like Reid, they were raised a hundred miles apart and had no obvious friends or associations in common.

Matt was certain Catherine would say the answer lay in one of two possibilities: either they hadn't yet uncovered the connection that surely existed between Reid and the Hendersons, or there had been another victim—someone killed *before* the Hendersons. Historically, a serial killer's first victim was often someone familiar to them: a neighbor, a co-worker, a casual acquaintance. Someone who unknowingly ignited the spark of violence and ended up on the killer's radar.

The FBI research team had already combed through unsolved homicides, but they hadn't found any missing couples matching the demographics of the three murdered pairs. If Garrett had started with a single victim—most likely a woman—it would be far more difficult to identify her, given the much higher number of unsolved single-victim murders.

Because Matt's Mobile Response Team had only been brought in three weeks ago, they were playing catch-up. It was impractical to follow the fourteen men who fit each point of Catherine's profile, but now they could home in on Garrett Reid. Matt lamented that they didn't already have more information about this guy. They knew he was born in Pasadena, California, and had worked at several resorts over the last five years, but there were gaps in his employment history. He had no criminal record, no active social media, and was living in an eight-hundred-square-foot one-bedroom apartment twenty minutes southwest of the resort, right off I-95.

An apartment that would be near impossible to bring any of his victims to without being seen.

Forensics confirmed the victims were kept alive for up to five days after their abduction—again, confirming Reid's apartment was impractical and he had access to a second location. While there was no evidence of sexual assault, each body bore signs of brutal torture: blunt force trauma, shallow cuts, stab wounds, and widespread bruising. Once dead, each victim had been wrapped separately in plain cotton sheets, then the couples were tied together at the waist with common nylon cord, and dumped in the ocean. The tide carried them to shore within days. Yet, Reid didn't own a boat and they hadn't identified a boat he could easily access.

Autopsies confirmed the victims were already dead before

entering the water. The lab was still analyzing trace evidence but hadn't pinpointed the location of the killings or where the bodies were dumped. The best estimate put the range along the coast—from South Carolina to northern Florida.

Jim Esteban, their forensic crime scene expert, believed the bodies had been discarded no more than two miles out from shore. Any farther, and the damage from currents or marine activity would have been more severe.

Reid had access to a secure second location, someplace he could hold the victims for days without fear of discovery. But he had maintained a normal schedule. No sudden leave. No extended absence. Catherine narrowed the search radius: the secondary site had to be within a four-hour drive. Eight hours, round trip. Close. Controlled. Hidden.

Matt's phone vibrated. It was Kara.

"Hello," he answered.

"Nothing," Kara said.

"I need more than nothing."

"You and me both," she grumbled. "Reid's apartment is more barren than my old condo. A set of four plates, bowls, and utensils in the kitchen. Two pots and a pan. Some condiments and one leftover Chinese food container that even I wouldn't eat, and I have a steel-lined stomach. Couch, chair, television—the TV is nice, new, wall-mounted. Queen bed, made. Some clothes and an extra maintenance uniform. Toiletries. But the place is immaculate. He's been here, but I don't think he lives here."

"Talk to the neighbors, see what they say—"

"Done. The place has eight apartments, four up, four down. Made contact with three neighbors, all have talked to him. He helps one of the older women with her trash every week, and the single mom with two kids? Says he's the nicest guy, didn't even hit on her but went out of his way to pick up a bunk bed she bought on Facebook Marketplace *and* helped her put it together. Everyone likes him. He's a good neighbor, works a lot, keeps to himself."

"Have they seen him with anyone?"

"No men, no women. He told his next-door neighbor that he took the job last fall because he wanted to see if he liked living in Florida, but wasn't sure he would stay. Didn't talk about friends or family, but if it got personal he talked about his job and the resort. He signed a year lease on October 3, two days after he was hired. He paid first, last, deposit. That was nearly four thousand upfront. Never been late."

"Nothing to connect him to even one of the victims?"

"Nope. No diary confessing to a crime, no calendar stating 'today I'm grabbing a blonde and her husband,' no ketamine or other drugs anywhere—and we looked deep—and no signs of violence. And there's no way he could get a body in and out of his apartment, dead or alive, without someone seeing or hearing. These walls aren't thick."

"Okay. Stick with the deputies while they finish processing, collect any information we can follow up on. I'll wait for you here."

"Roger that, boss." The line went dead.

They needed an expanded search warrant, and Matt wasn't certain they would get it with what they had. Though the attempted kidnapping of a federal agent might be enough.

John came back into the room. "Reid's lawyer didn't answer—we offered a public defender, but Reid wants his own guy. So we're on hold until he gets here."

"Status of the warrant?"

"I'm going before the judge in an hour," John said.

"We need to find his second location," Matt reiterated. "That info might be in his credit card statements, gas bill, any speeding or parking tickets, even utilities in his name."

"I'm working on it."

"His vehicle?"

"He drives a small pickup truck. I doubt he'd use it to move bodies, but it's not out of the question. It's already at the crime lab being processed. Bianca's team is sweeping every large vehicle on resort property. Vans, box trucks, oversized sedans. Anything that could hide two bodies." John looked glum, his earlier enthusiasm had flatlined. "This wasn't how I thought it would go."

"Me, either," Matt said. "But we couldn't let him overpower us or remove us from the property. It was too great a risk to the safety of my team."

"The plan was solid—I just expected, I don't know, *something* more. A secret room in his apartment, walls covered in photos of his victims, a memento from his kills. But there was nothing. His place, his car, so far both are completely clean. The guy lived like a damn ghost."

Matt exhaled slowly, staring at the wall that held the photos of all six victims. Their driver's license photos and their wedding pictures. Six people who had celebrated the happiest day of their life . . . and then were killed.

"We know what he's capable of," Matt said. "But without proof, it won't matter."

"We need something to fry this guy."

Matt agreed, but what could he say? Garrett Reid might walk. And if he did, someone else would end up dead.

2

Kara walked around the apartment building to get away from the crowd of cops who were going through every nook and cranny of Garrett Reid's sparse apartment.

Matt didn't have to say anything, but she could read between the lines: they didn't have a good case. Hell, they didn't even have a bad case. They had nothing against Garrett Reid for murder. They couldn't even prove he drugged their food.

She had argued with the task force that they needed to allow the suspect to restrain her and Matt, and preferably take them off-site before bringing in the cavalry. The sheriff's department didn't want to risk an innocent or team member being injured if the killer suspected a trap, so wanted the takedown contained within a controlled area. Matt concurred.

The plan had been to allow Reid—at the time, their unknown suspect—to restrain one of them, and then the team, who were watching through a hidden camera, would come in both entrances and take him into custody. Matt didn't like either him or Kara being incapacitated, but it was a good compromise.

Unfortunately, Michael thought he saw a gun when Reid reached into his pockets. Fearing one of them would be shot, he ordered the team to go in.

Reid didn't have a gun. It was a flashlight. But he *did* have zip ties and duct tape on his person. All victims had evidence of being zip-tied at the wrists and ankles, and one victim had a piece of duct tape in her hair. It was a small piece of evidence they may be able to match to what they found on Reid today. *Maybe.* Not enough to make the case, and they'd need days for the lab to confirm. Even then, the results could be inconclusive.

She would testify, of course. Reid had been *humming* when he checked first Matt, then Kara. He had touched her hair and said, *"This will be fun."*

Reid knew *exactly* what he was doing.

She shivered. He was creepy; creepier because he looked completely, totally normal. The guy was a killer. She felt it deep down. But when he reached into his overalls and Michael thought he had a gun, Michael ordered everyone in. Two more minutes. That's all they would have needed.

Yes, it was suspicious that he'd come in with a laundry cart big enough to transport both of them, checked to see if they were unconscious, and had zip ties on his person. But it wasn't a smoking gun.

From a tactical perspective, Michael felt justified going into the room at the first sign of a threat. Yet he'd told her in hindsight he wished he'd waited, and considered that he might sign up for more training. He'd been torn because the lives of his team were in possible danger, and went early. That, Kara understood.

This will be fun.

Dammit, she feared he would get away with it. They had to find *something* tangible to tie him to the abductions and murders.

She walked around to the back of Reid's apartment building. He lived in the first-floor end unit. The ground floors all had tiny fenced patios. The upstairs had balconies.

The six-foot fence surrounding Reid's patio had no gate; it was practically claustrophobic. Barely large enough for two chairs and a bistro-sized table, which was all Reid had. A canal bordered the property thirty feet to the rear; beyond that were acres of marshland. She shivered. Michael had reminded her there were more alligators in Florida than in any other state. She wished she hadn't known that.

She didn't like reptiles of any shape or size.

She glanced around making sure she didn't see any ground movement that might indicate an alligator was watching her. It was warm and quiet. Barely even a breeze. She turned to inspect the fence.

Two of the boards were loose. She pushed. They didn't budge. She pulled from the bottom.

Bingo.

Two boards came up together, revealing a space she could easily walk through—and so could Garrett Reid.

She walked around front and waited for Jim to finish giving instructions to the crime scene investigator. He came over to her. "Got something?"

"Maybe," she said.

"I hope so."

His frustration showed on his hangdog face as he wiped away sweat from his forehead. She didn't blame him. He'd gone over the autopsies of all six victims and had analyzed the extensive forensic evidence, but the salt water from the ocean had contaminated most everything. The sheet and rope were common and untraceable. Many lab tests were still pending or inconclusive.

Kara led Jim through the apartment to the patio in the back and showed him the boards. "He easily could have come and gone through this space without anyone seeing him."

"It's not a crime." But he looked critically at the boards. "I'll process them. If there's any blood or biological evidence, maybe it's still here, but this is Florida. The weather is not our friend."

Jim put his crime scene kit on the ground and opened the top, pulled out fresh gloves and put them on. "He drives a Ford Ranger. No camper shell, no tarp. Nothing he can easily transport two bodies in," Jim said as he took out his collection kit. "Still, the sheriff's department is processing the truck bed. They haven't found any trace evidence that the truck was used for transporting bodies, and there is no secret compartment under the bed liner."

"He could have a second vehicle," Kara suggested. "A van maybe, or a sedan with a big trunk."

Jim shrugged. "He could. Where is it? Only the Ranger is registered to him in the State of Florida, and no one at the resort has seen him in another vehicle—though the deputies are still conducting interviews. Maybe someone will remember something." He didn't sound optimistic.

Kara called Matt and told him what they found, thin as it was. "He needs a vehicle to transport two bodies. It can't be something that belongs to the resort because they would notice it missing."

"Flagler Sheriff's are already checking the ownership of every vehicle in the lot. So far, nothing."

"Maybe he uses a different vehicle every time," Kara said.

"Anything's possible," Matt said. "Are you heading back to the resort now?"

"I don't have anything else to do here, unless you need me."

"We're wrapping up because it doesn't look like Reid's lawyer is going to show today. I'll meet you there in an hour or two." He lowered his voice. "Ryder thinks we should stay the weekend. Everyone else is flying back to Quantico in the morning because our part of the investigation is over."

"It's not over," Kara said. "I understand that we were just brought in to identify the killer, but I'm worried he's going to slip through."

"I'll offer our help, but they have a good team and will continue the investigation, with the support of the Jacksonville FBI office. But what Ryder meant was we should stay, off duty. You, me, the full resort, without being watched by the team."

"Oh. Like a vacation?"

"Exactly."

"We can stay in the cottage?" That would be fun, she thought. She and Matt had been on-duty 24/7 for the last six days. She could use some R & R.

"It's already been processed and cleared, and it's paid for through Monday, though Ryder got us a flight back late Sunday because I have a meeting first thing Monday morning. I'll get it cleared with Tony, but I don't think he'll have a problem. He's always bitching that I don't take enough time off. I want to interview staff with Detective Fuentes tomorrow morning, then we'll take the rest of the weekend off to relax, go to a nice dinner."

"We've earned it," Kara said. "See you in a few hours."

Relax, she thought as she smiled and pocketed her phone. *Right*. Because both she and Matt were *so* good at doing nothing.

But a night of good food and great sex? She wouldn't pass that up. She and Matt had been pretending to be newlyweds but without the benefits. They'd kissed and flirted and there was a lot of pent-up sexual energy that would be explosive when they finally had privacy.

Yep, they had definitely earned it.

MONDAY

3

Ryder Kim, FBI analyst and overall logistician for the Mobile Response Team, walked into the conference room at five minutes to nine Monday morning for their post-operation team meeting.

Michael Harris and Sloane Wagner were chatting about what they'd each done on their first weekend off in weeks—Michael had worked on his house, Sloane had gone to a concert with friends from the Academy. Jim Esteban walked in behind Ryder.

"My sister and I went to a doubleheader Saturday," Jim said. "Needed yesterday to recuperate." When Jim was in DC, he lived with his sister, a widow. She was a veterinarian and owned a house only ten minutes from Quantico. He spent most of his free time in Dallas, where he had a basement apartment in his longtime home that he had gifted to his daughter and her growing family.

"What about you, Ryder?" Sloane asked. "Do not tell me you worked all weekend."

He hesitated.

"Damn, Ryder, I would have taken you to the game with me," Jim said. "You need to get out, have some fun."

"I didn't work," he said. A slight fib. He spent Saturday pulling together everyone's reports into one document, approving expenses, then he coordinated with the Flagler County Sheriff's Department and the district attorney on the paperwork and statements for Garrett Reid's arraignment later this afternoon. "Yesterday I went to a barbecue at a friend's house."

Why did everyone look surprised that he had a social life? True, he didn't have an *extensive* social life. Ryder didn't see the point of small talk and fake interest. He also didn't like talking about his personal life with his colleagues. He had few friends, but those he had were rock solid. The party yesterday, however, was bittersweet—the three-year anniversary of the death of a fellow soldier, a needless death and the primary reason Ryder decided to part from the Army and apply to Quantico.

He slid folders down the table, one for each person. "Catherine is on her way, and Matt is meeting with AD Greer at headquarters," Ryder said. "Zack is in Los Angeles giving his deposition in the political corruption case."

Last October, the team uncovered a major conspiracy involving all levels of local and state government, taking down a high-ranking FBI agent as well as an elected official. As the one who had cracked the financial network of money laundering and bribes, Zack had to be available to both the defense and prosecution.

"Kara?" Michael asked.

Kara was never late, so it was unusual that she wasn't here. However, since she moved out of the FBI Academy dorms last month into a house she'd purchased, she hadn't been coming in as early because her commute was longer than a five-minute walk across campus.

"She'll probably come in complaining about the traffic," Jim said. "Or she and Matt decided to take a longer vacation. God knows they both need it."

"Their flight landed at Dulles at one in the morning," Ryder said.

"More than forty-eight hours free time probably would have killed them both," Michael teased.

Ryder was relieved that Matt had come clean about his relationship with Kara Quinn, the LAPD detective on permanent loan to the Mobile Response Team. Ryder had figured it out from the beginning; it took the rest of the team a couple months. He greatly respected his boss, and Kara was an important part of the team—her way of looking at their cases was different than everyone else. It had been Ryder's idea that they take some time off after they wrapped up their undercover investigation on Friday, and Matt jumped at the idea.

Dr. Catherine Jones, the team psychiatrist, walked briskly into the room and sat in her usual spot, to the right of the head of the table where Matt usually sat. "I'm sorry I'm late," she said. "I was on the phone with the Flagler County district attorney to flesh out a few details since Matt is meeting with Tony. Reid will be arraigned this afternoon. There are a couple hiccups, however."

"I don't like the sound of that," Jim said.

"As you know, the search warrants didn't yield any useful evidence. I've gone over the reports and I believe he used his apartment only for official documentation. His secondary location could be closer than I suspected." She glanced at her watch. "Where's Kara?"

"Most likely stuck in traffic," Ryder said. He texted her and asked her ETA.

Catherine said, "She needs to talk to Detective Fuentes as soon as possible—her report was detailed, but there are questions regarding the moments leading up to his arrest and comments he made. If necessary, she'll need to testify on video during the hearing in order to put the comments in context."

Catherine glanced at her watch a second time, frowned, then

continued, "He asked for a lawyer, who evidently couldn't come until today."

"It shouldn't matter," Michael said. "We caught the guy red-handed."

"We have him on attempted kidnapping," Catherine said, "but the sheriff's department hasn't found any evidence tying him to the six homicides. Anson is charging him with assault, but that is thin—we can't prove he drugged the food—and while Reid's excuse for entering Matt's cottage is weak, it's still within the realm of plausibility. We need concrete evidence."

"They said they could handle the investigation," Michael said. "They didn't ask us to stay and assist."

Catherine put up her hand and said, "I'm aware, and I'll admit I was fairly confident that there would be connective evidence once the search was complete. We may be called back down to help, or provide support from here. Financials from the secondary warrant are coming in today, and our lab is still processing evidence." She glanced at Jim.

Jim nodded. "I'll be following up with the head of trace evidence later this morning."

Catherine made a note, then said, "I sent Matt a message right before his meeting with Tony that Michael and Kara may need to go back to Flagler County for a few days."

"Maybe we shouldn't have left," Michael said.

"Do we know anything about Reid's lawyer?" Sloane asked. "I would think he'd want to have a sit-down over the weekend to find out exactly what the charges are, talk to his client."

"When I spoke with the DA this morning, the lawyer had yet to arrive," Catherine said. "Florida asked for our help with Reid's background. Ryder has been working on his employment history, but there are holes, correct?"

Ryder nodded to the folders he'd already distributed. "Everything I have, you now have. Garrett Reid, thirty, from Pasadena, California. His parents claim they haven't spoken to him in the last six to seven years. The dad is a retired civil engineer with the county, the mom is a retired schoolteacher, and they've lived at their Pasadena home for more than forty years. We're tracking down his two older brothers now."

"The parents didn't help?" Sloane asked.

"Two LA FBI agents spoke to them in person on Saturday, but obtained minimal information," Catherine said. "They hadn't seen him, didn't care what he was doing. The agents came away with the impression that there was a family disagreement. Phone records support that they haven't spoken with him in years. Maybe his brothers will be more forthcoming. The local FBI office is checking with friends and other family. I plan to reach out to the parents as well, hopefully figure out why Garrett is estranged from his family and if that has any bearing on these murders. Depending on what we learn, I may ask Kara to speak with one or both of the siblings. She has an uncanny way of getting people to talk."

A rare compliment. Ryder was stunned. Maybe Catherine really had turned over a new leaf regarding Kara.

Catherine said, "None of the staff at the resort had anything but good things to say about Reid. He's competent, helpful, friendly. He rarely socialized with anyone outside of work. No one seems to know anything about his private life. He's been on staff for nearly nine months—two months before the first couple went missing. I have LA FBI digging deeper into the first two victims. We knew that Emily Henderson was raised in Santa Barbara, and while that's a distance from Pasadena, perhaps they knew each other in some way, crossed paths."

"And," Jim said, "we can't discount that he may have had earlier victims. Even if we can't find unsolved crimes that fit his profile, we may have missing couples or young blonde women who were his handiwork."

"True," Catherine said, "but I keep going back to why *here*? Why now? Why these couples? He was fishing in his own pool. Easier access? Convenience? Being an employee makes his crimes riskier. Did he relish that risk? Did he know Emily Henderson or did she remind him of someone?"

"We have far too many questions," Michael said, "and too few answers. Damn. I shouldn't have jumped when he reached into his pocket. He never used a gun before, but I thought he might have one as protection."

Ryder had been privy to the conversation where Matt told Michael he made the right call, but Michael said he shouldn't have made the mistake. If he'd waited five seconds, he would have seen it was a flashlight and not a gun. If he'd waited, they could have captured him in the act of tying up Matt and Kara, and that would have been harder for Reid to explain away.

"It was a tense and difficult situation," Catherine said. "Now that we have a suspect, even if he's cut loose this afternoon, there is a full, ongoing investigation. We'll find his mistakes. If Emily Henderson is connected to him in any way, we'll find the evidence. And I already asked LA FBI to look for any woman who fits the profile who was killed or went missing in Los Angeles County the year before Reid left. If he killed someone, that may have given him a reason to leave."

"Would he be able to wait five to seven years before killing again?" Sloane asked.

Catherine hesitated. "I don't know," she said cautiously. "I don't know enough about Reid. If the first murder was an accident, perhaps a girlfriend—someone who broke up with him or left him at the altar or turned down his engagement ring—then yes, I think a long cooling-off period would be expected. It could be the Hendersons were his first . . . or his second after a long period. But I don't want to jump to conclusions on this. We'll wait for the report from the LA office and go from there."

Ryder looked down at his silenced phone when it vibrated on the table.

"Excuse me, I have to take this," he said and stepped out of the room.

He answered his phone. "Yes, sir."

Assistant Director Tony Greer said, "Where the hell is Costa?"

"He's aware of your meeting. I'm sorry he's late."

"Don't apologize for him," Tony said. "He's twenty minutes late and isn't answering his phone."

"His flight was supposed to land at one-oh-five this morning. Perhaps it was delayed. Let me check." Ryder knew the flight landed, but would verify.

"I have a meeting with the director in ten, so Costa's going to have to sit and wait until I'm done."

Tony hung up before Ryder disconnected the call. He went to his desk and immediately looked up Matt's flight information—it had been on time. Then he called Matt's cell phone; he didn't answer so Ryder left a message, then texted him. He called Matt's house phone; that, too, went to voicemail.

His stomach tightened. Something was wrong. But he continued making calls.

Kara didn't answer her cell phone. Ryder left a message. She also hadn't responded to his earlier text message. He sent another with an urgent flag. Nothing.

He then reached out to the government liaison for the airline. After being transferred twice, he learned that neither Matt nor Kara had checked in or boarded their flight. They also hadn't canceled.

His bad feeling darkened. Something had happened to his boss. Never had Matt not been reachable without letting Ryder know where he was going and when he would be in contact again.

Catherine approached his desk. "What's wrong?"

"I can't reach Matt and he missed his meeting with Greer."

She frowned. "I swear, Kara brings out the worst in him. Are they at her place?"

Ryder bristled. He didn't like the tension between Catherine and Kara. They'd been getting along, more or less, for the last two months, but Catherine would dig at Kara whenever she found an opportunity.

If Matt had missed his flight, he would have called Ryder. Ever since the MRT was commissioned seventeen months ago, Matt had been diligent in keeping Ryder in the loop.

"Matt and Kara stayed in Florida for the weekend," he said.

"For shit's sake," Catherine mumbled. "I should have figured that when he canceled long-standing plans with Chris and me this weekend—by text."

"It was a stressful case," Ryder said, though he didn't know why he was trying to justify anything to Catherine. Matt and Kara weren't on duty this weekend, there was no reason they couldn't stay in Florida.

"They got to play newlyweds for a week, I think they had enough fun and games," she snapped. "We have a lot of work to do today, especially since the case against Reid is tenuous."

Ryder said, "I'm going to call the resort."

Catherine walked out, but he didn't breathe easier.

He called the resort and asked for Brian Valdez, the head of security. He already had a relationship with the man since Ryder had coordinated the MRT's undercover investigation with the resort.

"Agent Kim. How are you? We still can't believe it was one of our people. The sheriff's office has been all over the place this weekend. But we're relieved that an arrest has been made."

"I haven't been able to reach Agent Costa and Detective Quinn. They had a flight out yesterday evening, but can you please check to see if they stayed another night?"

"Sure, give me a minute." He put Ryder on hold.

It was eight minutes before Valdez came back on the line. "Agent Costa didn't check out. I spoke with housekeeping and they bypassed the room because of a Do Not Disturb sign on the door. It's still there."

"Will you please go down and check personally?"

"I'll call you back."

Ryder wanted to call in an alert immediately, but until he had more information from the resort, it would be premature.

He didn't go back to the conference room because he didn't have answers. He was worried, but there could be a logical explanation. Technology failed. One or both of them could have taken ill. There could have been an accident.

But Ryder couldn't shake the feeling that something was very, very wrong.

Valdez called him back ten minutes later.

"Agent Kim, I entered the room after identifying myself. No one is there, though their personal items are, including three firearms and two knives in the nightstand drawers. Two badges are on the desk—one federal, one an LAPD detective's shield. I'm reviewing security footage now to determine when they left, but no one on staff has seen them this morning."

"I need access to any footage you find," Ryder said. "I'll contact the sheriff to send someone to secure their weapons and ID. Did you see any cell phones?" He had already put in a request to track them.

"Yes, two phones were charging on the desk. You're concerned something happened to them?"

"Agent Costa would never leave his identification behind." Not even to go to the beach, Ryder thought.

Ryder ended the call as Michael stepped into his doorway. "What happened?"

"Matt and Kara didn't make their plane last night, neither are answering their phones, and they aren't at the resort—though their guns and badges are in their room. I need to call the sheriff."

"I'll call the sheriff," Michael said. "You get us booked on the next flight back to Florida."

"I need to inform AD Greer first."

"Whatever you have to do, but I'm going to be on the first plane down."

4

Tony Greer walked into the conference room less than ninety minutes after Ryder learned that Matt and Kara were missing. Tony was in his early fifties, of average height with the lean body of a lifetime runner. His steel-blue eyes looked around the room as he demanded, "Where are we in locating my agents?"

Ryder and Michael were the only people in the room.

Ryder said, "We've retraced their steps up until late Sunday morning." He crossed to the whiteboard and quickly ran through the details. He hadn't expected Tony to show up in person; he'd been prepping for a video conference. But he was ready, anxious to get this over with because he had all of them booked on a flight that left in less than ninety minutes.

"Matt and Kara were at the Flagler County Sheriff's Department Saturday morning from 8:00 a.m. until 3:45 p.m., except for a two-hour window where Kara joined Detective Fuentes to do a second search of Reid's known apartment and vehicle. Michael and Sloane were there until they left for the airport at noon. Matt and Kara arrived back at the resort at 4:10 p.m. They left at 6:20 p.m. for dinner off-site, taking an Uber to and from a restaurant in Ormond Beach approximately twelve minutes south. They returned to the resort at 9:30 p.m.

"At 8:30 Sunday morning they left their room and went to the gym," Ryder continued, "where they worked out then played three sets of racquetball, arriving back at their room at 10:50. They ordered room service at 11:10, which was delivered at 11:35 a.m. and signed for by Matt."

"And?" Tony said. "No one has seen them since eleven thirty yesterday morning? Nearly twenty-four hours?"

"Brian Valdez, the security chief, is in the process of interviewing every staff member who interacted with Matt or Kara. Housekeeping came at one that afternoon but there was a Do Not Disturb sign and they didn't enter. When the security chief bypassed the lock this morning, their weapons, credentials, and luggage were present. Flagler Sheriff's Department is checking the restaurant they ate at Saturday evening and will grab the security footage."

"They can't just have disappeared," Tony said. "Theories."

Michael said, "Our best guess is Garrett Reid has a friend who is trying to help him by making it seem like he's innocent."

"That's fucking ridiculous," Tony said.

Catherine walked into the room. "I don't know what happened, but whoever took Matt and Kara had a very small window to do so. Sloane just spoke with the head of housekeeping. They didn't enter the room, but while servicing the cottage next door shortly after 1:00 p.m., they spotted trays outside on the patio of cottage 14. They collected them and cleaned up. However, they are holding the room so we can search ourselves."

"Security footage?"

"Valdez is reviewing it now," Ryder said. "If he sees something, he'll call. I have reservations for the team to go down in—" he looked at his watch "—seventy-five minutes."

"By the time you land, I want answers," Tony said.

"We'll do our best, Tony," Catherine said, "but we have another issue."

"Nothing takes precedence over finding Matt and Kara," Tony said.

"The case against Reid is falling apart."

"How?"

"Flagler County has found nothing to tie him to the first six homicides. He fits the profile," Catherine added quickly, "all the way down. Single, thirty, Caucasian, attractive, nonthreatening, intelligent but working in a menial job which gave him access to the victims. The lawyer is going to ask to release him on a low bond, and we need to keep him in jail. If he called on someone to help make it look like he's innocent, they could be holding Matt and Kara until he's released, and then—well." She cleared her throat nervously.

No one wanted to think what Reid would do to them when he got out.

"If he's released, we stick to him like glue. Work with the local jurisdiction, but if we have to take this case, we will, understand?"

Ryder had never seen Tony so angry or worried. Tony and Matt had been friends longer than Tony had been his supervisor.

Ryder glanced at his phone, then said, "Our ride to the airport is here."

"Zack will be back tonight, he'll work from here unless you need him in Florida," Tony said. "You also have full access to my staff—they will get you anything you need." He looked at Catherine. "Does he have a partner?"

Catherine blanched. "I—I don't think so. Nothing has suggested that two people were involved in the abductions or murders. It would be unusual, but not impossible."

"It's one thing to help a friend out of a jam," Tony said, "it's another to kidnap a federal agent to get a friend out of a jam. Unless you've been involved from the beginning."

Catherine looked like she hadn't even considered the idea. "I'll review all of the files again on the plane."

"You're going?" Tony was as surprised as Ryder. Catherine rarely joined them in the field, preferring to work out of the office.

"It's my profile that gave Flagler County the idea for the undercover operation, and my profile that netted us Garrett Reid. If I'm wrong, or partly wrong, then I need to be there to watch and assess him."

"Keep me informed every step of the way," Tony said. "I've already talked to the SAC in Jacksonville, and he'll have agents at our disposal when and if we need them. I'll contact them now to send an evidence response team to process the room. If there is any trace evidence, they'll find it." He looked from Ryder to Michael to Catherine. "Find them, whatever it takes."

He turned and walked out.

Partner. Garrett Reid has a partner, Ryder thought.

"There are no signs that Reid worked with anyone," Catherine said as if reading Ryder's mind.

"Meet out front in ten minutes," Ryder said. He left the conference room and went to his office, closed his door.

A partner. That made sense. Matt and Kara were caught off guard. Hard to do, but not impossible.

Guilt ate at him. He'd convinced Matt to stay for the weekend. Maybe he hadn't needed a lot of convincing, but it had been Ryder's idea and Matt ran with it. Otherwise, they would have flown back Saturday after meeting with Detective Fuentes and the DA in the morning.

Ryder called Brian Valdez. "My team is coming down. We'll be there in three and a half hours. The Jacksonville FBI office may arrive before us—please allow them to search the room."

"I'll get a couple rooms ready for your team. I haven't even cleared out the conference room you were using because the deputies were here all weekend."

"I appreciate it."

"I may have found something," Brian said. "At 11:57 a.m., an individual we can't identify wearing a maintenance uniform with a baseball cap is seen pushing a laundry bin down a path near Agent Costa's room. The cottages don't have cameras nearby, but the path leading from the main hotel to the outlying cottages has some coverage. He is spotted on two of them, then disappears. I'm checking parking lots for additional footage, but haven't found anything yet."

"Email me what you have," Ryder said. "Thank you."

Ryder hung up. Catherine was standing in his doorway.

"Learn something?" Catherine asked.

Ryder told her what Valdez discovered.

"We need that footage," Catherine said. "We can enhance it, run it through facial recognition—maybe we'll recognize the individual."

"He's sending it to me and looking for more," Ryder said, "but there are no frontal shots."

"I still want to see it," she said. "There's a chance that someone Matt investigated is behind this, and it has nothing to do with Garrett Reid."

"That seems unlikely," Ryder said, then regretted it. He was an analyst, not an FBI agent.

Catherine said, "Perhaps, but I'm not ready to change my profile, not yet. I haven't been this wrong before, at least since . . ." She stopped herself.

Ryder raised an eyebrow. Though he had never discussed Catherine's background with her or anyone else, he knew the big picture. Two years ago her sister had been killed by a man obsessed with Catherine, and Catherine's profile about her stalker had been off. She had determined that he wasn't violent. She blamed herself, and then Matt. After a sabbatical, she seemed to be doing better, but Ryder knew how old traumas could return to wreak havoc in your life when you least expected it. He wondered if it was wise to have Catherine join them in Florida, but it wasn't his call to make.

Ryder glanced at his computer when a message popped up, reminding him that their driver had been waiting for ten minutes. He forwarded it to the team, then said to Catherine, "Our driver is here. We'll meet at the portico."

"Thank you. I'll tell the others."

"I've already messaged them," he said.

She gave him a wan smile. "Of course you did. I'll get my head together. I'm just worried about Matt."

"And Kara," he said pointedly.

"Of course," she said.

She left and Ryder pulled together the rest of his things. He checked his sidearm and extra clips, then secured them in the bag he would check. Though he was an analyst, Matt insisted that he carry while in the field. That meant Ryder qualified at the range just like a sworn agent.

The email from Valdez came in a minute later. Ryder texted the driver that he would be a few minutes, then sat down to watch the footage he'd sent. There wasn't much to go on. He'd study it more carefully on the plane. But he sent it to his contact at the computer lab with a note that this was the individual suspected of kidnapping Costa and Quinn and asking if he could enhance the video as soon as possible.

They needed a direction. But the best source of information was Garrett Reid, and he had no reason to talk to them. If he spoke, he would be incriminating himself.

But they had to try.

5

Matt slowly regained consciousness. His body felt like he was floating in a sea of molasses, his head heavy. He could hear his own voice shouting from a distance, but his jaw wasn't moving. It was his mind, ordering himself to wake up, get up, that something was wrong.

"Kara," he moaned and tried to move. Pain shot through him, jolting him fully awake. "Kara!"

He groaned, every muscle sore and tight as if it hadn't been used in days. His throat was parched, his mouth dry, his head pounded like the worst hangover he'd ever had.

His training clawed to the surface, every cell screaming *danger! danger! danger!* giving him a burst of adrenaline.

"Kara!"

He forced himself to move, then cried out as bruises all over his body made themselves known with stark pain.

He tried to get up and stumbled, fell on his face. He needed to collect his bearings, figure things out.

Slow, Matt. You can't help Kara if you panic.

First, feel around. The floor was cool against his skin. Smooth, concrete. He felt nothing but the ground. Then he listened. For voices, running water, the noises of a building.

Nothing except his own breathing and pounding heart.

Calm down, he ordered himself.

He took a moment, forcing himself to breathe easier. When his heart rate slowed enough, he focused on his surroundings. Faintly, he heard a distant buzz. Electricity, he thought. But it sounded louder than it should, like a large generator.

Finally, he forced his crusted eyes open through heavy lids. He saw nothing. The room was pitch-black.

He called out again. "Kara? Kara, are you awake?"

His voice bounced as if he were in a metal room. Not cavernous, but big enough that he hesitated walking without being able to see where he was going.

He pushed himself into a sitting position, felt around and found a wall. Also concrete. He leaned against it, getting his bearings and wishing for light.

Matt touched his body, realized he was wearing sweatpants and a T-shirt—what he'd been wearing earlier after the gym. Unfortunately, he didn't have his gun on him.

"What happened?" he mumbled. "Think, Costa, think."

His brain was fuzzy, his memories mixed up as he tried to put them in chronological order. The investigation . . . Reid was arrested Friday morning when he attempted to grab Matt and Kara. Saturday Matt spent the morning and half the day with the joint task force.

Then Saturday night . . . he and Kara put work aside and enjoyed a night alone. The team had returned to Quantico, and Ryder convinced him a little R & R was in order. Matt remembered that . . . Reid was in jail, the investigation shifted to Flagler County, they could let their guard down. All the teasing and anticipation during the week they were undercover had culminated in maybe the best sex Matt had had in his life. Then . . .

What?

What happened Saturday night?

Sex . . . dinner . . . sex . . . sleep . . . morning sex . . . then they went to the resort gym to have a friendly racquetball game. Matt won, but he had to earn it and was wiped out.

"Lucky you," Kara had teased as they walked back to their beachside cottage. "You get to decide on whether we eat first . . . or have sex."

"Food," he'd said, "I need energy."

She'd laughed and kissed him. He'd never seen her so relaxed . . . so *content*. They were both workaholics, but Saturday night they'd promised each other twenty-four hours without talking about work or the case. It had been bliss.

He'd ordered room service, and they enjoyed brunch on their patio. Their flight didn't leave until ten that night so they were discussing what they should do that afternoon—after eating, having sex, showering, and packing.

"Maybe we should check in with Detective Fuentes before we leave town," Matt had said as he drank coffee.

"I win!" Kara had fist pumped into the air.

He'd moaned. He had completely forgotten the bet he'd made her Saturday night over dinner that she would be the first to bring up work. They didn't actually bet anything except bragging rights . . .

Then what happened? Think, Costa! What happened after was crucial to figuring out where he was, where Kara was.

Matt remembered they were eating brunch on the patio. Kara was drinking a mimosa and enjoying the late morning sun. She'd said something . . . he didn't remember what . . . and then she got up and stumbled.

"What's wrong?" Matt had jumped up as Kara fell to the ground. His head felt thick and his vision began to fade.

"Poison. We need to throw up," Kara had said, putting her finger down her throat.

But she couldn't make herself puke, and was then lying prone. He'd tried to get to her, then felt a sting in his shoulder and . . .

Nothing. He remembered nothing else. His hand unconsciously went to his shoulder, still sore from whatever hit him. A small, hard welt had risen from his skin.

The sting . . . he'd been tranquilized. Their food had been drugged, then they had been tranquilized.

Except Reid was in jail awaiting arraignment. If he had been released, Fuentes would have told Matt . . . wouldn't she?

Matt didn't know what to think at this point, other than he needed to find Kara.

"Kara!" he shouted.

He didn't hear her, didn't smell her, couldn't even sense her presence.

Matt rose, his legs weak, but they held him up. In the dark, he couldn't tell the time of day, how long he'd been here. Based on his stiff, sore limbs, it had been hours since he'd moved.

Kara had felt the effects first, but she was smaller than he was. What had they been dosed with? And then the tranq—it had impacted him like a brick—was Kara okay? Was she conscious?

Was she alive?

Slowly, using his hand against the wall to judge where he was going as he looked for Kara or an exit, he shuffled along, mindful that her body could be anywhere.

He reached the corner almost immediately, maybe ten feet from where he'd woken up. From the corner he paced off the next wall. He stumbled over several items, unsure of what they were. Maybe a chair, maybe garbage. He counted off the size of the room. Ten feet. Twenty. Thirty. No door, no shelves, just what felt like cinderblock walls with the occasional small obstacle. At about thirty feet straight ahead he felt a metal door. At first he thought it was a way out, but as he searched for a handle, he noted it was flimsy metal and there were ridges equally spaced apart . . . a row of lockers? He walked along the row, counting. Twenty of them, each about eighteen inches wide. That made the room roughly thirty-foot square. The lockers ended and he felt another door.

Solid metal, but with a glass window. Thick by the feel, no light on the other side—either it was blacked out, or the other side of the door was just as dark as this room.

He tried the knob.

It wasn't locked.

Think, he told himself.

He'd been unconscious for hours. He was in a large cement room with lockers. First, he had to make sure Kara wasn't unconscious somewhere in this room. He hadn't heard her breathing, and fear that she was dead clawed at him.

He should also look for a weapon, check out each of the lockers.

As quickly as he dared, he finished mapping the perimeter of the room. There were some cabinets along one wall and he cut his hand on a jagged piece of metal. He found nothing he could carry. Slowly, he crossed the middle of the room, unnerved, listening for breathing, for any sign that he wasn't alone.

He walked into something and winced as pain radiated across his chest. He had bruises on top of bruises. He felt around—a table. He moved to the left and tripped. A chair. Dammit. Every direction he hit something else. He walked as slow as he could and counted seven tables. Just when he thought he was near the other side, his ankle hit something low and hard, he stumbled, and fell onto a damp cushion—a couch, he realized. A disgusting stench of mold wafted up. He coughed and rubbed his hands on his sweats.

Kara wasn't in this room. Maybe she was at the resort looking for him. Maybe she had been left behind, unconscious, and he was brought . . . here.

Matt found his way back to the lockers and opened each one.

Empty. Empty. Empty. No loose brackets or shelves or rods to extract and use as a weapon.

By the time he reached the door again, he had some strength back, but he felt drained and his head throbbed. He had a sense he was in a warehouse or factory, a building with solid walls. It felt abandoned, the humid air and smell of mildew and rot suggested it may have been damaged in a storm, maybe in a hurricane. Wherever he was, he couldn't hear the ocean or any traffic. No voices, no movement of people. Desolate. Empty. Hollow. Just that faint hum of electricity and the foul, rotting stench that filled his pores.

He needed to head toward the sound.

Someone had taken him. He couldn't imagine that the Flagler Sheriff's Department would have let Garrett Reid out of jail without informing him first. Reid wasn't even going to be arraigned until tomorrow.

Matt opened the door. The generator noise was now more distinct, though still too far away to gauge how big the building was. It sounded like it was coming from below. Two, maybe three floors down.

No lights in the hall and though Matt's eyes had adjusted to the dark, he saw nothing. It was darker than a moonless night.

Hand on the wall, he moved slowly, his shins still stinging from the low table he'd walked into.

He heard metal on metal at the far end of the hall, then a blood-curdling scream from the same direction.

"Kara!" he shouted.

6

Kara woke up with a start, every nerve on high alert as she realized something bad had happened. It took her several minutes to get her bearings.

Where the hell was she?

Faint lighting illuminated a small room that looked like a freight elevator. It *was* an elevator, she realized, about six feet wide and eight feet deep. The light came from a sickly yellow strip at the top on one side. The light strip on the opposite side flickered on and off.

She slowly pulled herself to standing. She felt ill, her head pounding, her stomach empty, her mouth dry.

How did she end up here? One minute she was having brunch and mimosas with Matt on their patio by the beach, the next . . .

They'd been poisoned. She remembered trying to force herself to throw up, but collapsing instead. Was Matt okay? Where was he?

Determined to get out, she pressed the buttons and the box didn't move. She pulled the alarm button. Nothing.

The elevator doors were propped open about four inches, stuck between floors. Looking out into the dark hall, she figured the floor was about a three-foot jump. If she could pry the doors open, she could slide out. She'd rather find a staircase than risk this rickety elevator.

She thought she heard something in the distance, but couldn't quite make it out. She didn't shout, fearing that whoever had taken her was somewhere in the building. Her best option was to get out of this box, find an exit, get to a phone, call Matt.

Which wouldn't do any good if he was trapped in this building with her.

Was he even alive?

Kara studied the doors, figured if she had the strength she could push them open just enough and slide out into the hallway.

She stretched, loosening her limbs.

Deep breath. Count to three.

Kara put her hands into the opening and pushed.

They were stuck. She wedged her shoulder in and used all her strength to split the doors open . . .

The elevator fell.

She screamed and jumped back barely in time to avoid having her arm severed as the hall floor came rapidly up toward her. As it was, she hit the elevator floor so hard, her breath was knocked out of her. Fortunately, the floor stopped moving. She was wedged to one side because there was a tilt that hadn't been there before. The hall floor was now above her. Barely enough room to crawl out . . . though the door had fully opened.

But she couldn't move. Had she broken her back? The fall wasn't that far.

She took small, slow breaths and slowly tested her limbs. Then her head, body. Nothing broken, but she felt like she'd been used as a punching bag.

"Kara!"

Matt? Sounded like Matt, but so far away and the ringing in her ears from the rickety elevator told her she must be hallucinating.

She looked at the opening. A cable had broken. How many held her up? Two? One? Could she move? Or was she just delaying the inevitable fall to her death?

The elevator was still stuck between floors, but now she would have to pull herself up and out. If it fell again, she'd be dead.

At peak health, she could do a couple pull-ups, but right now she had little strength.

"Kara!"

"Matt?" Her voice was hoarse. She coughed, cleared her throat. "Matt! I'm in the elevator!"

She heard him now, running down the hall.

"Stop!" she shouted. "Be careful."

"Kara?" He was above her. He knelt and she saw his face in the near dark.

She was relieved she wasn't alone, grateful that Matt was alive.

"I got the doors open, then the elevator fell six feet. Don't touch them."

"We have to get you out of there."

"Give me one sec."

"Take my hand."

"Stop!" she said. "Just wait. I think—I need to pull myself up without touching the sides of the elevator."

"Why?"

"It might be booby trapped." The more she'd thought about how the elevator fell when she was trying to get out, the more she thought she heard a pop, like something gave way. As if her actions had disengaged something that caused the elevator to fall. Maybe not a booby trap, but considering she had no idea why they were here or who brought them here or where they even *were*, she didn't want to take any chances.

"Tell me what you want me to do," Matt said.

"I need to pull myself up, but I don't know if I have the strength," she admitted.

"I'm going to lie down, I'll reach in and—"

"No. If the elevator falls, you'll be killed."

"What choice do we have?"

He was right. She had to get out. Her fear was paralyzing her.

"Okay, okay," she said. "I can get myself partly up, then you grab me and pull me out, fast."

He knelt. "Okay. Your call. Tell me when."

Just do it. Do it, do it, do it, she repeated.

Fear pumped adrenaline in her veins.

Now or never, she thought.

She jumped and grabbed the floor above her, using her legs to push against the cement wall in front of her to give her some leverage.

She heard a pop, the same sound she'd heard last time before the elevator fell.

"Matt!" she shouted and as she pulled herself up, his hands wrapped around her biceps and pulled her out.

The elevator brushed against her foot as Matt yanked her across the floor and into his arms.

The scrape of metal against metal sounded as the elevator plummeted, with a final crunch and thud as it hit bottom.

Her heart pounded as she clung to Matt. He was talking, but she couldn't hear what he was saying through the ringing in her ears.

"Kara!" He shook her.

"I'm okay, I'm okay," she repeated.

Then he hugged her again as they sat in the dark for several minutes. With the elevator gone, so was most of the light.

"What the fuck, Matt?" she finally said.

"What do you remember?"

She thought. "We were eating. I felt odd, and then . . . I

think—well, I tried to puke but I don't think I did." She rubbed her temples. "My memory is all blurry."

"You told me we were poisoned, then I felt a sting on my shoulder. I think we were tranq'ed."

She rubbed the back of her neck. "That would explain this welt. It still hurts. Do you know what time it is? It feels late."

"My watch. Totally forgot to even check it." He adjusted, pressed the side of his watch to light up the LED screen. "Well shit. It's after nine."

"We were out for *nine hours*?"

"Nine in the morning," he said.

She sat up. "The whole night? We were out for a full *day*?"

"Do you remember anything else? Did you see anyone? Hear anything?"

She thought. "No, but . . . I sensed something. Right before I felt sick, I thought someone was watching me. But I didn't see anyone."

"We need to find a way out."

"You don't have to tell me twice. Lead the way." He didn't get up. "Matt, are you okay?"

"I need another minute."

They leaned against the wall and Kara found Matt's hand, held it.

Matt said, "It was pitch-black, but now there's a faint light." He gestured with their joined hands at the area on the far side of the hall, past the elevator. The light flickered, but it only turned the black to dark gray.

"Maybe the elevator crashing set off an alarm or hit some switch or I don't know, jostled a wire?"

"No light the way I came." He gestured down a black hall.

"I say we go toward the light, but with extreme caution."

"Okay. Just a sec. I thought—hell, Kara, I thought you were dead."

"I feel like I was hit by a truck, but I'm alive."

She felt his lips on her forehead.

"Any chance Garrett Reid was released from jail?" she asked.

"They would have told me," Matt said.

Again, silence for a long minute before she asked quietly, "Did we arrest the wrong guy?"

"No," Matt said. "We caught him in our room. He put ketamine in our food—we have the tests to confirm."

Matt was right, though Kara had a bad feeling they'd missed something.

"The question," Matt continued, "is were we targeted because we're cops or for another reason?"

"Two killers targeting newlyweds?" Kara said with a bitter laugh. Then she stopped. "He has a partner."

"Oh, shit," Matt said. "That's the only thing that makes sense."

"Catherine never talked about him having a partner," Kara said. "Maybe we're thinking about this all wrong. Maybe this *is* someone else after us."

She didn't believe that. Who knew where they were? Who knew how to get to them?

"No, I think we're right." He touched her face. "You okay? I mean, nothing broken? Not bleeding?"

"Just sore with a pounding headache. I want to get out of here." She hated being trapped, not knowing where she was or what dangers she faced.

"Stick close. We don't know what condition this building is in, or if whoever brought us here is still around."

Matt got up, then helped Kara stand.

"What floor do you think we're on?" Kara asked. "The elevator hit pretty quick."

"My guess is the elevator fell two to three stories. This is some sort of multilevel warehouse. Maybe a factory. Abandoned. I woke up in what seemed to be a break room. Tables and lockers, but mostly empty, and there were no windows. Ready?"

"Yeah," she said and squeezed his hand as they walked cautiously down the hall toward the flickering green light.

There was nothing distinguishing on the walls to tell them where they were—no signage, no names, no directions. They tried each door that they came across and found them locked. At the end of the hall they turned and saw that the flickering was an exit sign.

"Staircase?" Kara said.

The door was different from the others; this had a push-in handle.

"I think so," he said and reached for it.

"Wait!" she said, pulling his hand back. "Remember, I think the elevator was booby-trapped, set up to fall when I opened the door."

"It's old. Maybe your added weight compromised the already decaying mechanisms."

"No. There was a popping sound. Twice. It felt like it was sabotaged. We really have to be careful, Matt. We have no idea where we are."

Matt didn't say anything, and she wondered if she was completely off base.

"We were separated for a reason," she continued. "If you'd found me first, you would have tried to pry open the doors and you could have been decapitated when the elevator fell half a floor. I'm not wrong. I have a bad feeling."

Obviously, she thought. They both had a bad feeling because they'd been abducted by the partner of a psychopathic killer and dumped in this abandoned building likely as a ransom to free the psychopathic killer. Or as revenge for arresting him.

"You're right," Matt said. "We have to assume that it was sabotaged, and we take each step with caution."

She let out her breath, squeezed his hand. "Okay. Nice and slow."

"Ready?"

Kara nodded. Staying here wasn't an option. No food, no water, and no one knew where they were—except the person who brought them here.

Matt opened the door cautiously. The stairwell was dark. The green exit sign barely illuminated the landing. The staircase appeared metal, but Kara could only see a couple steps down.

The air was musty, concrete and rust and a pervasive moldy stench. That didn't surprise her—Florida was humid.

"Stay right behind me," Matt said.

"You couldn't shake me if you tried," Kara said.

He put his hand on the railing, which wobbled. "I don't know how secure the staircase is, but it appears to be attached to the wall so we should be okay."

As soon as Kara let go of the door, it slammed shut, making her jump. The faint light disappeared, throwing them into darkness once again.

"Matt." Kara reached out, felt his back.

"Try to prop open the door."

She felt around but couldn't find the handle. "We're not getting out that way," she said.

In some secure buildings and hotels, once you entered the stairwell, you could only exit on the ground floor. But she doubted a warehouse would have that sort of security feature.

Someone had removed the handle.

"I feel like we're rats in a maze and the light was our cheese."

"Rats are usually rewarded when they find the cheese," Matt said, trying to look on the bright side.

"Not helping," she mumbled. "Watch your step. Literally."

She kept her hand on the small of Matt's back as he descended.

Matt tested each step in front of him before putting his weight on it. The stairs were metal and had some bounce, but seemed to be intact. A musty draft came up from below, which made him think that this was a tall building, at least three but likely four stories.

He counted stairs, to get a sense of the size. Ten steps and then he was on a larger platform as the staircase curved to the right. He felt along the railing to make sure he was right; he was.

"The staircase makes a one-eighty here," he said. "Ten more steps down."

"What if that door doesn't have a handle?"

"Then we go to the next floor. We're going to get out of here."

He tested the first step. Good. Second. Third . . . a sharp metallic crack and the stair gave way. His ankle went through, and a sharp pain made him cry out as the metal cut into his flesh. He leaned back, knocked into Kara, and the entire staircase seemed to sway.

"Hold on to the railing!" he shouted as the stair he had already tested started to bend.

"The whole staircase is falling apart!" Kara said.

Maybe she had been right about the sabotage, because metal like this didn't just crack and break, unless it was really old.

"I'm going first," Matt said, his breath ragged. "Stay here."

"Don't you dare die on me, Costa," she hissed. Kara sounded scared. She rarely sounded scared, which told Matt that their situation was dire.

Holding tight to the railing, he walked along the edge of the staircase. His ankle throbbed and he felt blood drip down into his sneakers. But no broken bones, so he counted his blessings.

The railing was jerky, as if some of the bolts were missing, and as he stepped he could feel the metal beneath him give way enough to know that there were other compromised stairs. He counted as he went, and when he hit the landing he breathed marginally easier.

"I'm okay," he called up to Kara. "Wait one sec while I feel things out."

The floor felt solid, no weak spots. He put his hands out and touched the door. Pressed. Ran his fingers along the metal. He found the seams, but didn't find a handle.

He and Kara needed to decide what to do next. He called to her, "Okay, walk along the edge of the staircase and hold the railing. It's unsteady, but as long as you avoid the center you'll be okay. There are seven steps after the broken one, they all sag toward the middle."

"I'm coming," she said, her voice rough around the edges.

He kept his hand on the railing and felt Kara's progress as she traversed the stairs. Then she was at his side and he wrapped an arm around her.

"I couldn't find a handle on the door. We should continue down."

"We can't see anything," she said. "What if the stairs just end? What if they collapse from our weight? The elevator was wood and steel, functional. The stairs are metal grates. It's clearly abandoned."

"There's electricity coming from somewhere," Matt said. "I don't hear it in the stairwell, but upstairs there was a faint hum. It sounded like a generator."

"Then maybe we can find a light source. Or a window. If the place is abandoned or sealed off for some reason—"

"I think it was flooded."

"Really? Why?"

"The moldy smell. It's familiar. When Dante and I were kids we used to explore abandoned buildings, many of which had been damaged in hurricanes and shut down."

Kara laughed, and that helped because it sounded like the old Kara, the brave Kara, the Kara who could help him figure out how to get out of this place.

"The by-the-book federal agent breaking into private property—I would never have thought."

"We all do stupid things when we're kids," Matt said lightly.

"Let me try to get through this door, okay? If there had been a handle at one point, maybe we can leverage it or wedge something in a space and open it. If we can't open it, then we go down."

"Alright," he said. He guided her hand to the door seams, then let her explore.

A minute later he heard the door creak.

"I got it," Kara said, her voice strained. "I found the holes where the handle used to be, but they're small, only big enough for my pinky fingers. I'm going to pull it open as far as I can. I felt it shift, so it's not locked, but it's heavy."

"You pull. I'll get my fingers in the crack and wedge it open."

"If I slip, your fingers will be chopped off."

"Don't slip."

"Matt—"

"Seriously, other option is going down the stairs, and you're right, we can't be certain all the steps are there." He didn't tell Kara about one of the buildings he and Dante had explored. The entire staircase had just ended halfway up. They couldn't see it at first, and when they started up, the stairs sagged. They barely got down before the entire staircase collapsed. He didn't want to think about encountering a gap in the stairs while going down with zero visibility.

"Okay, okay—find the crack. When you have it, I'll count to three then pull. But my fingers barely fit in, so I don't know how much traction I'll get."

"We'll try." Matt ran his fingers along the door and felt the crack. "Okay. Right here. You pull, I'll wedge, good?"

"Sure," she said without her usual confidence. "Okay, one . . . two . . . three." Kara pulled and Matt pushed his fingers into the narrow space. One of his nails split, but he wasn't going to let go. Kara grunted, and he worried that she had hurt herself.

But then his fingers went all the way in. "I got it!"

Kara stepped back a half step and Matt slowly opened the door.

The hall on the other side wasn't as dark as the staircase. There was faint yellow light coming from around the corner, creating a murky dark gray. But not totally dark. That was a plus.

"Ready?" Matt said.

"Let's do it."

They stepped into the hall. The door closed behind them, followed by a clash of metal on metal. Matt pushed on it, but it wouldn't budge.

"Rats in a maze," Kara repeated.

Matt took her hand. "We're going to get out of this," he said. "Just be prepared for anything."

7

Kara rubbed her sore fingers on her sweatpants. Now that they were out of the staircase, she felt a bit calmer, less claustrophobic.

For a split second when Matt had slipped on the stairs, she'd thought he was gone. It happened so fast, and her heart may have stopped for a beat. Then it pounded in her chest so hard that she couldn't hear much over the roar in her ears. Figuring out the door had given her that moment she needed to regroup and collect her bearings.

She wasn't lying to Matt; she *did* feel like a rat in a maze and someone had set up this entire building to torment them. It wasn't simply a sick joke; they could have died. They still could die. She could have died when the elevator fell. Or worse, broken her back at the bottom of the shaft and slowly, painfully, died over days.

She shivered. Matt squeezed her hand. "We're going to get out of this," he said.

"I know," she agreed without conviction.

They rounded the corner, and Kara saw a sign that surprised

her. Maybe because it was unexpected, here in this filthy, rotting building.

Women.

Cautiously, she pushed against the door. There was no resistance.

"We need water," she said. "The sinks might work. It might taste gross, but we're not going to get far if we don't have fluids."

"I'll stand at the door—I don't want to risk being separated."

Matt pushed the door all the way open and stood in the threshold, his back against the open door. The dim light from the hall reflected off filthy broken mirrors.

Kara saw distinct handprints on the cracked glass. Slowly, she checked each of the four stalls.

"Matt, I'm going to take a minute." If they really had been here for nearly twenty-four hours, she certainly wasn't surprised her bladder was full.

"Go ahead."

She chose the one stall that didn't have a door. The idea of being trapped again made her jittery, fueling her anxiety. She squatted, not wanting to sit. For all she knew, the toilet would fall through the floor and she'd go crashing down with it.

She looked up at her distorted image in the dirty cracked mirror across the room. The handprints were clear.

So was a message.

The Lord is my shepherd

At the end the "r-d" were crooked as they were written over a crack. Something had dripped. Blood, she thought with a shiver.

The dust and grime were thick; how long would the words last? Weeks? Months? Had someone been trapped here during a hurricane? Had they died here? Was there a ghost?

"Oh for shit's sake," she muttered.

"Kara? You okay?"

"My imagination is working in overdrive." She stood, every joint in her body creaking. "When we get out of here, I want to soak in a very hot bubble bath."

"I'll join you," he said.

"Look at the mirror."

"I saw it."

She walked to the sink and tried the handles.

Nothing.

"It was worth a shot," Matt said. "Are you okay?"

She shrugged. "Physically? Other than a whopper of a headache and a sore shoulder and bruises in odd places, I'm fine. I just really hate feeling trapped where everything is out of my control." She glanced at his leg and frowned. "Are you bleeding?" She squatted to inspect his injury. "Shit, Matt! This is bad."

He looked down at the surprisingly large dark stain on his ankle. "From the stairs."

She rolled up the leg of his sweats. He suppressed a moan when the material brushed against the cut.

"This is a deep cut."

"It's fine."

"It's still bleeding." She looked around but saw nothing they could use to put pressure on it. "There's gotta be something around here." She started to take off her tank, but he stopped her.

"I don't need your shirt."

"I'm wearing a sports bra."

He chuckled. "Yeah, well just keep it on for now. Down the hall there are some doors. Maybe we'll find something to bandage it up. But getting out of here is our first priority."

She didn't like the look of the cut, but he was right. She glanced down the hall. Junk littered the floor. A couple broken chairs, a file cabinet, a lot of paper strewn about. But the center of the hall was mostly clear, as if someone had walked through and pushed stuff up against the wall.

Maybe the person who cut their finger on the broken mirror.

The building wasn't completely silent. Matt was right, there was a faint electric hum. That had to be a good thing, right?

"We stay together," Matt said.

"No argument from me," Kara said.

Cautiously, they walked down the hall. Matt picked up a folder that was wedged between trash and an upside-down chair. Dirt fell from the front. He opened it; the pages were swollen from moisture. "Look," he said and turned the file to Kara.

"A cannery?" There must be farms in the area. Which meant lots of land and few people.

"Look at the bottom," Matt said.

Kara scanned the faded ink. "Georgia. We're in *Georgia*?"

Matt dropped the folder. "The resort is less than two hours from the border. Catherine said Reid would have a secondary location, and a place like this would fit. Remote, isolated, empty."

Kara stayed within reach of Matt as they navigated the cluttered hall until they reached the end of what appeared to be a T intersection. To their right was near-complete darkness, to the left a faint green light over metal doors.

Matt reached for her hand and squeezed it. "We stick together. Down there?" He gestured toward the eerie glow to the left.

"The green light is like a beacon, pulling us there, as if we're being led." She glanced right, frowned. "But I don't like the dark. We can't see where we're going, and after you nearly fell down the stairs . . ." She was torn. She hated being indecisive.

"Let's go right, slowly, stick close to the wall, and hold hands."

She nodded, let out a breath she didn't know she was holding. "Okay."

The corridor stretched ahead in dark shadows, littered with the broken bones of furniture, their shoes crunching on glass and scraps of metal. They stepped carefully, the last thing either of them needed was to slice their foot open. They couldn't see much, just dark shapes, so they tentatively felt their way through the maze of debris. The previous corridor had some junk, but nothing like this, as if someone had pushed all the furniture from every office into the hall.

Matt had the depressing thought that they were in a tomb. The air thick, old, and heavy. It had a taste, like dust saturated with mildew, like something that had been sealed in too long.

He shivered. Kara squeezed his hand tight, perhaps sensing his apprehension.

Just when Matt thought they had picked a dead end and was about to tell Kara to turn back, he saw a faint flicker of light, like the earliest dawn. A way out? A door? A balcony? A window?

"Did you see that?" Kara asked.

"Yeah," he said, his voice rough, his throat dry.

They had to scale what felt like a broken desk with concrete mixed in as they turned the corner. There, a dim, steady golden light cut through the dark. It was daylight. Not the eerie, artificial glow of the elevator or odd green lighting from the opposite hall, but outside. Freedom. It was a way out, it had to be.

Sticking close to the concrete walls, they steadily moved toward the light and discovered the source: a tall factory window, boarded from the outside. Light filtered through a jagged crack in the planks, thin and sickly. Matt ran his finger along the window; someone had painted the glass to block the light, but a section of the paint had been scratched off, letting in the morning sun.

He pressed his face to the glass, trying to see out. Though his vision was blurry, he saw something . . . but it didn't help.

"What?" Kara said.

"I see green. Fields, trees, that's it. There's no one out there. No buildings, no houses."

No one to help, he thought, but refused to give up hope. If he lost hope, Kara would, too. He had to be strong.

"No way out," Kara said.

"We'll find a way," he said firmly.

Matt felt around for a window latch. Maybe they could open the window—break it if they had to—pry off the boards.

"What's that?" Kara said.

Matt looked over his shoulder, his gaze moving to where Kara had squatted only a foot behind him. At first he didn't see anything, but as he shifted the thin ray of light hit the floor and reflected off something shiny and metal.

Kara picked it up. "It's a bracelet. Diamonds and gold. I don't know, they might not be real, but it seems odd to find this here."

She pocketed it, looked at Matt. "Can we get out this way?"

"No," he said. He didn't want to give up, but this wasn't the way out. He pushed on the latch at the bottom of the window. It didn't budge. "It looks like we're three stories up. We could break the window and possibly remove the boards, but it's a long drop."

"It's worth the risk," she said.

"Breaking our necks?"

"Just—break the window. Maybe we'll see someone. We can scream for help."

It was a desperate move, but they were desperate, Matt thought.

"Step back," he said. He squatted to pick up a broken drawer. He closed his eyes, turned his head away from the window, and hit the glass as hard as he could. He heard a crack, but it didn't shatter—the paint offered some protection. He hit it again.

"Try this," Kara said. She reached down and picked up what looked like a broomstick without the sweeper. It snagged on the debris. She yanked it and Matt heard a click, so soft he wondered if he imagined it.

"Wait," he said but it was too late. Kara had freed the stick, and at the same time a rumbling directly above them had Matt instinctively moving away from the window.

A crunch, a *pop!*, and glass shattered.

"Run!"

The ceiling above groaned. Dust sifted down in lazy spirals before the floor above gave way with a deafening *crash*. A rotted support beam dropped like a guillotine, slamming onto the floor where Matt had just been.

They ran through the maze of debris, Matt's calf burning, Kara swearing as she stumbled over furniture. Thick dust and chunks of plaster fell over them as they made it back to the fork in the hall. Another groan, like the sound of machinery slowly stopping, and more tiles fell from the ceiling behind them.

Then silence. Quiet except for his pounding heart. He grabbed Kara. "Are you okay? Are you hurt?"

"That wasn't a collapse. That was *triggered.*"

He agreed. There was no other explanation. Not in light of what they had already been through.

Kara's voice was borderline panicked. "Someone set this up. They're watching. Playing with us."

"It was a trap. I don't think they're watching. We moved something and then . . ." He didn't have to finish his sentence; Kara had lived through it with him. One saving grace of that collapse—it let in more light. That gave him a bit of hope.

"It's a game, we're the pawns, they're going to kill us."

"No. We're going to get out." He forced himself to sound strong though he was terrified that Kara was right. "Are you hurt? Talk to me, Kara. Were you injured?"

"I just . . . I just need a minute. Okay?" She was shaking. He was, too.

"Take as much time as you need, Kara."

She sat down and leaned against the wall.

Matt sat down next to her.

"I don't want to die here," she whispered.

"We're not going to die. I promise you."

"I'm holding you to that."

"We'll take five minutes."

"Thank you."

He kissed the top of her head. "I need five minutes, too."

He needed more than five minutes, but he feared the longer it took for them to find a way out, the greater chance they would, in fact, die here.

8

Catherine's head was splitting by the time she and Sloane arrived at the Flagler County Sheriff's Department Monday afternoon. Michael and Ryder were going straight to the resort, and Jim was heading to the crime scene lab to learn anything they might have found in the room. No one had spoken on the plane, each of them wrapped up in their thoughts and concerns, rereading files and notes and trying to figure out what happened to Matt and Kara. What had they missed. Where were they taken.

What did I do wrong? Catherine thought miserably. *What did I miss?*

Detective Bianca Fuentes and DA John Anson greeted them when they walked into the conference room. Neither looked happy.

"We have no physical evidence tying Reid to any of the murders," Anson said. "So far his phone records and financials are clean. We're still going through them, but this is a complete disaster."

Catherine couldn't help but recognize that on Friday, Anson

was on top of the world, confident his team would pull together evidence to seal the case. Now he sounded defeated.

"We have him on attempting to drug and abduct two federal agents," Catherine said.

"Do we?" Anson countered. "We have him on *possible* attempted kidnapping, but we can't prove he drugged the food."

Bianca said, "It's a tight window, and he is the only person other than the chef who could have done it."

"But we can't prove it," Anson snapped. "He could say he turned his back on the cart for two minutes and there's two minutes where anyone could have walked up and dropped ketamine into the coffee and juice."

Bianca scowled, and Catherine realized they were both exhausted.

She said, "You went through his calls, correct? He must have reached out to someone after he was arrested."

"I don't know what happened to your agents," Anson said, "but Reid hasn't made any calls other than to his lawyer on Friday. Did we get the wrong guy? Because from where I'm sitting, we have nothing on Reid other than *maybe* attempted kidnapping. And the judge may just buy his lame-ass excuse."

"The food he served our agents had been drugged with the same drug found in the systems of the other victims," Catherine said. "He was apprehended with zip ties and duct tape on his person."

"There were no drugs found in his apartment, his locker at work, his vehicle, or the kitchen," Anson said. "We can't prove *he* drugged the food. And Costa and Quinn aren't here to testify. His lawyer will say Reid is innocent because someone *else* abducted them. He, after all, was sitting in jail all weekend. The judge is going to buy it unless we have solid *physical* evidence that Reid has a partner. And nothing in your profile even hinted that he was working with anyone. In fact, it specifically states that he worked alone."

Catherine was well aware of what her profile said, and she was beating herself up over her mistake. Historically, if there was a killing pair, the dominant personality was almost always motivated by sexual violence. Because there was no sexual assault, she determined that there was a lone killer who targeted newly married women not for sexual gratification, but as punishment for wrongs done to him by a similar type of woman.

"My team here, and the LA FBI, are working around the clock to learn everything about Garrett Reid. The answer is there, but since we only identified him Friday morning, we're playing catch-up."

Bianca said, "Now that he has a lawyer, we can interview him again. I was going to do it alone, but since you're here, Dr. Jones, maybe you'd like to sit in."

"Yes, thank you," Catherine said.

"We jumped the gun," Anson said.

Catherine was glad he said *we* and didn't fully blame the FBI. Michael was already beating himself up on going in too early because he perceived a threat.

Anson rubbed his temples. "Thank you for coming back," he muttered. "We're all to blame for this fiasco, maybe I should have weighed in more on the plan. Maybe we should have allowed Reid to take your agents off the premises. Then we would have found *where* he killed six people."

"It was a risk that we didn't feel was worth taking—to Costa and Quinn, and to your deputies," Sloane said. "Everyone agreed."

"Quinn didn't," Anson said. "She argued against it, I should have listened to her."

"It was nearly unanimous," Bianca said. "We have to stop the what-ifs and should-have-beens. We talk to Reid again, get him to slip up. If we can't, then we lay it out for the judge."

"I know this judge," Anson said. "He's good, very law and order, but he really hates when he thinks we're overcharging."

"You're not overcharging," Bianca said.

"We can't prove much of anything," he said. "But I'll work through it. I'll find something—a felony—and make it clear that we intend to charge more."

Bianca said, "Let's see what his lawyer's game plan is. If he gets out this afternoon, we'll follow him. The resort isn't going to take him back. He's going to have to make a move at some point. Meet up with his partner, or maybe lead us to wherever Quinn and Costa are."

Anson walked away without comment. He was angry and worried about their case, and Catherine didn't blame him. She didn't have much confidence at this point, and she was worried about Matt and Kara.

"How do you think we should handle this?" Bianca asked.

"I read the transcript of your interview on Friday, and spoke with Michael," Catherine said. "We ask the same questions. Force him to recount everything, and any discrepancy, we push. Try to trip him up, get him to contradict himself. He may slip up or, if we're really lucky, give us a path to follow."

"The lawyer will be a buffer," Sloane said.

Bianca nodded. "He'll slow things down, prevent him from saying anything incriminating."

"Do you know anything about the lawyer?" Catherine glanced down at the notes she'd taken on the plane. "Franklin Graves?"

"Nothing. He's out of Jacksonville. I don't know how Reid knows him, but he's never handled a case in our county."

That was odd, Catherine thought. "He's not a public defender?"

"No. Reid had the number memorized, so I assumed they know each other." Then she paused, as if recalling the exact situation. "Actually, he left a message. I don't think he even talked to him. And he hasn't shown up yet, which is irritating.

We may not even have time to interview him again before his arraignment."

"Can you get the number he called?"

"I'll ask the sergeant to download the log. Why?"

"Research. How did Reid know this guy, and why him and not a public defender? Does Reid have money we don't know about?"

"He lives frugally," Bianca said. "We're still analyzing financials, but he doesn't have a huge chunk of change in his bank account. We have the contact information for his family, but your office wasn't able to get much out of them in person. Something like this is better in person, but we can't force them to talk."

"I spoke with the agent in Los Angeles," Catherine said, "and his impression was the parents were in shock and embarrassed. They claimed—and we have no evidence this is untrue—that they hadn't spoken to their son for seven years. I'll call and follow up, see what else I can learn. And I've left messages for his two brothers, but haven't had a callback yet."

Bianca nodded. "There are no calls to Reid's parents or brothers in the last year, which is as far back as we have, at least from his phone."

"What else have you learned?" Catherine asked.

"Your agent, the cop I mean, Quinn? She figured out how he may have been leaving his apartment undetected, through a hidden door in the patio fencing. But if this guy is the killer—"

"He is."

"Why wouldn't he rent a place that offers him more privacy?"

"Maybe to give him an alibi. His neighbors liked him, didn't think twice about him. He blends in. That's what he wants. Everything else about my profile holds," Catherine insisted. "He *may* have a partner, but Reid has above average intelligence and therefore he could have thought ahead, planned this all out. I contacted the FBI offices in the jurisdictions where he previously worked to reach out to his previous employers. They may have information on him, friends, colleagues. Someone he was close to that he might call for help."

"Help him by kidnapping two LEOs, so he appears innocent?"

It sounded extreme, and Catherine feared that not only was she wrong about the partner, but that she was wrong about Reid's psychology and motivation.

He had this *all* planned, Catherine thought. Extreme foresight. The timing, the lawyer, grabbing Matt and Kara. It was planned in case he was caught.

She would not underestimate him again, but she feared Matt and Kara would end up paying for her miscalculation.

"Finally," Bianca said as she looked down at her phone. "Reid's father is on the line. I've been trying to reach his family since I had the report from your agent. You with me, Catherine?"

"Yes, thank you." She turned to Sloane and said, "Will you determine what we're still missing on the financials and let Tony's assistant know? She'll light a fire under our people to get us everything today."

Sloane nodded, and pulled out her phone as Bianca and Catherine headed to a conference room.

Bianca picked up the phone and asked the desk sergeant to route the call then put it on speaker.

"Mr. Reid? This is Detective Fuentes. I'm with FBI Agent Catherine Jones. Thank you for getting back to me."

"I was surprised that I had a call from Florida law enforcement," Mr. Reid said. He had a soft, older voice. "Though I suppose after the FBI came by Friday I should expect anything."

Bianca slid Catherine a note.

Harold Reid, 66, married 40 yrs to Willa Reid, 62
Pasadena, California. Three kids, GR youngest.

Bianca said, "I'm calling about your son, Garrett Reid."

"I spoke to an FBI agent Friday evening. He said that Garrett has been arrested, but didn't give me any information. What did he do?"

Interesting, Catherine thought. No immediate denial, no *you must have the wrong person*, no anger. Just *what did he do?* As if his father was expecting something like this.

"The DA hasn't yet filed specific charges, but is looking at multiple counts of kidnapping and homicide," Bianca said.

Silence.

When Mr. Reid didn't respond, Bianca asked, "When was the last time you spoke to Garrett?"

"As I told the agent, it's been years. Seven years, at least."

"So you and your wife have had no contact with him? Not even on email or social media?"

"Not since . . ." His voice trailed off. "I don't see how we can help you. As I told the agent, we haven't talked to him, we don't know what he's doing, we have no responsibility for him. He's a grown man who is responsible for his own decisions."

Bianca glanced at Catherine, so she took over the questioning. "Mr. Reid," she said in a calm, professional tone, "I'm Dr. Catherine Jones, a special agent with the FBI. Your son will be in court this afternoon for his arraignment and bail hearing. It's important for us to understand his background, his familial ties, and whether he's had previous encounters with the law. While we know he hasn't had any federal arrests or arrests in Florida, we're still looking at all jurisdictions where he lived. We also are interested in speaking with his friends from before he moved to Florida last year."

"Again, Dr. Jones, I don't see how I can help you. I have three sons. Vince is a doctor, has a wife and two daughters, a good career, a good man. Never gave us any trouble growing up. Frankie, he's now a civil engineer, as I was. Frankie was a fun-loving child, athletic and happy. He had his fair share of scrapes, but always owned up to his mistakes. He married his high school sweetheart and they have four children, the youngest only two months now. As far as my wife and I are concerned, Garrett is no longer our son."

"You disowned him?"

"He dishonored us. He disowned us. We failed in some way. Believe me, I don't know what we did or didn't do. We didn't raise him any differently than Vince or Frankie. And Garrett was a smart boy, an attractive boy. He excelled in everything he did, from school to sports to making friends. He had the Midas touch, some might say. Whatever he did, he succeeded at."

"What happened?" Catherine said quietly.

"I—I don't see how this is relevant. It was years ago."

"We won't know what's relevant until we know," she said.

"There were many things," Mr. Reid said after a moment. "But it started when he was in college. We gave him money for tuition, room, and board. More than $30,000 a year for four years. We didn't realize until six months after he graduated that he'd also taken out loans in our name, loans we're still paying off."

"That's fraud, Mr. Reid."

"He manipulated my wife into signing the papers. It would be next to impossible to prove fraud. But yes, he conned his own parents." He sounded both bitter and embarrassed. "So we told him he had to pay the loans. Instead, he entered into an affair with my wife's closest friend—a woman twice his age who had a large settlement from her divorce. And he had *her* pay *his* loans. We—we didn't take the money. Garrett is charming, handsome, and smart. He works hard at not working. We haven't spoken since he left California when he was twenty-three. And I don't care to speak to him now. I am truly sorry for anyone he hurt. I never thought he would . . . he could . . . *kill* anyone. Steal from them? Manipulate people? Yes. But murder . . . it's going to break his mother's heart."

"But you believe it," Bianca said. Catherine saw the worry and panic on her face, that if Garrett's father was called to the stand, his testimony that he didn't see his son as violent might sway a jury.

"If killing another human being gave Garrett something he wanted? Yes. Yes, I suppose I do believe it. I need to go." He hung up before Catherine could ask another question.

Bianca asked Catherine, "What do you think?"

"Garrett Reid is a narcissistic con artist. I can't give a specific psychiatric diagnosis without a personal interview, but if we take what Mr. Reid said as true, he's a sociopath without empathy for other human beings. He wouldn't understand or care if they were emotionally damaged because of his con. Take seducing an older woman. He would have no guilt for lying to her, manipulating her, or stealing from her. He wouldn't care if she was an emotional mess when she realized what he had done—what she had let him do. More, he enjoyed it."

Catherine paused, considered next steps. "I want to talk to his brothers, who may be more forthcoming than his father. Any woman who had a relationship with him, starting with the mother's friend. Definitely his co-workers, both at the resort here and in other cities."

"How is this going to help us keep him in jail?"

"It won't, not today. But the more we learn about Garrett Reid, the greater chance we'll find out where he took his victims and who his partner is."

"So *now* you think he has a partner."

Catherine cringed at the tone, but answered professionally. "Yes. I don't know their role or how they met, but someone working with Garrett Reid abducted Matt and Kara."

9

While Michael worked with the Jacksonville FBI office to finish processing the room Matt and Kara shared, Ryder sat in the small Sapphire Shoals security office with Brian Valdez and reviewed the video Brian had compiled.

Video throughout the resort confirmed what Brian had told him over the phone, but Ryder was most interested in the clip of the person of interest spotted after Matt and Kara returned from racquetball.

It was his third time watching the segment of video where a maintenance worker was in view for only a few seconds pushing a laundry bin in front of him. He wore pants, which was part of the uniform, but also long sleeves, and was the only maintenance worker who seemed to be wearing long sleeves that Ryder could tell—Valdez confirmed that it was the correct uniform, but that most of the guys wore short sleeves. The suspect wore a hat low across the brow.

About five foot nine, with a slim build. Because of the ballcap, Ryder couldn't see his hair, but the skin at the back of the neck suggested the guy was most likely white.

There was a brief profile angle that made Ryder think this person wasn't a man; just for a split second, Ryder knew in his gut that this person was a woman.

But Ryder was an analyst; he never relied on feelings. He focused on facts, evidence, things he could prove or disprove. He couldn't state with certainty that their suspect was a woman. He need corroboration.

He saved that small fragment of the clip, then pulled up the section of video that Valdez had sent him earlier, the clip of the individual pushing the laundry cart away from Matt and Kara's room. Ryder didn't want to read anything into it because he *thought* their suspect was a woman, but was she walking like a woman? Could he make out breasts under the loose-fitting uniform, or was he making an assumption?

"Do you have this person on any other feeds?" Ryder asked Valdez when he returned. Ryder's eyes were dry and he blinked rapidly, forcing himself to turn away from the video.

"That's all we've found during the two-hour window, but my best guy is going through every recording for the twenty-four hours leading up to the abduction, as you requested," Valdez said.

"You're certain you don't recognize this person?" Ryder tapped on the frozen screen.

"No. He doesn't work here. I personally talked to the head of Maintenance—he's never seen the guy before."

Ryder hesitated, not sure he wanted to plant the idea in Brian's head. "Do you have any women working in Maintenance?"

"Sure, a few. Why?"

"Does this person look male or female?"

Brian looked at the still, then pressed Play, watched the ten-second clip. "Could be a woman, I guess. You're thinking because of how she walks?"

"That, but also the chin." Ryder rewound, then froze the image on the best profile shot he'd found. It wasn't sharp because he had to zoom in.

"I see that. It's not real clear, but could be a woman. But even if it was someone I've met before, I don't know that I would recognize them from any of these images. I'd say this isn't any of the women we have in Maintenance, but I wouldn't swear to it."

"You told Detective Fuentes that Garrett Reid didn't socialize much with staff but was still friendly and well-liked. Did she ask if he had a girlfriend?"

Brian nodded. "I told her I never saw him with a woman, and his co-workers said he didn't mention a girlfriend. You don't think a woman kidnapped your agents, do you?"

Ryder *did* think that—but he couldn't prove it. The only lead was a surveillance video showing someone, possibly a woman, pushing a laundry cart away from Matt and Kara's suite toward the parking lot. But there was no proof they were in the cart.

He sent the clearest images he could extract to the team, noting that this was most likely the individual who had abducted Matt and Kara.

He'd already forwarded all available video footage to the FBI lab—from twelve hours before Garrett Reid's arrest through midnight Sunday—along with the Ormond Beach restaurant surveillance from Saturday night. But without a clear image of the suspect, even the FBI's advanced software and facial recognition tools would struggle to identify them. Despite the footage being better than average, processing it would still take days.

Fortunately, Tony Greer had prioritized the case. The entire tech unit at the lab was working on it. Ryder sent the head of the unit the clip featuring the person of interest, along with time stamps, and asked for image enhancement and cross-referencing with the rest of the footage. Then he texted his theory to the team.

Time wasn't on their side. If this was a ransom attempt for Reid's release, a demand would have come by now. If it was retribution for his arrest, Matt and Kara were probably dead.

Ryder was still deep in reviewing security footage when Jim Esteban came in and sat down. He looked exhausted.

"Did you learn anything at the crime lab?" Ryder asked, tearing his eyes away from the screen for a minute.

"Nothing useful yet. It's a good team, and they're working closely with both the state lab and Quantico. But even if we bump everything to the top, some tests can't be done instantaneously. There's also analysis and verification. It's a process. I'm getting some of the preliminary reports tonight, and the ME and I concur on some of the chemical analysis. For example, we know the victims were drugged with ketamine, but there was another inconclusive test of a possible narcotic that we're going to rerun at Quantico. Some drugs break up faster in the system."

"Every little bit helps," Ryder said.

"Dammit, kid. This is Matt and Kara."

Jim pressed his fingers to his eyes and sighed.

"I know," Ryder said quietly.

"I tried talking to Michael. He's taking it hard, but he won't discuss it. He's like a wall."

"He blames himself for the case against Reid falling apart."

Jim scowled. "That's bullshit, and you know it."

"I didn't say I agree," Ryder said.

"We'll find them," Jim said firmly, as if to convince himself. Then he said to Ryder, "You think it's a woman."

"Yes, I do," Ryder said. He turned back to the computer screen, looked at the frozen image, then restarted the feed so he could go through it yet again.

"What does Catherine say?"

"She hasn't responded."

"Well, Michael's still working with the Jacksonville office, but I talked to him before I came in here. We have a good idea about what happened yesterday."

Ryder paused the recording again and gave Jim his full attention. "And?"

"Matt and Kara came back from racquetball and had breakfast on their patio, which overlooks the beach. There's evidence that someone was hiding in the bushes that separated their cottage from the neighbors'. The ground there is a combination of sand, rocks, and soil, so we don't have footprints, but there were freshly broken branches and the ERT is going over the entire area looking for trace evidence—blood, skin, hair. In your picture, hair was trapped in the ball cap. Still, the suspect could have taken off the cap or dropped a cigarette butt."

Ryder almost laughed. Highly doubtful, but the point was taken: criminals often left something behind by which they could be identified.

Jim continued. "We found a tranquilizer dart with dried blood on the tip. It's already on the way to the lab for processing, and since we have both Matt and Kara's blood types and DNA on file, we should be able to identify it quickly."

"They were shot with darts? I don't remember reading that there were any injuries consistent with a tranq on previous victims," Ryder said.

"Because there was nothing identified in the autopsies. I sent the information to the ME and he's going to review the reports and photos again, but if they had been shot with a dart, the wound might not have been noticed because of other injuries, time lapse, decomposition. And maybe the suspect used the darts with Matt and Kara because they are trained law enforcement and he didn't know if they were still checking their food."

"Or because she's a woman and might have needed them to remain unconscious for longer," Ryder guessed.

"Good point," Jim said.

"How fast would something like that knock them out?"

"Depends. A few seconds to a couple minutes. They'll test the dart for common sedatives. Could be one of maybe a half dozen—my bet is on ketamine or Telazol, but there are other options. Maybe a combination of drugs, if the shooter knows what they're doing. The fact that he or she took Matt and Kara gives me some comfort that they're still alive."

"And how long would they be unconscious?"

"I couldn't say." Jim leaned forward, put his hand on Ryder's knee. "You listen to me, okay? They're alive. They're stashed somewhere to make it seem like Garrett Reid is as innocent as the day he was born, but we know he's behind it. They will be fine. We *will* find them."

Jim sounded confident, but his voice cracked at the end.

"Anyway." Jim cleared his throat, continued. "There's a chance we can trace the drugs. Ketamine, not so much—it's very common—but if it's a mix or a different drug, we have a chance."

How long would that take? Ryder wondered. How much time did Matt and Kara have?

Michael walked in, his face rigid and unreadable. "Jacksonville is rushing the labs. We don't think that our suspect went into their room. Nothing appears to be taken or disturbed, but they printed the place just in case. Two agents went to the restaurant Matt and Kara ate at Saturday night, talked to staff—no one saw anything out of the ordinary, and the manager remembered them because Kara ordered tequila straight up." Michael's lips twitched a bit, but he didn't smile. "They talked to both Uber drivers, neither believed they were followed, and one said Matt talked to him about Miami when he found out the driver grew up in the same neighborhood. Neither driver has a criminal record, and both have family in the area."

Brian stepped into the crowded room. "Agent Harris, the staff that interacted with your agents yesterday are all waiting outside my office."

"Thank you," Michael said to Brian, then turned to Ryder and Jim. "You both good here?"

"I'm heading back to the morgue," Jim said. "We're going to take another look at the trace evidence, focusing on anything that may help us narrow down where Reid took his victims."

"Don't go anywhere alone," Michael snapped. "Jacksonville will assign you an agent."

"Is that necessary?" Jim asked. "I'm not the face of this investigation and I wasn't involved with the arrest."

"No exceptions," Michael said firmly. "Matt would insist, you know that."

Jim relented. "Fine."

"I'll have an agent meet you here and escort you to the morgue," Michael said. "Are you ready to leave?"

"Yes," Jim said.

Michael was on his phone as he followed Brian out of the conference room. When he was out of earshot, Jim said to Ryder, "See what I mean?"

"It's hard on all of us," Ryder said. "He's processing differently."

"He's going to implode if he doesn't acknowledge that he's worried. I'm going to talk to Sloane. She's good at getting Michael to open up."

He pulled out his phone and started texting, and Ryder went back to the security videos.

He had to find something—a face, a vehicle, anything that could pinpoint Garrett Reid's partner.

Time was running out.

10

Michael texted the head of the ERT in Jacksonville with the request to shadow Jim Esteban as Brian escorted him down the hall. "You can use my office for the interviews," Brian said. "Do you want to talk to anyone specifically first?"

"Room service, housekeeping, head of Maintenance, then whoever worked at the gym when Matt and Kara were there."

Brian jotted down a list. "Feel free to use my desk." He motioned to his chair, then stepped out.

Michael's first interview was with Jill Quiroz, a no-nonsense round woman in her late fifties with graying black hair and deep wrinkles around her eyes. She'd worked at the resort for twelve years. Michael had spoken to her on Friday when they arrested Garrett since she had also been on duty then. "I personally watched the chef prepare Mr. Costa and Ms. Quinn's breakfast," she said. "No one was poisoned on my watch."

"No, ma'am. We don't believe the food was poisoned," Michael said. The dart they had collected had indicated they'd been tranquilized, but he wasn't going to share that information with staff, not until they had a full analysis of the room.

"It wasn't," she said firmly. "I know the chef, he's a good man. And the food did not leave my sight from the minute I domed the plates until I personally delivered the cart."

She was angry, and Michael wasn't certain whether she was angry with him for asking questions or at the situation.

"You are now aware that Costa and Quinn are law enforcement?" Michael confirmed.

"Yes. That was made clear to me on Friday. I spoke to you and Agent Costa, remember?"

"Of course," Michael said with a small smile, even though his stomach was tight and in pain. The interviews were necessary, but he wanted to be out doing something . . . *more* . . . to find Matt and Kara.

He asked, "Yesterday, when did the call come in for room service?"

"It's in the log," she said.

"I want to confirm that it's accurate."

"11:10 a.m. Orange juice, champagne, blueberry pancakes, a protein omelet, and two sides of bacon. I delivered the cart at 11:35, maybe a minute or two after. I made certain the cart was never out of my view."

"Who answered the door?"

"Mr. Costa. They were sitting outside on the patio and I offered to set it up, he said he would take the cart, and then he tipped me."

"And his mood? Did he seem nervous, agitated, happy?"

"Relaxed," she said, "Friendly, polite. He's been polite his entire stay."

"Did you see Detective Quinn when you delivered the tray?"

"Yes. She was sitting in the sun on the patio drinking coffee, which appeared to have been made in the suite. It was in one of the blue mugs that we have in the room for guests."

"And their demeanor? Did either of them seem concerned or worried or preoccupied?"

"No, as I said, they were relaxed. They were—well, Mr. Costa seemed very happy. He did mention to me that he had won at racquetball and Ms. Quinn said something like he cheated. He winked at me and said, 'I never cheat.' He's very charming," she added with a smile.

Michael didn't know if he would call Matt charming, but he could see why an older woman might.

"Are they okay? You will find them?" she asked with concern.

"We'll find them," Michael said. He wasn't going to think about *not* finding them, or what his friends might be going through at this moment. He had people to interview, answers to find. Failure wasn't an option.

He would not fail his friends.

Don't think of Matt and Kara as friends. They are trained and competent. Colleagues.

If he made this personal, he wasn't going to get through the next hour, let alone through the day.

He asked Mrs. Quiroz, "Did you see anyone loitering outside their cottage?"

"Like I told Mr. Valdez, no. No one."

"Not necessarily a stranger—maybe a staff member?"

"No one," she repeated. "I delivered the cart, went back to the kitchen. I didn't see anyone except George and his new hire, I don't remember his name, working in the flower beds on the path."

Michael looked at his notes. He didn't have George on his list, so he made a note that he wanted to talk to him as well.

He then showed her the printout of the individual in the maintenance uniform that Ryder had given him. There was no clear shot of a face, barely a profile, but right now, it was the best they had.

"Do you recognize this person?"

She took a long look, frowned, shook her head. "No. Why?"

"We need to talk to everyone who worked Sunday morning, and we don't know who this is."

"Carlos, the head of Maintenance, would. Or Mr. Valdez. Maybe he's a new hire? I know I haven't seen him before."

Him, Michael thought. She assumed male. Maybe Ryder's instincts were wrong on this. The idea that a woman partnered with a killer . . . not unheard of, but not common.

"Thank you," he said. "You may send in the next person."

When she left, Michael texted Brian that he would like to talk to George in Maintenance who worked on Sunday morning. Brian responded that George didn't work Mondays, so he'd call him in.

Michael next talked to housekeeping. Two women, both young, were responsible for turning the room. Beth was the senior staff member and Anna didn't speak English, so Beth spoke for them and translated for Michael. "There was a Do Not Disturb sign on the door, so we didn't enter. We went back twice, but it was still there."

Michael confirmed the times they went to the room and asked if they saw anyone loitering. They hadn't.

"During your second pass you collected the room service trays."

"Yes. When we walked down the path to the next cottage, we noted that there was a room service cart outside the patio door. We collected the items."

"Was the door open?"

"No, it was closed."

"Did you look inside?"

"No, not specifically."

"But you would have noticed if people were in the room."

"If they were in the living area," Beth said. "We wouldn't be able to see the bedroom from the slider."

MAKE IT OUT ALIVE

Michael made note of that. "Was there anything odd or un-usual when you collected the plates?"

"No, except that one of the champagne flutes was broken, it probably fell over in the wind."

Michael didn't think the wind had done anything. If Matt and Kara had been sitting at the table eating breakfast and drinking champagne when they were shot with the darts, one of them could have dropped the glass. Or when the kidnapper put them in the cart, he or she could have knocked it over.

"Did you see anyone—either a stranger or someone you knew—while you were in or around the cottage?"

Beth shook her head. "I already told you we didn't. We were busy, we had many rooms to turn over."

Neither woman recognized the individual in the photo.

After Beth and Anna, Michael spoke with the head of Main-tenance, Carlos Rodriguez, a straight-talking man in his six-ties. Michael and Matt had both spoken to him on Friday after Reid's arrest. He had been crushed; he'd personally hired Reid last fall and said he was the smartest employee he had, that he could fix anything and did it with a good attitude, no matter what the job. Now his mood changed from shock and sorrow to anger.

"A partner. He has a fucking partner," Carlos said shaking his head. "Dammit, I still can't wrap my head around all this. Killing people. Women! I told my wife—she met him!—and she didn't believe it, either."

"Killers are rarely what we expect," Michael said. He showed Carlos the photo. "We need to talk to this person. Do you know who it is?"

Carlos frowned. "Brian already asked me—I said no. That's our uniform, but this person doesn't work for me."

"Are you certain?"

He narrowed his eyes at Michael. "Damn straight I'm certain.

I know every man and woman on my staff, and this girl doesn't work for me."

Girl. "Do you recognize the individual? Maybe another staff member, or someone you've seen around?"

"No," he said, then looked at the photo again, shook his head. "No. It's not a good picture, I mean I can't even see her hair color or anything. If you get something better, show me. If I know, I'll tell you."

"How easy is it to steal a maintenance uniform?"

He shrugged. "I couldn't say. Everyone is issued two uniform shirts, one set of overalls, and they're responsible for them. They can wear their own khaki pants or shorts in neutral colors, or buy additional shirts or overalls at a discount."

"Order through the resort?"

He shook his head. "A company we contract with—a lot of the companies use them."

Michael slid over a notepad and pen. "Can you write down their name and contact information if you have it?"

Carlos looked it up on his phone, wrote everything down for Michael. Michael thanked him, then when he left, sent the information to Ryder with a message:

Anyone can order uniforms from this site.

If anyone could order, they wouldn't find much—they could potentially have thousands of orders to go through in northern Florida alone. But if Garrett Reid ordered an extra uniform, especially one that was too small for him? That would give them a thread to pull.

Michael needed all the threads he could find.

Alena Porter, the manager of the resort, came in a few minutes after Carlos left. Michael had already asked Brian to bring in the woman who'd worked at the gym while Matt and Kara were there, but now he texted that Alena was here and said to ask Ms. Davidson to wait a few minutes.

Alena was a trim, attractive bleached blonde who looked younger than her forty years. Michael had met her several times over the last two weeks, and she was one of the few staff members who had been privy to the undercover operation. She'd worked at the resort for seven years, starting at the front desk, and had been promoted to manager last fall—two months before the first murders.

"I'm so sorry I'm late," Alena said as she sat down, straightening her knee-length skirt over her long legs. Though impeccably dressed in a summer-weight business suit, strands of hair had escaped her slick braid, and her makeup was less than artfully applied.

"You look frazzled," Michael commented.

"I have hardly slept since you arrested Garrett. The owners' group had been pleased this was resolved, and then I heard your agents are missing and that Garrett Reid may not be guilty. Monday's my day off, I was three hours away visiting my sister when Brian called me this morning."

Michael made note of Alena's whereabouts, just in case he needed to follow up.

"Reid is involved," Michael said. "He may be working with a partner."

She stared at him. "Two killers? Oh, jeez. What do you need? Has Brian been helpful?"

"Yes," Michael said. He ran through what they determined had happened yesterday and then showed Alena the photo of their suspect. "Do you recognize this person?"

She looked, shook her head. "I can't see their face. It could be anyone."

Michael put the photo back into his folder. "If Garrett makes bail this afternoon, what are your plans?"

Her eyes widened. "My plans? My plans for what? Why would he make bail? He's suspected of killing six people!"

"Because we're still investigating, and a good attorney could get him released with bond."

"That's insane. I have no plans for Garrett. He has been terminated. He won't be allowed on the property. Are you saying he may walk free?" She glanced at her phone, frowned, but turned back to Michael without addressing whatever she'd read.

"Temporarily," Michael said. He understood why the management would be upset, but Alena seemed personally agitated. "Do you have something to add?"

"No," she said quickly, too quickly, and she didn't look directly at him.

He asked, "Was anyone on staff close to Garrett? Did you ever see him alone with a man or woman, perhaps someone he was romantically involved with?"

She shook her head. "He was the last person I thought would be guilty."

Michael inwardly winced. He was tired of hearing how nice, helpful, and unproblematic Garrett Reid was. "Killers often don't look violent. So you know of no close friends? Girlfriend? Boyfriend?"

There was no reason, based on his history, to believe that Garrett was gay, but it was a thread they needed to close off.

"No. And I don't get involved in the private lives of staff. Carlos is Garrett's supervisor, he's the most likely to know about his personal life."

"I've spoken to him," Michael said.

Alena looked at her phone again. "Agent Harris, I have a minor crisis to deal with. I have two guests giving my assistant manager a difficult time right now, demanding a free stay because of this situation. The head of housekeeping is threatening to quit because in her words, 'There's a killer on staff,' and

I have two security officers who called in sick this afternoon, so I'm severely short-staffed."

Michael was interested in those security officers, but would talk to Brian about it.

"I understand if you need to go. I'll reach out if I have more questions."

Alena stood, walked to the door, turned back to him. "Agent Harris, I really hope you resolve this situation sooner rather than later. Our reputation is on the line, and while I feel awful that something bad happened to our guests, I have this resort and more than a hundred employees to protect."

He watched her leave, then texted Ryder.

Alena Porter was visiting her sister today. Verify her whereabouts.

Michael didn't think that the manager had anything to do with the murders. She knew about the undercover operation, and Michael couldn't imagine that she would have drugged and removed Matt and Kara from the premises, but he wasn't taking chances. He would cover all the bases.

The last person who came in was Hope Davidson. According to her employee file, she had worked here for the last four months and was thirty-five, though she looked younger. She was also very attractive and physically fit, which was to be expected of someone who worked in a gym.

She hadn't worked Friday or Saturday, so no one had interviewed her yet.

"I'm shocked," she said, clutching a bottle of water. "First Garrett, now this?" She shook her head.

"According to the security cameras, Agent Costa and Detective Quinn entered the gym at approximately 8:30 on Sunday morning to work out and then play racquetball. You assisted them."

She nodded, her golden-brown eyes wide. "When they were done with their workout, they came to me for equipment, and I showed them how to work the stereo. You can hook up to Bluetooth to play music through your phone."

"Did you notice anyone in the gym who was paying undue attention to them?"

She frowned, eyebrows furrowed. "I don't think so? I mean, it wasn't super busy—the Sunday brunch in the restaurant is popular, so I either get the hardcore workout people early, or the after-brunch people coming in for yoga or racquetball. Most people check out on Sunday, so it's not really that busy after eleven."

"How many people were working out or in the facility while Costa and Quinn were there?"

"Maybe . . . ten or eleven? There was a yoga class that started at ten—I don't teach that one, that's Denise. There were six people there, all women, and then four or five people in the gym. Oh! And that doesn't include the pool. There was a family at the pool and a couple people, but I don't know how many, I'm so sorry. I should know that, shouldn't I?" She bit her lip.

"It's okay," Michael said. He was used to dealing with witnesses who became upset when they couldn't answer all his questions. "I'm aware that the resort doesn't capture key cards to use the gym." Some hotels made guests swipe into the gym, but not Sapphire Shoals. "What time did they leave?"

"Around ten thirty, maybe a little after that? We only have two racquetball rooms, and there were guests waiting. They played real hard. I suggested they go to the pool to cool off, but the female guest—Kara?—she said they had plans."

"Did you notice anyone follow them out?"

She shook her head and looked concerned. "I really didn't. I had other guests to tend to, and I was training a new employee."

"That's okay. Thank you for your time."

She got up, started for the door, then turned to him. Her eyes had tears, but she blinked them back. "Did Garrett really . . . I mean . . . did he really kill those people? That's what everyone is saying."

They hadn't yet charged him with murder, but Michael wasn't surprised that staff was talking about it—it wasn't a secret that three couples had disappeared from the resort and were later found dead.

"It's an ongoing investigation," Michael said.

"But you arrested him. Right? He's in jail—that's what Alena said."

"He is in jail," Michael confirmed. He didn't know how long that would last. Catherine wasn't confident that the judge would deny bail, especially since they'd found zero evidence that he had killed anyone. Michael felt sick to his stomach that their entire case was falling apart.

"It's like, you don't really know people, do you? He always seemed like such a nice guy."

"Brian will reach out if we have additional questions. When do you get off work?"

"Usually I work five in the morning until one, but Brian asked me to stay because you wanted to talk to me."

"I appreciate your time," Michael said, and Hope walked out.

Michael quickly wrote up his notes, then sent Brian a text message that he'd like to talk to the employee in training, but that was a long shot.

He had nothing. Ryder was checking into their one small lead—the uniforms—but so far, zilch. He texted his Jacksonville FBI contact about the lab results from their room, though he knew nothing would be back this quickly, no matter how quickly they expedited it. He sent the team a status report.

And then he stared at the wall. He felt helpless. Matt and Kara had been missing for more than twenty-four hours and he didn't know how to find them.

11

Matt and Kara took a lot longer than five minutes to regroup after the harrowing experience down the hall when the roof collapsed.

"Okay," Kara finally said. "I'm ready. But we need to be super careful with any potential exits. Maybe they're all booby trapped."

"Agreed," Matt said and used the wall to help push himself up. He winced, tried to hide it from her.

"Hey, tell me the truth," she said. "How is your leg? No lying, Matt, I'm serious."

"It's sore, but it's not bleeding anymore. I'm good, I promise. I'll need a heavy-duty antibiotic when we get out of here—I'm sure there's rust and bacteria roaming around in my bloodstream by now."

"Gross," she said with a small laugh.

"Made you smile."

"You can't see me."

"I can tell." He took her hand and helped pull her up.

They headed down the hall toward the large metal doors with the eerie green light.

"This place is a fucking death trap," Kara mumbled as they walked carefully down the hall. This side didn't have as much junk blocking their way, which again told her they were being led in a maze. "And that light? Green for go? I'll bet it's a trap, too."

"We have to try. We don't have another option. But like you said, we'll be extra careful."

The large metal double doors were twenty feet down the corridor opposite from where the ceiling had partly collapsed. Matt inspected the seams for a booby trap like they had discovered in the elevator and staircase. Kara didn't realize that she was holding her breath until he nodded that it was clear.

Together, they pushed cautiously; the heavy metal door opened from the middle, the screech of the hinges echoing through the silence. They stepped side by side into a large room with high ceilings lost in shadows, a wave of humid air hitting Kara in the face. She had the sense of something vast and open and hesitated to move. The floor was slick with dirt and dust. A putrid scent of rusted metal, stagnant water, and stale oil hit her all at once, but it was the ghost of burnt rubber in the thick air that made her cough.

Cautious, she tested the floor in front of her. It was solid, hard concrete. As her eyes adjusted to the faint natural light that seemed to come in from a football field away, she realized that this room wasn't just any space—it overlooked a vast factory floor. High, cracked windows almost black with grime offered a fractured view of the machinery below. The factory floor seemed like a scene from an apocalyptic movie. Rows of enormous machines with gears frozen in place, conveyor belts motionless. Massive presses, grinders, and turbines that once hummed with power now stood cold and abandoned. Huge metal pipes snaked across the ceiling. Rows of unlit industrial lighting hung from beams in the ceiling that was at least three, maybe four stories high. Many of the lighting units were broken, and one tilted precariously on a single chain.

"Can we get down there?" she whispered. She didn't know why she was whispering; they were alone. She cleared her throat, looked around the room they stood in.

"Maybe," Matt said. He, too, took a tentative step. "This might be the control room, or maybe where management monitored the factory."

The room's large windows that once provided a view of the floor were mostly broken. As she moved, her feet crunched on shattered glass. There were a couple of desks, one that looked ready to use, and two that had broken legs and missing drawers. Two chairs had been pushed into the far corner. A long, wide counter along one wall with cabinet doors, most closed, and one hanging at an odd angle.

"There's a catwalk," Kara said, feeling a hint of optimism for the first time since waking up in the elevator.

The walkway was suspended over the factory floor. The thick beams of metal and rusting scaffolding made it look like it might crumble under the slightest weight, but it appeared intact.

Together, they approached the edge and looked down, realizing what had happened.

The factory floor was covered with water. Based on the size of the machines, at least a foot of water filled the space. That explained the dank, humid air. The machines themselves didn't appear ancient, and Kara wondered when the factory had shut down—and why no one had cleaned up the space.

"After what happened on the stairs, I'm not sure we can trust the catwalk," Matt said.

"It might be our only way out," Kara said. "I'm not eager to test it, but we may not have a choice."

At least they now knew what was downstairs, which was a

big plus in her book. Kara could handle known threats; it was the unknown that scared her.

A bank of old monitors and computers lined the wall opposite the cabinets. Most of the screens were broken or cracked, but there appeared to be a dull static coming from several of them. It was a security setup, with dozens of monitors that, when operational, would show the factory floor from different angles.

Surprised, she motioned to the computers. "Are the monitors on?" If there was electricity, maybe they could reach someone outside this death trap. Though just because there was electricity, didn't mean that there was internet.

Matt studied the computers quizzically. "I heard a generator earlier, but a lone generator wouldn't be able to power a building this size indefinitely. So the power could be selective—but why would these monitors be hooked up instead of lights?"

"Why did someone set up a generator at all after the building was flooded?" Kara asked.

"Possibly to pump out the water," Matt said. He walked to the monitors. One flickered and Kara jumped.

"I don't believe in ghosts," she said, "but this is very creepy."

She slowly walked around the room, their near misses still making her nervous. Movement in the corner caught her eye. She stared at the ceiling, saw nothing at first, then a red light blinked on.

Then off again.

"Matt, there's a camera in the corner."

Matt followed her gaze and then walked right over to it and looked up, inspecting.

Suddenly, static crackled in speakers near the bank of monitors.

"Well, hello!" a cheerful voice echoed.

At first Kara thought someone had walked in behind them. She whirled around, looking for the threat and searching for a weapon at the same time.

No one was there. The voice came through speakers attached to the monitors, tinny and almost unreal.

"You were fast," the voice—a woman, Kara was certain—said. She didn't sound angry; in fact, she sounded downright giddy. "I knew you were smart, but I'm smarter. Still, we're not quite ready for you, so you'll need to hold tight awhile longer."

A loud clank, followed by a screech, and then the metal doors slammed shut.

Matt ran over to the doors, Kara right on his heels, but there were no handles on this side.

Kara kicked the door; her toe throbbed.

They were trapped.

12

Catherine listened to Reid's lawyer make a compelling case for both dismissal of all charges and a low bail.

"Your honor," Franklin Graves was saying, "the police rushed to judgment. My client explained why he entered the suite where, in the course of his job on the maintenance staff of Sapphire Shoals, he saw two guests lying on the floor who he thought were unconscious. He went to help, not to do harm."

"Your honor," Anson stood, "Mr. Reid had a laundry cart that he wheeled into the room. He had zip ties and duct tape on his person. Two FBI agents came in and caught him squatting over Agent Costa. As you are aware, three couples have been abducted from the resort over the last seven months, and all of them have been found dead. Detective Quinn perfectly fits the description of the three women who were abducted and murdered."

Graves said, "If the police had evidence that my client killed anyone, they would have charged him with homicide. As it is, they are desperate and grasping at straws. My client has worked at the Shoals for nine months and has an exemplary employment record. In addition, he did not attempt to restrain anyone. The zip ties in his pocket are the same zip ties that are used in any number of tasks at the resort from wrapping wire to tagging equipment. Virtually every employee in his department has the exact same ties while working."

The judge said, "We're not litigating this case here. My job is to determine if there is probable cause to hold Mr. Reid. Mr. Anson, will you be charging Mr. Reid with homicide?"

"Detectives and my office are still investigating and—"

The judge hit his gavel. "Bail is set for $100,000 and I will see all parties back in my courtroom in one week, Monday, 9:00 a.m., for a preliminary hearing. You will have your ducks in a row, Mr. Anson, or all charges will be dismissed. Understood?"

"Yes, your honor."

"Court adjourned." He banged the gavel.

Bianca swore under her breath. "We're screwed."

"We need to talk," Catherine said quietly as she watched Reid. He whispered with his lawyer. Reid looked pleased. Not simply relieved, but pleased as if he expected the outcome but it was better than he thought.

He would run, she suspected. Graves's claims that Reid wanted to clear his name notwithstanding, he had to know they weren't going to stop looking for Matt and Kara. Anson was right not to charge him with homicide. Putting that in the charges would have started the clock. They would have to turn over evidence to the defense in discovery, and without anything of substance, the defense could easily have had the entire case dismissed.

Attempted kidnapping was enough for now; they could always add on charges as soon as they had hard physical evidence against Reid. When they arrested him for first-degree murder, they'd get his bail revoked.

Bianca followed Catherine out of the courtroom. Catherine

turned to the detective and asked, "How long until he's released?"

"Hour, take or leave."

"The lawyer seems competent. Have you seen him in action?"

"No. John hasn't even heard of him, and he knows most of the defense lawyers in northern Florida."

Catherine wanted to know more about the lawyer because it seemed odd that Garrett Reid, who had lived in Florida for less than a year, had a specific lawyer to call when arrested for a serious felony.

"Someone needs to follow Reid," Catherine said.

"My boss won't authorize that," Bianca said. "He's already angry about how this entire thing went down, and is playing CYA with the DA and media right now."

Catherine was afraid of that. "I'll have my people do it, but we're going to need to work together to build a case against him—and find my agents."

"Unless you're wrong," Bianca said pointedly. "Maybe he *is* innocent, and someone we haven't even considered is the killer."

Catherine tensed, expecting the reaction but still angry about it. "I'm not wrong," she said. "He's not innocent."

"You were wrong about the partner."

She nodded once.

It wouldn't be the first time she was wrong. So wrong that she may have gotten her best friend killed.

Like she got her sister killed.

She pushed her grief back deep inside. If she started thinking about Beth now, if she started remembering the bastard who killed her—and how wrong Catherine had been about the profile—then she wouldn't be able to do her job and she might as well go home, curl up into a ball, and cry.

John Anson stepped out of the courtroom. "We have one week to find something on this guy, or he's going to walk."

"We can make a case about kidnapping—"

"No, we can't. We don't even have the alleged victims, do we? And it will be pretty easy for the court to determine that Reid couldn't have been involved because he was in jail all weekend."

Catherine said, "My people will follow him. Can you please give me a heads-up when he's cut loose?"

John nodded. "I'm sorry about Matt and Kara. I hope we find them, but I don't know how to connect their abduction to Reid. We might think he's involved and knew about it—an accessory—but it's going to be damn hard to prove when he only made one call while in custody, and that call was to his lawyer."

"Do you know anything about Graves?"

"Nothing. He's a member of the Florida State Bar in good standing, which is all that is required."

Catherine had already asked Ryder to look into Graves's background, but she had hoped John had better information.

"What are the next steps?" John asked. "I'm open to any ideas on how we're going to prove this guy is a killer in the one week we have to do so."

"Dr. Esteban is working closely with the crime lab and medical examiner," Catherine said. "His primary focus is to find any trace evidence that will help us determine where Reid kept his victims."

"And?" John said, making a motion with his hand to hurry up, then pointedly looking at his watch.

Catherine tried not to be irritated at his attitude. "Agent Harris is reinterviewing staff at the resort. We may have found video of the individual who abducted our agents. The lab at Quantico is working on enhancing it and using facial recognition to identify the person of interest." She paused, said, "It may be a woman. The face is unclear, but the body type suggests female."

"None of this is going to give us evidence that Reid tortured and killed six people," John said with growing irritation. "One week—if I don't have something tangible, Reid walks and it'll be ten times harder to bring him in if we do find something."

John walked away and Bianca sighed. "We're fucked," she said.

"I need your help," Catherine said. "My team is going to be laser focused on what Garrett Reid does over the next forty-eight hours. Who he makes contact with, who he talks to. We need a warrant to tap Reid's phone." Catherine suspected he had a second phone, likely a burner or under a different name or business, which was how he communicated with his partner.

"I'll need to talk to my boss. He wants this guy, but he's going to take a lot of heat for the bail. And John is going to have to get the warrant, which I don't think will come from this judge." Bianca gestured with her thumb to the closed courtroom behind them.

"I can have my boss reach out," Catherine said. She wasn't sure Tony Greer would be of the right mindset at this point. He kept texting her for updates, but she had none, until now. And it wasn't good news.

Bianca said, "I'll talk to John first. I'll let you know what, if anything, we can do. Bringing in the big guns from the FBI—when the sheriff is already pointing fingers in your direction for the screwup—isn't going to get anything accomplished."

"Don't forget to let me know when he's leaving and who's taking him home."

Bianca gave a quick salute and left. Sloane approached Catherine and said, "I heard."

"You and Michael will follow Reid. I doubt he'll drive directly to where Matt and Kara are, but we need eyes on him at all times."

"Michael finished interviewing staff and is on his way in."

Catherine glanced around. No one was within earshot, but she kept her voice low. "Whoever took Matt and Kara was very familiar with the resort. He—or she, as Ryder suggests—

avoided most every camera and when they were in the range of one, they turned away or tilted their head and used the uniform and hat to avoid giving us a good image. They entered through the patio because there are no cameras beachside. There was a risk—someone could have seen them from the beach—but because of the way the cabins are laid out, it would be difficult to know exactly what the person was actually doing."

"We interviewed staff twice. Reid was never seen with someone who didn't work there. Oh," Sloane said, realizing what Catherine was thinking.

"Yes, I think his partner is on staff."

"And a woman."

"Possibly, but we can't state it with certainty."

"Ryder is positive," Sloane said. "He isn't usually so emphatic when he has an opinion. And I see it, too, but don't know if I see a woman because Ryder put it in my head. I remember the seminar you taught at Quantico last year—that the majority of female partners are subservient to the male partner."

"I'm not comfortable making that determination yet," Catherine said cautiously. Was she cautious because she'd been wrong about the partner from the beginning? Or because she didn't have enough information? "But whether or not the partner is a woman, it makes sense that Garrett Reid recruited from his immediate sphere. Sociopaths recognize sociopaths."

"If his partner is another employee, wouldn't that make her easier to identify?" Sloane asked.

"Our interviews on Friday and Saturday didn't reveal that he had a girlfriend, and we specifically asked the question about known relationships."

"Do you think it's realistic that an attractive, friendly thirty-year-old who has been living in Florida for nearly a year would never go on a date?" Sloane asked.

"He could have received his sexual gratification through the acts of violence," Catherine said. "For predators, not all sexual release comes from rape."

Michael strode down the corridor toward them, anger in every step. "He walked?"

"Bail," Catherine said. "Sloane, fill him in. I have to brief Tony." Something she wasn't looking forward to.

13

"Graves isn't taking Reid to his apartment," Michael said flatly as he followed the dark Lincoln that Reid's attorney drove from the Flagler County Jail north to 95 toward Jacksonville.

"Mm-hmm."

He glanced at Sloane. "You've been quiet," he said.

"Trying to figure out their game plan," she said. "They now know that Matt and Kara aren't newlyweds, that they're cops, so why take them?"

Michael didn't have an answer. He didn't like getting into the minds of psychopaths and trying to figure out why they did what they did. He left that to agents like Catherine, who were trained for it.

But Sloane had a point: if they didn't know Reid's game plan, they wouldn't be able to find Matt and Kara—and prove that Reid was a killer.

Michael pushed his fear to the back. He had been a Navy SEAL. He had faced danger and handled it like a pro. Why was he terrified now? If he didn't maintain control, if he fell apart, he would be no good for his team.

"Catherine said that his partner likely works at the resort," Sloane said. "It would explain how the partner could avoid security cameras. If she worked there, she may have known when they returned to their room. Maybe she had access to the room service log, or saw them walking back after the gym."

Michael said, "Are you suggesting that we may have interviewed his partner?"

Sloane shrugged. "Maybe. I don't know. We should talk to Carlos and Brian again, ask them to really think about anyone on staff who Reid may have eaten lunch with or socialized with. No matter how innocuous it seemed."

"We asked about a girlfriend—no one said he had one. No one claimed that he had any close friends on staff. And if his partner *is* on staff, we don't want to tip them off."

"All we need is an idea of who the partner might be, a profile, to narrow it down."

"Catherine was wrong from the beginning," Michael said bluntly. "She said Reid was a solo killer, she explained his motivation, and it all made sense and felt familiar—but if he is killing with a partner, especially a *female* partner, that makes her profile worth nothing."

"He *was* on the list," Sloane reminded him.

"The very long list of single men under forty who worked at the resort as a staff or vendor for less than a year."

"Catherine is beating herself up over her mistake. She blames herself that Matt and Kara were taken."

"If she has an idea, I'll listen," Michael said, "but right now I'm focusing on tried and true field work to find them."

Matt and Kara had been missing for more than twenty-four hours. It had been nearly a full day before the team even knew that they were gone. Michael blocked out how they might be suffering. It wouldn't help find them.

"Why Sunday morning?" Sloane asked.

"I don't understand the question."

"I'm mentally recreating the kidnapping. Matt and Kara could have been taken Saturday night. Going to the restaurant. Returning from the restaurant. If someone worked at the resort, they could have laid in wait in the cottage. Drugged them while they were sleeping. Any number of ways that seem easier than shooting them with a tranq dart on their patio and pushing them in a laundry cart. If it's a woman, she's strong to be able to lift Matt up."

Michael shook his head. "I doubt she's stronger than you."

"I'm strong," Sloane said, "but I couldn't lift Matt into a laundry bin. I could drag him somewhere, but there's no evidence that was done."

"My guess," Michael said after a moment, "she put the cart on its side and rolled him into it. Then she either rolled Kara into it, or righted the cart and picked Kara up. She probably doesn't weigh much."

"She's all muscle," Sloane said with a slight smile. "I can beat Kara in virtually every drill, but I'm a Marine. Still, I have to work to win. If I slack off, drop my guard even for a second, she'll find a weakness and exploit it."

She spoke with pride, not arrogance. Michael had watched the friendly competition between Sloane and Kara at the gym. Sloane had more training, better form, longer endurance, and at least six inches on Kara. Kara had tenacity, quick feet, and street smarts. He was glad that they were friends, because the tension between Catherine and Kara, until a few months ago, had been difficult. Sloane and Kara seemed to have hit it off from the beginning.

"But you're right," Sloane continued, "a woman could roll them into the cart, then right the cart with core strength and leverage. Still, a woman . . . I know women can kill, but these crimes seem particularly brutal for a woman to be party to. And with Reid in jail, if she was the submissive, would she take the initiative to go ahead and kidnap two people who she would now know are cops?"

"These people are all crazy to me."

"Don't let Catherine hear you say that."

"I don't get it," Michael said. "I really don't." He cleared his throat, trying not to be emotional. He needed to be the strong one on the team. Catherine was wringing her hands over her botched profile. Jim was convinced he had missed something in the physical evidence so was going through everything a third, fourth, fifth time. Ryder was sullen, worried, and blaming himself because it was his idea that Matt and Kara stay behind for R & R. Sloane was acting like an investigator, calm, methodically working through the crime, asking valid questions. She cared about the team, but she was new. She hadn't been with them from the beginning.

Maybe that wasn't fair. Maybe Michael was too emotional, too close. And the more emotional he felt, the harder he worked to bury his fears.

A moment later, Michael said, "Two people work together to kidnap couples, torture, kill, and dump the bodies in the ocean, but not so far offshore that they never turn up. In fact, they drop them close enough so that they *will* show up sooner rather than later. Once, I think it's personal. Twice, I think it's a psychopath. Three times? It's a game."

"A game," Sloane repeated with interest. "Maybe."

Michael was certain. But he wasn't a shrink, and he didn't understand most of the psychology that went behind twisted crimes like this. "Reid enjoyed himself during the interview," he said. "No concern that he was going to spend any real time in jail. He's clean-cut, no record, no debt, nice-looking, everyone likes him, and yet he kills people."

"There's always a reason," Sloane said.

Michael grunted. No reason would make sense to him, not for this level of violence.

Matt and Kara were smart, he told himself. They would find a way out. They'd get help. Call. Draw attention to themselves so that Michael and the team could rescue them. He had to focus on that, otherwise his concern for his friends and colleagues would cloud his judgment.

"I don't think the female partner is submissive," Sloane said after a couple minutes of silence.

"Does it matter?"

"I think so," she said. "If she was submissive, I think Reid would have raped his victims."

"Is that something Catherine said?"

"No, at least not to me," Sloane said. "It's not sexual violence they are interested in. It's physical control they want. Kidnapping. Restraining. Torturing. The women seem to have been tortured more than the men—"

"Which can be sexual," Michael said.

"Yes, but were the women tortured to manipulate their husbands? To force them to act? Or were they targeted simply because they're women? Some of the injuries don't make sense. The second male victim fell to his death, but his wife survived for several more days. Her wounds had even begun to heal—how does that happen? Did Reid hurt her, let her recover, then hurt her again?"

"If there's any trace evidence that could help us find Matt and Kara, Jim will catch it," Michael said. Though the truth was, Jim had already reviewed the autopsy reports and found nothing the medical examiner hadn't already noted.

An hour and twenty minutes later, they stopped down the street from Franklin Graves's office in a classy brick townhouse off North Main. The structure had two townhouses, one for Franklin Graves, attorney-at-law, the other divided into two offices—one a family therapist, the other insurance. "He owns the building," Sloane said, looking at her phone. "Ryder just sent me the basics. Bought it six years ago when he opened his practice in Jacksonville—Ryder is still working on finding out where he was before then, because he handles mostly civil cases now. Divorced with a daughter—the ex and the kid now live in Texas—and Graves remarried six years ago to Lily Warren and adopted the woman's then-five-year-old son."

Michael watched from across the street as Graves parked around back. From this angle he could see the parked car, but not the rear entrance of the building.

"Why come here?" he wondered out loud.

"To go over the case? Graves didn't spend more than five minutes with Reid before they went into the hearing." Sloane scrolled through her messages. "He employs a legal secretary, who's been with him since he moved here."

"Why would Reid call *this* guy?" Michael asked. "He hasn't done criminal defense, at least in the last six years. Could Reid have been a client back then?"

"There's no sign that Reid lived in Florida until nine months ago," Sloane said. "We've documented most of his residential history from when he graduated from high school until now. Maybe Reid called a lawyer who referred Graves."

"Who doesn't do criminal law?" Michael shook his head. It was odd that Reid would hire a lawyer more than an hour away in Jacksonville, who hadn't worked a similar case in years—if ever.

"Get comfortable," Michael said. "We're going to be here for a while."

14

Franklin Graves had nothing to say to the man who sat in his passenger seat, but if he screwed this up, his wife and son would be dead. So he told Garrett Reid the truth.

"The FBI is following us." His voice was raw, the adrenaline from his court performance giving way to the cold fear that his family was in danger.

"Doesn't matter," Garrett said. He was grinning, his fingers tapping a silent rhythm on his leg.

"They're going to charge you with murder." His voice cracked. He cleared his throat, his chest tight. The nightmare had started three days ago, and Franklin didn't know when it would end.

"Nope. Didn't do it because there's no evidence. No evidence means not guilty. They have nothing on me. Nothing!" Garrett chuckled. He was enjoying himself, the sick bastard.

"You attempted to kidnap two federal agents."

"It won't stick." He ran a hand over his hair. "Just call me Teflon."

Franklin swallowed nervously. What would happen if he couldn't get the charges dropped? Would his family die?

Garrett glanced at him. "What's your problem? You did good."

"I'm not a criminal defense lawyer, not anymore."

"Doesn't matter. You did what you needed to do, and soon we'll be out of your hair."

"You have to be in court on Monday."

"I'll be long gone."

"They froze your passport."

He laughed. "Ye of little faith."

"They're dead, aren't they?" Franklin said, his voice a whisper.

"They'd better be dead," Garrett said. "I wanted to be gone by now, but Audrey was still having fun. Damn feds. Serves them right."

Franklin was thinking about his family, not the federal agents. He decided not to say anything else. In the three hours he had known this man, Franklin realized two things: Garrett Reid was both smart and ruthless. And, maybe, crazy. He had to be crazy to think he could get away with murder when the cops were already onto him!

"Why me?" he asked. He didn't mean to say it out loud, but it came out anyway, so he kept talking. "There're other lawyers, better lawyers, people with experience who would be able to do a better job. Why me? Why my family?"

"Because Audrey knows you," Garrett said matter-of-factly.

Franklin almost said he didn't know anyone named Audrey, but decided to keep it to himself.

Garrett glanced at him with a frown. "What's your problem, Franklin? We're going to pay you. Don't tell me you have some warped sense of *ethics*. You're a fucking lawyer, you got off drug dealers all the time in Miami."

That was a long time ago, before he had a crisis of conscience.

He didn't want or expect money from these people. He just wanted his wife and son back, alive and well.

On Saturday, he'd gone to his office to catch up on some work; when he came home his wife and son weren't there. At first, he wasn't worried. Nathan had batting practice that afternoon and they could have gone shopping after. He called Lily; no answer.

When they weren't home by dinner, he became worried. He called Lily again; again no answer. Nathan didn't have a phone. He was about to call the batting coach to find out what time they left, when his phone rang; Lily My Love popped up on screen and he smiled.

"Hello, I was getting worried."

"Hello, Franklin," a woman said. Not his wife.

"Who is this?" he demanded.

"I can't believe you don't remember me," she said. "You will. But for now, your wife and stepson are just fine. They will stay fine as long as you do what I say."

He immediately thought that they were being held for ransom. He wasn't rich, but he had some money from the years he worked in criminal law, which he'd put in two trusts, one for his daughter, and one for Nathan's education. He'd do whatever he could to get his family back. But he also wasn't positive that this wasn't some sort of prank. He'd heard how sophisticated scammers were, that there were computer programs that could spoof a loved one's voice. Maybe this was a twist on that cruel con.

"What do you want?" he demanded.

"Right to the climax," she said, oddly.

"I'd like to speak to my wife. I can't take your word that she is okay."

"You'll have to."

"Then I'll call the police."

They could trace her phone, find her.

"You call the police, they both die, and it won't be pretty."

It was the tone more than the words that had Franklin believing this woman was serious.

"I need proof of life," he said quietly. "Please."

"Please, that's a nice touch. Say pretty please."

He straightened. Was she serious?

"Pretty please," he whispered. The woman laughed.

A few seconds later, he heard Lily's voice. She stuttered, "F-Franklin?"

"Are you okay? Is Nathan okay?"

"We're fine. Nathan is in a cage and I—"

"That's enough," Franklin heard in the background, and then the woman came back on the phone. "They're alive. They'll remain alive unless you disobey. I'll contact you tomorrow with instructions."

"How much do you want? What—" But she'd already hung up.

Franklin eased his sedan into the narrow lot behind his townhouse, his eyes flicking to the rearview mirror out of habit. He'd told Dotty not to come in for the next couple of days. She only worked part-time, so it didn't raise eyebrows. He didn't want her anywhere near this.

"Nice office," Garrett said, stepping out and glancing around. "Classy, but not ostentatious. I like it."

Franklin unlocked the back door. As soon as they walked in through the break room that had once been a kitchen, a woman leapt up from the couch in the waiting room, tossing aside a fashion magazine. "Garrett!" she squealed, launching herself into his arms.

They kissed—deeply, hungrily—and then Garrett spun her, pinning her to the wall. She laughed, breathless.

Franklin froze in the doorway, staring. He *knew* her. That face. Those eyes. But the name Garrett used—Audrey—didn't match the one in his memory. He couldn't quite place her, even though he recognized her. Not yet.

She turned and smiled directly at him, her fingers pressed playfully to her lips as if sharing a secret. Then she crossed the room with eerie calm, kissed Franklin on the cheek. He shivered.

"I need you for just a minute," she said, pulling out a phone. *Snap.* "Say cheese!" *Snap.* "Perfect." Her tone shifted. "Now go upstairs while Mommy and Daddy talk."

She gave him a gentle push toward the stairs. Garrett didn't say a word as he watched the exchange. Did he look confused? Or bemused? Franklin couldn't tell.

"My wife—" Franklin began, but she cut him off sharply.

"Shut up, Franklin." Her eyes turned from playful to cold in a blink. "*Go.*"

His instincts screamed at him to stay, to demand answers—but something in her voice, her smile, chilled him.

He passed his office then turned up the stairs to the second floor where he had a spare office for his occasional intern and a small conference room that housed his law book collection. He sat at the long table, his hands trembling. The silence below seemed unnatural, then he heard a crash and moan and laugh. Her laugh.

Who was she? Where had they met?

He hadn't represented her—he was sure of that. But he'd *met* her. Somewhere. She was unforgettable. Beautiful. Deadly. A siren.

His should call the police. Or the FBI. Or someone—*anyone*—who might help. But what if that was exactly what they were waiting for? One wrong move, and—

Because Audrey knows you.

The name rattled in his head like a marble in a glass. *Audrey. Audrey.* No. That wasn't it. That wasn't her name.

Her real name surfaced like a corpse breaking water.

Amber.

Los Angeles. Seven years ago.

He'd just proposed to Lily. She'd said yes. He was flying high, invincible. He hadn't wanted to leave for the legal conference, but because he was changing from criminal to civil law, he felt it would be helpful. After having dinner with an old friend, he didn't want to stay in his room. He sat in the bar and did a little work on his phone when *Amber* appeared. Young, stunning, relentless.

She'd propositioned him. Offered him a drink; he didn't drink. Only soda water with lime. He told her he was engaged. She told him no one had to know.

He told her *no*. Maybe he'd said something else . . . something rude. He couldn't quite remember. She'd leaned over to kiss him and he recoiled in surprise and anger.

Then he caught her dumping something into his drink. She realized he'd seen her; she rose and started to walk away.

Ten feet from him, she turned with a smile that never touched her eyes. "We'll meet again, Franklin. Someday when you least expect it."

The next morning he found a cryptic note under his door.

Now, Franklin stood, dizzy, grabbing at the table to stop himself from falling, then settling back into the chair. His hand shook.

Why now? Why her?

He picked up the phone, put it to his ear, stared at the numbers on the push-pad. Stared, trying to think. He wanted to go to the police. But if he did . . .

He saw Lily. Nathan. Two people he loved more than life itself. He couldn't risk their lives.

He put the receiver down.

What do these people want?

And why had they chosen him?

First, they had sex. Then Garrett listened as Audrey told him how she'd tranquilized the two agents and transported them. He was impressed, and said so.

She beamed. "I was afraid I dosed them too heavily, but even though they were restrained, I didn't want them waking up in the van. It would have complicated things."

He shrugged. "Doesn't matter how they died."

She didn't say anything, and he felt her body tense in that way that told him she had done something stupid.

"You did kill them, correct?" he asked calmly.

"Noooo," she said. "We already set up the factory for them. I wasn't going to let the new game go to waste!"

"They're *cops*. This isn't like the others. Shit, Audrey!"

"Don't swear at me," she pouted.

"I'm sorry," he said, though he was so frustrated he wanted to take out his anger on someone. But with Audrey, he had to be careful. He kissed her, nuzzled her neck, and said, "I don't want either of us to land in prison."

"They'll be dead soon enough," she insisted. "This is *fun*. Maybe more fun than the others. Except for Emily. She was definitely the most fun."

Audrey's nemesis Emily started it all, and Garrett hadn't minded getting revenge on the bitch who had hurt the woman he loved. So he agreed to get a job at Sapphire Shoals after Audrey learned where Emily would be honeymooning. He started two months before she and her husband arrived. And, he had to admit, it was exciting to use his engineering skills to create all the fun traps. Everything worked perfectly.

He'd agreed that they couldn't leave Florida right after the Hendersons disappeared, that it would be suspicious. Then Audrey got a job at the resort and said it was full of losers to con. At first, Garrett thought she was targeting conventions, men who were away from their boring daily lives were the easiest to lure. But then she said she wanted to "do it again" and he knew what she meant.

The other two couples were more work than fun, at least for Garrett. He simply didn't care. Sure, Audrey enjoyed herself, and deep down Garrett considered that the additional murders would help cover up Audrey's old connection to Emily, but still, Garrett was worried. Things had . . . escalated. Audrey had insisted one last time when Garrett wanted to bolt. He refused.

Then he saw Kara.

He'd been about to give his two weeks' notice when she and her not-husband had sat down at the bar by the pool. He'd been repairing the ice maker. No one really noticed maintenance workers, so he had lingered longer than necessary. She was petite and pretty, but she also looked stronger than the other women. She was . . . well, exactly his type. If he wasn't with Audrey, he might have asked her out. Except that she was married.

But she wasn't, he knew now. It had been fake.

He would have liked to have seen her fall apart. The first three broke too soon. He'd known from the minute he saw Kara that she wasn't like the others. He was intrigued and more than a little bit attracted.

Not that he would have said *that* to Audrey.

Unfortunately, he hadn't pegged her as a cop.

Audrey took out her phone and showed him the footage she'd saved. She watched him watch the video. "She *almost* got cut in half."

"It's too dangerous to keep them alive."

"Babe, they might be cops, but they're also lovers."

"It was an act."

She shook her head, leaned over and kissed him. She sat up, adjusted her shirt to cover her breasts. He zipped his pants. He had too much to think about; another round of sex wasn't in the cards.

"It *wasn't* an act," she said. "I watched them all weekend." She scrolled through her phone, clicked on another video. "I was careful, so this is from a distance. Look."

Garrett watched the video of the two cops who tricked him kiss as they stood outside a restaurant. Then they held hands and talked. They looked comfortable, intimate.

"They were together this weekend, *in bed*. If they were really just faking it to trap us, would they have stayed in the same room? And yesterday when they were in the gym? They were totally flirting. They kissed. It wasn't just a friendly kiss, it was a *wait until I get you alone* kind of kiss. I *know* when people are in love or in lust, and they have a lot of both going on."

"We have to kill them," he said. "They were supposed to be dead before I was released. *No more games.*"

Audrey loved games, and sure, it was fun most of the time, but before now he hadn't been really all that concerned about getting caught. Before Florida, no one had died. He hadn't thought much about the consequences because most of the people they played with would never go to the police. And, well, the sex was always amazing. The thrill of the honey trap always made him and Audrey super horny.

But his freedom was important. He wouldn't give it up just to play games.

"Baby," she pouted, "killing isn't the fun part."

"I can't drive up there and take care of it myself. The FBI is following me. You have to do it. *You* have to kill them."

She clicked her tongue. "First, Garrett, if we do nothing, they'll die. They won't be able to get out. The exits are traps, you did an amazing job! They'll go *splat.* So get a grip."

He didn't like when she minimized his concerns.

"Second," she continued, "we can lose the stupid FBI. It's more fun to play the game with *you.*"

He closed his eyes, put his head against her forehead. "I love you, Audrey. We have to think this through. This is no longer a game. This is *my life.*"

"It's *our life.* We're in this together, now and always."

He did love her, but dammit, he didn't want to be in prison. They had nothing on him—and he *should* be able to get out from under these stupid attempted kidnapping charges. But he couldn't risk it. He couldn't risk going back to court next Monday on the chance that they would put him behind bars. While he didn't see *how* they could find any evidence that he was involved with Audrey's games, he knew the FBI had advanced forensic and surveillance tools. So it was possible. They didn't know about her, which was good, but that didn't mean they couldn't learn about her.

"We need to use our escape plan," he said.

They had really good fake IDs and had always said if a situation became too hot, they'd go to a big city—New York would be best—and blend in. They had money saved up from their previous cons, it wasn't like they lived extravagantly. Audrey spent too much money, as if it grew on trees, but he would temper that bad habit. They'd lie low, rebuild their nest egg. Because if the cops found their factory in Georgia, they *might* be able to find evidence tying him and Audrey to the murders.

While it would be *nice* to clear his name, that was a pipe dream. They needed to disappear and regroup. Create a new plan. Get clear, solidify their new identities, come up with a different game. A better game. No one needed to die. The risk just wasn't worth it.

She was pouting.

"You know I'm right," he said.

She frowned and nodded.

"I'll come up with a new game, I promise."

He wanted to make her happy; he just didn't want to go to prison. She had to understand they were in a pickle right now.

She leaned into him. "What are you thinking?" she asked with a devious smile. "What kind of game?"

He smiled just as wickedly as she did. "Something just as fun, just as dangerous, but we'll take a few different precautions."

She ran her fingers down his neck. "What kind of *precautions*," she said, her voice low and sexy.

"No more than three months in one place. And no dropping bodies for just anyone to find. But first, we have to get out of this mess. Which means tonight, you kill the two feds. Leave their bodies. They won't be found for months, if not years. By that time, we'll be long gone."

"I can't do it tonight," she said. "I have to work in the morning, and if I miss my shift, they might get suspicious."

"They won't."

"They *might*. I get off at one, then I'll go. I'll be back before dark."

She was right that she shouldn't miss work, but damn, he didn't like knowing the cops were still alive and *might* be able to identify Audrey.

"Why can't you go now? It's only a couple hours there, you'll be back before dawn."

"Baby, it'll be dark, I don't like driving those roads late at night."

That was no excuse, but he wasn't going to push it.

"Alright," he said. "But leave right when your shift is over and make sure you're not followed."

"No one will follow me—they're watching *you*, remember?" She glanced upstairs and whispered, "What are we going to do about the lawyer?"

"He's your friend."

"Well, I don't trust him, so I took some precautions."

"I thought you had something on him." He assumed the man slept with her and she had pictures to show his wife. It was a good con, and one that had worked for them dozens of times.

"Well, now I do."

Garrett tensed, almost threw Audrey off him. "What have you done?"

"Calm down."

"He could rat us out, Audrey. You told me you trusted him!"

"He *can't*. Attorney-client privilege."

"You're not his client!"

"Don't be paranoid."

"Audrey—"

"I have them."

He blinked. "What are you talking about?"

"His family. They're at the house. I told them if they leave, I'll kill Franklin. And the kid is in the cage. The mom will never leave him there, because I'll kill him and she knows it."

Garrett's head was spinning. Audrey had kidnapped the lawyer's family? *A kid?*

"You're not making any sense. You told me you had a lawyer who would help and look the other way."

"And he is."

"What's this about his family then?"

"Look, I know Franklin. He fucked me over years ago, so now he gets what he deserves. I put him in my back pocket in case we needed him. And we did. You should be happy I have a long memory." She pouted again, her eyes watering. "He hurt me, Garrett."

"What did he do?" Garrett was beginning to second-guess their entire plan. He didn't like unknowns.

She put her chin up. "I don't like your attitude. I love you, and everything I've done, I've done because you're my one and only."

Garrett squeezed his eyes shut. Took a deep breath.

"Did they see you?" he asked quietly.

"Do you think I'm stupid?"

Now she was getting mad, and Garrett knew better than to make Audrey mad—she might do something *really* stupid.

"Of course not," he said. "But the police don't know anything about you, and while I don't want to go to jail, I don't want you there, either."

"Aw, you're so sweet." She kissed him. "I blindfolded them and I had a disguise just in case. They never saw me. So we're safe. And they won't leave." She still had Franklin's phone. She edited the photo of herself and Franklin so that she was blurred out and then she sent it to his wife with a message, which Garrett read over her shoulder.

I'm not joking. If you leave the house, Franklin is dead.
Maybe that's what you want?

"Not only do I have their total and complete fear, I have cameras everywhere. Sunday morning, she tested me. Nearly got her leg blown off. I called her. Made sure she understood that next time, Franklin would die—or her son. She got the hint."

"Sometimes, you drive me crazy."

"Like this?" She grinned and put her hand on his penis.

He moaned and shifted. "No. Like not understanding the risks."

She called upstairs. "Franklin! Get down here now!"

"I don't want an audience."

"Shh," she said and kissed him. "Trust me."

A moment later, Franklin came down the stairs. He stared at them half naked on the couch and blushed. He actually blushed. Garrett was now really wondering how this lawyer had screwed over Audrey.

"Franklin," Audrey said with a smile, "just so you know, this little game we're playing? We already won. I know where your wife and brat are—you don't. Remember that. I know everything about you, about Lily, about your properties and how much money you have in the bank. I know where your in-laws live, and I even know where your ex-wife and daughter live in Texas. And your daughter is going off to college next year, isn't she?"

His eyes widened and Audrey laughed. Garrett didn't think it was smart to push Franklin too hard—there was only so much humiliation a man could take.

Audrey said, "They're all safe if you obey the rules I laid out very clearly. Do you understand?"

"Y-yes." His voice cracked and he looked terrified.

"Good. Now go back upstairs so I can fuck my husband's brains out *again*."

15

Lily Graves hated the woman she'd never met before Saturday, but would never forget—or forgive.

That voice. That awful, singsong, arrogant bitch.

Lily crossed herself. She needed to remember not to lower herself to that level. She needed to remember her faith.

It was really hard to trust in the Lord when her son was suffering. But she was trying, praying for an answer to this impossible situation.

Lily stared at the photo sent from Franklin's cell phone and read the attached message.

I'm not joking. If you leave the house, Franklin is dead.
Maybe that's what you want?

Franklin looked terrified. Hollow. Dark circles under his eyes. Had he even slept in the last forty-eight hours? Probably not much more than she had.

The woman claimed she had been his lover, that they had a

passionate affair. Lily didn't believe her. Well . . . maybe in the back of her mind she thought it was possible, but that would have been in the past. He'd confessed to her that he'd lost his first wife in part because he had an affair with a colleague at his law firm. That between the affair and his long hours, Marissa couldn't forgive him.

But she and Franklin had always been honest with each other. Her ex-husband had been abusive and cruel; Franklin was neither. He was kind, he was responsible, and he loved them. Lily didn't doubt it. He had changed his practice, never worked nights, and only worked Saturdays when Nathan didn't have a baseball game.

He had never once missed a ballgame. When Lily worked—as a nurse, she worked three twelve-hour shifts a week—Franklin picked Nathan up from school and made dinner. He brought her flowers. Not on birthdays or Mother's Day, but randomly, once or twice a month, from a roadside stand near his office. Spring bouquets or a single yellow sunflower or long-stemmed white rose, her favorite.

He was the man she deserved. He was *present*.

Nathan's father had wanted nothing to do with his son, who as a baby had been sickly and small. He'd walked out on them when Nathan was three.

Now Nathan was almost twelve, healthy, and growing like a weed. He played baseball and was very good. His grades were nearly straight A's. Franklin had shown Nathan nothing but love and pride. He never yelled, even when Nathan on rare occasions deserved punishment. Franklin would talk to him, then together the three of them would come up with a punishment to fit the crime. Nathan loved Franklin, and Lily loved her little family.

Now they were all threatened. By a woman who had knocked on her door and then . . . Lily hadn't remembered much after. A glimpse of a blonde and then . . . nothing.

She'd been unconscious for hours. And when she woke up, the woman had been in her face, wearing an obvious wig and large sunglasses even though they were indoors.

Now she was gone, but Lily couldn't leave this damn house in the middle of nowhere. She would never leave her son. She believed the woman when she said Nathan would be dead if she stepped off the porch again.

She limped down to the basement of the farmhouse where Nathan was locked in a cell. Who had a jail in their basement? Who would put a child there?

If she were locked up, Lily would have told Nathan to leave. She had tried. At dawn, while Nathan slept, after the woman had left, Lily had tried to leave to get help.

The porch stairs exploded. She thought she was dead because of the sound, but the explosion was small and the damage to her calf was manageable. She had found a first aid kit in the kitchen and painstakingly removed splinters from her skin, then cleaned the cuts—dozens of small cuts. She was bandaging them when her phone rang.

"Next time, you'll be dead and your son will starve to death, so think twice about defying me."

Lily believed her.

He'd starve, or die from the gas that the woman threatened to release into the basement.

Lily couldn't bear the thought.

There was only one light in the basement, a bare overhead bulb. So she'd brought down a couple lamps and a mattress from one of the beds upstairs. She wasn't going to let her son sleep down here alone. It was damp and the stench of mold and dirt filled the space; it was cooler than upstairs but that was actually a blessing in the middle of the day when it was so hot.

She'd made them dinner—canned soup and grilled cheese. There wasn't much to choose from, but the woman had left them two grocery bags of food. No fresh fruit or vegetables or milk, but two loaves of bread, cheese, eggs, frozen hamburgers, and canned soup. Lily had written out how long the food would last if she had one meal a day and Nathan had two. They had ten days; this was the third day.

Her son would not go hungry.

"Mom," Nathan said when he accepted the mug of soup through the bars, "you need to go find help."

"I'm not leaving you."

She could have called 911. From the far corner of the front porch, she had cell service. But the woman claimed to have cloned her phone and would see any call she made, any message she sent. She believed her when she said she would kill Nathan before help arrived.

Lily found the canisters of gas in the basement. There was a digital panel and phone attached to them. The panel was lit with numbers that meant nothing to her. If the gas was released, Lily would be here with her son. He wouldn't die alone.

"Did Dad call?"

"No. He's okay, though. The woman sent me a photo."

Lily had looked everywhere for tools to cut through the bars; there was nothing. The farmhouse appeared to have been abandoned, though there was electricity to the property. There was some furniture, but most of the house was empty. The basement had been flooded at one point, but most of the water had been pumped out, only a few puddles remained in the low spots. Still, there was an overriding stench of mildew and rot, like something had died down here. A rat or an opossum or . . . she tried not to think about it.

They didn't talk for several minutes while they ate their soup. When they were done, she collected the bowls, but she didn't want to leave him yet. "Ready for a game?"

The first day they were here, she'd found an old deck of cards that was missing the ace of spades and four of diamonds. She'd also found several boxes of books in a closet. They'd been working through them. She'd read eight Harlequin romances—all published more than thirty years ago—and Nathan was reading *All Creatures Great and Small* by James Herriot. Lily had read that book when she was a child.

"Mom, I've been thinking. Maybe if we turn off the power, that'll kill the cameras. And you can go out a window, not the front stairs."

"I'm not risking it. I'm not risking you." She looked over at the cabinet where the canister and phone taunted her. "Let's play a game, okay?"

"Sure, Mom."

They played rummy in silence for several minutes, then she said, "If I can get you out of this basement, we'll go. But I'm not leaving you down here alone." She reached out and took his hand. "I'm not leaving you," she repeated.

"I love you, Mom."

16

Seven and a Half Years Ago

When Garrett Reid walked into the Odyssey Restaurant in the hills above the San Fernando Valley, he didn't know his life would forever change.

Love did that to a guy.

He'd gone to the Odyssey to seduce an older woman to carry him through the next few months. It wasn't that he didn't have any money—he had plenty, thanks to his smart management of resources during his time at college. But he was bored, and he didn't like being bored.

Older women were so much more interesting than girls his own age. First, they could have adult conversations about virtually any subject. Second, they appreciated sex. College girls had hang-ups and most fumbled along or faked it. Older women knew exactly what to do to turn him on . . . and themselves. They actually *enjoyed* sex. They *wanted* to be seduced, and Garrett was very good at the game.

Blanche Richardson had taught him more about how to please a woman than the dozen girls he'd slept with in college. He didn't count his first time—he and Becca had both been virgins, they were both fumbling around and that was . . . different. Special and, well, he didn't want to think about her.

Blanche was smart and while she may have been fifty-one, she was attractive and classy and in amazing shape. The three months he lived with her had been incredible.

College girls didn't want to have sex every night. Blanche expected it. And she expected to be fully satisfied, which made him eager to do everything he could to please her.

The happier Blanche was, the more she gave him—in and out of bed.

Then her son found out and nearly killed Garrett, so he was outta there.

The second woman he spent only a week with—and he learned a lot of lessons. At first, he thought he'd have a few months of living the high life in Beverly Hills, but Sheila was crazy. She told him the first night that he'd given her the best orgasm of her life, the next she said she'd cut off his dick while he slept because all men were pigs.

Yeah, he got out of there fast. Just because a woman was attractive, rich, and had the right zip code didn't mean she was sane.

But now he had a target *and* a plan: Vicki Montero was forty-nine, recently divorced, no kids, and had already dated a guy not much older than Garrett. She was loaded, and Garrett figured if he played his cards right, he'd have a place to live for at least six months while he worked out a longer-term plan.

Hell, maybe he'd marry her if the sex was good and she wasn't crazy.

Vicki was sitting at a table in the bar drinking a martini. Garrett already had his in—research was his best friend.

But then he saw Audrey.

He didn't know her name at the time; he only saw a beautiful woman. The *singularly* most beautiful woman he'd ever laid eyes on. She was blonde—his personal preference—but that wasn't the reason he noticed her. It wasn't even her beauty that drew him in.

It was the way she looked at him when he crossed her path. The subtle cat-like gaze, eyes narrowed, as she assessed him.

She was in her late twenties—maybe five or six years older than him, but that made her even sexier. She was sitting with a man in his late forties who had that air of Big Man on Campus. He looked like a former jock who expected beautiful younger women to fall at his feet.

Audrey was everything. Classy. Gorgeous. And smart. He could see her brains as they worked—she had a plan.

They were kindred spirits. In that moment, he knew he'd met his other half, his fate.

When she looked at him, she knew it, too.

A thrill ran down his spine.

He approached Vicki Montero. Just because he had spied his possible soul mate across the room didn't mean he could forget about his current plans.

Audrey watched him. She touched the inner thigh of the man with her.

The next hour became a game of cat and mouse. He began the seduction of Vicki Montero. The dual relationship tracts excited him. When the blonde excused herself to step outside, Garrett excused himself and followed her.

"I have a date," she told Garrett.

"So do I."

She raised an eyebrow. "It seems we both like older lovers."

"Do we? Or maybe we haven't found the right lover."

"I need two weeks."

"Why?"

She smiled slyly. "I'm Audrey."

"Garrett. Why two weeks?"

"I'm in the middle of something important. Go play with the old woman for a while, and meet me here two weeks from tomorrow."

"I'm going to kiss you."

She tilted her chin up defiantly, with a glimmer of lust in her eyes.

He leaned in, she stepped back, hit the wall. He smiled, leaned in closer, his lips an inch from hers. She smelled dark and dangerous and sexy.

"In two weeks," he whispered and went back inside without the promised kiss.

Clara Dolan much preferred the name Audrey, she decided, and when she was done with her current mark, she might officially change her name.

It would really tick off her mother, an added bonus.

She returned to the bar after she composed herself. That encounter—that almost kiss—was unexpected. She had never instantly lusted for a man before in her life. But when Garrett walked in, she saw something in him that drew her to him, a moth to a flame. If she didn't have something important to do, she would have left with him right then and there.

He had skills. The way he charmed the old bat was a master class in seduction.

But Clara had her own game to play, which was why she gave him a fake name. She hoped to see him again . . . but if she didn't, then no harm, no foul.

She wasn't going to miss the opportunity to destroy her nemesis. Even for a hot guy.

Emily Masters had it coming, the bitch.

She'd stolen Clara's boyfriend. She'd stolen Clara's promotion. She acted like the oh-so-sweet girl next door when she was really a conniving little bitch.

And now she was getting married! What did he see in her? Truly, she must have drugged him or something if he agreed to marry that whiny, ugly little bitch.

Clara didn't want him back, not after he got into Emily's pants. Obviously, his taste was mediocre. But she still tried to break them up because really, he couldn't possibly think that *Emily* was a better woman than *Clara*. But their relationship didn't fall apart.

So Clara decided to ruin her wedding.

She smiled at Richard Masters, Emily's father. Emily's *married* father. Clara would make sure that his wife and daughter both knew he'd strayed . . . a couple days before the *I do*s. It would make Emily miserable. Maybe she'd call off the wedding, though Clara didn't really much care. She just wanted to hurt her, the perfect little Daddy's Girl.

Garrett may have been good at seducing older women; Clara was a master at seducing men of all ages.

Except for one asshole who had a stick up his ass. Someday, that arrogant, self-righteous prick of a lawyer would get what was coming to him. No man refused Clara.

Seduction was the easy part. The hard part—and the fun part—was ensuring she got everything out of the aftermath that she wanted.

Two weeks later, Clara ordered a two-hundred-dollar bottle of champagne as she waited for Garrett.

Everything had worked out even better than Clara planned.

Emily still got married—Clara didn't care about that—but after her father was disinvited to the wedding, Emily had cried for days and looked like a wreck even with all the makeup. The reception was at a hotel and Clara watched the festivities from the hotel bar.

She loved throwing a bomb and walking away.

Then *he* walked into the Odyssey. Garrett. As hot and sexy as she remembered.

She poured him a glass of champagne and asked, "How's your girlfriend?"

He took the offered glass, sipped, assessed her. "Satisfied. *Very* satisfied."

Clara said, "I only share if there's something in it for me."

He leaned forward. "I don't share."

His eyes were dark then, dangerous, a hint of violence.

Her stomach twisted in excitement. "This will be fun," she whispered before she realized she had spoken.

He smiled then, his eyes sparkling with lust and humor. He really was perfect in all ways. "Tell me what you did these last two weeks."

She told him everything. How she seduced Richard Masters. Not that it had taken any effort, he had wanted her from the minute he saw her. They had a "wild" affair that she "accidentally" exposed to his wife and daughter. "He didn't know what hit him," Clara said. "Emily knew. She knew I set up the whole thing and that made it even better."

"What did she do to you?"

"What didn't she do? Stole my boyfriend, took my job—the lying bitch maneuvered behind my back. She has been a thorn in my side ever since she came into *my* business. But I won. Her wedding was yesterday, and she was miserable the entire time. It won't last."

"It won't?"

"No."

"Maybe I can help, Audrey."

In that moment, she fell in love. In that moment, she knew there would be no one else for her except Garrett Reid.

"Maybe you can," she said, leaned forward, and kissed him. Lightly. Teasingly.

He grabbed her wrist and held it tight. "If this is going to work, there will be no secrets, no lies, no games between us."

Then, she almost told him her real name. She almost told him everything about her life. But at the last second, she decided to keep it to herself. After all, she had a trust fund. It would be best that he didn't know quite how much money she had, at least not yet.

Maybe she'd tell him later.

She stared at him. He'd grabbed her, yes, but there was no violence in his eyes, just lust. And, okay, a hint of danger, which was super exciting. The idea that she was going to keep a secret from this man gave her a spark of fear, but that ignited her own lust. "No games?" she said, her voice quivering. "What about sex games?"

He smiled. "Sweetheart, sex between us will always be fun, but it'll never be a game."

17

Present Day

Matt sat slumped in the corner, his back pressed against cold concrete, watching Kara pace like a caged animal. His leg throbbed
with each heartbeat, a dull, insistent pain that both grounded
him and made him feel helpless.

They'd smashed the camera hours ago. Futile rebellion, but at
least they couldn't be watched anymore. After that, they'd pulled out
every monitor, every cable, trying to send a signal—anything. Matt
reasoned that if the camera was broadcasting somewhere, he could
tap into that and get a message to his team. But nothing worked.

Kara had torn through every cabinet like a storm, her hands
bloodied from forcing jammed drawers. No food. No water.
Nothing but yellowed paper, shattered glass, and the stench of
decay. She'd spent nearly an hour scraping her fingers raw to
twist bolts off a metal leg, detaching it from the desk, and now
she gripped the makeshift weapon like it was the last fragment
of control she had left.

"You need to rest," Matt said quietly, voice hoarse.

She didn't look at him. Her eyes darted along the catwalk across from them, too far to walk to, but he knew what she wanted to do: jump.

Her lips moved silently—calculating. The distance? The risk?

"I think we can make it down," she said. "I've gone over it a hundred times. That catwalk—the closest one—it's probably unstable, but it's only a twenty-foot drop. If we can hang, then fall, it's survivable. Bruises, maybe a sprain. But we can't stay here. We have to try."

"Not tonight," Matt said firmly. "It's pitch-black. If we screw up, we might break a leg. Fall on something we can't see. Or get caught in another trap."

"There's a door on the far side. It's blocked, but I don't think it's sealed shut."

She couldn't know that, not from this distance, but Matt didn't say that.

"We can get out—if we make it down, we get out that door."

"Kara," he said, almost pleading. "Sit down."

She froze. Then shook her head slowly, like a child refusing to accept a cruel truth. "No. I *can't* sit. I can't just . . . wait to die in here."

He looked at her—really looked. The moonlight through the dark factory windows gave just enough illumination to show him a hint of her anguish. Her cheeks were sunken, lips cracked, eyes ringed with exhaustion and something deeper: fear eating her from the inside out.

"We need to conserve our strength," Matt said gently. "Just a few hours of sleep."

"Strength?" Her voice cracked. "What strength? We haven't eaten in nearly two days. My mouth feels like sand. My hands won't stop shaking. We were drugged, Matt. We were *taken*. If we wait . . . we won't have the energy to move when it *is* time."

She was spiraling, fast. Matt could see it. She gripped the metal stick tighter, fingers white.

"Kara. Please."

"No, Matt. We *have* to try—" She turned on him suddenly, stick half raised like she didn't even know it was in her hand. Her breath caught, and then she dropped it. The clang of metal on concrete echoed loudly in the stillness.

Her body crumpled.

"I don't know what to do," she choked out, collapsing to her knees. A sound ripped from her—a raw, animal cry of grief and terror that shattered whatever composure Matt had left.

He forced himself to his feet, biting down on the pain, and limped to her. He dropped beside her and pulled her into his arms.

"I'm here," he whispered.

"I don't want to die in here," she sobbed into his chest. "I feel like we're already ghosts."

Matt held her tighter. He didn't speak. What could he say? He felt the same way, completely helpless.

There was really nothing either of them could say. They both knew the danger of their situation. They both knew the risks. The odds weren't in their favor.

Then Kara, voice barely audible: "Do you think they're even looking for us?"

"Yes," Matt said, firm now, because he had to believe it. "They know. Our team knows. They're looking. And if they don't find us tonight—we find *them* at dawn. We won't spend another night in this damn tomb."

Slowly, her sobs faded. She hugged him tightly, shaking, clinging like the world would fall away if she let go.

Matt was just as scared. He could feel it creeping in with every hour—the weakness, the doubt. But they had one thing left.

Each other.

And until morning, that had to be enough.

18

Catherine shut the door to the sheriff's conference room before answering the call from Garrett Reid's brother.

"Thank you for getting back to me," she said.

"I talked to my dad," Vince Reid replied. "He said Garrett's a suspect in a homicide?"

"Yes. Multiple homicides."

"Shit," Vince muttered. "Don't call my parents again. They're retired, they're heartbroken, and they don't deserve to be dragged into this."

"I hope I won't need to. But we have to understand Garrett in order to stop him from hurting anyone else."

"I haven't spoken to him in over five years."

"What was he like growing up?"

"I'm ten years older. Frank's less than two years younger than me—we're close. Garrett came along years later. Cute kid, good at baseball. Our parents were always at his games, bought him the best gear. He was a star player—until he hit tougher leagues and realized other kids were just as good, or better. He quit. Could've been great, if he practiced and accepted that there were other good players. But he hated being second to anyone."

Catherine made the note. It was a very interesting point, and she considered how that might play into his psychology with a partner.

"He was smart," Vince continued. "Straight A's. Got into UCLA. Our parents saved for college, paid his tuition and housing. He never visited them, rarely even returned their calls. Six months after he graduated, they found out he'd taken out loans in my mom's name. Tricked her. She thought she was signing something else. He pocketed the money they gave him and stuck them with nearly a hundred grand in debt. They're still paying it off. When I confronted him, he said they didn't need the money because they didn't have a mortgage."

A narcissist, Catherine thought. *No remorse. No conscience.*

Possible. But she still needed more information, because sociopaths were complex. They didn't always fall neatly into known patterns of behavior.

"What did he study?" she asked.

"Mechanical engineering, at least at the beginning. Like I said, Garrett is very smart. But he hates work. He works hard at avoiding work, so halfway through his second year he switched to English lit with a minor in math, because he already had most of the math requirements done. Said all he had to do was read a book and parrot the professor."

"And he graduated?"

"Yeah. With honors," Vince snorted.

"Why did you stop speaking to him?"

Vince hesitated. "Does that matter?"

"It might."

"When the loan scam came out, he walked out of our parents' house and moved in with my mom's best friend. She was recently divorced. Twice his age. I'm sure he used her for money, then moved on. It destroyed my mom's friendship—who sleeps with someone their son's age?"

He exhaled hard.

"Then he tried to seduce my wife. Came over when I was working a thirty-six-hour shift. Bella had just had our first daughter. She'd left her career, felt isolated and overwhelmed. Garrett charmed his way in. Played the loving family member. She wanted to believe he could change, make our parents proud again." He paused.

"What happened?" Catherine asked.

"He kissed her. She told him to leave. He didn't. Picked up our baby and started walking around with her. Wouldn't give her back. Bella was crying, terrified. And Garrett—he laughed. Thought it was funny.

"She *begged* him to give the baby back," Vince continued. "Said she'd sleep with him if he did. He told her she wasn't his type, handed the baby over, and walked out. It was like a game to him, to emotionally break my wife."

Catherine's voice was low. "I'm sorry."

"I confronted him the next day. Punched him in that smug, self-satisfied jaw. Wish I'd broken his nose. Told him if I ever saw him again, I'd kill him. I'm not proud of that, but he—he crossed the line. He always did. He laughed it off and walked away."

"What about your other brother, Frankie?"

"He hasn't seen Garrett, either. He would have told me."

"Any old friends? From high school or college?"

"I don't know. Everyone likes Garrett at first. But I doubt he kept any of his friends. In college, he was more interested in women."

"A girlfriend?"

"A lot of them. None I remember specifically. I don't even think I knew names."

"You mentioned older women?"

"After college. He lived with that divorced friend of my mom's."

"Do you remember her name?"

"Blanche Richardson. She moved to Florida a few years ago—maybe Fort Myers?"

Catherine jotted it down. "Do you know how to reach her?"

"No. And even if I did, I wouldn't. My mom cut her off years ago."

"What about someone from high school?"

"Becca McCarthy. Garrett dated her for two, three years. Maybe longer. My parents liked her. I met her a couple times, she was pretty and smart. I think they broke up when they went to different colleges. As I said—people really like Garrett. Until he screws them over."

Catherine asked Ryder to find Blanche Richardson and Becca McCarthy. She gave him all the information she had, which wasn't much.

It was after nine in the evening and she had a splitting head-ache. She hadn't eaten since breakfast that morning, which was never good, but the thought of food made her feel ill. Her cell phone rang and she almost didn't answer; it was her husband, Chris. She hadn't told him what happened to Matt because he had been in surgery this morning when she left; all she'd said on his voicemail was that there was a situation in Florida, and she was traveling there with the team.

Matt was one of their closest friends. The best man in their wedding. Their daughter's godfather. She had to tell Chris what was going on.

"Chris," she said. "Hello."

"I'm sorry it took me so long to call you back—there were complications."

"No apologies. Is your patient okay?"

"She's in critical condition, but I'm hoping by morning I'll be able to upgrade her. What about you? What's wrong?"

She told him what had happened to Matt and Kara.

"They're missing?" he asked, shocked.

"Abducted from the resort Sunday morning. Garrett Reid has a partner. I missed it."

"Everyone missed it," Chris said.

"*I* missed it. I'm the profiler. I should have seen it."

"Why? Are you God?"

"Chris—"

"Catherine, you can't blame yourself for this."

"Like hell I can't. This isn't the first time I missed a profile and someone I care about—someone I love—got hurt."

"Catherine, don't do this to yourself."

"I can't stop thinking about Beth, about Matt, that I should have seen it."

"Do you see it now?"

"I don't know. I can't tell if I'm pulling things out of thin air. He has a partner. That much is certain. But I haven't had time to study the murders again, to see if it *was* obvious and I just didn't see."

"Catherine, sweetheart, breathe."

"If Matt dies, it's my fault."

"It's not. Who's with you down there?"

"Everyone."

"You know what to do. You know how to find them."

"They've been missing for nearly thirty-six hours. Every minute that passes puts them in greater jeopardy."

"Trust the team," Chris said. "No one is slacking."

That was true. "We're meeting at the resort when the sheriff takes over surveillance of our suspect, but I'm scared for Matt and Kara. Ryder blames himself—because he suggested that they stay for a mini-vacation. Michael is angry he didn't stay in Florida with them, but he's closed himself off, won't even discuss anything but the work. Jim is working far too hard, thinking all the answers are going to be in evidence he has already looked at a half dozen times."

"How many times have I heard you say that the only person responsible for a crime is the person who committed the crime?"

She smiled tiredly. "Quoting me to me?"

"You're a smart woman, darling. You'll find them. You know," Chris said, "when I'm faced with an inexplicable case at the hospital, when I don't know why a child is ill or unresponsive, I go back to the beginning. The first time the child showed signs that something was wrong. Haven't you also said that you can trace a killer from before they started killing? What was his trigger?"

"Knowing what I know about his childhood and college years, I would never have guessed that Garrett would turn into a killer. A con artist, a manipulator—yes. He seduced older women, manipulated them into bed and out of money."

"He didn't kill them."

"No. And there are no outstanding warrants, no arrests, no restraining orders, no investigations. No one filed a complaint against him for theft, fraud, or assault. He's clean as a whistle."

"Then maybe it's the partner who brought violence into their relationship."

"What if the partner is a woman?" Catherine said.

"Is she?"

"We have some evidence that his partner is a woman. Which . . . well, I'll be damned."

"You figured it out."

"Maybe. Maybe. I have to go. I love you, Chris. Give Lizzy a hug for me."

"Will do. I love you, Catherine."

19

By the time the team gathered in the Sapphire Shoals conference room, it was nearly eleven o'clock. Ryder had brought in a buffet for the team and even though Catherine hadn't eaten all day, she only nibbled on some cheese and crackers, her stomach tight with anxiety.

Jim was the last to arrive, looking as drained as Catherine felt. He ran a hand over his long, hangdog face, grabbed a sandwich, and sat down.

"I may have something," he said, but without much enthusiasm. "I flew samples to Quantico. They'll be there first thing in the morning. The state lab could handle it, but Tony has assurances from the director that anything from us will be prioritized."

"What kind of evidence?" Catherine asked.

"First, the county lab processed everything in their room and discovered a strong prescription-strength muscle relaxant in the coffee mugs. While the mugs they drank from were removed, it's likely all the mugs had been lined with the drug."

"What would that do?" Michael asked.

"Make them feel sick, tired, disorientated."

"Can we trace it?" Sloane asked.

"No," Jim said. "It's a very common prescription. We can look for it among our suspect's belongings."

"But they were shot with a tranquilizer gun," Michael said. "Why do that if they were drugged?"

"My guess," Jim said, "is that there was no guarantee they would drink the coffee, or that they would both drink coffee at the same time. By this point, the suspect would know they were cops, right? So I'm thinking she drugged the coffee, but couldn't guarantee it would knock them out before they could call for help. So she waited for a reaction, then hit them with the tranq. Also, even if she's a good shot, if she hit one of them, the other might have time to get to safety or apprehend her. Drugging them first makes their reaction time slower."

"Extreme foresight," Catherine said. "A planner. She didn't want to leave anything to chance."

"Two other things stand out," Jim said as he picked at his sandwich. "First, an unusual algae found on the second couple is typically found in freshwater, like stagnant ponds, not the ocean. Initially dismissed, it's actually distinct and potentially traceable, so we've prioritized that analysis. Second, trace amounts of rust were found on all the victims."

"That was in the original reports," Catherine said.

"Right, but after the lab analysis, we have more information. The state lab identified yellow rust on an iron alloy, suggesting a high-moisture environment—probably near standing water, like a swamp or pond. While they couldn't pinpoint the source, we have good samples of the alloy. If we can identify its exact makeup, it might help locate where the victims were held. There was also plant matter mixed with the rust—too small for testing at the local lab. Quantico might be able to match areas where the algae and rust overlap and identify the alloy. I'll be back at the morgue tomorrow to examine more tissue samples. It's clear, however, that all the victims were held somewhere damp, moldy, with nearby stagnant water. The more we learn, the closer we get to a location."

"Thank you, Jim," Catherine said. "That's good work."

"Not good enough," he grumbled.

"Every piece of information helps," she said.

"Why didn't Reid go to his apartment?" Sloane asked, changing the subject. "He had his lawyer take him to a hotel in Jacksonville. The sheriffs are watching him, but why wouldn't he want his things?"

"Maybe because he thought we'd be watching there," Catherine said, "or he thinks it'll be easier to disappear from a hotel."

"It will be," Michael said, "if that's his plan."

"Which is why there will be multiple teams of law enforcement watching him," Catherine said.

"I hope it's enough," Sloane said. "I can go back after the meeting."

"We all need sleep if we're going to be sharp in the morning," Catherine said. "But I wanted to share a new profile first. It's rough and I don't want to commit to anything yet. I need the insight of everyone on the team to make sure we're heading in the right direction. After interviewing Garrett's brother and father, then reviewing everyone's notes, I have a better understanding of his personality and possible psychopathy."

She glanced at her notes. "Initially, I assumed, based on the victim similarities, that Reid worked alone and the female victim was a surrogate for someone in his past. But we now know he's working with a partner, and that she's female changes everything."

"So you concur with Ryder that his partner is a woman," Michael said.

"Yes," Catherine said. "I talked with experts at Quantico,

and probability based on analysis of the image we have leans 90 percent female.

"Garrett Reid is a con artist," she continued. "He seduces older women, and this is backed up by interviews and info from his brother. He's well-liked by staff, especially older female staff. He's charming, diplomatic, well-educated. He manipulates and seduces. However, I don't think he's a natural killer."

Ryder, who rarely spoke unless asked a direct question, said with some surprise, "Are you saying the dominant killer is the female partner?"

Catherine nodded. "I was skeptical at first, because it's rare for a woman to be the dominant in a male-female partnership. But in this case, while I won't say that she is the leader, she's certainly his equal. Based on his clear narcissism, I don't see him as subservient to her. They are partners in every sense of the word. They've worked together to con individuals or couples, using sex as the weapon. We don't have any unsolved homicides that fit our parameters in the cities where Reid has worked, which suggests that either they recently started killing, or their victim profile changed. I am inclined to think recent because victim type rarely changes."

"*They,*" Jim repeated flatly. "They're working together because they enjoy killing. That's messed up."

Catherine had been refining her profile, but doubts still lingered. She couldn't afford to be uncertain. "Garrett has a romantic relationship with his partner. He's been with her for at least two years, likely longer. He trusts her. He gave no hint that he had a girlfriend during his interrogation. No one on staff suspected he was in a relationship, but confirmed that he didn't date staff or guests. This is a strong bond, one that will be hard to fracture. They believe they are in love, and that their crimes are a sign of devotion."

She slid a one-pager across the table with details of the six victims laid out in two columns. "The male victims died from blunt force trauma or blood loss, but also sustained other, non-fatal injuries—such as the first male victim had a broken ankle. The female victims survived for up to three days longer than their husbands, enduring multiple injuries—cuts, bruises, extreme dehydration, broken bones—though not the same bones. The women were the primary victims in a cat-and-mouse game. Reid and his partner toyed with them before they grew tired of the game and killed them. Each woman died in a unique way: one was impaled with a wooden stick, but we haven't yet identified the wood. One died from internal bleeding. One drowned."

She paused, watching her team absorb the information. "I believe the women were targeted out of jealousy."

"Hold on," Sloane said, "you're saying that the female partner is jealous of these women, and that's how she picked them? Did Garrett have a relationship with any of them? Or express an interest in them?"

"Doubtful," Catherine said. "I think they were targeted because of their type—blonde, attractive, successful, and married. The female partner feels inadequate compared to the victims. Perhaps she feels she's not 'good enough' for Garrett, or that Garrett has a type that she doesn't fit into. My guess, when we find Garrett's first girlfriend—Becca McCarthy, his high school sweetheart—she will be a classic girl next door type, at least in her appearance. She will be successful and intelligent, like our female victims. And that success is likely the primary trigger."

Catherine took a sip of water, continued. "All three victims had advanced degrees and personal success—a lawyer, a doctor, a CFO who was also a tax attorney. They were all thirty-five or younger. That was why we made Kara's undercover background a lawyer. That, even more than their physical looks, tells me why they were specifically targeted. Reid's partner may be a natural blonde; if not, she will dye her hair. She is attractive with outward confidence, but also jealous of attractive and successful women. She hasn't accomplished what she wanted in life—academically or professionally—and she hates women who have succeeded. That is the *primary* reason they were targeted. There could be secondary reasons we can't know without identifying Reid's partner. Likely, their appearance is a factor in who was targeted, but whether the appearance was because of Reid's attraction or his partner's jealousy, I can't say."

"We need to comb through all of Matt and Kara's notes and see when and to whom Kara mentioned her fictional background," Ryder said. "If anyone asked questions or seemed unduly interested in Kara's life."

Michael added, "And you think the partner works here?"

"Yes," Catherine replied. "She likely started within three months of Garrett Reid, before or after. She's older than him, but not middle-aged. I'd guess between thirty-five and forty—but that's a guess. I wouldn't limit our pool of suspects based on age."

"Reid worked here, his partner works here," Jim said. "They could have accessed Kara's registration and the false address we used that would lead them easily to her fake employment."

Catherine conceded the point, but also knew accessing guest registration was limited to the front desk and management. Possible to access, but they had flags on Matt and Kara's fake backgrounds. If anyone looked them up—address, employer—it would have triggered an alert.

"We'll look again at those staff members," Catherine said.

Ryder looked up from his laptop. "I found Blanche Richardson. She moved from Pasadena to Fort Myers over seven years ago."

Catherine considered the distance from Flagler County to Fort Myers. "It's a long drive for a face-to-face. I'll call her in the morning."

"I'm a pilot," Sloane reminded them. "If we can get access

to a small plane, I could be there and back in four hours, interview included."

"No one works alone," Michael said. "We can't make an exception just because you're flying out of the area, Sloane. But I agree it's important to talk to her. Catherine, can you ask Bianca or Brian to go with Sloane?"

Catherine nodded. "But we still would need a plane. I'm sure Tony would approve it, and, Sloane, you don't need to fly if we get a charter."

Jim raised an eyebrow. "Is it really that important to meet her in person?"

"It's about body language and how people react in person," Catherine replied. "A phone call won't give us that. I can't risk missing something important."

Sloane thought for a moment. "What if we involve the local FBI? I could direct the interview over the phone, over FaceTime or on speaker, but another agent would be in the room to assess Richardson's reaction. It would save time, as well."

Catherine considered, then nodded. "That works. You lead the interview."

Sloane made a note, and Michael said, "We need to reinterview every woman who fits the profile."

"She'll be single," Catherine added. "She may or may not have a boyfriend, but she won't live with him, and he'd be a pawn to her, part of her game. She believes that Garrett Reid is her true love."

Ryder said, "I just skimmed through Matt and Kara's reports again. Kara's law background came up three times: once in the hotel bar, once in the gym, and once when Matt was talking to a guest the morning before the abduction attempt."

"I remember the gym incident," Sloane said. "Bridget Thomas. She kept showing up wherever Matt and Kara were and chatting them up. She lost her husband last year and is lonely. This is her first trip without him."

"She's currently still a guest," Ryder confirmed, "but is scheduled to check out tomorrow."

"She might have seen something," Catherine said. "We need to talk to her."

Sloane raised an eyebrow. "You think a sixty-year-old is working with Reid?"

"No," Catherine said. "I think Reid would seduce a sixty-year-old, but we're looking for a more confident, calculating killer. Mrs. Thomas may have overheard something, seen someone watching Kara. Michael, can you approach her?"

"First thing in the morning," Michael replied. "I'll have management flag her so that if she checks out earlier, they'll call me."

Ryder added, "The third time Kara's background came up was when Matt was talking to a guest in the gym the morning before the first kidnapping attempt. The guest asked where his 'hot wife' was, and they had a conversation about Kara being a lawyer. That guest is gone now, but I can track him down."

"Get his name and contact info, talk to him," Catherine said. "We'll start with Bridget Thomas."

After a long silence, Jim stood up. "We all need sleep if we're going to be any use to Matt and Kara. Let's reconvene at six."

"Agreed," Catherine said. "I'll reach out if anything new comes in."

20

It was midnight. The moon had shifted in the sky and only a faint, eerie glow permeated the warehouse. Near-total silence—no traffic, no voices, no music, not even a dog barking. The only sound was the faintest hum of the generator somewhere on the bottom floor and a couple crickets that echoed from far below.

After Kara's borderline panic attack, they'd stretched their limbs, then cleared a space in the corner and sat there, leaning against the wall and each other, exhausted, thirsty, weak. There was nothing else they could do.

They fell asleep. Or passed out. Until Kara startled awake, her heart racing.

"Kara," Matt murmured.

She listened. It took a minute for her to tamp down on her fear and actually hear anything other than her ringing ears.

Matt shifted, then winced.

"Are you okay?" she asked.

"Yeah. The stretches earlier helped."

"What time is it?"

He pressed his watch. The dim light was comforting. "12:02 a.m."

They'd slept for less than two hours.

Kara had thought a lot about what the team was doing to find them, starting with interrogating Garrett Reid. Would he talk? What could they offer to a killer? Life instead of the death penalty? They certainly wouldn't offer him freedom.

Would he even care? He could feign ignorance. Laugh in their face. Taunt them.

Or use the fact that Matt and Kara were missing—or dead—as proof that he had nothing to do with six murders.

She hadn't wanted to wait to try the catwalks, but Matt was right, it had been too dangerous earlier, when it was nearly dark.

"I'm sorry I snapped at you," she said as she put her head on his shoulder.

He put his arm around her, rested his head against hers. "No apologies, from either of us. We're tired, hungry, angry—I get it."

"You were right. It would have been a suicide mission to try and cross the beams when it was getting dark."

"Not just that," he said, "but this place is filled with traps. The elevator, the staircase, the door—it would make sense that they might create a trap on the catwalks. It's more than a two-story fall—you might survive it, but—"

Kara jerked up. The fall. Booby traps. "Matt, the *fall*—one of the male victims, he had injuries consistent with a fall."

"Kevin Blair, I think. The second victim."

She nodded, even though he couldn't see her.

"He could have fallen down the staircase. Or the catwalk," she conceded. "Dammit. They were all here, weren't they? I saw blood—what I thought was blood—in the bathroom."

"Either Reid has skills we don't know about, or his partner is an engineer."

"Reid worked in Maintenance. He could fix anything, remember? When we looked at the short list, we noted that Brian Valdez said Reid was their go-to guy for mechanical repairs."

"The elevator was set to fall with you in it," Matt said, his voice catching. "They couldn't do that multiple times."

"Why not?"

"I think the damage to the shaft would be too great. It hit hard."

"Maybe they set up different . . . oh, I don't know, traps? Like . . . an escape room. But this is an escape building. There has to be a way out, because there was a way *in*."

"Promise me that any exit we find, we don't rush through it," Matt said. "We investigate first, think through every possibility, no matter what."

"Agreed."

She tried to relax again. She wanted to sleep. The idea of staying awake for the next six hours, thinking through everything they'd done over the last week, made her dull headache worse.

"We'll get out of here," he said with more confidence than she felt.

"Yeah," she said.

"We *will*," he insisted. "There has to be a road directly here, a way for Reid's partner to bring us in."

"You're right," she said, leaned back into Matt. "Why not just kill us?"

"Ransom, most likely."

"They'd better not let that bastard out," Kara muttered.

"They might play along, but they'll have a plan. Our team is the best," Matt reminded her.

"I know."

"You don't sound like you believe it."

"I do, I'm just—tired."

"Sleep some more."

"I'll try."

She closed her eyes and breathed in Matt. He smelled awful, but so did she. Sweat, dirt, mold. She was glad she wasn't alone.

"I love you, Kara."

"Don't."

"Why?"

"Because you sound like this is the last time you're going to say it."

"I love you. See, not the last time."

She grunted a small laugh. "I love you, too."

"We're getting out of here. I promise. We, you and me, are in a good place, and nothing is going to screw with that."

"We are in a good place, aren't we?" she said thoughtfully.

They'd met on a case fifteen months ago in Liberty Lake, Washington, when Kara had found a dead body and ended up assisting Matt and his newly formed Mobile Response Team in tracking down a serial killer. At first, it was mutual lust. Then . . . over many months . . . she realized that she loved this man. Matt knew it first, but then again, Matt was supremely confident in everything he did and felt. It took her a bit longer, but she knew the moment when it was real for her.

Last October, they'd been on the roof of her old condo in Santa Monica. Her entire world had fallen apart, and she learned that the people she had trusted the most had betrayed her. Except Matt. Matt was there for her and whatever decision she made. It wasn't a switch flipping when she realized she loved him. It was a dam breaking. There was no putting the water back in the lake or the genie back in the bottle or whatever cliché she could think of; it was out and she felt a peace she had never felt before.

It couldn't end like this. Locked in an abandoned building by a pair of serial killers.

"We should get married," Matt said.

"Matt," she said, a firm warning in her tone.

"Well, we should."

"We just agreed we were in a good place, and now you want to raise the stakes?"

"Not tomorrow," he said with a humorous lilt in his voice.

"Oh, goody."

"I want kids."

She stiffened. His arms wrapped around her tighter.

"Don't you?" he added.

"I don't know," she said. A year ago she would have said no fucking way was she bringing a baby into this messed-up world. "I mean, you'd make a great dad."

"You'd make a great mom."

She snorted.

"Seriously," he said, "you would."

"I am *not* maternal."

"I've watched you talking to kids, to victims, to witnesses. Winnie and her little niece in St. Augustine. And remember Hazel in Friday Harbor? You knew exactly how to get information out of a three-year-old."

"By letting the firefighter talk to her."

"You always rewrite history to make yourself look less heroic, Kara."

"I'll concede that I'm good with kids who have been dealt a bum rap. But kids aren't babies."

"They were at one time."

"Why are we talking about this now?"

"Because we have a future, and we have to find a way out of this so we can enjoy it."

She considered that. She loved Matt, and if he really wanted to get married and have a kid, she would think about it. But that sort of commitment—not marriage, which she could probably handle. But a child? The responsibility of bringing a life into the world, of protecting and providing for a helpless infant? It terrified her.

"Have you ever thought about adoption?" she asked, surprised that she was having this conversation.

"Not really. You don't want to be pregnant?"

"I don't care. I mean, being pregnant is temporary. It's the baby that I'm terrified about. But it's not really about that. I guess, well, I haven't really thought about having my own kids because I always pictured myself adopting older kids. There are so many out there who have crappy lives, no parents, or their parents are in prison, or . . . well, I don't know. Abusive or something." She paused, thought about the Santana family— she hadn't thought about them in years.

"What?" Matt said. "What happened, Kara?"

How did he know? How did he always know when she was aching inside?

She took a moment, because even now her feelings were raw. "Back, nearly five years ago? I was undercover. Met these kids, Ben, Juan, Sienna. She was only six. The boys were ten and eleven. The three of them were abandoned by their parents, left to fend for themselves in a drug house. Ben, the oldest, was forced to work for a dealer. The building was so run-down—no heat, no food except what the dealer decided to give them, no one who cared anything about them. The people hanging around were all part of the crime ring I was investigating. But . . . I couldn't just walk away."

"I know you, Kara. You didn't leave them there."

She shook her head. "I called Lex, and he got CPS involved. I didn't want them caught up in the system, but it would be better than living in the middle of filth and drugs. And I could still keep my cover.

"The next day, CPS came knocking . . . and did shit. Why? Because the asshole drug dealer said there were no kids. CPS walked through, literally *saw* toys, but no kids, so there were no kids. They walked out, apologized for bothering him. The kids had been told—I didn't know this at the time, but learned later—that whenever anyone official came they were to hide and be quiet, or they'd be punished. It was messed up."

"What happened to them?"

She didn't say anything for a long minute, trying to get her emotions in check. "It took time, but I got the boys to trust me. And eventually—even though I shouldn't have—I told them I was a cop and I was going to find them a good home. I told them to be ready, and I would take them at the first opportunity it was safe."

"Oh, God," Matt said and squeezed her tighter.

"They're okay," she said quickly. "But it was close. Too damn fucking close."

She would never forget the sound of gunfire, Sienna clutching her neck with her skinny arms, Ben shaking, and Juan trying to shield all of them when he was shorter and skinnier than Kara.

"I wanted them. They were so brave, so smart, so damn young . . . They'd been given crap parents and a crap life. Social services couldn't find their parents at first—later I learned their father was in prison for a double homicide and their mother was dead of a drug overdose. I'd just turned twenty-six, and bringing three kids into my little condo? I wouldn't be able to work undercover, and it's not like I was making the big bucks as a cop."

"What happened to them?"

"They went into the system. They were separated, and believe me, I fought to keep them together. But there were no foster homes that could take all three. They had no one. And I wanted to—but—well." She wiped at a tear. "Anyway. After that, I told myself I would adopt. Because these kids are here on the planet, they need someone that cares because the adults in their lives are screwups, drug addicts, killers, worse."

"Worse than a killer."

"There are some people who are worse than killers, yes."

"You know, sweetheart, there's no law saying we can't have a baby *and* adopt."

"I'll take it under advisement," she said. But she was pleased that Matt didn't think she was foolish for wanting to adopt in the first place. "But not now. I'm not ready, and like you said, we're in a good place."

"Not now," he whispered.

Not in the next year. Hell, she was only thirty-one, she wasn't ready for kids whether they were newborn or older.

But it didn't make her squirm thinking about it. Because of Matt.

Matt dozed off again. She wished she could. She was so tired, the adrenaline that had been pumping through earlier was gone, leaving her physically drained and weary.

And then she, too, finally drifted off.

21

Audrey Reid lay next to her husband, her lover, her best friend, and listened to his even breathing, her hand on the steady beat of his heart.

She loved Garrett more than life itself. She would do anything to protect him, anything to save him.

But he shouldn't have been caught.

It was partly her fault. He'd wanted to leave after the second couple, Jenny and Kevin. She wrinkled her nose. Jenny was a complete and total bitch and deserved everything that she got, walking around as if she was better than everyone.

But they stayed on staff so that it wouldn't be suspicious, and started planning their next trip. She wanted to go back to Las Vegas, because that's where they got married five years ago. That's where they fully committed to each other. Body, soul, life.

That's where they were when she first killed a man.

She didn't count the unfortunate accident in Scottsdale. That wasn't her fault. She just got a little carried away and, in her defense, she thought he was playing possum. She'd walked away clean from that . . . but still, it was sort of exciting. She never told Garrett everything because she wasn't certain he would understand . . . later, when Garrett learned their target had died, he asked her about it.

She'd lied, told him that the old fart was alive and well when she walked out.

Then, they had to lie low for a while because the entire country was on pause, but that gave her and Garrett time to really get to know each other. To just *be* together. And it was paradise. They headed to Vegas as soon as Garrett was able to land a job there. It had become their habit—first Garrett got into a position, then she applied for work. They were always hiring young, attractive women, so it was easier for her to find something after he got inside.

Vegas had been amazing in so many ways. They needed to go back and renew their vows, make a fresh start. Garrett might have to change his name this time—she'd changed hers so many times she sometimes forgot that she was born Clara Dolan. She'd legally changed her name to Audrey Reid after they got married, but she had never used that name at any of her jobs.

Though next time, they would. When they got to Vegas, they would go into it as a couple. No more of this sneaking around, no more watching Garrett flirt with other women because that was his game. She didn't like it. She didn't know what Garrett saw in the old women he seduced. She knew what she saw in the men—victory, money, pride that she hadn't lost her touch.

So, while staying here in Florida was partly *her* fault because she had spotted the Avilas and knew they needed to be put to the test, it was also *his* fault because Garrett saw Kara Costa—Kara *Quinn*, Audrey reminded herself—and looked at her a moment too long.

Audrey hated her. Hated her with a passion. Because there had been something in Garrett's eyes, a lust she hadn't seen with any of the other women they conned . . . or killed. The older women were a game—Garrett enjoyed playing with them, sleeping with them, stealing from them. They weren't a threat to Audrey.

But Kara Quinn was pretty, she was confident, she was successful . . .

No, she's not *successful. That was all fake.*

That it was fake, that they had tricked her and Garrett (but mostly Garrett) grated on her.

She rolled over, pulled her laptop off the nightstand, and booted it up. They were in a Jacksonville hotel. The police were watching outside, but they didn't know her from Adam, and of course she and Garrett hadn't walked in together. That would have been a big red flag.

She glanced over at Garrett, considered waking him up so he could watch with her, but decided against it. He was right about one thing, and she hated being reminded of that.

Matt and Kara were FBI agents. They weren't like the others. They might—and that was a big *might*—find a way out. It was doubtful; they had spent a month setting up the factory again after the Avilas had died. But . . . it was a teeny, tiny concern.

First, she checked on Lily Graves and her brat. They were sleeping in the basement. It was really weird that the mom brought a mattress down to sleep next to her son. Audrey didn't really know what to do with them. Of course Franklin would have to die—he had *humiliated* her—but she made sure the woman hadn't seen her. Yet . . . she wasn't certain about the kid. He may have spotted her before she put on her wig and glasses.

She didn't want to kill him, but . . .

Maybe he wouldn't remember. When this was over, she could make an anonymous call and tell someone where they were.

They had enough food for a couple weeks if they didn't eat too much, it wasn't like they would starve or anything.

If the house lasted that long.

Everyone who died was guilty of *something*, Audrey reasoned. Most of them were cheaters. The women Garrett seduced— they were just stupid, and they hadn't killed any of them. Most didn't even know they had been conned. See? *Stupid.* The men Audrey conned were thrilled to have sex with a beautiful young woman. Of course, after she married Garrett, she never slept with any of them. Her body belonged to her husband now. She teased, seduced, maybe gave them a little taste, until the drugs took over and she and Garrett could stage the scene.

They always paid. Because they were horny bastards who thought with their dicks.

Audrey logged in to the factory site. She watched the re- cording of Kara nearly being sliced in two in the elevator. She thought for certain she would bite it then, but even though she got out, it was fun to watch. Then the recording of Kara pee- ing in the bathroom. Audrey laughed. Garrett stirred next to her, but didn't wake up. Audrey stifled another giggle as she watched the recording of the two of them trapped in the con- trol room. That was how they were going to die. They walk on one of the three catwalks and fall to their death. Or better, like Mitch Avila, fall on their back, hit their head, and drown. She could still hear Sheila crying, alone in the control room. They left her there for another day because they both had to work. By the time they got to her, she was hysterical. She begged them to save her husband, thinking they were there to save them . . . then she ran over to the edge and pointed. Audrey couldn't stand her theatrics, one light push and plop.

Sheila joined her husband on the floor below. It was easier getting a dead body out from the ground floor, anyway.

Audrey switched to the live feed. The external cameras showed all was quiet—no vehicles, no sign of trespassers. She didn't expect there would be—the bridge was out and there was only one way to get to the abandoned factory. Then she checked on the control room . . . nothing. No feed. She checked the settings and all the other cameras were working, but the control room was out.

Frowning, she rewound the recording and saw the moment that Matt had found the cameras. And when he destroyed them.

That *prick!*

She loaded the recording from the camera on the factory floor that Garrett had mounted on one of the conveyor belts so it was halfway up, angled at the control room. It was wide-angle so it saw a lot, but the quality was distorted. From that camera she watched on high speed as Matt and Kara stood at the broken window and talked, inspected the catwalks, and then they disappeared from view. They didn't come back and then the recording stopped and showed real time.

It was 12:45 a.m.

Audrey quickly checked the camera outside the metal doors; the doors were still shut, and there was no sign that they had gotten out that way. Good. They were still trapped in the control room.

They would die on the catwalks in the morning, probably just waiting for sunrise before they started. They would be weak, careless.

And if they survived the fall?

They still wouldn't get out of the building alive.

She hoped.

No, they wouldn't. Every trap was perfectly set.

Dammit, this was all Emily's fault.

Eighteen Months Ago

Garrett was working and Audrey was bored.

When Audrey got bored, her mind worked in overdrive. She had *so* many ideas, really great ideas, and when Garrett came by tonight she would share them all with him. He would go through her targets one by one and help her pick the best one. He was *so* good at that. And he never made her feel stupid if one of her ideas wasn't great.

After all, she had hundreds of ideas, *of course* one or two weren't well thought out. But always, he would find her best idea and they would work together to plan the operation. Garrett called it a "con" but she didn't like that word. It was too . . . common. This was an operation, a grand heist, *an adventure!*

She knew who she wanted to target—a convention of financial planners was coming in next week. She already had the reservation list downloaded from the system and had gone through all the names. She picked ten probable successes, ten men who would absolutely hit on her. But there was one she *really* wanted to take down a couple pegs. He was all bragging about his daughter online. She got into Harvard Law. She was top of her class. She was engaged. She was blah-blah-blah. All fake for the world to see. Because Audrey knew that he would want to screw her, and she also knew he would pay anything to prevent his oh-so-perfect daughter from finding out.

Since she was done with her operational plans—she loved that phrase—Audrey went to social media. Checked out what her mother was up to . . . boring. Clicked through to her mother's friends. Sophia got divorced—no surprise there, her husband had been keeping a mistress their entire marriage. Douglas married a trophy wife last year, who was now pregnant. Gross. Click. Click. Click.

She checked on her old boyfriends. She did so periodically, but didn't tell Garrett. It wasn't that Garrett would be upset, she didn't think, but she didn't want her husband to think she was still hung up on any of them. She wasn't. She just wanted to know what they were doing.

Audrey nearly screamed when she saw Charlie's most recent post. A photo of Emily. That bitch. With a man.

Congratulations to Emily and Josh! I'm so happy for you both to embark on your new life together.

Below that was an engagement announcement. Emily and Josh were getting married a year from now. In Florida.

Audrey dug deep into Emily's life. She hadn't given that bitch a second thought since she exposed her father as a cheater. Well, she had celebrated when Charlie finally came to his senses and left her not even two years after they got married. And now . . . she was getting married *again* and Charlie was *happy* about it?

Two hours later, Audrey had learned everything out there about Josh and Emily. They were moving to Florida because that's where Josh was from, bought a house and everything! They were getting married at a church—could they even do that since Emily was divorced? Whatever. Audrey found out which church and maybe she could find a way to ruin the wedding—again. But she'd done that before, so it wouldn't be as fun to do it again.

When Garrett got home she told him everything. He listened, then said, "You'll figure it out. You always do."

She fell in love with him all over again. Because he *got her.* He *loved her.* He *trusted her.* Mostly, he thought she was smart.

Two months later, she did figure it out—after online stalking every person in Josh's family to find out where they were going on their honeymoon.

Besides, it was getting a bit heated here in New Orleans. Time to slip away and find new jobs in a new state with a new plan.

The first of which was to find the right property for what she wanted to do. She couldn't tell Garrett everything, but most lies had some truth, so when she told him her family had a run-down, abandoned property in southern Georgia that would be perfect for what they planned to do to Emily and Josh, he didn't even question it.

She would take Emily Masters down a peg or ten, then she would kill her.

And have fun doing it.

TUESDAY

22

When Michael walked into the resort conference room at five thirty that morning after getting not much more than three hours of sleep, Ryder was already sitting at his computer, hollow-eyed and pale with dark circles under his eyes.

"Did you sleep?" Michael asked as he poured himself a cup of coffee.

"Some," Ryder said. Michael didn't know if he believed that. "I'm tracing Garrett Reid's last seven and a half years. I think I found something interesting in Scottsdale, where he worked at a resort for a year right after he left Los Angeles. A suspicious death."

"Suspicious? Not a homicide?"

"The ME ruled it inconclusive, possible accidental drug overdose. But the suspicious part is that the deceased was the CEO of a Seattle-based tech company with no history of drug use, and the bartender told detectives that he had been flirting with an attractive woman in the bar."

"Security footage?"

"It's not in the information I could access," Ryder said, "so I left a message for the local detective, but it's not even three in the morning there."

Ryder gestured to a closed whiteboard. "You can check what I've added to the board and what I'm still missing, but close it up when you're done. I don't want staff to see where we are."

Michael opened the two doors and looked at the timeline that Ryder had created. He took a photo with his phone, then closed it. "This is good," Michael said.

"Catherine said Garrett didn't meet his partner here. That they have too much trust built up for this to be a new relationship. Which suggests that he met her somewhere between Los Angeles and here."

The timeline was almost complete, but there were a few gaps.

Seven and a half years ago, Garrett had left Los Angeles for Scottsdale, Arizona, where he worked for fourteen months at an exclusive resort. Catherine had spoken to his supervisor, who refreshed himself with Garrett's file. Good employee, rarely tardy, no serious complaints from staff or guests. He hadn't remembered him personally. At the time, Garrett worked as a bartender. Next to that entry, Ryder had written:

Dennis DeMarco, 48, from Seattle, Washington, died of asphyxiation from possible accidental drug overdose in his suite. Reid left two weeks later.

"But the police didn't rule DeMarco's death a homicide."

"Still under investigation, but a cold case and not getting any attention," Ryder said. "I want to know if Reid worked the night that DeMarco died."

"If he did, was he the one who told police the CEO was flirting? Would he have known the woman? Or was this how they met?" Michael wondered out loud.

After Scottsdale there was a six-month gap before Garrett

ended up working as a bartender at a hotel casino in Las Vegas. That gap could have been because of hospitality closures in 2020. He was there for a year, then had a brief stint in Dallas before taking a maintenance position at a major convention hotel in Nashville, which lasted just over two years. After, there was a year-long gap before he took a job as a bartender in New Orleans. Ryder had a question mark and *Texas* written during that time gap.

"Does it seem odd to you that he moved back and forth from bartending to maintenance?" Michael asked.

Ryder shrugged. "He has experience in both. Maybe it's whatever position they were hiring. I've reached out to each of the supervisors to get a copy of his application. Especially the first job in Scottsdale—they would have asked for references or previous employment. Brian gave us his application for the Shoals, but the only references were his supervisors in New Orleans and Nashville."

"It's a good thread," Michael said, though he sounded more confident than he felt. How was this deep dive into Reid's background going to find Matt and Kara? Each day—each *hour*—they didn't find them, the chances of their survival went down exponentially.

None of the victims had lasted more than four days.

Ryder glanced at Michael, looked as if he wanted more reassurance, but Michael didn't have anything left in the well. He was already walking an emotional thin line. "Anything you need, let me know," Michael said. "I'm meeting Mrs. Thomas in a few minutes. She's an early riser."

He left before Ryder could say anything else. Michael didn't want anyone to tell him they would find his missing team members, and he didn't have any optimism to share. He had to keep working, gather information, do everything feasible to locate them. Action would find them. Hope wouldn't get them anywhere.

Mrs. Thomas was waiting for Michael in the lobby as they had arranged. She was in her early sixties with dyed red hair and pale blue eyes. Trim and tan, she wore white cotton pants and a filmy blue blouse over a white tank top. "We can use an office to talk," he suggested.

"No," she said with a smile. "It's a beautiful morning, I think we should sit outside."

She put her arm through his as if they'd been friends for years, and escorted him through the lobby to a small private patio on the other side of the restaurant. A short brick wall separated them from the sand.

"I was very surprised to have a message from the FBI this morning."

"And I was surprised that you responded so quickly. Thank you."

"I'm a morning girl, always have been. Born and raised on a farm in North Texas."

Michael didn't want small talk, but if he was rude she might not talk at all. As if sensing his tension, she leaned back and asked, "So how can I help the FBI? Is it about the man who was arrested on Friday?"

"Partly. We're talking to several guests about what they saw and heard over the last week. You had a conversation with Kara Quinn—she was going by Kara Costa—at the gym one day last week?"

"The cute little blonde girl? Oh, yes, what a sweetheart. And I never guessed that she was a police officer!"

"Word travels fast," Michael said.

"Well, everyone was talking about it on Friday, and Mr. Valdez was very forthcoming when I asked him what was going on, then I talked to Kara again on Saturday."

"Oh?" Michael asked. He hadn't known that.

"Yes. She was getting coffee. An early riser, like me. I was reading the paper in the lobby because it was a bit cool. I really enjoy how the resort has a physical paper—I hate reading on those screens. Anyhoo, she said hi. I asked her to sit, said that Mr. Valdez told me she and her partner had arrested one of the employees. I wanted to know more, but she didn't tell me anything I didn't already know. I asked about her partner—she said he was sleeping in, but they were going to the sheriff's office. I mentioned they didn't have any time off? I mean, they were here for a whole week or more—longer than me! And didn't they get a break? She said they were taking tomorrow off to enjoy the resort before going back to Virginia."

"When you first met Kara, you asked her about her job."

"Well, that was before I knew she wasn't a lawyer."

"What I mean is, how did you learn that she was a lawyer, before the arrest?"

"Oh. Well, gosh, let's see. I saw them on the beach when I arrived last week. I may have said hello or something—but then a couple days later we were in the locker room at the gym, and I commented about how hard she was working out. I like yoga, keeps me limber as I creep toward sixty-five. And she said yoga annoyed her and she didn't like how painstakingly slow some of the stretches were. I liked her bluntness! So we talked. She said her husband was a lawyer. I said my husband, God rest his soul, had been a county prosecutor for thirty years. She said they were both in private practice—it's how they met, on the job. And I asked what kind of law, and she said her husband did tax law and she handled contract law. I told her that sounded more boring than yoga and she laughed. Later, the three of us had drinks in the bar by the pool—I really thought they were married. They were so cute together." She leaned forward, added almost conspiratorially, "You know, I think they really have feelings for each other. I can tell. The way he looked at her when she wasn't looking?" Mrs. Thomas sighed. "But that's probably discouraged if they work together."

Michael didn't share Matt and Kara's relationship status, but asked, "I'd like you to think back to the gym and the pool bar—not what you talked about, but who you saw."

"Is this about the guests, the honeymooners, who were killed?"

"You heard about the murders?"

"Of course—several guests have talked about it, but staff hasn't said anything. The Delmonicos checked out yesterday because Mrs. Delmonico freaked out, was talking about three couples who went missing and were killed, and that an employee had been arrested while trying to abduct two more people. It's a shock, but you all caught him, so I thought she was overreacting—I read the newspapers, all the women were pretty blondes, and Mrs. Delmonico is not only not blonde, but not very attractive, though she tries, bless her heart. That wasn't very nice of me to say, was it?"

"I can't fault an honest opinion, Mrs. Thomas."

She smiled. "They weren't very nice people, but that's no excuse for me being rude."

Her face paled. "Why are you asking all these questions about Matt and Kara if they arrested the kidnapper? Are they missing?"

"Yes, they were taken late Sunday morning. That's why I want to find out if you saw anyone who acted overinterested in them when you were having drinks. Staff or guests, male or female."

She was thinking, but her expression suggested that she was thinking too hard, and Michael didn't want her to make something up just to please him—it had happened before, especially in friendly interviews.

So he said, "Maybe not while you were talking, but you are observant—maybe you saw someone watching them, or paying too close attention to what Matt or Kara were doing. Anything odd or unusual or that gave you pause."

"There was one thing, but maybe I'm making a mountain out of a molehill."

"Let me be the judge," Michael said and smiled politely, even though he was getting antsy because he had a lot of people to talk to this morning. He spared a quick glance at his watch and hoped she didn't notice.

"It was on Wednesday, maybe, when I had a drink with them at the pool. I was walking back to my suite to call my daughter—she's pregnant with her fifth child, said she's done but we'll see!" She laughed lightly. "Anyway, there was a woman lying in the sun with a book, but she was looking at Matt and Kara."

"How do you know she was looking at them?"

"Well, I said something like, 'I just finished that book, it's wonderful.' It was a historical novel about nurses in Vietnam. She said, 'I haven't gotten far.' Yet it appeared she was more than halfway through the book, so I glanced back and saw her staring at Matt and Kara. I said, 'Aren't they cute?' And she said, 'It won't last.' Then she went back to the book."

"Would you recognize her?"

"No—I really don't think so. She looked familiar, but I assumed because she was a guest and I had seen her in passing. She wore dark sunglasses and a floppy hat."

"Hair? Skin? Age?"

"She was a little tan, though lathered in sunscreen. I didn't see her hair, because of the hat. I remember she wore a red bikini. I wouldn't know her age, I couldn't really see her face. Thirty to forty, maybe older? Nice figure, the bikini suited her."

"This was Wednesday?"

She nodded. "Mid-afternoon. Just before four. That I know because of the call to my daughter. But certainly that woman has nothing to do with anything!"

Michael thanked Bridget for her time, though he wasn't sure that it was time well spent. Still, he called Brian. "Are there security cameras on the pool area?"

"No," he said. "Did you find something?"

"A woman, possibly a guest, watching Matt and Kara on Wednesday. Are staff allowed to use resort facilities?"

"Off duty, yes. It's a perk."

That got Michael thinking, but he didn't know if following this thread would get them any closer to finding Matt and Kara.

Sloane accepted the use of Brian's office and closed the door. Catherine was on another call, so Sloane was taking this interview solo. She'd coordinated with Agent Sylvia Black out of the Tampa FBI office, and encouraged her to make contact early, as this was a critical investigation and lives were at stake.

At 7:45 in the morning, Sylvia called Sloane and put her on speaker. "Agent Wagner, I'm here with Mrs. Blanche Richardson and told her why we wanted to speak with her. She'd like to cooperate, though indicated that she hasn't seen Mr. Reid since before she left Los Angeles."

"Thank you for your time, Mrs. Richardson," Sloane said. "And I apologize that we came to your door so early."

"I'm up before six every morning," she said. "How can I help?"

"Did Agent Black tell you why we are inquiring about Garrett Reid?"

"He was arrested."

This was when Sloane wished she was there. Seeing facial expressions was important. But she had talked to Sylvia earlier and the senior agent knew what to look for and would interject if warranted. "Are you surprised?" Sloane asked.

"I don't know," the woman said. "Maybe. Why was he arrested?"

"Attempted abduction of two law enforcement officers," Sloane said.

Mrs. Richardson laughed. "Garrett? That's—almost unbelievable."

"He's a suspect in a homicide investigation," Sloane said bluntly.

"Murder? *Garrett?* I—I don't see that."

"How would you describe your relationship with him?" Sloane asked.

She was silent for a moment, then said, "You think I'm a fool."

"No, ma'am."

"So does my son. He thinks Garrett manipulated me, that he used me. Maybe he did, but I didn't care because I used him as well. We had a mutually beneficial relationship based on very selfish common ground."

"Can you explain further?"

"You want details?"

"If they are relevant."

"Relevant to what?"

"I need to understand who Garrett is, what motivates him, why he would kill someone he didn't know."

"Murder," Richardson said, her voice full of doubt. "That I have a very hard time believing, Agent Wagner."

"Who was Garrett Reid when you were involved with him?"

"Attentive. Inventive. Intelligent. I was quite demanding of him in bed, and he was more than willing to learn everything I had to teach him." She paused. "I had a good marriage, but it wasn't sexually satisfying. When my husband passed suddenly, I was upset because I loved him and he was a good man. But I never had a real orgasm with him."

Sloane did not need to know this, and was about to interrupt when Richardson continued. "I tried, but my dear husband didn't have the same drive I did. This isn't something I could explain to my son. I never strayed in our twenty-seven-year marriage. Not once. But I told Garrett my fantasies, and he fulfilled them. I knew he wanted a comfortable place to live,

good food to eat, a state-of-the-art gym to work out in, luxu-
ries that I had more than enough to share. In exchange, he gave
me complete and total physical satisfaction and treated me like
a queen. I never harbored any fantasies that he loved me, and
I didn't love him, not like I loved my husband, though I think
we both loved the image of us."

"How did the relationship end?" Sloane asked.

"My son. Dear boy threatened to kill poor Garrett. Garrett
doesn't like conflict, and even though I told him to ignore Johnny,
he walked away. Well, we had one more amazing night together,
and then he left. I harbor no ill feelings. Garrett taught me as
much about myself as I taught him about what makes me—what
makes most women—happy. Garrett is not a violent man, Agent
Wagner. If he killed anyone, I'm certain it was an accident."

She sounded confident, Sloane thought.

"Did Garrett tell you any of his plans after your relationship was over?"

"No. We never saw each other again, though I talked to
him a few times on the phone. I heard he had brief affairs with
a couple of other women my age, but they were short-lived. A
few weeks, at most."

"What about his ex-girlfriend, Becca McCarthy?"

"What about her?"

"Did you know her?"

"I'd met her. Garrett and my son went to school together, and
I'd met Becca at high school events. They were cute together."

This conversation was weird for Sloane. She didn't understand how an intelligent woman could have a relationship with
a man young enough to be her son—who had gone to school
with her son—and sound so matter-of-fact about it.

A real-life Mrs. Robinson.

"Why do you care about Becca? As far as I know, she and
Garrett split up when they went to different colleges."

"Like I said, we're trying to piece together Garrett's background."

"Becca was his first love, as it often is with high school sweethearts. They grew up and apart—again, very common. But he still loved her. He didn't say it, specifically, but I could tell."

"So he *did* talk about her with you."

"In passing. None of the girls he dated in college held a candle to Becca, he said once."

"Has he contacted you since he moved to Florida?"

Silence.

Agent Black said, "Mrs. Richardson, did you know Garrett has lived in Florida, north of Daytona Beach, for the last nine months?"

"No," she said somewhat curtly.

"Does that bother you?" Sloane asked.

"No," she said. "I left Los Angeles for Florida three months after Garrett and I split. I was angry with my son for interfering in my life, and I wanted a fresh start. I'm happy here. I have friends, I have a lover, I'm content. I assumed Garrett would stay in Los Angeles, though I heard that he'd taken a job at a resort in Scottsdale."

"And in the nearly eight years since you split, you only talked to him on the phone?"

"Correct," she said. "Maybe two, three times. The last time was the week before I moved. I had already sold the house and had the furnishings I wanted shipped, so I was staying in a hotel. I called him for a, well, I guess you would say a booty call. He said he couldn't, that he had plans he couldn't break. I told him if he was ever in Florida to look me up. And that was it."

She was upset, Sloane realized. Upset that he had been here for months and hadn't reached out to her.

"If that's all," Mrs. Richardson said, "I have brunch plans."

"Yes, thank you for your time."

Five minutes later, Sylvia Black called Sloane. "She was upset at the end," Sylvia said.

"I thought so."

"She cared about him more than she let on at the beginning of the conversation."

"You believe her that she hasn't spoken to him?" Sloane asked.

"Yeah, I do," Sylvia said. "She was forthcoming. Not at all embarrassed about the affair, though is it an affair if neither of them are married? Anyway, she didn't know he lived nearby, and I doubt she lied about not talking to him. Did any of it help?"

"Maybe," Sloane said. "It gives us more insight into his personality, but I don't know if that's going to help us nail him for murder."

The personnel manager at the Scottsdale resort returned Ryder's call and promised to send Garrett Reid's application. Ten minutes later, it arrived via email and Ryder read through it.

He'd listed his parents' home address as his last address, even though Ryder knew that he hadn't lived there since he left for college when he was eighteen. He'd included two references—Blanche Richardson and someone named Jeff Maddox. Ryder made note of his address and phone number, then ran it through the FBI database. He wasn't in the database—which didn't necessarily mean anything, just that he wasn't wanted for a federal crime.

Ryder did a Google search on Jeff Maddox in Los Angeles and there were more than two dozen people with that name or a variation of it. He narrowed it to the Westwood address, but quickly realized that this was a person Reid knew in college who likely no longer lived there. Digging into social media, he found the correct Jeff Maddox. He'd graduated from UCLA the year after Reid, now lived in Austin, Texas, and worked for a computer software company. His social media showed that he was married with two kids and attended church regularly.

Ryder itched to call Maddox, but sent all the information first to the team. Catherine immediately responded and asked Michael if he could contact Maddox for an interview ASAP.

Michael responded that he would, then he stepped inside the conference room and said to Ryder, "Bridget Thomas saw a woman watching Matt and Kara at the pool, but there are no security cameras in the area, and the woman wore sunglasses, a hat, and red bikini. Brian is looking through security footage from outside the pool deck to see if he can spot her. What's this Maddox thing?"

Ryder told him about the reference and that he may have background on Garrett that would be helpful.

Michael said, "Sit in on the call, you know more than I do about Garrett's background."

Michael closed the door to give them privacy, and Ryder dialed Maddox's number, putting the phone on speaker.

Maddox gave them a bit of the runaround, and then said he'd talk if Michael would text him a photo of his badge and ID. After they got that out of the way, he said, "What do you want to know? Is this like a background check or something?"

"Or something," Michael said vaguely. "You're talking to myself and analyst Ryder Kim, both of us with the FBI Mobile Response Team."

Maddox said, "Is Garrett in trouble?"

"What do you think?"

"I don't know what to think. You called me."

"Mr. Reid has been arrested," Michael said. "We're pulling together information about his background, so if you can help we would appreciate it."

"Wow," Maddox said. "Well, I haven't spoken to him in years. Maybe saw him once or twice after he graduated. I wasn't really into his scene, you know?"

Ryder slid a note over to Michael giving him the basics of what he knew about Maddox and that they had likely lived together in college, based on a shared address in Westwood during that time.

"Let's start at the beginning. You know Garrett from college, correct?"

"We were roommates. I was a freshman, he was a sophomore, and I swear, I would have flunked out if Garrett hadn't helped me. The guy is a genius."

"How so?"

"Just super smart. He explains things well. He was an engineering major. He changed after his sophomore year, I don't remember to what, but he was still smart. I told him he should like get a master's or something and teach college. I was a computer science major. It's what I do now, programming. But I had to take these advanced math classes, and I just didn't get it. Until Garrett tutored me. And he didn't even ask for money or anything, just helped me because we were roommates. So even when . . . Well, no matter what, he was a friend."

Ryder caught Michael's eye and saw that Michael had the same thought.

"Even when *what?*" Michael asked.

"What was he arrested for?" Maddox answered the question with a question.

"Felony kidnapping, and he's a suspect in multiple homicides."

"*Murder?* Oh my God. That's—wow."

"What did you remember, Mr. Maddox?" Michael pressed.

"You're not going to tell him I talked to you or anything, are you?"

He sounded wary. Was he scared of Garrett?

"No," Michael assured him. "This is just for our records. We're building a case, and I need to know everything about his past."

"Well. Like I said, we were roommates," Maddox said, at first talking slow, then seeming happy to share what he knew.

"Garrett doesn't really care about people. Okay, that's not quite right. He's friendly and will help people out and seems all genuine about it, right? But then when you look at him, you realize he just doesn't care about *you*. He helps . . . but that's easy. It's easy for him to give you answers or explain a problem because he knows it. And he likes people to think he's smart and all that. I mean, he is smart. But if you like, um, tell him your mom died? He shrugs."

"Did that happen to you?" Ryder asked. "Did your mom pass away?"

"Yeah. She died my junior year. Garrett, me, two other guys were renting an apartment off campus. I was really broken up. My mom—well, she was the greatest. When she died—it was a stupid accident—I was destroyed. My oldest sister was pregnant and losing mom was super hard for her, too. I mean, I know guys are supposed to keep all this inside and just be a rock? And I was, for my sisters, because they needed me to be. I took over all the arrangements and sometimes, I wanted to just talk about things, and Garrett . . . he didn't understand, he didn't *want* to understand. And then . . . he said my mom had been hot. That was *so* wrong. My mom was my *mom*. You know?"

His voice cracked and Ryder said, "I understand what you mean." He glanced at Michael, and Michael nodded that his interjections were appropriate and to jump in when he saw fit.

"I knew Garrett dated older women, and I'm not talking like thirty to his twenty. I ran into him after he graduated and he was with someone old enough to be his mom. We just didn't share the same values, you know?"

Ryder said, "He put you down as a reference for a job at a resort in Scottsdale, Arizona. Did you provide him with a good recommendation?"

"Yeah, probably. I don't remember specifics, but a couple times people called me for a personal reference and I always said he was a nice guy, we'd been roommates, and he was super smart. Never late on the rent, things like that. All true. Just not . . . emotional or sensitive to people. I didn't say that to anyone, of course, because seriously, I wouldn't have graduated without his help. People can be good and bad, you know?"

"When was the last time you saw him?" Michael pressed.

"Well, I ran into him at the Odyssey about six months after his graduation. I was working there as waiter when I saw him with a woman."

"The Odyssey?"

"It's a real nice restaurant in the hills in San Fernando, north of LA. I usually only worked weekend events—they do a lot of wedding receptions and parties—but sometimes if I was free and someone called out, I'd go in and wait tables. Good tips. I was doing that the last time I saw him."

"And he was with an older woman. Do you know her name?"

"He pretended he didn't know me, and I was fine with that because it was weird. And then—get this—he was flirting with another woman while on a date with someone else. Total sleaze-ball move."

"Another older woman?"

"No—someone closer to his age. She was pretty, would have been a knockout except over–made up. Not like a hooker or anything, just too much stuff," he finished lamely.

"You wouldn't by chance know who she was?"

"No, but the bartender did. He said she came in a couple times a month, usually with a rich guy. I don't know anything about her, though I don't think I ever saw her again after that night. Again, I didn't work there much other than for events."

"Could you describe her?" Michael asked.

"Not really. Twenties, thirty tops, pretty, blonde—though I don't think it was natural. Tall with long, long legs. Dressed classy. That's really all I remember."

Ryder was writing everything down when Michael asked, "Who was your manager then?"

"Um, the event manager was Leo Tanaka—I worked for him. The general manager was Jim or John or Jess or something like that—I didn't really know him."

"This is helpful, thank you," Michael said.

Ryder spoke up, "One more question, Mr. Maddox. Do you know Becca McCarthy?"

"Becca? Well, sure."

"How?"

"She was Garrett's girl in high school, and she visited him a couple times in college, though she went to Point Loma. But they split up . . . I don't remember exactly what happened. I mean, they had broken it off after high school, but they still kinda saw each other. Then they like had a fight or something, because she stopped coming by."

"Was it her decision or his?" Ryder asked.

"I don't know. Mutual? Maybe? He didn't talk about his personal life at all. Hell, I didn't even know he had two brothers until he graduated. He didn't talk about his family *at all*. And like the day after he told us he and Becca were through— and the only reason he told us was because she was supposed to visit and we'd promised to get lost for a couple hours, you know—he was fine. Told us Becca left, wasn't coming back, and never mentioned it again. But . . . I think he really loved her. Just a few things he said, like comparing other girls to Becca. No one was good enough, no one as pretty, or as funny, or as smart, stuff like that. Even after they split, he was so matter-of-fact and talked about her as if she were perfect and no other girl could live up to her."

"Do you know how to reach Becca?" Ryder asked.

"No, I haven't seen her since. Sorry."

Michael thanked him for his time and ended the call. "I screwed up."

"No, how?" Ryder asked.

"I didn't even think to ask about the girlfriend."

"I did. That's why you wanted me on the call, right?" Ryder finished writing up his notes. "Michael, we can't all do everything. That's why we're a team. We pick each other up."

Michael nodded, but looked away. Ryder didn't know what to say to help Michael. They were all struggling not knowing where Matt and Kara were, not knowing whether they were alive.

"Do you think you can find this Becca McCarthy?" Michael asked Ryder.

"Yes. Knowing that she went to Point Loma helps. They may be able to help me track her down, but I still have at least an hour before the administrative building opens."

Michael stood. "I'm going to reinterview the female staff."

He walked out and Ryder put his head down for a minute. He had lied to Michael; he hadn't slept at all last night. And he couldn't sleep now. He breathed deeply, recentered his emotions, then got up.

He had more threads to tug. He needed to start pulling until he found something—anything—that helped the team identify and apprehend Garrett Reid's partner.

23

Kara's eyes snapped open. Her heart was racing, every inch of her tired body sore and bruised. The air around her was thick, humid, cloying, and for a second she didn't know where she was, almost couldn't breathe. Panic flared, and she tried to sit up but found the effort almost impossible. A dull throb pulsed through her head and her limbs felt unnaturally heavy.

"Matt?" Her voice was rough, disoriented. She coughed, a dry, hacking sound. She could barely process the noises around her: the distant drip of water, the faint buzz of a faraway generator, and the overwhelming stillness.

"It's okay." Matt's voice came from beside her, soft, steady. His arms tightened around her. "You're okay."

Kara blinked, tried to focus. Matt's back was pressed into the corner of the concrete wall; she was spooned into him. Her head rested on his arm, which felt oddly comforting, but now that she was awake, she realized that Matt had to be uncomfortable. She herself felt like she'd been run over by a truck.

"I'm fine," she said, trying to convince herself that this was all normal, that they would get out of this situation, though she felt anything but fine. Her head was spinning, her muscles stiff. The realization hit her like a punch—*they had slept.* They had actually slept while trapped in some abandoned flooded warehouse in Georgia, a hundred miles or more from where they'd been abducted.

With a wince, she pushed herself up, vertigo threatening to pull her back down. Her limbs ached like she'd been stuck in one position for hours. Her mouth was dry, her empty stomach gnawing at her.

"We need to get out of here," she said, her voice barely more than a hoarse rasp.

"We will." Matt shifted, and she saw pain flash across his face.

"Your ankle—is it okay?"

"Fine."

"I don't believe you."

"It's a dull throb," he said. "Honestly, every one of my muscles feels bruised, and I had a dream—or nightmare—about a juicy cheeseburger just out of reach."

She moaned, but smiled, just a bit.

He took a long look at her, his eyes dark but resolute. "You're right, we can't stay here much longer. We *will* get out."

"And get a cheeseburger?"

"I promise."

Kara forced herself to stand. Her legs were weak, as if they had forgotten what it was like to be used. She stretched, feeling the tension in her shoulders, the cramp in her stomach. "I can't believe we slept," she muttered, her gaze drifting across the room. The faint light that filtered through the grimy windows barely illuminated the factory floor below.

Matt glanced at his watch. "It's 7:10 a.m."

"Wow," she said. "That long?" Time felt like it had completely lost all meaning. Maybe they hadn't slept. Maybe they'd fallen unconscious again.

"The windows face west," Matt explained, looking around. "So it's still pretty dark out from our angle."

Kara's hands clenched at her sides. "This whole thing is driving me kind of crazy." She glanced out at the catwalks. She'd figured it out last night—how to use the catwalks and beams to get down to the flooded floor below. But her mind was a mess, and she was trying to sort through all the possibilities to find the solution again.

"You're fine," Matt repeated. He wrapped his arms around her, pulling her into him for a brief moment, his embrace grounding her. Kara felt the tension in her chest loosen. The reality of their situation was still there, but with Matt by her side she had confidence they'd get out of this.

She gave him a light kiss. "We have to get moving."

Matt let out a breath. "Alright, let's do this."

She looked at him, searching his face for the kind of reassurance she knew he couldn't give. "You sure about this?"

"No, but we're only getting weaker. We need water, at the very least. And now that we disabled the cameras, Reid's partner will come back. Neither of us is in a position to fight, and if she has a gun, we're really screwed."

Kara scanned the factory floor, the web of catwalks hanging from the ceiling across from them, stretching like an endless maze of rusted metal. "I've thought about what might happen if the catwalks break. If we fall . . . it's about two stories down. That's not enough to kill us, unless we hit our head on the machinery. Still, we could break something."

"We may be able to use the equipment to help," Matt said. "Cross the catwalks, then drop down onto a machine. Whatever decision we make, it's going to be dangerous."

Kara squeezed his hand and started toward the nearest catwalk. "If we don't make it, Matt—"

"We will make it," he said firmly, cutting her off. His confidence made her heart thud in her chest. "I'll go first."

"No," she said. "I'm lighter."

"What does that have to do with it? If the catwalk holds me, it'll hold you."

"Matt, I'm doing it," she insisted. "First, your ankle is messed up."

"So?"

How did she convince him? "Want to flip for it?"

Now he smiled. "You have a coin?" Then he said, in all seriousness, "Okay, you go. But listen carefully, Kara. If you get down there and I don't, you get out of this place. Promise me?"

"I'm not promising anything like that. I'm not leaving you behind."

"Kara—"

"You wouldn't leave me. I'm not leaving you."

"Just—"

She kissed him. "Shh."

Kara knelt and inspected the metal. She couldn't just walk out from the control room onto the catwalk, it was about two feet away. She would need to jump, which was a risk even if she wasn't concerned about sabotage. She took one of the monitors they'd pulled from the wall when they were looking for a way to communicate with the outside world, and carefully tossed it onto the walkway. It hit hard, bounced, then fell off, plopping into the water below with a thud and splash.

This catwalk went straight across from the control room to the opposite wall, where there was a ladder down to the floor. She hoped to get all the way across, but if there was any danger or threat of collapse, if she could get just halfway, there was a conveyor belt she could drop onto, the top of it only a few feet from the bottom of the catwalk.

Now or never. She walked to the door, then ran and jumped onto the catwalk, grabbing the handrails as it swayed back and forth. But it held. She heard Matt swear behind her. She turned, gave him a thumbs-up, then she started across the metal grate, her tennis shoes giving her traction. The catwalk continued to sway, but it held. She stepped carefully, her mind running through all the booby traps they'd already encountered. The staircase that chewed up Matt's ankle. The falling ceiling. The elevator.

Her confidence grew as she progressed, but still she moved slowly, purposefully.

Suddenly, the support chain to her left broke, hit her arm, then made a deafening sound as it clanked against the metal and hung from where it was attached to the rail. It jerked heavily, made the entire structure wobble. She froze. The catwalk creaked ominously.

"Kara, get back here!" Matt called.

"No, it's okay."

She took another step. Good. Another. Only twenty more feet and she'd reach the top of the conveyor belt. Her first opportunity to get off. She glanced back at the end of the swaying chain and it looked clean, as if it had been sawed off.

Maybe she should go back. But it was only another few feet . . .

Suddenly, three chains broke simultaneously in front of her, and Kara screamed as she lost her balance, tilting sideways and down. She would have fallen to the floor below, but her hands clutched at the rusted edges of the walkway, holding on as she dangled above the factory floor, a chasm of dark, murky water. How deep was it? Would she fall, hit her head, drown? Was it so shallow that she'd break her back?

Matt shouted her name, but the sound was muffled by the ringing in her ears. *Focus, Kara. You need to focus.*

The catwalk groaned, and her world tilted again. Kara looked frantically around, the top of the conveyor belt too far from her. She didn't have the strength to use the catwalk as makeshift monkey bars to get over to it, but the edge of the belt was directly below her, sloping out of the huge machine. If she could reach it, maybe—just maybe—she could avoid a deadly fall.

With a burst of energy, she shimmied down the broken catwalk, muscles straining, until she could drop onto the conveyor belt, now only six feet below. She hit it hard, sending shockwaves of pain clear through to her bones. She gritted her teeth, forcing herself to roll down the belt, not off the side. She tumbled, slid, then hit the water-covered floor with a thud.

She gasped, her body screaming from the impact, but she pulled herself up out of the water and stood on shaking legs. The water reached her knees.

"Kara? Kara!" Matt shouted.

She couldn't respond at first. She started to laugh and cry at the same time, tried to respond to Matt, but couldn't quite catch her breath.

"Are you okay? Kara, dammit!"

"Yes!" she managed to shout. She waved her arms above her head in a sign that she was okay. She took a deep breath. "Nothing broken!"

"Go," Matt called down to her. "Get help."

"Like hell," she said. "I'm not leaving here without you. Remember?" She looked up to where the catwalk was hanging down like a crooked ladder. "Can you use the catwalk as a slide? Shimmy down or something?"

She squinted to watch Matt. He was standing near where she'd jumped onto the catwalk. He wouldn't be able to reach it now.

"Matt, check out the other catwalk, but be careful. Find a way to drop down. Please," she added almost to herself.

Matt's heart had skipped a beat or three when the catwalk partly collapsed, but now he had his breathing under control as he looked down at Kara standing knee-deep in the dark water. She was alive, that's all that mattered. She had made it. He wished she would leave, find a way out, but if their positions were reversed, he'd never leave without her.

"Give me a minute," he called down.

She put two thumbs up, then climbed onto the conveyor belt and sat down.

Kara was alive, but that didn't mean the danger was over. He looked at the catwalk she'd crossed; it was still shaking and ready to completely give way, plus it was swinging too far for him to reach. He couldn't take the same path as she had—even if he could leap and grab onto the metal, he had at least seventy pounds on her. The catwalk would likely collapse as soon as he put his weight on it.

They'd mapped out the entire area last night, before it got dark. There were several catwalks, none that looked stable, and only one left that was close enough to access, if he jumped. And by jumping, he might force the entire structure to collapse.

But there was no other choice.

The catwalk was five feet away, attached to the wall, but with no railings to help him balance. He stared at the support bolts. They looked intact, but the catwalk Kara crossed had held until she was nearly to the middle.

This was the only way.

He swallowed hard, and headed to the far side of the control room.

"Matt?" Kara called up to him, her voice echoing in the cavernous room. "I told you last night that was too narrow."

"No other option," he shouted.

He pushed the desk up against the half wall, and brushed the broken safety glass away. He climbed up into the opening and heard Kara curse.

He wasn't going to die today.

Careful but determined, he balanced on the thin ledge and used the last of his strength to leap over to the narrow catwalk.

He hit it hard. It creaked and groaned beneath him, but stayed attached to the wall. His legs dangled over, but his hands were curled around the rough, rusting metal.

He breathed deeply, held on tight.

"I'm okay," he called down to Kara when he'd caught his breath.

"Go to the right about twenty feet," Kara shouted. "There's a ladder mounted to the wall. It'll get you most of the way down, then you'll drop about five feet."

As she spoke, Matt felt the walkway sag. It was the only warning before the metal snapped and he fell. In the distance, he heard Kara scream, and for a split second Matt thought he was a dead man.

He hit the water hard, the impact sending ripples across the flooded factory floor, then he hit the concrete bottom and the air was knocked out of him.

Kara watched Matt fall and she heard his body hit with a sickening thud. She screamed and may have shouted his name; she didn't know. She ran as fast as she could toward him, water splashing. She fell, got up, then her shin hit something hard and sharp and she stumbled and fell again. She forced herself to get up, get going, find Matt. What if he was unconscious? What if he drowned? What if he broke his back?

Damn damn damn! He could *not* be dead. Not dead. Not dead. Not dead.

He didn't surface.

Her heart pounded, her body felt numb, her head was spinning as she navigated as fast as possible across the factory floor.

He hadn't surfaced.

"No no no no no," she repeated as she reached down to where he had fallen, feeling for his body, touching his arm, pulling him up.

He sat, coughing water out of his lungs, his face pale and drawn but alive.

He was alive.

She sat in the stagnant water with him, wrapped her arms around him, pulling him close. "You're okay. You're okay."

He held her.

"Is anything broken?"

"No," he said, his voice raw. "I think I'm okay."

"You scared the hell out of me."

"Ditto."

They helped each other up and Kara winced. Yeah, she had really done a number on her leg. She didn't know what she'd hit, but it hurt like hell. She didn't say anything.

She scanned the factory floor, desperate for any sign of an exit. There, at the far end of the room, was a door. It was a faint silhouette against the gloom, but it was a door.

A way out.

They started toward it and her left leg gave out.

"What's wrong?" Matt asked.

"I cut my leg. It's fine."

He steered her to one of the many conveyor belts that traversed the floor. They supported each other until they both sat heavily on one of the belts, their feet still submersed in the standing water.

She looked down and saw blood seeping through her sweatpants at the same time Matt said, "You're bleeding."

"It's fine."

"It's not fine. It's deep."

He leaned over and pulled her sweatpants up to her knee. Blood poured steadily from the deep gash.

He took his shirt off over her protests and tied it tightly around her calf. "This water is probably filled with thousands of bacteria and—"

"Your leg is cut up and you just fell from nearly two stories, so I don't want to hear it," she said.

"My cut has clotted. Sore, but not bleeding."

"Let's just get out of here and then I won't even fight you about going to the hospital."

He smiled at her. It was small, but it was there, and that made her feel like they just might get out of this alive.

"Five minutes," he said.

"Tell me the truth—is anything broken? The water isn't deep." She inspected him, looking for blood or protruding bones. She squinted, examined his eyes, looking for signs of a concussion.

"What are you doing?"

"You hit hard." She felt the back of his head, searching for bumps or blood.

He leaned into her and rested his head on her shoulder. "Five minutes," he said and held her.

She forced herself to relax, tried to ignore the throbbing in her leg. For five minutes they sat there until their breathing evened out.

"Okay," Matt said. "We go to the doors, but approach carefully."

"I hear you," Kara said.

They headed toward the double doors, but she started to get that bad feeling she always had when her instincts told her something was wrong. Her stomach clenched—she felt like a million tiny bugs crawled over her skin. She stopped.

"Kara?" Matt said, his arm around her waist, supporting her.

"I don't like this."

"We can't stay here, you need medical attention, and we don't know when she's going to return."

"The door—it's too easy."

He looked down at her and frowned. "It was not easy getting down here."

"Booby traps. This is the only door we can see, you think

they wouldn't have done something to it? Like the elevator? The staircase?"

"We're on the ground floor. We can't fall any further. With all this standing water, I don't think there's a sub-basement, or if there is it's not accessible from here or it's completely filled with water."

"There was a charge on the elevator. Something that sparked and sent the elevator down. If something sparks and we're standing in water? We know there's electricity—the cameras had to have something charging them, and they can't all be run on batteries, right?"

"There wouldn't be enough electricity to electrocute us—it would take a real strong jolt."

"Do you want to take that chance?" She sounded panicked, and she didn't want to panic, she just wanted to get out. Though the factory floor was huge, she felt as if the walls were closing in on her. "I feel like I'm in the damn Zoo of Death," she muttered. "We go through that door and a deadly spider is waiting for us. Or worse, a snake. I hate snakes."

Matt squeezed her hand. "So does Indiana Jones, and everything turned out okay for him."

"You're not funny," she said, but she smiled anyway.

"Let's think this through logically." Matt's voice was calm and confident. "The killers set up this factory like a giant escape room. We were directed down halls and paths simply because that was the only way we could go. Now we have this door that's so obviously a way out—you're right, it could be sabotaged. There could be something dangerous on the other side, something we can't see. So we don't just open the door and take our chances."

"Okay," Kara said, beginning to feel better as her mind worked through the situation as Matt laid it out. "Logically, would this be the only exit?"

"No," Matt said. "When we were looking last night, remember the exit on the far wall?" He gestured across the factory floor to the exit she couldn't see because rotting equipment stood in the way. "It was blocked by fallen equipment. We could try to move it, but . . ."

"But that could also be a trap."

"I'm more concerned that the door is locked or bolted and moving the heavy equipment will sap the little energy we have left. But yeah, it could also be a trap."

"If everything's a trap we're stuck here."

"No. We're going through those doors," Matt said.

"But—"

"We're going to be smart about it. We'll find a way to push them open, with a long pole or something like that."

There had once been handles; they had been removed, Kara noted.

"Let's start looking," Kara said. "How far do you think we need to be?"

"As far away as we can get," Matt said. "Maybe ten, twelve feet?"

Kara was pretty good at identifying danger, but she couldn't imagine what was on the other side. Hell, she couldn't have imagined half of what they'd already faced in the last forty-eight hours.

"But you're staying put," Matt said. "I don't want you walking on that leg any more than necessary. I'll look around for something long enough to give us distance from the doors, but strong enough to push them open, okay?"

Reluctantly, she agreed. It was easier to agree than argue.

24

Matt and Kara had been missing for forty-eight hours.

Catherine was stuck. Jim was back with the ME and talking to Quantico about the lab results, but hadn't returned with anything actionable. Michael was finishing the third round of staff interviews. Sloane had good information from Blanche Richardson, but only about Garrett's personality.

Still, everything Catherine was learning about Garrett's personality was shifting her profile of him. What particularly stuck was that Blanche still cared about him. He hadn't hurt her—physically or emotionally.

Garrett was kind to the women he used. He was honest—they knew he wanted money and nice things, and they happily gave him everything he wanted because he gave them something *they* wanted. She didn't think it was just about sex, though that was certainly part of it. It sounded as if Garrett listened, which made him a good observer of human nature.

Jeff Maddox also had keen insight. The fact that he appreciated

Garrett's help and intelligence while distancing himself from Garrett because of his lack of empathy showed Catherine that Garrett was either uncomfortable with emotions or incapable of feeling them.

Becca McCarthy was an outlier. Both Maddox and Blanche believed that Garrett had once been serious about his high school sweetheart. That indicated he had some sort of emotional core, though it was twisted and off-kilter.

And the biggest takeaway: no one suggested that they had seen any violence in him. Just the opposite. Garrett Reid walked away before confrontation. Even his parents and his brother said he wasn't violent. He had no history of violence, though he had tormented people emotionally—such as hitting on his sister-in-law and seeming to enjoy her discomfort. What his college roommate said was key—he just didn't care. He didn't connect with people emotionally, but could fake it when it benefited him.

If he truly had no natural leanings toward violence, did that mean his partner, his *female* partner, was the violent half of their relationship? Did he kill to make her happy?

He had participated in the killings, assisted in the abductions, yet . . . the murders were hands-off. They weren't personal acts of homicide—like stabbing, or strangulation, or even poison.

One victim fell to his death. Another bled out. Another died of blunt force trauma, but it was a repeated trauma that resulted in internal bleeding, which killed him. One drowned. Perhaps Garrett and his partner were one step removed from the deaths. They all died by circumstance, not by a specific act.

Catherine was reasonably certain that Garrett didn't personally know any of the victims. She suspected that wasn't true of his partner. One of these victims—most likely one of the women—was personal. One of these women had a connection to the partner, Catherine would stake her reputation on it.

She looked at the photo of Emily Henderson. An accomplished lawyer at thirty-six. Newly married. Attractive, whole-some, girl-next-door . . .

Thirty-six. She was also the oldest of the three women—four, if Catherine included Kara. Did that mean something?

The first victim—or victims, in this case—were almost always connected to the killer, but they hadn't found any con-nection between these victims and any of the potential suspects on their list. Ryder was looking at a suspicious death in Scotts-dale during the time that Garrett Reid worked there, but it seemed like a long shot.

Yet . . . what if one of the women working at the resort had a connection? That was a much narrower pool to work from.

She called Ryder. "Do you have a list of single, Caucasian female employees under forty?"

"Michael has it. He's been including them in his interviews all morning."

"Okay, thank you." She should have known that Ryder and Michael were on top of it. "Have you received a report from the sheriff's department regarding Reid's activities?"

"He hasn't left the hotel."

She straightened. Why hadn't she thought of this last night when she learned Graves took him to a hotel? "His partner—she was there."

"Excuse me?"

"They need to see each other. She was at the hotel last night. Ryder, we need to go there now and look at the security foot-age."

"Do you want me to have Michael meet you?"

"Can you come? You're the fastest with computers and we need to work fast."

"Yes. I'll contact the security office at the hotel and have them get the recordings ready, then have a car brought around to the lobby."

"I'll be there in five minutes."

For the first time since Catherine learned that Matt and Kara were missing, she thought they finally had a break.

Michael read the text from Catherine.

Michael frowned, pocketed his phone.

"What?" Sloane asked.

"Nothing. Let's talk to Alena Porter again."

He walked out of the conference room, Sloane on his heels. "You don't think Catherine is right," she guessed.

"I don't know," he mumbled. He didn't want to get into this now, and he didn't like to criticize other team members when they weren't around to defend themselves.

"Michael, I know I'm new on the team, but don't ice me out."

"I'm not."

"Then talk."

He stopped walking, glanced around to make sure no one could overhear them, and still kept his voice low. "Catherine used to be one of the best profilers in the Bureau. After her sister was killed, she has second-guessed herself repeatedly, and she was wrong about Reid. She never considered, or considered and dismissed, that he has a partner. Because of that error—a major error, not a little whoops—Matt and Kara could be dead."

He hadn't meant to say that, because he had been working to convince himself that his friends were alive.

"Profiling is not a science," Sloane said.

"I know. But when you act like your word is gospel, you can't be wrong."

"So you think she's wrong about the hotel."

"I don't know, and that bothers me. I don't want to doubt anyone on my team, but I'm asking myself if this is a good use of our time. Ryder is our rock. He's the backbone of this entire operation, whether he knows it or not, and the most computer savvy among us. We need him working the backgrounds, following up with Reid's employers, finding Becca McCarthy.

Having him escort Catherine to view security footage when she could have asked a deputy to take her?"

He was talking fast and getting angry, because anger kept him from falling apart.

But he recognized it and stopped. He didn't want to dump on anyone, and his frustration wasn't getting the case solved. "Sorry," he mumbled, turned and walked out of the security building.

"It's okay, Michael," Sloane said, following him across the courtyard.

It wasn't, but he didn't say anything as he opened the side door of the main building and held it for Sloane.

Maybe Catherine was right. But was it going to help them find Matt and Kara? That was the million-dollar question. He felt as if they were barely treading water.

Michael asked the concierge for Alena Porter.

"I haven't seen her yet," he said. "She doesn't generally work on Mondays and Tuesdays."

"She told me she would be here," Michael said.

"Let me check. Please wait."

He stepped away from his desk and went down the hall to the management offices.

Michael scrolled through the list of all female staff members that met the criteria Catherine established. Alena made the cut, so Michael wanted to talk to her again. He also wanted Sloane's impression.

There were two women on the list who Michael hadn't spoken to at all, though they'd been interviewed by Matt or Detective Fuentes on Friday. One worked in Housekeeping, and one was a bartender. Both in their early thirties and single and had worked at the resort for less than a year. And then Hope Davidson, who worked in the gym and saw Matt and Kara on Sunday morning.

He wanted to talk to them in their working environment.

See what their reaction was when he and Sloane walked in. Nervous? Confused?

He knew that women could kill, but it was difficult to put any of these women into the murderous role of Reid's partner.

The concierge returned. "Alena isn't in her office and hasn't answered her page. However, her assistant said she is somewhere on the property. Shall I have her reach out?"

Michael slipped him his card. "My cell number is on the back. I need to talk to her as soon as possible, and I'm happy to meet her anywhere at the resort."

"As soon as she calls in, I'll give her the message."

Alena Porter spent all morning—on her day off—writing memos, changing protocols for security, and a very uncomfortable thirty minutes talking to the lawyer of the resort ownership group. Then she was late for her meeting with the event planner for a fiftieth wedding anniversary celebration two weeks from now.

Her head was spinning, and she worried she might just lose her job when this was over. They claimed she'd done everything right, but as her dad always said, shit rolled downhill.

And in the back of her mind, she couldn't get that photo of the female maintenance worker out of her head. She knew that person, but she didn't know why or how.

It wasn't that she *knew* them, but she'd seen someone who looked just like her walking through the resort, and there was just something familiar about the memory that she couldn't place.

The concierge texted her that the FBI wanted to speak with her again, and she said she'd be back at her office in an hour. She had nothing to add, and her vague feeling that she *might* know the woman in the image was just that . . . a feeling. Nothing she could articulate. Someone she saw in passing who was . . .

She felt an itch, sort of like the hair rising on the back of her neck but all over her body. She detoured from going back to her office and headed to the gym instead.

She'd seen that uniform, she realized. Sunday morning, it was in one of the lockers. She thought it was strange, but hadn't really focused on it. Staff were allowed to use the facilities during their days off—it was a perk. And while they had programmable locks available for guests, no one on staff used them unless they had valuables.

She entered the locker room via the poolside entrance and went over to the locker where she had seen the uniform. If it was still here, she would definitely reach out to the FBI—they might be able to find evidence on it. But when she opened the door, it was empty.

"Alena, are you looking for something?"

Alena yelped, a hand to her chest, then laughed slightly when she recognized the woman. "Hope, you startled me!" She closed the door to the empty locker and said, "I thought I saw a uniform in here Sunday, and the FBI is asking questions about a woman in a maintenance uniform. Did you see it?"

"No," Hope said.

"Have you talked to the FBI?"

"Yeah, twice now. Do you need something?"

"No, thank you. I'll talk to the FBI about it, it's probably nothing."

"Good idea," Hope said. "By the way, since you're here, I wanted to show you something in the yoga room—we might need to get Maintenance in to fix the mini-fridge."

"Just put in the work order," Alena said.

"Well, I have an idea about that, not just a repair, but we might be able to do something fun with the area, something we did at one of my old gyms. But if you don't have time . . ."

"Sure, since I'm here." Alena followed Hope through the gym and into the yoga studio, which wasn't currently in use. She only half listened to Hope's idea, then said, "Sounds good, how about if you bring it up at the next staff meeting and if there's a consensus, we'll do it."

"Great!" Hope reached into the refrigerator and took out two flavored waters. "Want one?"

"Thanks, it's hot in here. Is there something wrong with the A/C?"

Hope unscrewed the cap. "No, it's just from hot yoga this morning, though it's almost back to where it's supposed to be." She motioned to the opposite wall, which listed the schedule each day. Alena never understood the allure of yoga, but their guests enjoyed the classes. "Should be comfortable in an hour for the next class."

She took the water from Hope and drank half of it as they walked out into the gym. Hope walked behind the counter and Alena headed toward the hotel. She still felt hot from the yoga room. Maybe she was coming down with something.

Her phone vibrated and she saw a text from the concierge. But her eyes ached and her vision blurred momentarily. She would deal with the FBI tomorrow. All she wanted now was to take a nap, and pray she didn't come down with a cold. Not when she had so much on her plate.

25

Michael immediately dismissed Paula Stuart, one of the women Catherine indicated fit the parameters of Reid's partner. While she fit the basics on paper, she was barely five foot three with such long, thick red hair that there was no way she was the woman in the photo. Still, Michael asked her questions about housekeeping in general, what she observed over the weekend. Michael thanked her, then he and Sloane walked to the main bar, where Alyssa Prescott was just coming on her shift.

Alyssa was thirty-six, tall, blonde, attractive but with a hard edge, as if she had seen everything and nothing fazed her. She also sported a colorful tattoo sleeve.

"Valdez said you might be coming in for a chat," she said after Michael introduced himself and Sloane. She looked them both up and down, offered water, which Sloane accepted.

"Thank you for making the time," Michael said.

"I really don't have a choice, do I? Valdez said anyone who gave you guys any shit would be written up." She put the water in front of Sloane, then turned to a tray and started to efficiently wedge limes and lemons.

Her confrontational attitude surprised Michael. "Have you met Garrett Reid?"

"Yep, it's not that big of a place, and he works maintenance. He also used to be a bartender, and we chatted a few times when he came in to fix the ice machine, which goes out at least once a month."

"What did you chat about?" Michael asked.

She shrugged. "This and that. Nothing serious. Pros and cons of working the bar. Dealing with guests, management, whatever."

She finished with the citrus, placed the pieces in the appropriate trays, and then pulled out a box of cocktail napkins and set them up at strategic intervals along the bar.

"He has nearly every drink memorized. I asked him why he didn't want to work the bar. He said he liked to fix things." She shrugged, squatted and straightened the bottles behind the bar.

"Did you like him?" Sloane asked.

"I didn't want to screw him, if that's what you mean."

"I didn't mean anything," Sloane said. "Most people we've spoken with said he was friendly and personable. Did you agree?"

Alyssa looked at Sloane as if considering a response. "Look, if I told you I think he was a creep, you wouldn't believe me because probably everyone now remembers something that makes them like him less. But truth? He was fine. He didn't hit on me, which I can't say the same for a lot of the staff. He was chatty and smart."

"But?" Sloane said.

"It's just a feeling, and it's not something I can really quantify."

"I'm interested in your feelings."

"Garrett is a great conversationalist, and he knows a lot of shit, always willing to help out, whatever." She leaned against the bar and crossed her arms in front of her chest. "But if you really look at him, like make eye contact? There's something . . . calculating there. Like he's cataloging you and putting you into a prelabeled box. I mean, we all do it when you work in the service industry. We shelve people into good tippers, assholes, drunks, complainers—it's probably not fair, but when you work with a lot of people every day of your adult life, there's a dozen categories that everyone will fall into. But with Garrett it was . . . different. I can't explain it any better than that. And it doesn't help you keep him in jail, does it?"

"It's good insight," Michael said. "Were you familiar with the guests who went missing?"

"The second couple," she said. "They came in several nights when I was working. Both drank maybe one too many, but they were happy drunks. Cute together, if you're into that sort of thing."

"Was anyone watching them? Giving them undue interest?" Michael asked.

She stared at him. "You arrested Garrett. Who else are you looking at?"

"We believe that Garrett is working with a partner," Michael said, gauging her reaction.

"Really? Wow. Garrett? For a guy who was that good-looking and friendly, he was a loner."

"It may not have been someone who was seen with Garrett."

"Staff often comes in after shift for a beer, to chat with me or Doug, because usually one of us is on until closing. If the weather is crappy, we're crowded. If it's nice, most people go out to the poolside bar. I wouldn't have noticed unless someone was being rude or something."

Michael put the photo down in front of Alyssa. "Do you recognize this person?"

Alyssa shook her head. "I don't think so. I don't think she works here."

Michael and Sloane exchanged glances. Alyssa was the first person who immediately thought *female* when she saw the photo, without prompting.

"I've only been here a year, but I know most of the staff, and there's only three women who work in Maintenance—none of them have her build."

Michael took the picture back. "Thank you for your time."

They left the bar and walked back to the main building, where the gym took up the southwest wing. The concierge waved at them.

When they approached his desk, he said, "Alena called in ten minutes ago. I gave her your message. She should be back in her office in less than an hour, but if you need her immediately, she was in the main ballroom working with an event planner."

"We'll come back. Thank you."

Instead, they headed to the gym to talk to Hope Davidson again.

Hope was straightening towels on the shelves in the gym lobby. Six or seven guests were working out on the equipment, and a game of racquetball could be faintly heard in the background.

"Agent Harris," Hope said. "Do you need something?" She glanced at the clock. "I'm getting off in a few minutes."

"We're following up with everyone we already spoke with, just to clarify a few things," Michael said.

"Oh. You don't mind if I keep working? I have plans and don't want to work late."

"Go ahead," Michael said.

She finished folding towels and made sure they were perfectly straight in the shelving unit.

Michael confirmed everything she'd already told him about Matt and Kara's morning before they disappeared. She moved over to the free weights, grabbed a bottle of disinfectant and a rag, and cleaned each one individually.

"Do you remember the Blairs and the Avilas?" According to her employee file, she had started working here two months after the Hendersons were killed, and only a week before the Blairs went missing.

"Those are the missing couples, right?"

"They were murdered," Michael said.

She shook her head and frowned. "So awful."

"Did any of them come into the gym?"

She shrugged, carefully put a heavy weight into its appropriate slot. "Maybe. I really don't remember. Maybe if you had pictures?"

Sloane pulled out her phone and showed Hope photos of the Blairs, then the Avilas. Hope tapped on the second picture. "She came in for yoga once when I was working. I just said hello and goodbye, didn't have a conversation with her."

"You don't recognize the others?"

"No, I'm sorry."

She grabbed a clean rag and walked over to the window separating the now-empty yoga room from the main gym. She sprayed and wiped.

"I have a photo if you can look at it?" Michael asked.

She stopped for a minute, looked at him expectantly. He showed her the woman dressed as a maintenance worker. "Do you recognize this person?"

She shook her head. "No. Sorry." She went back to cleaning with a quick glance at the clock. "I have ten minutes until I'm off, and I need to clean the women's locker room. Do you want me to stop at Brian's office on my way out? Are you still using it?"

"That's not necessary," Michael said. "Just one more question. You mentioned you didn't really talk to Garrett Reid since you started working here, correct?"

"Yeah. Just a few times, in passing."

"Did you ever see him with anyone? Like a girlfriend?"

"No," she said. "I only saw him when he was working."

"Thank you again for your time. I'll call if I need anything else."

"Great." She gave them a quick smile, then headed to the women's locker room.

When Michael and Sloane were back in the security office, Sloane said, "She was off."

"How?" he asked, grabbing a water bottle from the mini-fridge. "She didn't contradict her previous statement in any way."

"She was busy when we were talking to her, but there was really nothing she was doing that couldn't wait five minutes. For example, she folded already neat towels. She cleaned already clean equipment. She kept looking at the clock."

"She said her shift was almost over."

"It all had the feeling of nerves to me."

Michael thought a moment. "She didn't seem nervous when I spoke with her yesterday, and I didn't notice she was nervous today."

"Where's her application?" Sloane asked.

Michael sorted through the employee files that Brian had retrieved for them. "Here." He slid it over to Sloane since he didn't know what she was looking for.

She opened it, skimmed the sheets. "It says here she's from Las Vegas, Nevada . . . has worked in a variety of hotels . . . bingo."

"What do you see?"

"Her references. She has some holes in her employment history, but look—she worked in Nashville when Reid was there. It's not the same place, but . . ." She frowned, pulled out her phone and typed something.

Michael leaned over and read the file. "You think they met there?"

"Maybe," she said as she scrolled. "Okay—yes—she worked at Fitness Square, which sounds like a business, right? And she didn't include an address, only a phone number. But Fitness Square is actually the name of the gym at the resort where Reid worked." She jumped up, opened the whiteboard where Ryder had written the Garrett Reid timeline. "She started there three months after Reid, and left only two weeks before he did. This could be it. This could be where their paths crossed."

"Where was she the year Reid was unemployed?"

"She worked at a restaurant in a Dallas hotel."

"And after? When Reid was in New Orleans?"

"Nothing here. Whoever interviewed her put a sticky note that she had a lapse in employment because she was caring for her sick mother." Sloane snorted.

"You don't believe that?"

"Not really. Maybe she did have a sick mother, but I think she didn't want her résumé to match up exactly with Garrett's when they both applied to work here. That's why the small cheat on the fitness place in Nashville."

Playing devil's advocate, he said, "She started here at the beginning of the year, months after Garrett."

"I think that was intentional. I think we can prove it."

Sloane picked up the phone. A minute later, she asked for the human resources manager of the New Orleans hotel where Garrett had worked. Five minutes later, she ended the call and said with a thin smile, "Hope Davidson worked for the hotel as a cocktail waitress. She simply didn't put it on her résumé."

"Let's go ask her about that," Michael said and motioned for Sloane to follow him back to the gym. "And find whoever she was training on Sunday to see if they saw or heard anything." He hadn't followed up with the individual because there hadn't been a need at the time. He glanced at his notes. "His name is Will. I didn't get his last name."

Hope wasn't behind the counter. Another woman was there, "Jane" according to her badge. Michael had only spoken to her briefly because she didn't work weekends.

"We were here speaking with Hope earlier," Michael said. "Can you let her know we have a couple more questions?"

Jane said, "She left."

"Do you know where she went? Did she leave the grounds?"

Jane shrugged. "She said she had an appointment. It's slow, so I said whatev."

"Is Will here?"

"Will?"

"A new hire she was training on Sunday."

"Oh, Will Kirk. He's not really a new hire. He's a lifeguard and wanted to pick up some extra hours so I guess he's helping out in the gym on the weekends."

"Where can I find him?"

"If he's working, he's at the pool."

As they walked toward the resort pool, Michael called Catherine. "Hope Davidson lied on her employment application."

"How?" she asked.

"She worked at the same New Orleans hotel as Garrett Reid during almost identical times, and they also overlapped at the resort in Nashville. There's no way they didn't know each other."

"Did you ask her about it?"

"She's already gone for the day. But I may have something more—I'm going to interview the staff member she was training on Sunday when Matt and Kara were in the gym. There was no reason to verify her alibi, but now?"

"As soon as you know, call me. If we can find just one discrepancy in her statement, I can get a warrant."

Michael ended the call and found the very tanned Will Kirk in board shorts and a staff T-shirt. He sat on a tall chair under an adjustable umbrella where he could easily see the entire vast pool.

They both showed their badges and said, "We have a couple questions."

"Fine, but I can't leave. I can get someone to relieve me and meet you in like fifteen or twenty minutes. Management told us to cooperate."

"We can talk here," Michael said. He didn't want to wait; they needed to jump on this immediately.

"Sure," Will said. "What do you need?"

"Were you going through staff training on Sunday morning in the gym?"

"Sort of, I guess?"

"Specifics."

"I'm going back to college in the fall, so I'm trying to make some extra money this summer. My boss said they could use extra help in the gym on weekends if I wanted to pick up some more hours. Hope was showing me the equipment, most of which I knew how to use because I work out there after my shift. And you know, basic jobs like refilling the water, checking the locker rooms, scheduling classes, things like that. I was just there for a couple hours for the walk-through."

"When was that?"

"I was supposed to be there from nine to noon, because I start my lifeguard shift at noon. But she, like, disappeared on me. I thought she was in the women's locker room, so I called in there, but she didn't answer. I waited around, but I had to go—I was already late."

"What time did you leave?"

"Well, at 12:15 I went into the locker room to change—" he motioned to his shirt and board shorts "—and when I came out she was behind the counter. I said, hey where'd you go? I'm late for my shift. And she said she never left, that she was in the women's locker room." He shrugged. "Maybe she was and didn't hear me."

Michael didn't believe that.

"What time did she disappear?"

"I don't know."

"When was the last time you saw her?"

He thought. "Around 11:20. I don't know the exact time, but about then. She had fresh towels we'd just folded, and she said she was going to restock the women's locker room and check supplies. She told me to wipe down the equipment, so I did."

If she left the gym at 11:20, that would give her plenty of time to change, grab a laundry cart, and go to Matt and Kara's cottage. It would give her enough time to tranquilize them but not remove them from the resort property.

"It wasn't the first time," Will grumbled.

"What do you mean?"

"Right when I got there, she said she had to run to the office and left me. We had people in racquetball, people coming in for classes, people asking about the equipment, and she was gone for twenty minutes."

Michael remembered what room service said—Kara was drinking coffee out of one of the blue room mugs. Forensics had found a narcotic in the base of the remaining mugs. There were no cameras around the cottage, but there were cameras right outside of the gym. If they could get Hope coming or going around nine Sunday morning, that would give them one more small piece that fit the evidence. She could have entered their room and poisoned the coffee mugs, then returned to the gym.

"Thank you, Will. We may have more questions."

"Is Hope in trouble?"

"We have questions for her," Michael said. "How long have you known her?"

"Just the last month. This is my third summer working here. I think she started in January or something. I don't really know her. The first time I actually talked to her was on Sunday."

Michael and Sloane went back to Brian's security office to review videos outside the gym Sunday morning. He texted Catherine with what they had learned, but he wanted something more—something that would guarantee no judge would deny them a warrant.

"Bingo," Sloane said. "She left at 9:03 a.m. and returned at 9:20 a.m. And there's no sign that she went to the hotel office."

Not a smoking gun, but they were getting closer.

"What about at 11:20?" Michael said.

"She didn't leave the gym," Sloane said, sounding defeated.

"But," Brian said, "each locker room has an exit into the pool area and there are no cameras on those doors."

Michael and Sloane both looked at him, surprised. Michael asked, "Can she get back in through the locker room?"

"Yes. The locker rooms are accessible from both the gym and the pool. We don't have security cameras for privacy reasons."

"That's how she did it," Sloane said. "She could change in the locker room, incapacitate Matt and Kara, then return the same way and no one would know."

"But she didn't leave the resort," Michael said. "If she didn't leave the property, where were Matt and Kara until her shift was over?"

"Whichever vehicle she used to transport them," Sloane said. "If they were unconscious, she could have left them for an hour, easy."

"A van," Michael said. "It would have to be a van because nowhere on camera did we find the same disguised maintenance person returning toward the resort pushing a laundry cart. But a cart could be rolled into a van."

Brian said, "Security keeps a log of all vehicles in the lot, makes sure they have either an employee sticker or guest pass. Every vehicle was accounted for on Sunday, as I told your team."

"You still have a list of license plates?"

"License, make, and model."

"I need that list. We'll go through it again," Michael said. "Is there another parking area? One that isn't monitored?"

"Not on the property—though there's a beach lot adjacent to ours, open to the public."

"How close?"

"Separated by a walkway. We use it for event overflow parking."

"That's it," Sloane said.

Michael agreed. "And can I assume there are no cameras on that lot?"

Brian shook his head. "Not ours, and not the county. Do you still want the list?"

"Yes," Michael said. "For every day this week. Maybe they slipped up."

He wasn't holding his breath, but it was a small chance.

Michael called Catherine and filled her in on everything they'd learned.

26

Audrey had left work thirty minutes early. She told Jane that she had an appointment. The girl just shrugged and waved her off. Now *Jane* was stupid. People thought Audrey was dumb? Hardly! Audrey had smarts where it counted.

When she got in her car, she bit her lip and hoped that leaving early wasn't going to make her look guilty. No, of course not, she wasn't a suspect. She didn't have a good feeling about all this, especially talking to the FBI twice in two days. Especially after they showed her the photo. But if they thought it was her, they would have arrested her, right? Or asked her *is this you?*

It was a bad photo, didn't show her face. No one would be able to identify her from it.

Well, almost no one, but she had taken care of that one little problem. She hoped Alena passed out before she talked to the FBI again . . . but honestly, what did it matter? It wasn't like a uniform in the locker room that was accessible to everyone on the property was going to point a finger at *her*.

But she needed to buy some time, and getting Alena out of

the picture for a day would buy her that time. Enough time to get her stuff, kill the two agents, and run away with Garrett. A day, that's all she needed.

Audrey was a little concerned that the hunky black FBI agent had brought in the woman with the sharp eyes. Agent Wagner. She'd barely said a word, just *watched* her, asked a couple questions, maybe to try and throw her off. It was unnerving and creepy, as if they knew something she didn't.

She hated when people knew more than she did. It made her feel dumb, and she was *not* dumb.

Audrey went to her car and immediately logged in to the factory cameras. She needed to see where they were and what they were doing.

The units in the control room were still out, but she had a couple angles that showed the flooded factory floor. The woman, Kara, lay on a conveyor belt, unmoving. Was she dead? That would make Audrey's life *so* much easier. The man was walking around the perimeter, clearly looking for a way out. Why hadn't he just opened the door and been done with it? She would just leave their bodies there, no need to dump them and reset the factory for the next couple, because she and Garrett were done with these games.

They would come up with something new, something *better*.

Maybe by the time she got up there—it was a three-hour drive—the FBI agent will have walked through the door and been crushed to death.

She reached under her seat just to make sure her gun was still there. She didn't like guns; they were crude and not at all fun. What was the thrill of shooting someone? It was almost *unfair*.

But right now, she really didn't have a choice. For Garrett, she would take care of this. For Garrett, she would do anything.

She loved him, and more importantly, he loved her.

Garrett was right—when this was done, they would have to

bail completely. She'd pick him up at the hotel in Jacksonville and they'd head north. Dump the car, get a new one. They had enough money to lie low in New York City with identities she'd already bought them.

She had enough money to do anything she wanted. Garrett thought she'd just done well with their honey traps, but he didn't know the half of it.

She might tell him. Or not. A girl had to have her secrets, right?

She liked reinventing herself. She'd done it before when she became Audrey Reid. Well, first she was Audrey Dolan—she had to buy that identity so Garrett wouldn't be suspicious. That's who he thought she was. But Audrey Reid was her married name, legally.

Now she and Garrett could live out in the open as a married couple under completely different names. Names were nothing, just labels. They'd be Rhett and Annabelle Dubois. She already had the identifications. Their five-year anniversary was coming up. No more honey traps, no more flirting with old women. They would be normal. And when they started running low on funds, they could plan a few carefully designed cons along the way to ensure they could support themselves. If she had to, she'd seduce some rich asshole and rob him blind, like she used to.

Those really were the good old days.

Audrey arrived at her house twenty minutes later. She was antsy, and she always got antsy when something was wrong. She trusted her instincts. They had saved her many times—in who she targeted, what she asked for, how far she could push. Her instincts had never failed her, so now she ran through the house grabbing what she really needed: money and her fake IDs. She packed a small suitcase with her essentials, just in case she couldn't come back. But she could buy anything she wanted.

It wasn't like money was a problem.

Mostly, she needed to leave her Honda Civic behind. It was registered to Hope Davidson, and if the FBI were suspicious of Hope, they might start looking for her car.

She loved her house, but she loved Garrett more. She had the important things—cash and the new Dubois identities for her and Garrett. Because she *was* smart, and she thought of everything. Once things had escalated with Emily and her dickless husband *Josh*, she'd made sure they had an escape plan.

Fifteen minutes, in and out. After she killed the two agents, she'd find a way to sneak Garrett out of the hotel and disappear, all before dark.

Oh, and kill the lawyer. He was always going to die for treating her like dog shit. What to do with his wife and kid . . . she didn't know. She'd hid the key to the cage in the house, so she could call Lily Graves and tell her where it was, or she could just let the woman figure it out herself. *If* she could figure it out in time. One thing Garrett had taught Audrey over the seven years they had been together was to always have a backup plan. Audrey took that lesson to heart.

They should have killed Franklin Graves as soon as Garrett was free. She'd been thinking they might need the lawyer for something else, but truthfully, he was now a liability.

She pulled the van out of the garage. It wasn't registered to Hope Davidson, because Audrey wasn't an idiot. No one knew she had the van, except Garrett. Once she completed all her tasks, she would get rid of this van for another vehicle, and she knew exactly where to get one.

As she pulled onto I-95 heading north, she saw the sign that said Jacksonville, 57 miles.

Maybe she should grab Garrett on her way to Georgia.

She liked that idea.

She *really* liked that idea. She'd much rather have Garrett with her now, because she didn't want to return to Florida. Go to the factory, take care of business, then disappear. She had a couple places they could stay, watch the news, make plans.

She was thirty minutes away when she called the hotel on her prepaid phone and asked to be connected to room 513.

Garrett answered on the second ring. Hearing his voice filled her heart.

"Hello?"

"Hey, baby," she cooed.

"You shouldn't be calling me here." Did he sound angry?

"Are you mad?" she asked.

"No. But it's too risky."

"The lawyer said they didn't get a warrant to wiretap you, so we're good."

"Where are you?" He sighed, and her brain registered annoyance. He was annoyed? With *her*? She had to be wrong.

"Just left my house heading to you know where. But I'll be going through Jacksonville in thirty minutes. Let me pick you up, we'll take care of the problem together, then just disappear."

"The cops are still out front."

"You can sneak out. Please, honey, I'm worried."

"I'm fine here. Take care of the problem and come back tonight, okay? When it's dark, I have a way we can slip out of the hotel unnoticed."

"I need to get rid of the van."

"How are you going to get back?"

She frowned. "I'll figure it out."

"It's a two-hour drive from Jacksonville. You can't Uber it, an Uber driver will remember you!"

"I said I'll figure it out!" She was on the verge of tears. He sounded angry with her, and she hated when he got mad at her. It was always because he thought she did something dumb, and she was *not* dumb.

"I'm sorry," he said, his voice calm and conciliatory. "I didn't mean to sound mad. I'm worried. I can't have anything happen to you, baby. I love you."

"I love you, too," she said. "I'll drive to the boat, then take the boat out and down the coast. I'll be back in Jacksonville by sunset. No one can trace it to us, and I'll leave it at an empty pier on the St. Johns River. Then I'll take an Uber to the hotel."

"Someone will call it in."

"So? We're going to be leaving, right?"

"Like I said, I have an idea, but we have to be careful."

"Maybe you can meet me at the dock tonight," she said.

"Babe, I can't leave right now. It has to be after midnight." He paused. "You know, maybe you shouldn't come back tonight. I can slip out easier on my own."

"You don't mean that."

"It's for your own protection, Audrey. We need to be extra cautious right now. You do what you need to do, and don't call me again, just in case they're listening in."

"They can't, not without a warrant, and Franklin is on top of it—or *you know what.*" That's why she had kept Franklin alive, to get them inside information. She was relieved that she hadn't made a mistake not killing him yesterday.

"This is to protect you, Audrey," he said. "I love you."

"I love you, too. But, Garrett—"

"I'll find a way to call you later, once I get out of here. Okay?"

"Fine," she said.

She reluctantly ended the call as she passed the first Jacksonville exit. "Bye, Garrett. I'll be back soon," she said out loud to herself.

Maybe.

She didn't like the way he sounded on the phone. He seemed worried and depressed, and he should never be worried about anything. And he sounded . . . different. Was he going to leave her?

No, he wouldn't. That was silly. He loved her.

First things first. A two-hour drive. Two bullets in the stupid blonde, Kara, and two bullets in the asshole FBI agent, Matt. Then drive to the coast, get the boat, and go to her love.

Before Garrett, she was lost. With Garrett, she'd found her purpose. She hoped he wasn't mad at her. He sounded mad. She didn't like it when people criticized her. If he was mad, he thought she had done something wrong. She hadn't. She had done everything they had planned, it was *others* who messed it all up.

Yeah, maybe she should have killed the cops at the beginning, but what fun was that?

Garrett would see it, too.

Before she met Garrett, Audrey was Clara Dolan. The only child to two brilliant college professors who never expected to have kids until, after fifteen years of marriage, her thirty-nine-year-old mother became pregnant.

When Clara proved to be average academically, they were sorely disappointed. They had her tested repeatedly, sent her to the best schools, expected her to suddenly do well in school, write brilliant essays, and understand advanced math. After all, she was the prodigy of Gerald and Piper Dolan, of the genius IQ.

But Clara was average in every way except one: her looks.

Clara had been told she was beautiful from before she knew what beautiful meant. Strangers would go up to her mother and say, "Oh, your daughter is beautiful!" or "Those eyes! She's going to be a knockout" or "I've never seen such a beautiful child."

When Clara was six, she wanted to be a model. Her parents said no. They had a bunch of reasons, but Clara thought it was primarily because her mother was jealous of her beauty and didn't want Clara to get the attention she clearly deserved. Also, they'd have to hire someone to take her to auditions and photo shoots and if Clara had a photo shoot, it might put a damper on their social life. When Clara was nine, she wanted to be an actress. Her parents, perhaps because they realized she was never going to be a rocket scientist, relented and let her take acting lessons. Clara overheard her father tell her mother, "Acting isn't about intelligence, it may be a good fit for her. She is a pretty girl."

But three years later, Clara overheard her instructor tell her parents that she had no talent. They offered to pay him more to keep working with her—he declined. They sent her to camp that summer and never discussed it, never told her why she was dropped. But she knew the truth and saw the disappointment in their eyes.

They thought she was so stupid she couldn't even act.

Clara realized at a young age that her parents didn't value her looks, but everyone else did. Her parents wanted a smart child, and Clara tried. But she wasn't like them. She didn't care about school, and it was hard. She was always a disappointment, and she didn't like being made to feel stupid. *She* knew that she was smart, just not in the same way as her parents.

When she was twelve, Clara overheard her mother telling her book club that she thought Clara had been switched at birth with her real daughter, and she secretly had a DNA test done. And, unfortunately, Clara was in fact her daughter.

That's when Clara just stopped trying *or* caring. She wasn't book smart, so what? She wasn't *dumb*. She wasn't *an idiot*. She was hardly *stupid*. She just didn't get math—who the fuck cared? She didn't like reading, was that a crime? And why did it matter if she knew anything about history or art or why gravity worked? She just didn't care about any of it.

She was beautiful. She was the most beautiful girl in school. Everyone said so, so Clara focused on her natural talent: using her looks to get her everything that she wanted.

In high school she learned that men would do anything a pretty girl asked. That took her far. She also learned that women resented her simply because she was beautiful. It's why Emily Masters thwarted Clara and stopped her from getting a promotion, because Emily resented Clara's good looks and charm and wealth.

Clara learned to use her attributes to not only get what she wanted, but to pay back everyone who had hurt her.

Then, she'd found Garrett. It had been love at first sight.

And she would not lose him.

They would need to lie low for a few months, but she couldn't wait to plan out their future.

New York City, here we come!

But first, she had two FBI agents to kill.

27

Matt was worried about Kara. She never complained about being in pain, but he'd seen the cut when he tied his shirt around it. It was deep. The dark, filthy water wouldn't help it heal, and could be dangerous. She needed a hospital, a hefty dose of antibiotics, and someone to clean and stitch the wound.

His ankle was messed up, but it wasn't broken, he didn't even think it was seriously sprained. The cut burned, but it wasn't as serious an injury as Kara's gash. His chest hurt. He'd thought he might have had a cracked rib earlier, but now he was certain. It only hurt if he moved abruptly, so he tried to be cautious. Still, cracked ribs were rarely even taped up anymore. He pushed through the discomfort to find a way out.

He'd inspected the two doors without touching them. They were heavy metal doors that had, at one point, been automatic—a large button to the side suggested that when pressed, the doors would swing out, wide enough for large carts to be pushed through. The other side of the doors was most likely storage, or offices, or the way to the loading dock—he couldn't see enough to be certain. He didn't test the button or doors now, but if they were electronic, the water had likely short-circuited them. There was a narrow window in each door, but they were blackened on the other side.

While the doors went from the factory to another room or a lobby or suite of offices, they would also lead to the main entrance. They had to find a way to get them open without risking themselves.

The first time they'd crafted something to push open the doors, they had barely budged. Even though they were heavy, they had enough momentum that they should have opened, unless something had blocked them. He feared they were bolted from the other side and they would be stuck here, sitting ducks in the middle of the flooded factory until Reid's partner returned . . . or they died of dehydration.

But they *had* budged, just a bit, so Matt thought rather than a lock, something heavy blocked them.

He had Kara sit on the conveyor belt, out of the water, while he carefully walked around the entire factory floor looking for another way out since the swinging doors felt too much like a trap.

Matt had inspected the pile of junk in front of the exit on the far side. He was glad that he was cautious—he poked it with a metal rod and it creaked and shifted. Several rusting rebars were seemingly randomly placed in the pile, but when he stood back and looked, he realized they were all at dangerous heights—his head, his gut, his groin.

He remembered one of the male victims had been impaled with something round and imperfect. The ocean salt water had messed with forensics, but Matt now wondered if it could have been rebar. If his memory served him, the size of the hole would be about right. If they got out of this—*when* they got out of this, he told himself—he would ask Jim about it. Hell, they'd bring in an entire forensics team to go over this factory. Chances were they'd find evidence that all six victims had been here.

He returned to Kara. She was lying down with her eyes closed, pale and unmoving.

He touched her. She opened her eyes. "Hey," she said.

"You okay?"

"Conserving energy. Find anything?"

"Not a way out. But I have an idea. Stay put."

Matt had determined that any narrow rod, no matter how strong or tough, wouldn't provide enough force to push open the door, especially against the water pressure. He needed something heavy with a large surface area.

A stainless steel basin that had been part of an eyewash station was moveable. He winced as he tried to push it. Kara saw what he was doing and got up.

"I got this," he said. "I'm going to turn it lengthwise and then push it through the door. If there is anything dangerous on the other side, hopefully the distance gives me time to get out of the way."

"I don't like this."

"I'm out of ideas."

"So am I," she said.

"Let me try, okay?"

He grunted and shifted the six-foot-long basin. He hoped that was long enough to protect him if there was something on the other side that was set to collapse, like the ceiling upstairs.

He pushed. The doors didn't give. Again, he feared they were completely blocked.

He pushed again, and they moved, just a bit.

Kara came over to him.

"You don't—"

"Yes. I do. We're in this together, Matt. And I'm not completely helpless."

"You've never been helpless," he said. "On three, we push as hard as we can, then we jump back, okay?"

She nodded. He counted. "One. Two. *Three.*"

Together, they used all their strength to push the basin through the doors.

A loud, thunderous crash had them turning away from the doors, shielding their heads. Metal grated on metal, creaking, then splashing, as heavy objects fell into the water on the other side of the door that was now partly wedged open by the basin. Matt's arms covered Kara, expecting something to fall on them, even though they were still on the factory floor. The water moved in waves as objects continued to fall.

A minute later, silence, though the clamoring still rang in Matt's ears. Simultaneously, they turned and looked.

Through the door they saw what looked like a junk yard. A mountain of twisted objects—a desk, chairs, rebar, cans, jagged metal trays. The debris now blocked the doorway.

Had they walked through the opening, the heavy pile of junk would have fallen on them. They'd probably have died instantly, or been trapped under the shallow water and drowned.

Cautiously, Matt pushed at the sink, hoping that if there was anything else ready to fall he'd jar it loose. The pile shifted, but nothing more fell from above.

The door was partly blocked, but it was open.

"We'll have to climb over it," Matt said. "But there's a lot of sharp metal, I'll go first and see if I can clear a path."

She took his hand, squeezed it. "Don't die on me," she whispered.

"I wouldn't think of it."

Matt climbed onto the sink, then he wiggled it with the weight of his body. It didn't budge, and nothing fell. Carefully, he pushed aside some of the debris. He looked over the pile into a large room.

Another set of doors was on the opposite side, along with windows. They were so filthy he couldn't see through them, but they brought in enough light that it gave him hope.

The exit. Freedom.

"Almost there, Kara," he called back to her. "Follow in my footsteps to get over the debris."

Matt determined the best way through was to crawl over the basin that he'd used as a wedge, then pivot left, where there appeared to be a narrow path without dangerously sharp and rusting metal protruding in every direction. He shuffled through the water, not wanting to step on something sharp enough to puncture the soles of his shoes.

As soon as he was through, he called back to Kara. "Okay, your turn."

She followed his steps exactly and met him on the other side of the debris without incident. They both breathed easier, but Matt still proceeded cautiously.

The dirty windows provided enough outside light to cast shadows all around and give them decent visibility. The water softly rippled.

Matt and Kara traversed the room, walking cautiously toward the windows. As they neared, Matt saw a door. A simple double-door over which was an unlit exit sign. He stopped.

"You saw something," Kara said. "What?"

"Stay here."

"Don't do anything stupid," she warned him.

"Give me one minute to check things out." He slowly approached the door, his eyes focused on something that only momentarily reflected from the sun outside. He squatted two feet from the exit.

"Well, shit," he muttered.

"What is that?" Kara asked, still behind him.

"I don't know, but if we open the door, it'll trip a wire." He looked up. "Holy shit, I feel like the Road Runner."

Kara followed his gaze and saw a net sagging with more than a dozen bowling balls.

"These people are crazy," she said.

"Stay away from the wire," he warned. He went back to the

pile of trash and found a heavy metal gear that he could easily grip. He returned to the window next to the door. "Turn around, shield your eyes," he said.

He put his arm up to shield his own eyes, then with all his strength threw the gear into the window.

Glass shattered. The window was paned, but the metal was weak. He worked on bending it enough for them to get through. "Okay," he said.

Kara turned around. "Are you sure?"

"Yeah. Step over the wire, careful . . . okay. You go first."

Kara did; Matt followed.

They were out. Free. He greedily breathed in the fresh, humid Georgia air.

The sun felt amazing on his bare back, but he didn't take the time to enjoy their escape. Watching where they were going, he navigated away from the building, then turned back and looked at the structure.

Four stories tall. Painted on the front in large, faded black letters: Sweetwater Cannery, Clinch County, GA.

"Where the hell is Clinch County?" Kara said.

"Southern Georgia, borders Florida. There's not much here. A lot of creeks, swampland, farmland, a couple small towns. I'd be surprised if there were more than six thousand people."

"How do you know that?"

He smiled. "Just smart that way," he said. "So, good news, bad news."

"We're out of there. That's all good news."

"Based on the state of the factory, how long I think it's been abandoned, I suspect this was taken out of commission during Hurricane Helene, about a year ago. Remember that?"

"Vaguely. I think we were in Los Angeles at the time."

"Being born and raised in Florida, anytime I hear about a hurricane, I need to know where it is and who is affected. It hit southern Georgia pretty hard, and based on the damage and the fact that the building is still pretty sound, it fits. It's not cost effective to get it up and running again—these places operate on a thin margin. And this has been here for over a hundred years."

"How can you tell?"

He pointed to a stone on the corner of the building. Kara squinted. "1923. Wow. It's historic. So that's the bad news?"

"No, the bad news is we're going to be doing a lot of walking to find a house. Maybe miles. Are you okay to walk?"

"I'll make it."

"Your leg."

"We're both beat up, Matt. We don't have a choice. We can't stay here because neither of us is in a condition to fight and we don't have any weapons. But neither of us is going to make it two miles without water. Can we eat that fruit?"

"What fruit?" He shielded his eyes from the sun and looked to where Kara pointed to a thick gaggle of bushes. "Blackberries. Yeah, we can eat those. They grow all over southern Georgia, both wild and in crops. Blackberries, blueberries, strawberries."

"I thought Georgia was the Peach State or something."

"Peaches, too, but not this far south."

They walked over to the bushes. Matt sampled one. It was warm from the heat and a bit overripe, but it tasted like paradise. "Not too fast," he said, looking around. "One at a time." He didn't want either of them getting sick.

They were on a deeply pitted gravel road that hadn't been maintained since the hurricane swept through. A wide creek flowed on the other side of the blackberry thicket—wild blackberries usually grew along rivers and creeks. He didn't see any maintained crops—the fields around the cannery were fallow, with ragged bushes of blueberries bursting through here and there. Farms were also victims of hurricanes.

But they could follow this road and would eventually hit either a house or a county road. They would have to be cautious about flagging down a car in case Reid's partner was on her way here, but they could hide and assess any approaching vehicle. If they found a house, they'd call in the cavalry.

"Okay," he said after slowly eating a dozen berries. "We walk along here so we can grab berries as we move. That will help with energy and dehydration. If we hear anything, we hide—we don't know when Reid's partner will return. But first, I'm going to destroy the generator."

"Where is it?"

"Based on the sound, it's on the other side of the factory."

"Why? There's no reason to, and they could have it set as a booby trap, too."

"Because I don't know if there are cameras out here, and I don't want them to know which direction we go. It'll buy us a little time, at a minimum. It won't take me long. Sit here, under this tree, and wait for me."

"Matt—"

"Trust me."

"Okay." Kara sat, pulled another blackberry off the bush. "Ten minutes, or I'm following."

"Fair enough."

He kissed her because he was so relieved that they were alive and help was imminent. "Eat the berries slowly," he warned her, then headed to the other side of the factory.

Kara watched Matt walk back toward the factory and she sat heavily on the ground, feeling both relieved and ill.

Her leg throbbed. She knew it was bad. Not like fatal bad, but the cut was deep and that disgusting water sitting in the factory probably wasn't helping matters. She didn't dare untie Matt's shirt to check the damage—there would be time enough to do that when they were in a more secure location.

She leaned against the tree and ate another berry. She went slow as Matt had warned because her stomach felt queasy. She certainly didn't want to puke. What she would give for a cold water bottle. Hell, a warm water bottle would suit her just fine. She closed her eyes, enjoying the sun on her face.

"Kara! Kara, wake up!"

She felt a sting on her cheek and batted Matt's hand away. "What? Jeez."

"Thank God," he muttered, his hands on her forehead, her neck, his fingers inspecting her leg.

"Ow! Stop!"

"You lost consciousness."

"No," she said. "The sun felt good, maybe I fell asleep. Damn. I should have been watching, in case—"

"You weren't responsive," he said slowly. "Look at me."

She did, and saw the panic on his face. "I'm okay," she said.

"Can you make it?"

"Yes," she insisted. "Or, you can leave me and get help. I can hide in the bushes—"

"No way am I leaving you. We'll rest whenever you need to, okay?"

"I didn't mean to scare you." She ran her fingers across his bare chest, trying to lighten the mood and wipe the fear off his face. "This would be kind of sexy, if we both didn't stink to high heaven."

He helped her up, and she bit back a cry when she put too much weight on her cut leg. Instead, she forced a smile. "You can nurse me back to health," she said. "That'll be fun."

"Getting you into bed is always fun," he said lightly, but she saw the concern on his face.

"I love you," she said seriously. "You're stuck with me, so get that look off your face. I'm okay, I promise."

"I'm holding you to that," he said. "Lean on me."

"I might have to, just a bit."

They slowly walked down the gravel road, Kara limping but managing just fine, she thought. They stopped a couple times to eat berries and rest. After the third stop, she looked across the field and thought she was hallucinating.

"Matt, is that a house?"

She pointed not at the end of the gravel road, but across the field, to a cut-out in a grove of trees.

"Maybe it's a mirage," she said, feeling disorientated.

Matt looked. "You were right the first time. It's a house."

"What if it was flooded and abandoned, too?"

"Maybe it was, but I don't know how long this road is, and honestly, Kara, you look like shit."

"Jeez, always the Casanova, aren't you?"

"Abandoned or not, it's shelter, and if we're lucky, we'll find water. So we go there and lie low, and if it's safe, I can leave you to get help."

"Sounds like a plan," she said, and they detoured across the field.

28

Catherine and Ryder arrived at the luxury hotel in Jacksonville where Garrett Reid was staying. They were greeted at the front desk by the security chief, Kristin Gee, who escorted them to her office.

"I have the feeds cut and saved for your review," Kristin said.

"Thank you," Catherine said. She motioned for Ryder to work his magic and watched over his shoulder, hoping to catch a glimpse of Garrett's partner. She didn't want to predispose herself into believing that it was Hope Davidson, who Michael and Sloane had identified as the likely accomplice, so she laid out photos of not only Hope but the other women she'd identified as possibilities.

Kristin had helpfully cued up the moment when Garrett entered the evening before. There were seven entrances to the hotel, and they viewed four entrances at a time on the large screen.

It took an hour, even running through the feeds at triple speed, but then Ryder spotted someone familiar.

"That's her," Ryder said, stopping the recording and enhancing the image. "That's Hope Davidson."

Catherine looked. The woman had her hair up in a wide-brimmed hat and was wearing sunglasses. "Are you certain?"

"Yes. I'll prove it."

He started the tape again at normal speed, saw what elevator she went in, then pulled up the elevator feed. She didn't take off the hat or glasses, but the elevator angle caught a good image of her profile as she adjusted her hat. Ryder clipped it, then brought up the image of the unknown maintenance worker and put the profiles side by side. Close, Catherine thought, but it wasn't enough.

"We need more."

"Hold on," he said. He typed rapidly, then three photos of Hope Davidson popped onto the screen—including one body shot. They had been taken at the resort and posted on the resort website, and except for the one head-on image where she worked behind the gym desk, they were candid—Catherine didn't know if Hope was aware they had been taken.

Ryder then waited until she exited on the fifth floor, froze the screen, and clipped the image of her full body and matched it near perfectly with the full body shot he had from the website. Then he switched the feed to the hall camera, and as they watched, she walked down the hall and knocked.

The door opened and she smiled and looked up, giving them the perfect profile shot as she entered. They couldn't see Garrett Reid, but that was his room.

"That's her," Catherine said. "This is enough to get a warrant. I'm calling Tony."

Michael and Sloane drove to Hope Davidson's house in Palm Coast, north of the resort in a very nice subdivision walking distance from the beach. Sloane looked up the property while Michael was driving. "An LLC owns the house. I guess she's leasing it, but damn, this is much nicer than Reid's place. Three bedrooms, three baths, decks and views from virtually every room. Last sold for three quarters of a million nearly a year ago. Maybe she comes from money, because there's no way she can afford this on her income."

"We only have a search warrant at this point. Tony is still working on getting her financials and phone records. He was lucky to get this so quickly."

"Because she lied to you in your interview," Sloane said.

"We rarely prosecute anyone for lying to a federal agent if they haven't committed another crime, but if she knew about Garrett's activities, she's an accomplice. If she's involved, she's a killer."

"You think she simply knew what he was doing and took Matt and Kara to give him an alibi? Or was she actively involved from the beginning?"

"I'm having a hard time picturing her willingly killing six people, but the evidence, though circumstantial, is more damning than anything we have on Garrett at this point." Michael recognized that even though he'd been an FBI agent for five years and had seen both men and women commit violent crimes, he still had a difficult time processing that a woman could be party to such extreme brutality. "She's the one who abducted Matt and Kara."

He could almost hear Kara's teasing voice in his head: *"You're such a sexist. Women can be as evil as men. Worse, because you don't expect it."*

He missed her. He worried about Matt, but it was different with Kara. They didn't always see eye to eye. They had some fundamental differences about the law and justice. Michael wholeheartedly believed in the system. He believed that in the end, it worked, even if it was flawed. He would die for his country—he had put himself in the line of fire not only in the Navy but in the FBI because it was his duty to serve. The

Navy had saved his life, helped him escape a cycle of drugs and violence that had killed his brother, taken his mother, destroyed the lives of almost every friend he'd had growing up.

Kara didn't see the world in black-and-white, and was more apt to bend—or break—the rules. She didn't trust the system as he did, and maybe she had reason to be cautious. But in the end, she cared just as much about the people they helped. And she always had his back. She never hesitated, and even if she questioned, she was at his side.

He didn't love her like Matt did. But he loved her, and he wanted her back. He even missed her teasing him about his impeccable wardrobe.

Sloane reached out, rested her hand on his forearm. "We're going to find them."

"What if they're already dead?" he whispered. "I don't know if I could do the job anymore. I—"

"They're not dead."

"You don't know that."

"I believe they're alive," Sloane said. "We have to believe it. Let's see if Ms. Hope Davidson has anything incriminating in her house."

Michael *wanted* to believe his friends were alive. He wanted to believe that he would see them again, that they would be no worse for wear, and they could pick up the next case as if nothing had happened. But he couldn't shake this dread that he might never see them again.

He worked to control the fear, calling upon all his training to focus on the mission. Right now, his mission was to find evidence to prove Hope Davidson and Garrett Reid were killers, and locating where Matt and Kara were being held.

Or where they would find their bodies.

They knocked on Davidson's door; no one answered. Sloane rang the bell as Michael walked the perimeter and looked in one of the garage windows. He returned to Sloane. "The Honda registered to her is there, but there's an oil spot in the second space. I think she has another vehicle."

"There's nothing registered to her in Florida."

"Maybe from Louisiana or Tennessee or under a different name," Michael guessed.

He knocked loudly on the door again. "Hope Davidson! This is the FBI. We're coming in."

He waited a beat and when he heard no one approaching, took out his gun and motioned for Sloane to break the window and unlock the door. She did so, and then pushed the door open. Again, Michael announced their presence.

"Clear the house, then we can search," Michael said.

Hope's house was as lovely on the inside as it was outside. Impeccable furnishings, tidy rooms, bright beach colors, views from every window. Once they determined that no one was home, they holstered their weapons.

"I miss Montana," Sloane said, "but I sure wouldn't hate living here."

Michael said, "You take the garage, her bedroom, and the guest rooms. I'll go through the living area, den, and kitchen."

"Are you looking for something specific?" Sloane asked.

"The warrant is clear—we can search wherever it is reasonable to find documents relating to her employment, finances, property, or physical items that may connect her to the homicides—dirty clothing, blood, anything that belonged to the victims. A journal confessing to all six murders would be nice, but short of that anything that tells us where she is, how she knows Reid, where she's from, how to find her."

They split up and silently looked through drawers, cabinets, books. They didn't toss the place; while some cops might get a thrill out of messing up a killer's home, most cops treated an individual's property with respect, even if they were a murder suspect.

The one thing Michael noticed right off: there were few personal items in the open. No photos on tables or the walls, no to-do lists or notebooks or mail. In the den, her files were meticulous and clearly labeled. He took photos of everything, then scanned through the files. Bills, insurance, LLC paperwork . . .

That was interesting. There was paperwork for several LLCs, all with slight variations in their name. SmartGirl Properties, SmartGirl Fun, SmartGirl Business. The paperwork was in the name of Audrey Dolan. He took pictures of the key pages and sent them to Zack Heller, their white-collar crimes expert who had returned last night from Los Angeles where he'd been testifying on one of their previous cases.

Sloane came up from the garage. "You're right about the oil stain, it's been there awhile, plus there's fresh oil so the second vehicle was only recently moved."

"I'll look for insurance papers for a second car, but I found an LLC. I'm having Zack run it, maybe they own the second vehicle."

"What's the LLC? Is it the same LLC that owns the house?" Sloane asked.

Michael looked at his notes. "There's multiple companies, all starting with 'SmartGirl.'"

"The house is owned by SmartGirl Properties, LLC," she said.

"That's one of them," Michael confirmed.

Sloane went upstairs to the bedrooms, and Michael continued going through the desk but didn't find anything else of interest.

Five minutes later, Sloane called down. "Michael! I got something and you will not believe it."

He went upstairs and saw that Sloane had spread papers and photos across the dresser and was systematically taking photos of each.

"This woman has multiple IDs, different names. They were all in that box." She gestured to a box at the end of the dresser. "I found it in her closet, but it wasn't hidden. Just sitting on a shelf. I glanced inside, thinking there'd be family photos or jewelry. There's no jewelry, but there's an empty velvet box. And a photo album."

He opened the small photo album with eight digital prints behind plastic. The cover read *Silver Bells Chapel*, Las Vegas, Nevada. The first page was a photo of male and female hands, with wedding rings, and the date. The other seven pages were of the bride and groom at the cheap altar, slicing a small cake, and kissing.

Garrett Reid and Hope Davidson.

"She's married," Michael said, shocked. "To Reid."

Sloane handed him the marriage certificate between Garrett Reid and Audrey Dolan.

"Audrey Dolan is the name on the SmartGirl LLCs," he said. "Next month is their five-year anniversary. What else did you find?"

"She has documents under the names Audrey Reid, Audrey Dolan, Amber Dunning, and Hope Davidson, all out of Nevada. There's a birth certificate for Clara Dolan, born in Glendale, California. They all look legit, but they can't all be real, right? My guess is the birth certificate is her real name—it has an official seal and date stamp issued a month after her birth—but it will need to be verified."

"Send copies of everything to the team. I'm calling Tony."

When Catherine learned that Garrett Reid was married and that his wife had a false identity and worked at the same resort, she called John Anson and told him they needed to bring Reid back in to interview.

"I can't force him to come in," Anson said. "He'll have to come in on his own, and there's no reason for him to do so. We may have to wait until Monday and ask the judge to revoke his bail—but he didn't lie about being married. We never asked him and no one mentioned it."

"We need to bring him back into questioning because of this new information," Catherine insisted. "Matt and Kara's lives are in danger—certainly we have cause."

"The best I can do is see if I can get a warrant to arrest him for obstruction, but that's going to be a long shot."

"I can bring him in on federal charges," she said, though she had no idea what they might be. She'd have to talk to the AUSA and that would take time—time they didn't have.

"Good luck with that," Anson said with a short laugh.

"I already had the FBI put out a BOLO on Hope Davidson, with her real name and other aliases."

"She brings in a lawyer, she's not going to talk," Anson said, "and we have no evidence. That she has multiple identities isn't covered by the warrant. Meaning, we can't arrest her for discovering false identification while searching for information about the whereabouts of your agents."

Catherine was getting very frustrated with the DA. "John, she and Reid worked together at two different resorts over the last few years. They went out of their way to conceal that information from their employer. She used a false name in employment, and hell, I don't know, we can maybe get her on tax or social security fraud if she has multiple social security numbers to go with all her names. We need to bring her in—she's Reid's partner." Before he could object, she added quickly, "We have multiple FBI offices in every city where they worked interviewing staff and anyone who might have known them, and the LA office is working on finding out who Clara Dolan is—if it's in fact Hope's real birth certificate. We have our white-collar crimes expert looking into each identity as well as the LLCs that we uncovered, one of which owns the property she lives in."

"And all that may be thrown out if the information was obtained in a fraudulent manner if not covered by the warrant."

"Unless her identities lead us to Matt and Kara."

"You're stretching it."

"And you're being too cautious!"

"I don't want two people to get away with multiple homicides," Anson snapped, "and you could be tanking our already tenuous case."

"If we save Matt and Kara, it's worth the risk," Catherine said. "These two have dropped bodies across the country, I'm positive—Emily and Josh Henderson were not the first two victims. We just have to connect them to unsolved murders in the cities where we know they lived."

"You're grasping at straws."

"It's all we have."

Anson sighed. "If Graves can convince Reid to come in for a second interview, I'll be there. But I doubt it'll work. They're holding all the cards right now."

Catherine had to try. She called Franklin Graves's office; voicemail picked up. She left a brief message that she would like to arrange an interview with his client, that it was both important and time sensitive, and left her number. Then she called his cell phone number and left the same message.

She went back to the security office where Ryder had continued to review all recordings to find out exactly when Hope Davidson, aka Audrey Reid, had left the resort. He was on the phone and writing on a notepad. He glanced at her, and she knew he had learned something important. A moment later, he ended the call and said, "Becca McCarthy has been missing for over seven years. She disappeared driving from Los Angeles to Santa Barbara where she was in graduate school."

"I assume there was a police investigation?"

"Yes. Her parents lived in Pasadena not far from the Reids. She came home for two weeks at Christmas, and her parents said Garrett came over for dinner the day after Christmas. He told them he had a job offer in Scottsdale and was looking forward to moving. Becca confided in her sister that Garrett had asked if she would consider relocating to Scottsdale when she graduated in the spring, that he still loved her and if they were in the same place at the same time maybe it would work. Becca said she would—because seeing him again brought back all the memories and she still loved him.

"Garrett came over two days before Becca left to say good-bye," Ryder continued. "She said she would visit him in February and according to her family, they were both excited about this quote, 'new phase of their relationship.' She disappeared on the drive back to Santa Barbara. They found her phone in her car by the side of the road, but never found her body. They brought out dogs to search the area."

"What happened to her car?" Catherine asked.

"Mechanical trouble. Forensics were inconclusive whether it was an accident or intentional."

"If she was walking for help, she would have taken her phone."

"She called for roadside assistance. An hour later they arrived and Becca was gone."

"What did the police think?"

"That someone saw an attractive woman standing by the side of the road and took advantage of the opportunity. It's gone cold," Ryder added.

"Did they interview Garrett?"

"Yes. He showed no sign that he was involved, and seemed upset by the news. In addition, he was already in Scottsdale and his alibi was ironclad—he was training that night with his manager and other staff. The family didn't suspect him then, still don't. They said Garrett and Becca had wanted to explore their relationship again, but neither was in a rush. Becca planned to graduate, and confirmed to her parents what she'd said to her sister, that she'd visit Garrett in Scottsdale and if the feelings were still there, she would move in with him."

"Did you tell them—"

"I didn't talk to them," Ryder clarified. "I spoke to the detective in charge of the missing persons investigation. The detective always looks at current and former partners, and Garrett had no motive, no opportunity. Becca had a college boyfriend for a couple of years that the detective seriously looked at and still thinks he might be involved—he doesn't have an alibi and he had the opportunity, since he lived in the area. But motive was murky and they had no physical evidence."

"Clara Dolan," Catherine muttered.

"Garrett's wife?"

"They met at some point, possibly before they left Los Angeles. She was born in Glendale, which is only a few miles from Pasadena. A big city, but this all seems too coincidental. Could they have met in college? Through friends? I have LA FBI working on getting her history. We'll talk to her family, maybe they know Garrett." Clara Dolan's birth certificate showed her to be only five years older than Garrett—maybe they had a relationship back then. Maybe Garrett didn't want his ex-girlfriend in the picture and had Clara, who had no connection to Becca McCarthy, take her out. Definitely possible . . . but Catherine would need to prove they knew each other seven years ago.

And maybe . . . just maybe . . . Garrett was serious about getting back with his ex and Clara didn't like that and took the competition out.

Another possibility.

"One more thing," Ryder said. "I have a photo of Becca McCarthy."

He turned his phone to show her.

Twenty-three-year-old Becca was blonde, with an engaging smile and sparkling blue eyes. She was very pretty, the stereotypical girl next door. Though her hair was longer, she looked surprisingly like Kara—if Kara had a lighter, whimsical side. In fact, this last week while they were undercover, Kara had played the part of a happy bride . . . making her look even more like Becca.

All the victims had the same general look, which was why Catherine had believed that Garrett was a lone killer targeting a specific type, but Kara came closest. Not to Emily Henderson, but to Becca McCarthy—Garrett's first serious girlfriend.

Did Garrett choose the victims because the brides reminded him of his missing girlfriend?

Or did Clara choose the victims because the brides reminded *her* of his missing girlfriend?

Where was Clara the day Becca McCarthy disappeared?

"Ask the detective to send us everything he has on Becca McCarthy's disappearance," Catherine said.

"It's already on its way," Ryder said, refreshing his email.

Catherine's phone vibrated. It was Michael.

"Do you have something new?" she asked.

"Alena Porter, the Sapphire Shoals manager, is unconscious and on her way to the hospital," Michael said.

"What happened?"

"Before we talked to Davidson, I was looking to speak to her. She was supposed to be on site, but then we were told she went home sick. She fit the profile, even though we were leaning toward Hope Davidson, so I asked Detective Fuentes to follow up. When she arrived at her house, she found Porter unconscious in her vehicle, which was parked in the garage with the door open, ignition off—as if she came home, tried to get into the house, then passed out. She's unresponsive."

"People do get sick. Do you think she was poisoned?"

"Yes," Michael said. "Fuentes retraced her steps and learned that immediately before she left, she went to the gym. She had told her assistant that she'd be back in her office, but then left from the gym saying she wasn't feeling well. Hope—Audrey Reid—was still there."

"You're thinking what exactly?" Catherine asked, though she was beginning to see what Michael was seeing.

"That Porter may have been suspicious. She didn't recognize Audrey from the photo, but perhaps there was something else that triggered a memory, before or after she saw her at the gym."

"Have Fuentes follow up with the hospital to find out her status and what might have happened," Catherine said.

"Fuentes already has a deputy there and we'll know when and if she regains consciousness. I'll go back to the gym and talk to the other staff."

"Let me know," Catherine said and then filled him in on what she and Ryder had learned. "We're getting closer, Michael."

"It's taking too long," he said and hung up.

29

Catherine didn't want to leave Jacksonville before she spoke with Franklin Graves. She reached out again; again, no answer. She wondered if he was avoiding her calls and if it would be worth her time to go to his office. She was about to ask Ryder what he thought when Jim called her.

"Catherine, forensics came through," he said, sounding excited. "I've spent most of the day going back and forth between Quantico and the Florida State Lab. We took the rust samples, water samples, trace evidence, and lung samples from the victims, then isolated common particles. I'm 99 percent confident they were all kept captive in a warehouse or factory that was flooded during the last hurricane, and I'm 90 percent confident that the location is southern Georgia or northern Florida. It could be farther out, but taking the entirety of the evidence I think I'm right."

"That's great work, Jim." But was it already too late? Matt and Kara had been missing and presumably without food and water for more than forty-eight hours. They were drugged, and based on what Jim uncovered, trapped in a dangerous warehouse.

But between the two of them, they would figure a way out, wouldn't they? Except they hadn't reached out, they hadn't called anyone for help.

"The tech lab is currently running possible locations based on known flooding, but they might not have a complete list," Jim said.

"It would need to be remote and abandoned, but accessible by vehicle."

"I agree. I gave them the parameters and they know it's a time-crucial situation. We're going to find them, Catherine." He sounded more optimistic than she felt. The more time that passed, the less confident she became.

"As soon as we get a list of possible locations," she said, "we'll bring in every FBI office, sheriff's department, troopers—Tony has already given law enforcement in the region a heads-up, so we can cover a lot of ground in short time."

"We'll have something more in a couple hours. I'll call you back." He ended the call.

A couple hours. Hope Davidson—Audrey Reid—Clara Dolan—whatever name the woman went by, was in the wind. Had she run . . . or was she on her way to kill Matt and Kara? If the latter, they didn't have a couple hours.

Ryder slid over a piece of paper. "Piper Dolan is Clara Dolan's mother. Her father, Gerald, is deceased. Here's her contact information. She's still in California, it's eleven in the morning there."

"Thank you." She looked at the address. It was in Bel-Air, one of the most expensive and exclusive Los Angeles neighborhoods.

She cleared her throat, pushing aside her worries. She was usually the calm agent, the unemotional agent, the agent who didn't snap or yell or demand when things got tough. And she certainly didn't cry.

She called the first number on the list. A woman answered and, when Catherine introduced herself, said she would bring the phone to Mrs. Dolan.

It took several minutes before Piper picked up the line. "This is Piper Dolan. To whom am I speaking?"

"Dr. Catherine Jones, FBI Special Agent."

"Doctor?"

"Forensic psychiatrist," Catherine said.

"And you wish to speak to me?"

"Yes, ma'am. It's about your daughter."

A faint sigh in the background. Then Catherine heard Piper speak to someone else. "Marissa, please contact Mrs. Brockway and tell her I'll need to reschedule lunch." A moment later, she said, "I assume you have bad news for me."

Her tone reminded Catherine of her own mother. Charlotte Harrison thought she was superior to most everyone, and Catherine had been a distinct failure in every way—from who she married (into a middle-class family, not the fact that Chris was a surgeon); to Catherine's career choice (that she had "wasted" her medical school education to work in law enforcement); to the worst sin of all: that Catherine had brought violence into the family that got her sister Beth—the child who was perfect in every way—killed.

"Your daughter, who has most recently been using the name Hope Davidson, is wanted for questioning in the kidnapping of a federal agent and police detective."

"Hmm," Piper said shortly. "I see. I can tell you two things. First, I haven't spoken to or heard from Clara in nearly eight years. Second, Clara is capable of hiring her own lawyer, so I shall not be helping her in that way."

"It would help if I understood Clara's background and

whether she has ever been in trouble with the law, or shown any tendency toward violence."

"I do not know my daughter. I barely knew her as a child as we had nothing in common. She had no interest in school, books, history, art. Frankly, she showed no interest in anything except herself. She was a beautiful child from the minute she was born, and she knew it. She wanted for nothing. Gerald and I worked hard to educate Clara, to give her a solid foundation on which to do something productive with her life. She threw it all away."

"Have you disowned her?"

"I wouldn't say something so common as disowning a child. She received her trust fund when she was twenty-five, and we wrote her out of our will. The Dolan estate will be split in quarters between my niece, nephew, the Getty Museum, and UCLA, where I am a tenured professor."

"What do you teach?"

"I have doctorates in sixteenth-century English literature, European art history, and Russian literature. I'm currently teaching a graduate class in sixteenth-century English literature."

"Your husband was also a professor?"

"Yes, though I don't see the relevance. Gerald passed five years ago."

"What is Clara's trust fund worth?"

"I only know what it was when she was given full access to it. Ten million dollars. It was established by her grandparents. I would not have been that generous with a child who showed apathy in everything except seducing men."

Ten million dollars was a tidy sum. It explained the house and resources that Clara had. It could have grown quite substantially over the last ten years.

"Who manages her trust?" Catherine asked.

"I will text you the law firm who established it. I wouldn't know if Clara still uses them. I doubt it. She wanted to cut ties with us, and that suited my husband and me just fine."

"Do you care at all that she's wanted for multiple felonies?"

"No," Piper said bluntly. "Clara was a beautiful child, as I said. On the outside, you have never seen such an exquisite beauty. I assure you, the cliché 'beauty is only skin deep' could have been coined to describe my daughter."

There had to be more here than a mother who hadn't seen or spoken to her daughter in years and showed absolutely no interest in what she has done since.

"Do you know a man named Garrett Reid?"

"No. Dr. Jones, I may have canceled my lunch, but I am a busy woman."

Catherine ignored the clear message that Piper wanted to end the call and asked instead, "Clara left Los Angeles for Scottsdale more than seven years ago with a man named Garrett Reid." That was a guess on Catherine's part, but she felt she was right, or close to it. Though initially they believed that Garrett and Clara had connected at one of the resorts where they'd worked, now they knew both of them were from the Los Angeles area and they'd married five years ago, and if Piper hadn't spoken to Clara in nearly eight years—which was around the time Garrett had left—it reasoned that they left together. "They were married in Las Vegas two years later."

Another irritated sigh. "What do you want to know, Dr. Jones? Just ask me. If I know, I will tell you."

"Did anything unusual happen in the months before Clara left town? In your last conversations with her, did she say anything that gave you pause?"

"I suppose salacious gossip is what psychiatrists are more interested in," Piper said derisively. "I rarely saw Clara after she moved out of the house when she received her trust fund. I rarely spoke to her when she lived here. Gerald and I traveled extensively, including spending two years teaching in Oxford. Sometimes, I wish we had stayed." She sounded wistful at the memory, then she cleared her throat and said, "I have never seen

Clara react violently with anyone. She took pleasure in hurting people emotionally, not physically. She was wicked, Dr. Jones. Purely Mephistophelian. That means—"

"I know what it means," Catherine interrupted. She detested being talked down to by anyone, especially someone who reminded her far too much of her own mother. "Did you witness or hear of anything that Clara was involved with in the months before or after she left?"

"She had an affair with her co-worker's father and, as I learned from someone I trust, made sure the woman knew what had happened at the most inopportune time: less than a week before the girl's wedding. The revelation that Clara and Richard Masters had been involved in that way put a damper on the entire wedding, and, ultimately, the marriage quickly ended in a divorce."

Masters . . . "Was Clara's co-worker a woman named Emily Masters?"

"Yes. They had been friends, I thought. Though when Emily won a promotion over Clara, I should have seen something like this coming. Clara does not handle failure well at all."

"And this happened about eight years ago?"

"Seven and a half years, I believe. Sometime during the holiday season. Clara left town shortly after—maybe a month or two later. I can't be certain. We saw her on Christmas Eve when she came to get her most treasured belongings because she said she'd found her 'one true love.'" She said it with such contempt and derision that Catherine was a bit shocked, though in hindsight she shouldn't be, considering the whole of the conversation.

"Do you have a name?"

"No. Perhaps it's that Garrett Reid you mentioned. But I didn't believe it. Clara has been in love many times, and it's always her one true love, the one man who sees through her beauty to her brains." Piper laughed and Catherine got a chill.

"What happened to the other men in her life?" she asked.

"Donovan was her high school sweetheart, a smart young man from a good family. He went to Harvard. She couldn't follow. She wanted to go to Harvard so badly to be with him, but she didn't have the intellect for it, and we weren't going to overpay for her to be accepted. Then she dated this boy, Charlie, for a time. I met him once, he was . . . polite." She said it as if that was the only complimentary thing she could come up with. "He married Emily Masters long after he and Clara broke up. He and Emily divorced, as I mentioned before."

"Do you have their last names?"

"Is this all you need, Dr. Jones?"

"Yes," Catherine said.

"Charlie Rowe and Donovan Prince. I will send you the contact information for the law firm my parents used to establish the trust, though I doubt you will get anything from them without a warrant. And I will also send you the contact information of my own lawyer, who you will need to contact if you would like to speak again. Good day."

The line went dead.

"Are you okay?" Ryder asked.

Catherine nodded slowly. "I wasn't expecting that level of coldness."

"From what I could hear, she sounded unfazed."

Catherine gave Ryder the names of the two men Clara had been involved with prior to Garrett. "We found the connection to the first victim, Emily Masters Henderson," Catherine said. "Clara knew her. Find out where they worked, what they did, how to contact Charlie and Donovan. I'm going to call the trust fund lawyer."

Unfortunately, Catherine quickly learned Clara had transferred her trust fund out of their control and into her own bank. They gave Catherine the name of the branch, but that was all they would share. Catherine didn't even attempt to contact the bank; she knew they wouldn't give her any personal information without a warrant. She sent the information to Tony and Zack. Perhaps with the information about the LLCs that Michael and Sloane found, Zack would be able to learn more about Clara's finances. Maybe, like the beach house here, she had other property in one of her names or any of the LLCs'.

She had a thought and sent a text to the team:

Check specifically boat ownership in all of Clara's names and LLCs. Likely she used her own boat to dispose of the bodies. If she has one, figure out where it is docked, etc.

Catherine assumed the woman had enough money to vanish—so why hadn't she? Why kidnap Matt and Kara instead of fleeing after Garrett's arrest?

Was it because Kara resembled Becca McCarthy? Or because Clara needed to complete her plan? Some killers were driven to act—inaction simply wasn't an option.

Or because she truly loved Garrett Reid and refused to leave him?

She reflected on what Michael and Sloane had discovered at Clara's house. Clara liked order and luxury, kept mementos of her life and identities hidden in a box—but nothing from her victims. Once dead, the victims no longer mattered.

Garrett hadn't kept trophies either—not in his apartment, at least. Catherine believed Clara had chosen the targets, or heavily influenced Garrett's choices.

Leaning back in her chair, Catherine closed her eyes. Though exhausted, she didn't need sleep—just five minutes to think. She'd focused so much on profiling Garrett Reid; now it was clear Clara Dolan was the key—possibly even the mastermind.

Clara came from wealth and intellect. Her parents were older when they had her—Piper was forty when she gave birth. Established professionals. Their Bel-Air home was likely worth millions. Piper had sounded like old money—probably went into academia out of genuine interest and intelligence.

Clara, though beautiful, wasn't academically inclined. Catherine suspected she lacked aptitude and rebelled early. She was likely very normal, but with academically focused parents who prided themselves on their intellect. Clara's normal achievements wouldn't have been celebrated. If something didn't come easy, Clara wouldn't bother. Over time, that became her norm. She leaned on her looks and craved attention for who she was, not who her parents wanted her to be.

Seducing Emily Masters's father to sabotage her wedding showed emotional manipulation and keen insight into human behavior. Clara knew how to read people and exploit their weaknesses. But if the goal had been to ruin Emily's wedding—and it worked—why kill her years later?

Was it revenge? Or was Clara simply continuing a pattern? Were she and Garrett at the resort to run a scam, and seeing Emily was just a coincidence? Or did they choose Sapphire Shoals because Emily would be there?

Catherine had told her team the victims were likely chosen for their appearance and success—things Clara lacked or resented. Yet Clara was objectively a beautiful woman, so it was who these women represented: successful in their fields, newly married and ostensibly in love, and—the key point—they all looked at least marginally like Becca McCarthy.

Was that Clara's hang-up . . . or Garrett's? Catherine honestly didn't know, and she could go either way—depending on if Garrett was involved in Becca's disappearance.

But Emily was the first victim here, in Florida.

Catherine sat up. "Ryder, I need Emily's background. She wasn't a lawyer when she knew Clara. They must have met at work, since Clara's mother said Emily was her co-worker, someone promoted over her. Where was that?"

Ryder replied, "Emily went to UCLA, majored in English

lit, received a master's in communication. Worked in Marketing for a publisher in New York, then came back to LA and went to law school while working for a major hotel chain in Orange County. That could be the connection." Before Catherine could respond, he added, "I'll get you their contact info."

"No," she said. "You contact them. Find out everything you can—confirm Clara's employment, timeline, if she and Emily knew each other there. Her mother said they were friends, but I don't know how much Piper Dolan paid attention to Clara's life. We'll get a warrant, but see what you can get now without one. I'm going to talk to the ex-boyfriends."

Donovan Prince worked in New York City for a financial services company and wouldn't take her call. Catherine left a message. If he didn't call back in an hour, she'd ask someone from the New York field office to visit him in person.

Charlie Rowe lived in Huntington Beach, California. He was a computer programmer who worked from home and answered the phone on the second ring.

Time wasn't on their side, so Catherine was blunter than she normally would have been. After a brief introduction, she asked, "Mr. Rowe, were you aware that your ex-wife Emily was killed seven months ago?"

"Yeah, her mom called me. Em and her new husband were both killed while on their honeymoon. I didn't know the FBI was investigating the murders."

"We are assisting local law enforcement," Catherine said.

"What do you need from me? We've been divorced for five years. I was happy she found someone. I even met Josh a couple of times, before they moved to Florida—he was a nice guy. I didn't harbor any bad wishes or anything."

"Why did you get divorced?"

"That's really not any of your business, is it?" He sounded only mildly irritated.

"I'm a forensic psychiatrist and putting together a comprehensive timeline of Emily's life. It's important that I understand her psychology because that helps me understand the killer's psychology."

"Oh. Well, there was a lot of stuff going on in her life. I'm pretty laid-back. Maybe too laid-back. When we got married, her parents had just split, she was a mess, and she said more than once that our marriage was cursed. I tried to let it go, but it bugged me. I loved Emily."

"Do you know why her parents split up?"

"Sure, that really has nothing—"

"I know why," Catherine said.

"You do?" He sounded surprised.

"Clara Dolan had an affair with Emily's father."

"What a mess that was."

"You also went out with Clara?"

"Yeah, but that was ages ago. We went to the same community college. Clara's boyfriend had gone to college on the East Coast, my high school girlfriend had dumped me, we hung out. And it kind of developed into friends with benefits. But it was never serious."

"What was Clara like when she was, what, eighteen, nineteen?"

"We were both nineteen. She was gorgeous. Adventurous. We had fun."

"Why'd you break up?"

"We were nineteen and she started getting serious and I was like, no, I'm going to a four-year college. I was just saving money going to community college for two years. She didn't like that. She didn't like when I said I had to study. I'm pretty smart, but I was taking all the hefty math and science classes so I could get into a good college. So we split up. Like I said, we really weren't that serious and I didn't want to be, but I liked hanging with her."

"How did you end up reconnecting in Orange County?"

"Oh. Well, I went to college in Arizona, took a job there, didn't really like it, and we were Facebook friends. She mentioned there was an IT position with her company—she worked for a hotel resort—I applied, and got it."

"Did she try and rekindle your relationship?"

"Maybe? I don't know, really. I was just glad to be back in California, and living in OC. I met Emily a year later and knew she was the one."

Catherine had to think like Clara . . . Did Clara believe Emily had stolen Charlie from her? Did Clara think Charlie owed her something for helping him get the job? There had to be more to it . . . and Catherine suspected it had to do with Emily's educational background.

"When did Emily start law school?"

"She was in law school when I met her. She was going at night while she was working."

"How did Emily know Clara?"

"Why all these questions about Clara?"

"Again, I'm just trying to put together a comprehensive background."

"No, this is different," he said.

What did Catherine say to that? "Clara's name has come up in the course of our investigation into Emily's murder."

"Oh. Wow."

"How did Emily know Clara?" she repeated.

"Clara worked at the hotel. She didn't need to work—she had come into a lot of money when she got her trust fund, which was after we had split. But she liked being around people, and she was good at her job."

"Which was?"

"Personal trainer. She pretty much made her own hours. Emily worked in Marketing. They didn't really work together, but

I thought they were friends. At least friendly, you know. Until Clara applied for a different position. She'd been at the hotel for like two years maybe? And said she wanted something new. She had a marketing idea and wanted to work in the marketing department. Well . . . Emily didn't think her idea was any good, and she didn't hire Clara into the open position. Clara told me Emily got promoted over her, but I think that was kind of a stretch. Emily did get a promotion, but Clara had no chance at it. Then Clara accused Emily of stealing her idea and quit. She was mad, I get it, but Clara wasn't the sharpest tack. She wasn't dumb," he said quickly. "She was great with people, but when it came to details or math or budgets? She couldn't be bothered."

"Thank you, that helps."

"You don't think Clara . . . I mean, she wouldn't *hurt* anyone."

"I don't think anything yet," Catherine said, "but I appreciate your time."

She ended the call. She did think something, but nothing she wanted to share with Charlie Rowe.

Clara lived in her own world. She saw slights where there were no slights. Emily didn't steal her boyfriend—Clara and Charlie had split long before Emily came along. Emily didn't steal her job, but Clara would have considered it a slight that Emily may have prevented her from getting a position that she wanted. Especially if they were friendly. The accusation that Emily stole her idea was likely built on a slim premise or stray comment.

Catherine looked again at the timeline. Clara had quit her job at the hotel two months before the wedding. And that's probably when she seduced Emily's father for the sole purpose of exposing the affair and putting a damper on the festivities. She did it to be mean, but Catherine suspected she got satisfaction out of emotionally destroying a family.

Destroying the Masters family was Clara's way of destroying her own, though she would never admit it . . . and she probably wouldn't even recognize it if Catherine laid out the breadcrumbs.

Why was Clara, who had a ten-million-dollar trust fund, working as a personal trainer? Was she bored? Wanted to meet people? Maybe to seduce or scam them? Did she find joy in tricking people? Did the murders evolve because she became bored with seduction? Or because she and Garrett had married and she didn't want to sleep with other men?

How did she meet Garrett Reid?

Michael called her. "We're done at Hope Davidson's house. Jim said that Matt and Kara are likely being held in southern Georgia—I don't want to drive in the opposite direction and go back to the resort, I want to be closer to where they are being held."

"The hotel here in Jacksonville has allowed us to use one of their conference rooms," Catherine said. "I need to talk to Reid's lawyer, but he hasn't returned my call. Meet me here, and we'll head over to his office to have a conversation with him."

"Can we do that?"

"Yes. He doesn't have to talk to us, but he needs to know what we're dealing with—who he's dealing with."

"What are we dealing with, Catherine?" Michael asked bluntly.

She hesitated, only a moment. She was confident, but her previous errors still weighed heavily on her. "I believe, based on what others have said and the crimes committed, that Clara Dolan is a psychopath. I believe she has Antisocial Personality Disorder. Her deceitfulness, using multiple names, impulsiveness, reckless disregard for safety, rationalization for her acts, lack of empathy for her victims. There are a few traits that don't quite fit, but psychopathy is not a hard science, and people are unique. Most people with mental disorders aren't killers, but those who start killing do so with complete inner justification of their actions. Without a formal interview, I can't state this all with certainty."

"And Garrett Reid is the same?"

"No. Reid isn't a naturally violent person. He's certainly a sociopathic con artist, but I don't believe he would have ever turned violent without Clara's influence. He naturally avoids confrontation. Which is why I want to talk to his lawyer. We're going to offer him a deal."

When Michael ended the call, Catherine turned to Ryder. "I need everything about Becca McCarthy and her disappearance, every detail you can find no matter how trivial. That's how we get Reid to turn on his wife."

Then she called Tony. She would have to convince him to pull out every favor he had to offer a deal to a suspected killer.

30

By the time Matt and Kara crossed the field, Kara had stopped talking altogether. She leaned into him, her weight dragging on his shoulder with every limping step. She could still walk, but was in obvious pain. The T-shirt he'd tied around her calf was red with her blood.

Matt ached all over from the fall. His body felt like a single, pulsing bruise. His ankle throbbed, but held. The sun beat down on his bare back, searing his skin. He was probably burned, even with his darker complexion. Kara, pale and blistering red, fared worse. They'd eaten a few berries, enough to dull the edge of hunger, but not their thirst.

At the edge of the field, he stopped. The house loomed ahead—weathered, listing, half boarded up. A hurricane, probably the same one that had flooded the factory, had left its mark. But there, above the sagging porch, a single light glowed.

Electricity. Maybe someone was inside.

This was the rural South. Sometimes you met the kind of

people who'd offer you a drink and a hot meal. Other times, they'd run you off their land with a shotgun. Matt didn't like the odds, but he didn't have a choice.

He considered that the house belonged to whoever had taken them, though that seemed unlikely. Once the cameras had gone dark in the factory and he disabled the generator, whoever was watching them would have come to investigate if they were this close. Still, unlikely didn't mean impossible.

He couldn't risk Kara.

He eased her down beneath the shade of an oak tree, her back against the rough trunk. "I'm going to check it out. Stay here. Don't move unless you have to."

"Roger that," she whispered, her eyes already closing.

She didn't protest. Didn't insist on going with him. That said more than anything else: she was worse off than she'd let on.

If this house turned out to be the wrong kind of refuge, Matt didn't know if either of them could run.

Matt kept his hands in the open and to his side to show that he wasn't a threat as he approached the property. While he was still fifty feet away from the base of the broken steps, he called out, "Hello? Is anyone home? I need some help. Hello?"

He walked slowly forward, listening.

"My name is Matt Costa," he called out. "I'm an FBI special agent and I've had some trouble. Is anyone home?"

He was only a couple feet from the bottom stair when he heard footsteps running inside, then the front door burst open. "Stay back! Don't come any closer!" a woman shouted.

"Okay," he said, keeping his hands up. "I don't mean to bother you."

"Back up!" she demanded.

Matt took two steps back. This woman wasn't their kidnapper, he was nearly certain of it. She was in her late thirties with long dark hair braided down her back. She looked terrified, even as her voice commanded that he stay away. She wore dirty surgical scrubs and scuffed white shoes that reminded Matt of every nurse he'd met.

"Are you a nurse?" he asked.

Her eyes widened in fear. "How do you know that?"

He motioned to how she was dressed. "My partner is injured. We were trapped in the abandoned factory across the field—"

She interrupted him. "You have to go right now. *Right now!*"

"My partner has a deep cut and has lost a lot of blood. She needs medical attention. I understand that you might not want to let strangers inside, and I don't have any identification on me, but I can give you a number to call to verify I am who I say I am. They'll send help."

"You don't understand," she said, her voice quivering. "Just please go."

"I can't," he said softly. She had no weapon. He didn't want to scare her, but he couldn't walk away. He didn't think Kara would make it much farther. "My partner and I were held hostage in the factory across the field for the last two days. No food or water." He took a step forward. "I won't come in, if you insist, but if you can bring us something to drink," he took another step forward, "and call my boss—"

"No! Stop!" Tears started streaming down her face as she clutched a small gold cross on a chain around her neck. "If you take one more step my son is dead. Please, just stop."

Matt did as she asked.

"What is your name?" he asked.

"You have to leave."

"I'm Matt Costa. My partner is Kara. I can get help if you have a phone."

The woman wiped her face. Her hand was trembling.

"We don't need to come inside. If you could call for me, that would be great."

She continued crying.

"What's your name," he asked again.

"L-Lily."

"Hi, Lily. I'll help you any way I can, I promise."

"My son is trapped in a cage in the basement. If I do anything to try to get him out, he'll die. There's a gas canister down there, poison. She will set it off—she told me she would. I'm not going to risk my son's life for you or anyone. Do you understand that?"

Matt attributed his fatigue and pain for being slow on the uptake, but he finally put two and two together. They were less than two miles from the factory; a field separated them. *She* was the same *she* who had taken Matt and Kara from the resort.

"I understand," Matt said. "If you let me help you and your son, I can get you out of this."

"I'm not risking my son's life because you think you can help. What if you fail?"

"Someone is keeping you here against your will," Matt said. "Just like my partner and me—someone put us in that factory. It's the same person. We nearly died getting out, but we got out. What kind of gas is down there?"

"I don't know! There's no label on it, but it's in a canister with a phone attached. She says if she calls that number, the phone will set off the canister. My son is locked in a cell. Who has a cell in their basement?" She shook her head.

"What else did this person tell you?"

Lily clearly didn't want to say anything, but maybe because she was terrified and he was her only lifeline for help, she relented.

"My husband is being forced to do something he doesn't want to do. We were taken here to make sure he complies."

"Who is your husband?" A cop maybe, someone involved in the investigation.

"Franklin Graves."

Matt didn't recognize the name. "Is he in law enforcement?"

"He's a lawyer."

"A prosecutor?" Maybe he worked with Anson.

She shook her head. "He was a criminal defense attorney in Miami, but he doesn't do that anymore. He works civil cases now, helps people. I don't know what they want from him, I only know that she told me if Franklin does what they want, they'll let Nathan and me go."

"They? You said she, now you say they?"

She bit her lip. "Because she said 'we,' but I don't know. I want to believe she's crazy, but sometimes people are just cruel. Leave. The cameras all point to the house, but if you take another step—oh, dear Lord, she'll see me standing here talking to someone!" She buried her face in her hands and sobbed.

"I'll get your son out. I'll disable the gas or break the lock or . . ."

She shook her head. "Then they'll kill my husband."

"Do you have a phone? Anything to communicate?"

"Anything I do on my phone, she'll see it. She cloned it."

Matt knew the woman was scared, but he had to find a solution.

"I *am* an FBI agent," he said. "I can get your husband protection within minutes."

"What if we don't have minutes? What if she sees you and kills my son?"

Matt understood her fear. He understood that Lily's only concern right now was protecting her child first, her husband second. He would feel the same. But there had to be an answer.

"Okay. Go inside, look at the gas container, study it. Tell me exactly what you see. Wires, plugs, dials, everything. Come back and describe it to me. I'll figure it out."

She stared at him, unmoving.

"Lily, please. The woman I love, my partner, is dying under that tree." He gestured to the large oak tree where he'd left Kara. "I will do anything to save her, and right now she needs you—she needs a nurse to clean her wound and give her water and food, at least until we can get her to a hospital. And in exchange for your help, I will save your son. I need to know what the device looks like, how it is secured, if there are any wires or cords. I can help." Matt didn't know what else to say to convince her.

She gave him a short nod, turned, and went back into the house.

Matt hoped Lily could do this. He needed her to do this.

He walked back to Kara. She leaned against the tree, eyes closed. But her chest was rising up and down, up and down. He sat next to her, where he could still see the porch. He hoped that the woman made a decision quickly.

"Kara," he said quietly.

"Hmm."

"There's a mother in the house with her son. A woman brought her here, threatened to kill her and her son, and is using them as leverage with her husband, who's a lawyer. I don't know what they think he can do, but my guess it's Garrett and his partner who did all this."

"Yeah. The voice we heard. Also a woman. Same person?"

"Likely. I don't see how unrelated criminals with a penchant for kidnapping would leave their victims this close to each other."

Kara grunted a laugh at his poor attempt at humor.

"How are you doing?" he asked.

"Okay."

She wasn't okay. She didn't even ask about the woman or what his plan was.

"The mom is named Lily. She's scared and believes that if she allows us in, gas will be released in the house and kill her son, who is locked in a cage."

"That really sucks," Kara said. "What crazy person locks a child in a cage?"

Her voice was stronger now. Angry.

"I'm going to help her disable it, if she lets me."

Kara reached out and grabbed his wrist. Her grip was weak, but her voice was clear. "Be careful."

He kissed her forehead. "I'll wait here until Lily comes back. I don't know how long it's going to take."

"Okay," she said and put her head on his shoulder.

Lily Graves went down to the basement where Nathan was leaning against the bars. "I heard you talking to someone," he said. "Can they help? Why are you crying? Are you okay?"

Nathan didn't sound scared, he sounded hopeful. Protective. He sounded far older than his years. He shouldn't be forced to grow up so fast. He'd be twelve next month. But he sounded almost like a grown man. She blinked back tears.

"A man who says he's with the FBI, but I don't know. He has no shirt and is wearing sweatpants."

"He said he was with the FBI? You think he's lying? Why would he do that?"

"Why does anyone do what they do?" she said, exasperated. "I don't know, pumpkin. I don't think he's with that woman, but I don't know that he is a good person."

"Mom, we need to trust someone. I heard him say his partner is hurt. Is that true?"

"I didn't see a partner. What if he's trying to lure me out? What if he is part of that woman's twisted game, trying to trick me into leaving the house?"

"Do you really believe that?"

She didn't. But four days being trapped in this house, barely sleeping, worrying that the gas would go off and kill her son, the best thing in her life, the child she vowed to love and protect from the minute she felt him move in her stomach . . . She felt gutted.

"Mom, if someone's hurt, you have to help them. You just have to."

"If that woman looks at the cameras and sees that I brought someone in here, we could all die."

"Mom."

He reached through the bars and took her hand. When had he grown up? Her baby was becoming a man.

"Are you sure?" she asked, her voice catching.

He looked her straight in the eye and, without hesitation, said, "Yes."

31

Matt carried Kara into the house and put her on the couch in the living room. The house was just as hot as outside, but at least they were out of the sun.

"I could have walked," Kara muttered.

"Lily is a nurse," he said.

The woman still looked terrified and said, "You have to disable the gas. Please, right now. If she sees you here, she'll kill my son."

"Okay, show me your son, then please take care of Kara?"

"I'm not letting you alone with my son."

"Lily," Matt said with as much calm as he could muster, "Kara has a serious cut on her leg. You're a nurse. Please look at it, see what you can do. You can trust me."

"Not with my son."

Kara said, "Matt, go. Take care of the kid. I'm fine."

Matt knew she wasn't fine, but said, "Can you bring her some water first?"

Lily left the room then returned with a bottle of cool water.

"The refrigerator isn't great, but there's electricity and it keeps things cold enough."

Matt handed it to Kara. She took a small sip, handed it back. "You take some."

"Kara—"

"Matt. Stop arguing with me. Take some, give it back, save the kid."

Now she sounded more herself.

He drank a big gulp, the cool liquid soothing his raw, aching throat. He gave back the bottle to Kara and said, "Drink it slow, but drink all of it." He glanced at Lily. "You mentioned cameras. Where are they?"

"Outside facing the house—she knew when I left. She had to have been watching because she . . . did something."

"What do you mean by that?"

"I stepped off the porch to see what was around, hoping maybe I could see someone who could get help. I started back inside and when I stepped on the top step, I heard a bang and the stair collapsed. I was lucky I didn't break my leg. She called me and said the next time I disobeyed, my punishment would be worse . . . and that's when she told me about the gas canister."

Matt had seen the broken stairs outside.

"Any other cameras?"

"In the basement, kitchen, the hall. I didn't find one in the living room, but a couple were well hidden, so I don't know for sure."

"I'm not a technical person, but based on our experience in the factory, I don't think she has the cameras on motion sensors. She needs to log in to whatever system she's using and look at the feeds. I would say let's disable all the cameras and then get to work, but if we miss one, she'll see what we're doing anyway. So let's get your son out of the cage first, then I'll figure out a way to get us all out of this mess."

"If I leave, she'll kill my husband," Lily said. "I believe her."

So did Matt. "Once your son is safe, I can use your phone and get help for your husband. I'll find a way. I can go out and look for help if I need to. But doing nothing is not an option."

"Okay," she said quietly, then reached out to grip his hand. "Thank you, Matt."

Sunlight filtered weakly through narrow, grimy windows high on the brick walls, casting faint beams across the partially finished basement. The air was heavy with the scent of rotting wood and musty earth. Water stains bloomed like bruises on the crumbling foundation. Under the creaky wooden stairs, the basement sloped down and the dim bare bulb above the stairs reflected off stagnant water left over from the flood or subsequent storms. Matt couldn't see far into the darkness, but it was creepy. He heard the slow, steady, *drip drip* of water in the dark.

Lily must have opened two of the hopper windows, though the hot and humid outside air did little to erase the stench of mold and mildew. A sharp cleanser scent hit him as he reached the bottom step, and he wondered if Lily had tried to clean up.

A small jail cell had been built into the corner to the right of the staircase, floor to ceiling and six feet square. It had been there a long time, the rods attached to the wall with large metal screws. Lily's son—Nathan—sat on a blanket against the wall, a book and water within easy reach. As soon as he saw them, he jumped up. He looked to be around twelve, take or leave a year, with dark hair that kept falling in front of his hazel eyes.

"Are you really an FBI agent?" he asked Matt.

"Yes," Matt said. "Special Agent in Charge Mathias Costa. My friends call me Matt. Are you okay? You're not hurt, are you?"

"I'm fine. Are you going to get us out?"

"That's my goal," Matt said.

"She's going to kill my dad—will you help him?"

"As soon as we get you out of here, we'll find a way to help your dad."

He glanced around and immediately saw two of the cameras—one in the corner of the cell, by the ceiling, and one above the bare light bulb.

Matt inspected the jail cell, shaking each of the bars, looking for any that were loose.

"I already did that," Lily said. She stood off to the side, at the base of the stairs, her face full of concern, eyes darting back and forth from Matt to her son.

"There's a lock here," Matt said. Though the cell had been here for a long time, the lock was brand new—a durable Master lock, the kind you could buy at any hardware store. "I assume you looked for a key or a bolt cutter?"

"First thing I did. I couldn't find anything."

"Kara, my partner, is good at picking locks. If we can find the right tools somewhere, and she can make it down here on her bum leg, it's an option."

"You think so?" Nathan said, hopeful.

"Yes," Matt said honestly. "But first, I want to check the gas. Try to determine what we're dealing with, and if I can disable the device."

"Your partner is hurt," Nathan said.

"Yes." He glanced at Lily. "She's resting upstairs now, and when we're done here, your mom will help her."

"Mom," Nathan said.

"I'm not leaving you alone with a stranger," Lily said.

"You're a nurse. Go help her. They're FBI agents."

She looked from Matt to her son, clearly torn. "We don't know that."

"Mom, I'm okay."

Matt said, "The faster Kara is on her feet, the faster we can get Nathan out of here."

Lily said to Nathan, "If he does or says anything wrong, you scream and I'll be here."

"I promise," Nathan said.

Lily sighed, said, "The gas canister is over there." She gestured across the room. Matt couldn't see anything but shelves cluttered with junk and a broken work bench.

Reluctantly, Lily went back up the stairs. Matt breathed easier.

"This has been really hard on her," Nathan said.

"I can imagine," Matt said. "You, too."

"Yeah, but . . ." He shrugged.

"You're a good son," Matt said. "Let's find a way to get us all out of this nightmare."

He looked around. A mattress and blanket were outside the cage along with a deck of cards and a stack of Harlequin romance novels. Lily had slept down here with her son, staying by his side, because they were scared. She'd found books and a game. She was doing everything she could to hold it together after being threatened with the lives of the two people she loved most: her husband and child.

Matt looked around again, checking out the structure. For being flooded, it seemed sound. The basement was held up by thick support beams along the ceiling, and pillars roughly six feet apart went deep into the floor, reinforced with cement footings. The portion of the basement with the cell was eighteen feet by twenty-four feet, a good-sized room. It narrowed under the stairs, but he couldn't see how far back the space went.

Along the far wall, an old furnace had been knocked off its foundation and was lying at an angle, muddy nearly to the top. By Matt's estimate, the basement had been flooded halfway up the wall, but it had drained either naturally after the hurricane, or had been pumped out. The cracked concrete floors revealed dark, damp veins where water still seeped in from the outside.

Matt crossed the room and first visually inspected the shelves.

To the left was a workbench that was missing two legs. The workbench had been completely cleaned off, and the door on the front was partly open.

He squatted, carefully opened the door. Lily had already found the gas canister, so he wasn't worried about tripping something just yet, but it was in the back of his mind that Garrett's partner liked to set traps and he needed to be on alert.

An army-green industrial canister was tucked into the workbench. A label had been removed, part of the corner visible, which did not identify the contents. The canister was simple: valve, ring, and safety cap. There was a stripped-down phone strapped to the canister, and wires extended from the mechanism to the safety cap.

Matt frowned at what he thought he saw and squatted to get a closer look.

"Do you know what it is?"

"No," Matt said. "The gas isn't labeled. Definitely a phone with wires here."

"So it'll kill us?"

"I don't know. I'm not taking chances. Just give me a sec, okay?"

Matt glanced over at Nathan. He was standing at the bars, his hands gripping the metal, watching Matt. "I'll figure it out." Though he was tense, he smiled at the kid to reassure him, then turned back to the device.

He wished Michael was here. It appeared to be a simple bomb, but simple bombs were often the most volatile. Michael would know exactly what to do.

But it was just him now, and he had to make a decision. He stared at the bomb, willing a solution to come to him. Sweat poured off his brow, from the heat and from the threat in front of him.

Matt was beginning to truly hate Garrett Reid's partner. It was an odd feeling for him—he didn't hate criminals. He'd faced many violent predators and desperate criminals, and while he didn't like most of them, he pitied some and had no feelings for others. He pursued them, investigated them, arrested them, testified against them. This distinct feeling of hatred made him uneasy, as if he wasn't in control of his own emotions.

This woman had put him and Kara in a damn warehouse full of dangers. That, he could have dealt with. He was a cop, he was trained. But she also kidnapped a child and his mother and terrified them. Locked a kid in a cage and threatened to kill him, kill his father.

Matt didn't use the word *evil* lightly. He couldn't remember a time when he thought one of the criminals he pursued was *evil*. Some came close. But this woman seemed to take pleasure in setting up these deadly games—for the newlywed couples, for him and Kara, for Lily and her son. He could still hear her gleeful voice coming out of the tinny speakers at the warehouse.

A game. That's exactly what this was to her. And if someone got hurt or died, they'd lose and she'd move on to another game.

This damn basement was a trap—a cage for the child, cameras to keep the mother in line, a cloned phone to prevent her from seeking help.

He breathed in, breathed out. Focused his attention on the task in front of him. Worried that no matter what he did, it would be game over for all of them.

The wires went from the phone to the safety cap, which wasn't completely attached. Between the base of the cap, where it could be securely attached over the valve, and the valve itself, was a chunk of white putty the size of a golf ball. The wires went into the putty.

Carefully, Matt reached out and with his pinky pressed gently on the putty. It had the clay-like consistency of C-4.

Where the *fuck* did this woman get C-4?

Then Matt remembered what Kara had told him about the elevator—that she'd heard a bang and spark when she pushed on the door and the elevator fell. It could have been rigged with C-4, and the electricity in the lighting plus Kara pushing on the door could have set it off.

It almost didn't matter what type of gas was in the canister—something as benign as oxygen could create a fireball that would kill or severely injure whoever was in the basement. But Matt didn't think this lone device could take down the house.

Unless there were more like it that Lily hadn't found.

"Matt?" Nathan said, cautious.

Did he ask Lily for permission to pull the wires? He was 99 percent certain that once the wires were removed, the bomb would be inert.

Lily wouldn't do it, Matt was certain. Even a tiny risk to her son was too great. But if Garrett's partner decided at this moment to look at her camera, she would see that Matt was here. She might set it off, killing him and Nathan.

"Nathan, I need you to trust me," Matt said. He forced himself to remain calm, even as his heart raced.

"Okay."

Matt walked over to the mattress and leaned it up against the cage, a weak buffer between Nathan and the bomb. "Sit down in the far corner, behind the mattress. I can disable it."

"The gas?"

"It's not the gas you have to worry about. It's a bomb. Even if the gas ignites, it'll be short-lived. I don't know what type of gas, so the fumes might be dangerous, but it's the fireball that is our main concern. If it goes off, this should protect you." Matt hoped.

"Okay," he said. He didn't ask for his mom, or for her permission. Maybe he knew, like Matt, that Lily would never agree to this.

"What happened?" Matt asked as he adjusted the mattress to better protect Nathan should something go wrong. "How did the woman get you here?"

"She came to the house. Said her car broke down, asked if she could wait on our porch until the tow truck came. My mom invited her in. And then she took out a gun."

"You saw her?"

"She had on this big floppy hat and sunglasses, at least when she was talking to my mom."

"But?"

"I saw her put them on, before she came to the door."

"You saw her. You can describe her."

"Yeah. That's not good, is it? In the movies, if you see the bad guy, they kill you."

"No one is killing you or your mother," Matt said. He pushed at the mattress; it was as secure as he could make it. Then he walked back to the device.

Matt counted the wires. Six. He couldn't see if there was a mechanism that might detonate it if he bumped or moved it, so he grasped the first wire as close to the C-4 as possible and pulled it out.

32

While Michael drove them to Franklin Graves's office, Catherine spoke to Tony on the phone.

"This isn't a good idea, Catherine," Tony said after she explained her plan to talk to the lawyer and convince him to help. "The entire case could be thrown out. Reid could literally get away with murder."

"Reid is working with Clara Dolan, aka Hope Davidson. She's vanished—left work early, went home, and disappeared again. If Matt and Kara are still alive—and I believe they are—Clara's going after them. If we can save them, it's worth the risk."

"I agree. But most people won't. Matt and Kara are law enforcement officers—they know the risks. We don't let killers walk because they threaten our people. We don't negotiate with terrorists."

"Becca McCarthy was Garrett's high school sweetheart. His college roommate and even a former lover said he cared for her—maybe the only person he's ever truly loved. They reconnected just days before she vanished, and now she's presumed dead. Her family believed they were reconciling."

"Or he killed her because she rejected him."

"That was my first thought, but her parents and sister said she didn't reject him—she was planning a visit in February."

"Maybe he didn't want her to. Maybe he planned to end it. Maybe the idea of a commitment panicked him." Tony brought up all good points that Catherine had considered.

"They broke up in college, dated others, then saw each other again by chance."

"You've told me—told everyone—that Garrett Reid is a sociopath. So does he have feelings or not?"

Catherine winced. People misunderstood psychology. Human behavior didn't fit neatly into boxes.

"He doesn't feel empathy for his victims," she said calmly. "But that doesn't mean he's incapable of strong attachments. I believe Clara killed Becca because she feared Garrett would leave her for his first love. Clara dyes her hair lighter because she thinks Garrett prefers blondes. She's beautiful—Garrett values that. All the women he has dated were attractive. But Becca was different. She was wholesome, kind."

She paused, struggling to distill her theory.

"Garrett and Clara may have killed before, but definitely Clara," Catherine said. "I think their primary crime, their joint purpose, was to con wealthy men and women. They have been moving across country, west to east, and picked the Sapphire Shoals to continue with their cons. Maybe Clara snapped when she saw Emily on her honeymoon—maybe that was the trigger. Or maybe she picked this resort because she knew Emily was going to be here. The other victims? Clara enjoyed killing them, picked them because of their type, not because she knew them."

"Catherine, I trust you. But this will be a hard sell," Tony said.

"My point is, Clara kills these women because they remind her of Becca—or because Garrett is reminded of Becca. I need some leeway."

"I don't have any to give."

Michael pulled up in front of Graves's office and stopped the car.

"I'm going to lay everything out to Graves. I need the flexibility to offer Reid a plea."

"You're not a lawyer."

"Garrett Reid is a passive killer," Catherine said. "I don't think he would've killed anyone if not for Clara. When he learns she killed Becca, he'll talk. I need something to offer him."

Tony was silent. Catherine braced for him to shut her down. She might go through with it anyway. Losing her job meant nothing if she could save Matt.

"You can't offer a deal. That's up to the Flagler County DA. But you can say you'll recommend reduced time—if he cooperates and Matt and Kara are found alive. Be careful, Catherine. If this blows up, the Mobile Response Team is finished."

He hung up.

Catherine stared at her phone. She didn't know if this was the right move—but she knew she had to do everything to save Matt.

"I don't like breaking rules," Michael said quietly. "Because when we do, bad guys walk. But this time? I don't care. I couldn't live with myself if we didn't try everything to find Matt and Kara. Even if Reid gets off on a technicality. Besides, we have no solid evidence he killed anyone. Just a pile of circumstantial. It could take weeks—months—to build a case. Matt and Kara have been gone for more than forty-eight hours. They don't have that time."

Catherine nodded in agreement. "Let's go."

They walked up to the townhouse and tried the door; locked. They rang the bell. No one came to the door.

ALLISON BRENNAN

"His car is out back," Michael said.

Catherine didn't like this. Had Garrett killed his lawyer? Unlikely. They had followed Graves when he took Garrett to the hotel. They had a dedicated security guard watching the camera on the fifth floor. Garrett hadn't left his room except to use the gym, and someone always had eyes on him. Thirty minutes after he returned to his room, he ordered room service.

But Clara . . . would she have killed the lawyer who got Garrett out of prison? Maybe, if she thought he was a liability.

"I don't think we have probable cause to enter," Michael said.

"I've left two messages, his car is here, he hasn't been reachable."

"Let's call his legal secretary," Michael said.

Michael was right, though Catherine didn't want to delay. Time was not their friend. But told Michael to call.

After a brief conversation, he hung up and said, "She spoke to Graves an hour ago and he was in the office. She said he was tired and under strain, but told her not to come in."

Catherine called Franklin's cell phone. He didn't pick up. She said, "This is Dr. Catherine Jones with the FBI. We need to talk. Open your door, I'm standing out front."

She hit End, then waited.

Five minutes later, she heard movement, then the door opened and Franklin Graves stood there. He looked hollow and defeated. He had on the same clothes he'd worn to court yesterday. His trousers were wrinkled, his shirt sleeves rolled up and three buttons unbuttoned, no tie. His eyes were bloodshot. He looked much older than forty-five.

"I can't help you," he said but without emotion.

"Garrett Reid has a partner, his wife," Catherine said. "Her real name is Clara Dolan, but she's been using both Audrey Reid and Hope Davidson."

Franklin didn't look surprised.

"You knew."

He shrugged, opened the door. Though he didn't formally invite them in, Catherine and Michael entered. The townhouse smelled of stale food and body odor. Franklin shuffled to the couch and sat down heavily, his head in his hands. Michael closed the door.

Catherine took the secretary's chair, rolled it over across from him, and sat. Michael stood to the side.

"I believe," Catherine said, carefully choosing her words, "that Reid's wife is extremely dangerous. She abducted two federal agents in an attempt to help make her husband look innocent, and their lives are in grave danger. Clara left work at quarter to one, went to her house. She left her car there, and we don't know what she's driving, but she has nearly two hours on us. We need to find her, and I'm willing to put in a good word for Garrett if he cooperates. I'd like you to help facilitate this."

"I can't."

"I understand the ethics. I'm not asking you to violate your lawyer-client duties. I'm asking you to let me talk to him so I can save the lives of two law enforcement officers."

"You don't understand. You have no idea who they are. Especially Amber."

"Amber?"

"That's what she told me her name was when I first met her." He laughed, but there was no humor. There was only a dark hollow pain. "Amber, Audrey, Hope, who knows? *He* calls her Audrey. She has my wife and son. She promised to let them go if I do what she wants. I'm doing it."

"What does she want?"

"I thought at first to make sure Reid was released on bail. I thought that was it. Then she said I needed to 'wait in the wings' for a few days. And I'm sitting here, waiting, not knowing if Lily and Nathan are still alive. So no, I'm not going to facilitate anything. I can't risk losing them. They're innocent, Agent Jones. I don't care if I die or go to prison, I will do anything to save them."

"Then talk to me. I have information about Garrett's wife that he doesn't know. When he learns it, he'll turn on her."

Catherine didn't know if she was right. Her gut told her she was, but her gut had also told her that Garrett Reid was a psychopathic killer when, in fact, he was a co-equal or submissive partner going along with the murders for reasons she didn't quite understand.

"I've seen them together. She's insane. He is, too, going along with all her games. He humors her, he's not going to turn on her."

Something clicked. "He humors her? How so?"

Franklin shrugged. "They had sex right there." He looked at the other couch in the waiting room. "He didn't want to, he's worried about going to prison, but she insisted, and he went along with it. Oh, he enjoyed it, don't get me wrong."

"Does Garrett know she kidnapped your wife and son?"

"Yes."

"Did he know before he was released?"

"I don't think so. He was . . . angry about it. I thought maybe he'd insist she let them go, then he just gave in to her. They had sex again. They're like rabbits." He shook his head. "I'm not going to help you."

"We can protect your family—"

"You can't. She has them. You can't do anything. They're going to kill me anyway, I'm just praying they'll spare Lily and Nathan. They're innocent in all this."

"Then help us save our team and your family!" Michael interjected, speaking for the first time. "This fatalistic attitude isn't going to help anyone. You're sitting around feeling sorry for yourself, while people we care about, people *you* care about, are in danger."

"If I knew where they were, I'd tell you."

"I believe you," Catherine said. "Garrett Reid knows where they are. And if you agree to let me talk to him, he'll tell me. But time's up. Clara Dolan is on her way to kill everyone who can identify her. When she's done, she'll kill you and she and Garrett will attempt to slip away unnoticed. You help us, we have a chance of stopping her."

He hesitated. Catherine pushed. "Why did they pick you?"

He laughed, genuinely laughed, then tears streamed down his face and he ended in a sob. "I asked myself that over and over and it wasn't until I saw Amber—Audrey—that I realized why."

"Why?" Michael demanded. "Why you? Did you have an affair with her? Did she con you? Seduce you?"

Franklin was shaking his head. "No. That's the thing. I didn't sleep with her, and apparently, that was my sin. My sin was staying faithful to Lily, not succumbing to Audrey's seduction."

"When was this?"

"Seven and a half years ago. I was at a conference in Los Angeles and went to the bar because I didn't want to sit in my room. I was drinking soda and lime—I rarely drink alcohol, and never alone. I'd had a nice dinner with a friend of mine, we'd been in law school together, and I was very happy. I'd proposed to Lily the week before and knew this marriage would last. I was divorced, mostly my fault, though we've become friendlier over the years." He paused.

Catherine said, "Go on."

"I was sitting there and she had been at the bar. I had noticed her—any man would, she's a beautiful woman—but that was it. I didn't give her any signals. She came to me, sat down. Offered to buy me a drink. I declined. She flirted. I was polite, but firm, and told her I wasn't interested. She tried to change my mind, distracted me, but I was a criminal defense lawyer for more than a decade and she raised my hackles. And she poured something into my soda. I rose, was about to tell the bartender, when she got up and walked away. The next day there was a note under my hotel room door. It said, *I won't forget or forgive. You owe me.*

"I dismissed it, but apparently, this is what I owe her. My family, my reputation, my life." His voice cracked.

"We will find her and arrest her. I need to talk to Garrett."

"He won't talk to you."

"Yes, he will." Catherine hoped.

Franklin shrugged, got up. "He's at a hotel."

"We know. We have eyes on him. We'll drive."

33

When Matt and Lily left for the basement, Kara tried to keep her eyes open, but she was exhausted and her leg throbbed. She knew it was bad and worried it would take weeks to heal. The last thing she wanted was to be on desk duty while her team solved cases.

Kara was certain that desk duty was one of Dante's levels of Hell, right below forced small talk, but above going to the hospital. Chances were when they got out of this, she'd have to do all three.

She finished the water bottle, her stomach queasy from the first fluid in more than two days coupled with the blackberries she'd eaten. But she didn't puke. She leaned into the couch and let out a long breath.

Movement had her reaching out, eyes flashing open. She grabbed the wrist that was reaching for her head.

"I thought you were sleeping," Lily said.

"I—I guess I dozed off."

"I put a pot of water on to boil. When I searched the house

the other day I found an old first aid kit. The previous owners cleared out most of the personal items, but I found some old clothes and towels. They're a bit musty, but they'll do."

"Great. Go at it." She motioned to her bloody leg.

"You should change. And shower."

Kara perked up. "You have a working shower?"

"The water isn't hot—there doesn't seem to be a functional hot water heater. And there's no soap. But Matt said the factory you were in was flooded, and if that water was standing around for months there's a lot of bacteria and dirt. Don't touch the wound, but rinse off. I could only find men's clothing, but there are some shirts long enough to, um, cover you."

"Thank you," she said.

"But hurry, please? She could look at the cameras at any time. Your partner said he'll figure out what to do, but . . ."

"Trust Matt. He won't let anything happen to your son."

Lily helped Kara up, then Kara limped down the hall to the bathroom. The floor of the old house creaked and groaned.

The bathroom was small, with a pedestal sink, cracked toilet, and tiny shower. Fine for her, but she doubted Matt would be able to easily turn in it.

A towel, washcloth, and T-shirt were folded on the toilet seat. Kara stripped, grimacing as she untied Matt's shirt. Blood rolled down her leg as the wound reopened.

She put her shoes to the side, but the clothes not only reeked of body odor and disgusting flood water, but were damp and dirty. She pushed them all into a corner, except put her panties in the sink and soaked them in water. She wasn't overly modest, but she didn't want to walk around sans underwear.

The water was cool but not icy cold. Still, she winced as it ran over her sunburned body. As she got used to the temperature, she stood under the weak spray and let the water flow over her. It hurt and felt good at the same time. She looked down and saw brown and red water swirling down the drain as the grime and blood rolled off her body. When the water started to run clear she'd shift, and it would flow dark again.

With a groan, she reached over and grabbed the washcloth. It was thin and rough, but she wiped down her body, avoiding her injured leg. When she looked at the rag, it was dark with grime.

She could have stood under the trickle of water for an hour, but she rinsed as quickly as possible. The last thing she wanted was to be caught naked by whoever had taken them.

She dried herself off with the towel and more dirt and blood came off. She folded the towel over the shower door because they might need it again, then she pulled on the T-shirt. Lily was right—it fell nearly to her knees. It smelled musty, but not disgusting, and definitely not like her ruined clothes. She squeezed water out of her underwear as best she could, considered letting them air dry, then pulled them on. They might have to get out quickly. She dreaded putting on her gross shoes, but carried them out with her. She would need them if they left the house.

Her leg ached as she limped back to the living room, blood dripping to the floor.

"Kitchen," Lily called to her.

Kara stepped into the kitchen. It had the basics, including a lopsided table in the middle and three chairs. She sat on one.

"Put your leg on the other chair," Lily said as she carried a pot of steaming water from the stove to the table where she had also set up a first aid station—two towels, a first aid kit that looked like it was older than Kara, and another bottle of water. "Drink. You need fluids."

She didn't have to tell Kara twice.

Lily sat down and looked at the gash. Though it was bleeding again, it wasn't as bad as before, Kara surmised.

"I don't have gloves, but I washed my hands."

"I think I'm more likely to get an infection from the factory than from you, so I'll take my chances."

"I need to wash the wound with the hot water and I see some

foreign matter in there—probably from when you were walking through the field. This is going to hurt."

"Is there any tequila around? Whiskey? Bourbon? I'd be a cheap drunk since I haven't eaten in a couple days."

Lily shook her head and didn't smile.

Okay, no humor with this one, Kara thought. "Well then, just do it."

Kara winced as Lily washed out the wound, then took tweezers and pulled out . . . stuff. She didn't want to look and see what it was. She was still tweezing when Matt came up the stairs from the basement, which opened into the kitchen. Lily jumped up.

"What happened? Is Nathan okay?"

Matt held up a soft-looking golf ball.

"What's that?" Lily asked.

"She wanted you to believe that it was C-4."

Lily's eyes widened. "That's an explosive!"

"C-4 is, this is not. It's a high-grade clay that has the look and consistency of C-4, but won't ignite. She told you that she could remotely release the gas and poison your son?"

"Yes."

"I inspected the gas. I don't know what's in the canister, and it could be dangerous. But there is no way to release the gas, and definitely not with inert clay. It *looked* dangerous because of the wires and phone, and I thought it might be a real explosive, but once I disassembled it, I knew it was harmless."

"But you didn't know! You could have killed my son."

"I know what I'm doing, Lily. We need to get Nathan out of that cage. Kara can do it."

"I can?" she said. "You have a lot of confidence."

"In you, always," Matt said and caught her eye.

Lily looked from one to the other. "What's going on? Why would she put a fake bomb there and say it's real? Does that mean she isn't going to kill my husband?"

"The woman has killed at least six people," Matt said bluntly.

"Oh my God," Lily said, then crossed herself.

"She's capable of killing, but for now she needed you to be compliant. What better way than to threaten your son."

Lily turned to Kara, implored her. "You can break the lock?"

"I'm not Supergirl, but . . ." She glanced at Matt. "What kind of lock?"

"Common Master lock with a keyhole."

"I need really fine tools. Strong, flexible metal. Paperclip would be best, but I might be able to work with a bobby pin or a barrette, if it's small enough. And I need pliers. Unless of course you have a lock pick set handy."

"I haven't found anything like that," Lily said, her hopes falling again.

"I'll look," Matt said. "I'll find something. You finish bandaging Kara's leg."

"I need to check on my son."

Matt nodded and stepped out of the doorway.

Lily ran down the stairs and Matt sat in the chair she had vacated.

"That was stressful," Matt said.

"I'll bet. You okay?"

"I'm more worried about you."

"I got a shower. Cold water, no soap, but I feel a million times better. With you sitting there, I realize we both must have stunk to high heaven."

"Is that a hint?"

She smiled. "Not a hint, Stinky."

He took her hand, kissed it, then looked at her leg. "That needs to be bandaged."

"She will. She cleaned it out."

"It hurts?"

"Yep. I won't be running any marathons . . . but I never have run a marathon, so nothing's changed."

Lily came back up the stairs, each one creaking as she ascended. She was wiping tears from her face. "Thank you," she said quietly. "She could come back. She has a gun."

"Did you see her face?"

She shook her head. "No, neither of us did."

Kara felt Matt tense next to her, and wondered if he knew something Lily didn't.

"I'll find the tools Kara needs. You finish bandaging her leg. We'll all feel better when Nathan is out of the basement."

Matt got up, ran his fingers up her arm. There was something else going on, Kara knew. She wondered what he'd learned down in the basement.

Lily handed Kara two Tylenol packages. "They're expired, but they might help with the pain. Take all four."

Kara did, and averted her eyes when Lily opened a tube of Neosporin. She rubbed it into Kara's wound. That hurt worse than the tweezers. Then she wrapped gauze around it, followed by an ACE bandage. "That's all the gauze that was in there, so I hope it doesn't start bleeding again."

"I hope we're out of here before dark," Kara said.

"My husband has seen both of them," Lily said quietly.

"You know that she has a partner?"

"I don't know what is going on, but she talked about her husband. How Franklin owed her. She—she claimed they had an affair, but it's not true."

"You're sure about that."

"Yes. I'm not being a Pollyanna."

Kara wasn't positive, but she let it slide.

"She sent a photo of herself with my husband. She put a smiley face over her own, but Franklin looked so scared, so shaken. It was her way of telling me that I had to stay here or he would be hurt. And I think . . . her way of reminding him that she had us."

Lily looked at Kara, tears in her eyes. "They're going to kill him, aren't they? She told me that they wouldn't if he did what they want and I stayed put, but they're going to because he saw them." Now it wasn't a question.

"Not if we get out of here and stop them. Let's go downstairs so I can check out the lock and free your son."

"You can really pick a lock? I thought that only happened in movies."

"I was an undercover detective in Los Angeles. I picked up some useful skills over the years."

Kara tested her leg. She could walk on it, but it was stiff and sore.

"Be careful," Lily said. "Lean on me."

"I need to use it. It's just a cut."

"It's a deep cut, and you've lost quite a bit of blood. When Nathan is out, we'll have something to eat."

"She left you food?"

"Enough for a week, maybe ten days, if we're frugal."

"We'll be out of here long before that," Kara said.

She tested the wood railing, and it appeared to be secure enough. Using it for support, she carefully walked down the stairs, remembering what happened to Matt in the factory. They creaked, but nothing gave way. Lily had been up and down the stairs multiple times since Friday, and Matt was heavier than both of them and they hadn't broken, so Kara tried not to panic.

Though she certainly didn't like the creepy, dark basement they were in and would hate to be trapped down here. She got a whiff of a foul odor that made her nose sting a little, then it went away.

She smiled at Nathan. "Hey, how are you doing?"

"Good, now," Nathan said. "Matt said the whole thing was fake."

"Well, there could be gas in the canister, and we don't know what other surprises she has for us here, but hopefully we'll be gone before we find out."

"Matt said she locked you in a factory. That there were traps, and there might be traps here."

"So far, so good. We're going to get you out."

Kara inspected the lock. New, basic. Thick—it would be nearly impossible to cut through unless she had bolt cutters—but it had a keyhole, not a combo lock. She could break a combo lock with enough time, but it was much harder for her.

Lily said, "Why did she lie about the gas? Could she have lied about other things?"

"Yes, she could. But I'm taking her seriously. Matt and I nearly died in that factory. There were more than a half dozen traps we sprang. Maybe the gas canister was a last-minute idea, because she didn't know that her partner was going to be arrested. She had to set things up quickly."

Kara walked over to where the canister was still under the workbench. They weren't out of the woods yet. The woman could have more traps up her sleeve, and Kara didn't want to be caught in another one.

Matt came down the stairs. "I found paperclips and a couple safety pins. No pliers."

"I see you washed up a bit," Kara said. She almost laughed. He'd washed his hands and face and run water over his head, but the grime had dripped down his neck. Fortunately, he'd found a T-shirt.

"I can still taste the factory," he said and wrinkled up his nose.

Kara looked around the cluttered basement. Junk, broken glass, junk . . . She carefully picked through the items and found a small, dirty toolbox. It hadn't been opened in some time and it took her a minute to get the clasp unstuck. The metal box creaked as she opened it. Inside were tools . . . and water. "Gross," she said.

Matt walked over and handed her the paperclips. "You're

clean," he said and tilted the box so the water drained out. It smelled rank.

Then he turned the box over and let the tools fall on the floor. "So you don't have to dig through this gunk."

Lily came over with a dirty towel and handed it to Matt.

"Which one?" Matt said to Kara.

She looked. Hammer, wrench, several pliers. "Those." She pointed. "The needle-nose pliers with the broken handle." She might be able to do it without them, but pliers would help.

Matt picked them up with the towel, then wiped them down and handed them to her.

Kara stood under the bulb to get the best light and used the pliers to straighten a couple of the paperclips. The bobby pins were coated in plastic. She stripped the plastic off with the pliers. They were probably too flimsy, but they would be backup if she needed them.

She asked Matt to hold the lock for her so she didn't have to squat and go at it from below.

She took a deep breath, then slowly let it out.

Kara held one of the paperclips with the pliers in her left hand, inserted it into the keyhole. Then with her right hand used another paperclip and slowly moved it around until she could feel the mechanism. It took her three tries, and then the lock popped open. She sighed in relief. Matt pulled the lock out and Lily rushed over. He put up his hand to hold her back and said, "Wait."

"Why?" Lily said.

"Remember, she has tricks." Matt looked up at the ceiling. Nothing seemed disturbed, where anything could fall on Nathan. Still, he said, "Nathan, stand in the far corner." The boy complied. Matt slowly opened the door.

Nothing happened.

"Okay," he said.

Nathan ran out and hugged his mom. "Can we go?"

Lily looked at Matt. "You can find my husband? Have someone protect him?"

"Yes," Matt said. "First, let's disable all the cameras upstairs. And let me look at your phone. Even if she cloned it, I can communicate with my team through a message board or app. I'll find a way."

"And she won't know?"

"She might. But we have to try. Where is he?"

"We live in Jacksonville, but the case she wants him on is in Flagler."

Kara caught Matt's eye. "He's defending Garrett Reid," she said.

"Why would they want a civil lawyer for a criminal case?" Matt wondered.

"Whoever he's working for, he's out on bail," Lily said. She handed Matt her phone. "She sent me a photo of her and Franklin at his office. As proof that she was with him."

"How do you know he's out on bail?" Kara asked.

"She told me when she brought us here that as long as Franklin got her husband out of jail, he'd be alive and she'd let me know. If he didn't get him out, he'd be dead on Monday. And I got that picture Monday evening."

"Well, shit," Kara said. "They released Garrett Reid. How did the case fall apart? How did he have the money for bail? Husband? They're married? How did we not know that?"

Matt shook his head. Obviously, he couldn't know the answers, either. He said, "Lily, trust me. I will reach out to my team. I won't call or text them so hopefully she won't see what we're doing. This is the way we save your husband. Give me his full name, home and work address, all his phone numbers. We'll get him protection and let him know you're safe."

"Are we safe here?" Lily said.

"I don't know, but Kara can't walk far."

"I can," Kara insisted.

"Right now, we're safe here. We can hear a vehicle long before they arrive. I'm going to send the message and then we're going to cut the power. That should disable all the cameras, even the ones we can't find." He looked at Lily. "May I?" He held out his hand.

She reluctantly handed him her phone. "Please, Franklin is a good husband, a good father. I could not bear if he dies because I didn't listen to that woman."

"I will do everything in my power to make sure he's safe."

34

Catherine sat across from Garrett and Franklin in the sitting area of the hotel room. Garrett was not happy about this, and told Franklin he had nothing to say.

"That's fine," Catherine said, "but I have something to tell you. You're going to want to hear it."

Garrett stared at her, mouth set, but she saw the curiosity in his eyes.

"I know you're married, Garrett. We executed a search warrant on the residence of Hope Davidson. We know her name was Audrey Dolan when you married her because we found your marriage certificate. You may or may not know, but her real name is Clara Dolan. And she is a suspect in the disappearance of Becca McCarthy."

At the mention of his ex-girlfriend's name he flinched, a tiny crease popping out on his forehead. But he didn't speak.

"I don't know when exactly you met Clara, but it was in the months before Becca came home from graduate school for the Christmas break. You went over for dinner one night. Her family likes you. You and Becca talked. She told her sister and her parents that she planned to visit you in Scottsdale, because you were taking a job at a resort there. She thought that maybe you both had grown up enough where you might have a relationship again. Driving back to school, she disappeared."

"I had nothing to do with that," Garrett said flatly.

Franklin, in a monotone, said, "You don't need to answer her questions."

"I loved Becca," Garrett said, ignoring his lawyer. "Her father told me the police think some asshole predator picked her up while she waited for a tow truck."

"I don't think you hurt her," Catherine said. And watching him now, she went with her first instincts—that Garrett really had nothing to do with Becca's disappearance, and had no idea that Clara had killed her. Something Catherine felt deep in her gut was true, but she couldn't prove.

"Clara found out that you had dinner with your ex-girlfriend— a lovely young woman, very smart, and your first love. She suspected you still loved her, and if Becca returned those feelings, you'd dump Clara immediately. That was not going to happen, not to Clara. She gets what she wants. She killed Becca—I believe Becca was the first person Clara killed. I don't know what she did with the body, but there are a lot of mountains and ravines in the Santa Barbara area.

"Instead of Becca, you took Clara to Scottsdale. You moved from resort to resort. You married in Las Vegas. She lied on her marriage certificate. Her name isn't Audrey, it's Clara."

"Then you have the wrong person." Garrett's voice exuded confidence, but a hint of doubt clouded his eyes.

"You didn't know," Catherine said with a nod. "Interesting. Because Clara Dolan has a ten-million-dollar trust fund she's been living on. How do you think she was able to buy that lovely beach house?"

"I'm done," Garrett said.

"If you help us find our missing agents, I'll help you by going to the DA and asking for leniency."

"I said I was done. I don't need leniency because I didn't do anything, and you have no evidence that I have."

Michael reached over and showed Catherine a text message on his phone from Ryder.

Zack found something. He's on video chat now. You should be here.

"Think about it," Catherine said. "I'll give you fifteen minutes to consider whether you want to spend the rest of your life in prison, or maybe get out before you're wrinkled and gray. But if Matt and Kara die, you will face the death penalty."

"I didn't take them," he said calmly.

Catherine rose. "Accessory to the murder of federal agents is a capital offense. My guess is that Clara has no intention of returning here to get you."

She walked to the door with Michael. Garrett said, "Where are you going, Franklin?"

Franklin said, "I'm not staying here alone with you." And he followed Catherine out.

"Stay in the hotel," Catherine told Franklin.

"I'll be in the bar," he said and strode down the hall to the elevator. He glanced back at Catherine. "I'm not drinking," he added. "I just need to think. I really hope we're doing the right thing here, or my family is going to pay for our failure."

Catherine and Michael walked into the cramped security office. Ryder, Jim, and Sloane were sitting around a computer screen that showed Zack Heller, the team white-collar crime expert. He was talking fast, as usual.

Ryder said, "Excuse me, Zack, Catherine and Michael just came in."

Ryder moved over, but Catherine waved for him to stay. She stood behind him. "What do you have?" she asked Zack.

"I'm still working through all of Dolan's SmartGirl LLCs, but I have two things. First, her current lawyer for the LLCs. He's not returning calls, but Tony sent someone to his house. We have a warrant for the records. Second, I have all the LLC filings. The one labeled SmartGirl Fun is small, just over a million dollars. SmartGirl Business is worth about five million dollars. They both have moderate investments and pay Dolan a monthly stipend totaling eight thousand a month. The Smart-Girl Properties account is the largest and buys and sells property. The house in Flagler County is there, as well as several other properties she owns all over the country. The LLC has done extremely well buying property low and selling high. Its assets are now in excess of fifteen million. There have also been periodic deposits of large sums into the business account that I haven't been able to trace yet."

Ryder said, "She owns property or has owned property in every city she or Garrett worked in, except for New Orleans. There, the LLC rented an apartment in the French Quarter."

"When Jim sent his report," Zack continued, "I searched the records for all property in northern Florida and southern Georgia. The property LLC owns five hundred acres of farmland in Clinch County, Georgia."

"That's it," Jim said. "That's where the victims were. Where Matt and Kara must be."

"Send me plot numbers, an address, anything you have," Ryder said. "I'll map it out."

He opened his laptop as Zack said, "Sending now."

Catherine said, "Keep digging, specifically property within a day's drive of Jacksonville. She's going to run. If we don't find her in Clinch County, we'll find her at one of her other properties."

"I'm on it," Zack said and the screen went dark.

"Sloane and I will head out there now," Michael said. "Call

with updates and exact location, and call the sheriff's office as soon as you have a location."

"I'll reach out now, put them on alert," Catherine said. "I should go with you."

"Only you can break Garrett Reid," Michael said. "He knows more than he's said, and if we find that Matt and Kara are . . ." He couldn't say it. "You said she's not coming back."

"I could be wrong," Catherine said.

"But you think the odds are she'll run."

Catherine nodded.

"Then get everything out of Reid. I don't think he believed you that her true name isn't Audrey. He knows her as Audrey. Prove she's not who she told him she was, and I think he'll talk."

Catherine's lips curved up. "So you're the shrink now."

"I'm a man who has once been deeply in love. We don't like being played for a fool."

Michael opened the door to leave and Ryder said, "Wait. I think—I think Matt just emailed me. It's through some else's X account."

"Whose?" Catherine asked.

"I don't know, but it came in through my junk mail. I could have missed it."

"Read it," Michael said.

Ryder cleared his throat. "'It's Matt—we're safe for now. Garrett has a female partner. Attractive blonde, thirties. Garrett's lawyer is Franklin Graves and is being blackmailed—Garrett's partner abducted his wife, Lily, and son, Nathan; they are with me. Get him protection ASAP. We're in an abandoned farmhouse approx. one mile west of the flooded Sweetwater Cannery in GA. Lily's phone is cloned; don't respond or call. I'll be in touch when I can.'"

35

Matt put a towel in the still-warm water that Lily had used to clean Kara's wound, squeezed it out, and thoroughly wiped his face and hands. Then he ran his head under the sink, the cool water refreshing. When he dried, Lily handed him half a peanut butter and jelly sandwich. "Since you haven't eaten in a couple days, you need something, but not too much at once." She had also refilled all the water bottles and put them in the refrigerator.

"Thank you," he said. He was still filthy, but he hadn't wanted to shower and take the chance that Garrett's partner might show up.

Kara came into the kitchen and said, "The living room and eastern corner of the porch have the best vantage points to see anyone approach."

"Go to the living room, but stay inside for now. I'm going to find the breaker box and turn off the power. That should render the cameras useless. Then we'll make a plan."

"I can walk," Kara said.

Not far, he thought, but didn't say. Kara was generally realistic about her capabilities, but she always pushed herself too hard.

"If the message got through to Ryder, they'll find us before dark." Sunset was around 8:30. It was now four. Ryder would call the sheriff, the local FBI office—Jacksonville was closer than Atlanta. But the sheriff would be able to respond faster, and would know exactly where they were based on the flooded cannery. If that was the case, help could arrive in less than an hour.

If Ryder got the message . . .

"I'll be back in a few minutes," Matt said and left.

He walked carefully down the porch steps, recognizing that they had been sabotaged much in the same way that the stairs in the factory had been sabotaged. Had Lily triggered the only trap? Or were there more?

Matt was on edge, every nerve tuned to his surroundings. The house *looked* safe—but if there were traps, he might not see them until it was too late. He wanted to leave, to vanish into the woods, but waiting out there for help that might never come didn't seem much safer. At least with the house there was water and shelter.

"Stop it," he muttered. "Lily and Nathan have been here since Saturday."

Still, the unease wouldn't let up. That fake bomb on the gas canister—was it just a distraction? A warning? It felt like Garrett and his partner had more planned. Something worse. While logically Matt could believe that Lily would have triggered any booby traps—like the small explosion on the porch stairs—he couldn't be certain.

He circled the house slowly. No generator. So someone was still paying the electric bill. The waterline from the flood was obvious—two feet up the siding, right to the porch. No wonder the basement was so waterlogged. Even with a sump pump, there was still water in the lower slope of the basement. Maybe the house wasn't salvageable, which was why it had been abandoned.

Had Garrett found the place like this? If so, why the electricity? Matt itched to call Ryder, to hand this whole mess over to someone who could dig into property records, ownership, utilities—*anything*. The house was mostly empty now, but someone had once lived here.

Matt found the electrical panel and cut the power. The low hum vanished, leaving only silence—and the creaks of a century-old farmhouse settling in its bones.

They were isolated. Woods on three sides, farmland to the east. No other houses in sight, just the distant silhouette of the old cannery barely visible across the field he and Kara had crossed earlier.

He decided then that he didn't want to stay here. Even with the cameras off, Matt didn't trust Garrett or his partner. They were too smart, too deliberate. They had set up the factory and the house as a series of traps, and Matt was certain they hadn't caught them all.

They'd grab supplies, only what the four of them could carry, and hike into the woods. It wasn't cold at night—they wouldn't freeze—and he'd keep within sight of the house, in case rescue showed up.

If Ryder got the message.

He circled again, eyes scanning the foundation of the house. Basement windows. A heavy cellar door down a half flight of slick, mud-caked stairs. Water had pooled outside it, thick and foul-smelling—like chemicals and sewage. Flood damage? Or was the septic system ruptured?

The sunlight glinted off something in the mud. Glass?

He squatted, inspected the flash. It was a ring. He picked it up, turned it around in his fingers. A diamond wedding ring, caked in mud. He wiped it off and it looked familiar . . . then it hit him.

He'd seen this ring in photos of Emily Henderson's wedding. The ring hadn't been found on her body, and they'd considered it was either lost during her ordeal, or the killer kept it as a souvenir.

Emily Henderson had been in this house. He opened the cellar door. It creaked as he pulled, but wasn't locked. On the inside of the door he saw matted blond hair stuck into the rough boards, as if ripped out by the roots because the long strands had been caught on something.

Emily had been here. Had letting her escape been part of the game? To think she'd been saved only to force her into a more deadly trap?

He went back inside the house and announced to the group, "We can't stay here." His voice was low and firm. He caught Kara's eye, and she nodded. She was with him, even though she hadn't seen what he'd seen.

"Is she coming back?" Nathan asked.

"That, I don't know, but it's a risk, and I don't want to be trapped in here. Plus, Garrett and his partner set traps all over the abandoned factory, and I fear we're missing something here. I suspect at least one of the other victims was kept here."

Lily sucked in her breath, eyes wide.

Matt said, "We'll hike into the woods. If my team got the message, someone should be here within an hour, and we'll see them long before they reach the house. If they didn't get the message, we'll head out at dusk and find help."

"Okay," Kara said. When Lily hesitated, Kara told her, "It's the smart play here. If that woman checks the cameras and sees they're out, we don't know what she might do."

"Leave your phone here," Matt said. "She might be able to track it. If no one comes in an hour, I'll risk calling my team directly. She'll know on her end, but we need to make contact."

"You're right," Lily agreed and put her phone on the couch.

"I'll get the water," Nathan said and went to the kitchen.

"I refilled bottles and put them in the refrigerator," Lily called after him. "Thank you," she said quietly. "Nathan knows what's going on. He's nearly twelve, observant, but I didn't want to scare him."

"He's a strong, smart young man," Matt said. "You should be proud of him."

Lily blinked back tears. "Thank you. I'll help him. And get some food, too."

She followed her son. Matt turned to Kara, touched her. He needed to touch her to make sure she was okay. "I found Emily Henderson's wedding ring outside in the mud, near the cellar doors that lead to the basement."

"That cage," Kara said, disgusted. "What game were they playing?"

"The Hendersons were the first. Maybe they didn't have the factory set up yet."

She sighed, leaned into him. "You've been a rock."

"So have you."

She shook her head. "Last night I was a mess."

"You didn't act like it."

"Yes I did. I felt trapped. I hate feeling like I have no way out, like a rat in a maze. I panicked. You didn't waiver. You were calm, you were there. I don't know how to explain it. But I felt . . . like we were going to make it. Together. I just wanted you to know."

He kissed her. "I wasn't calm on the inside. I've been in a lot of dangerous situations, but the last few days have been the worst."

"Ditto," she said with a half smile.

Nathan came into the living room with a grocery bag of water bottles and food. "Where's your mom?" Matt asked.

"She went upstairs to get blankets."

"I'll help her," Kara said and got up.

"You can't go up and down stairs with that bum leg," Matt said. "You and Nathan go out to the oak tree. We'll meet you there."

"It's you and me, kid," Kara said and steered Nathan toward the door.

Matt's foot hit the first stair just as the whole house groaned, a low, hungry sound that filled him with dread. The floor tilted under his feet. A sharp crack echoed somewhere in the basement, support beams splintering. He froze for a half second, heart hammering.

Crunch.

The sound came from below, deep and sickening, a *crunch crunch crunch*. The stairs pitched and shuddered. Matt grabbed the railing for balance. The old wood flexed unnaturally beneath his hand.

"Lily!" he shouted as he ran halfway up the stairs, needing her to hear him. "Get down here now!"

In a gut-punch moment, it all clicked: the chemical tang he'd smelled in the basement, the steady drips that he'd dismissed as water. Another trap, just like Garrett and his partner had done in the factory. A chemical solvent dissolving the old wood of the support beams. Acid or lye, something that worked slowly over time until the house collapsed.

He feared turning off the electricity had accelerated the collapse. Or their captor had noticed the cameras were down and somehow set off the chain of events. Either way, they had to get out now.

"Lily!"

Lily appeared at the top of the stairs, blankets bundled in her arms, face pale and panicked.

"Drop it! Hurry!" He reached out his arm, urging her to run down the stairs.

The house lurched again, sharper this time, like a boat slamming against the dock. Lily stumbled forward, blankets spilling from her arms, as she tumbled down the stairs.

The banister snapped under her weight and she fell. Matt tried to catch her, but she rolled over the edge into the hall.

He rushed over to Lily and helped her up. The floor shifted again. The boards in the old wood floor visibly separated beneath their feet. Matt grabbed her around the waist as the house continued to fall apart around them.

He heard Kara screaming for him, and he prayed she had left with Nathan, that she didn't come back inside, that she didn't risk her life. He was *not* going to die in here.

Behind them, the stairs caved in with a thunderous crash, an entire section folding in on itself.

The house had gone crooked, like it was being swallowed sideways into the basement. He heard nothing except the screaming of wood, glass, metal. Every step was a fight uphill. Walls buckled. The floor dipped then rose. A cabinet fell in the kitchen with a deafening *bang*, hitting him in the shoulder and causing him to lose his grip on Lily. The table slid across the scarred linoleum floor.

"Keep going!" Matt shouted above the noise of destruction. He reached out for Lily again, sparing a glance behind him when he couldn't feel her.

She tripped and went down hard on one knee. She screamed and reached out.

"I got you!" he said as he yanked her up just as the table slammed into his side, knocking the wind out of him. He barely held on to her wrist. He would not let go.

The windows blew out one by one all around them, glass bursting inward. The sting of shards slashed his cheek, but he didn't stop. He saw the light from the open front door. It was higher than it should be as the center of the house was falling down into the basement . . .

And then he smelled it.

Gas.

It hit him like a wall: thick, raw, metallic. The stove. He looked—just a glance—and saw the pipe ripped loose from the wall, the stove askew.

"Faster! It's gonna blow!"

The front door swung open and closed as the house undulated, a gaping escape that looked farther away than it should have. He lunged toward it, dragging Lily as the floorboards dropped away in chunks behind them.

Almost there. Almost there.

The floor heaved. The house jerked to the side like something had punched its foundation. Lily's fingers slipped from his.

"Matt!" Lily screamed.

He lunged for her, but she was gone.

Audrey turned onto the long gravel road as the factory loomed in the distance. She smiled.

Her factory. Her prison.

When she'd bought this property last year, it had been the farmhouse she was most interested in. It had a cage in the basement! That's when her plan for Emily Masters Rowe soon-to-be Henderson fully gelled. She'd break Emily. It would be easy.

The factory just came with the land, practically giving it away, and she hadn't even gone inside.

Until Emily and her pathetic, crying husband escaped.

Garrett had to go back to work. No choice. If he disappeared now, the questions would start—too many questions. The police were already sniffing around the resort, asking about the Hendersons. But Garrett wasn't nervous. They had planned this down to the smallest detail. No direct connection. A clean alibi. By the time the newlyweds vanished, Garrett was already halfway through his shift. Six hours later, when no one was looking, they drove through the night to the farmhouse in Georgia with two unconscious bodies in the back of the van.

They pushed them through the cellar doors like sacks of meat and the bodies rolled down the stairs. Splashed into the water in the basement.

Maybe they could just let them drown, Audrey had thought. But that wasn't fun. And when they heard Josh and Emily moving and groaning from below, they knew they had to restrain them.

They went around to the front of the house, down the basement stairs, and dragged the two half-conscious people into the iron cage, the prison that had been built in the corner. Garrett had thought it was odd and disturbing that someone had a jail cell in their basement, but Audrey thought it was exciting. Her own prison!

For bad, bad girls who looked down on her. For bad, bad girls who took things from her. Her man. Her job.

Garrett had to go back to work. Audrey stayed behind.

When Emily and Josh stirred—groggy, confused, scared— Audrey's hands trembled. This was new. She'd never had prisoners before. But fear melted fast. Curiosity took over. Then glee. She turned it into a game.

And it was delicious.

She put Emily on trial. Dragged her into the center of the cellar like some medieval court, tied her to a chair, and listed every petty, poisonous thing Emily had done to Audrey. Stolen Charlie. Stolen her idea. Stolen her promotion. She presented the "evidence" with theatrical flair—the acting coach who kicked her out of his classes clearly didn't recognize talent—grinning while Emily sobbed and shook her head. Denial, denial, denial.

Until the hunger set in.

After a day and a half without food or water, Emily cracked. She confessed everything through tears and cracked lips. Josh, her new husband who sat crying in the cage, told her he loved her.

Pathetic.

And then Emily thought Audrey would let her go. Begged her.

"Please. Please let us go. I won't tell anyone."

Right. Did she think that Audrey was stupid? That she'd fall for that?

313

Yet . . . Garrett wasn't due back until tomorrow. Audrey still had time. So she invented another game.

A dangerous one.

She left the basement to set up the traps, and an hour later returned, unlatched the cage, and whispered, "Run."

She assumed they'd take the road—the obvious way out—straight into her row of bear traps, perfectly hidden beneath leaves and dirt. But they didn't. They bolted through the fields instead, toward the old abandoned factory.

Wrong move. And for a minute, Audrey was worried. That she had made a mistake, that they would get away, that she'd have to leave everything behind, including the love of her life.

Except, it ended up being the perfect move.

Audrey retrieved her gun then followed them silently through the fields. They were crying, telling each other to be quiet, breathing heavily, slowing down as they fought the increasing wind. Audrey stayed fifty feet behind, the moon only a tiny crescent obscured by clouds. It was going to rain tonight. It was all she could do to not laugh out loud. They thought they were getting away!

Maybe she'd shoot them and dump them in the creek. Except . . . if someone found them, they'd find her farmhouse and the factory and Audrey wouldn't be able to use her new prison again.

Audrey watched from the edge of the overgrown field while Emily and Josh stood outside the door and debated what to do. They were both angry, upset, and Audrey knew their so-called love was fake as they argued. Emily wanted to hide. Josh wanted to find help. Finally, Audrey grew bored and fired her gun into the ground. "Time's up," she said.

They ran into the factory and Audrey came in behind them, just in time to watch as Josh ran into a pile of junk and impaled himself. Emily screamed, but didn't even try to help him as his body jerked and blood poured out of both his mouth and the hole the rebar made in his chest.

The bitch. Typical.

Instead she ran farther into the factory. As Audrey pursued her, she realized this factory had so much potential! It would be far more fun to play here than in her farmhouse prison.

Emily ran blindly, falling, splashing through the water, trying to push herself up, wearing herself out.

Adrenaline could only take you so far, Audrey mused.

Thunder roared in the distance, and Emily screamed, tripped, collapsing in the shallow water that had flooded the factory. Audrey came up from behind, shined her flashlight. Emily was sobbing, gasping, falling into the water and pushing herself up. She was bleeding, too, her face all cut up. Emily reached out for her, begging for help, calling her by a name no longer hers.

"Clara . . . please . . ."

Audrey just smiled. And watched.

Watched her fade.

Then she handcuffed her to a piece of machinery and Emily didn't even fight her.

The next twelve hours were intoxicating. Audrey wandered the factory's maze of metal and rot, every corner a potential trap, every hallway a perfect dead end. She could see it all so clearly now.

This wasn't just a hiding place.

It was an arena. A stage.

With Garrett's help, they would build the most exquisite escape house the world had ever seen. It would be a masterpiece. It would be so much fun.

And it had been fun until the stupid FBI ruined it.

Audrey stopped the van next to the hidden door around the side of the factory. She loved having this game room. She was going to miss it. The two agents deserved to die slowly for what they did, but her gun was going to have to end them.

It really wasn't fun to shoot people. She'd only done it once, and that bitch hadn't even had the good sense to fall over and die and make Audrey's life easier. No. She had to run, creating untold problems until Audrey finally caught up with her.

That was then. Now Audrey was smarter.

She pulled up her phone and checked the cameras to make sure her prey were still on the factory floor.

Frowned. The cameras weren't working. Those fucking asshole feds! What had they done?

Then she realized she didn't hear the generator.

Gun in hand, she walked around the side of the factory and stared at the broken window.

No.

No!

When had they gotten out? It couldn't have been long ago, because there wasn't anyone around. No cops, no sheriff, no feds, no one. But her heart pounded; she couldn't stay here for long.

There was blood—good, they were hurt. Maybe dying. She walked along the unpaved road a few feet, looked toward her house, which she couldn't quite see.

Could they have . . . ?

She pulled up her phone and looked at the cameras at the farmhouse.

They were down, too.

She growled. These people were just *impossible*. They couldn't just play by the rules! She hit the archive and watched in high speed for a few minutes.

Damn, damn, *damn!*

She would just have to take care of all of them.

Audrey started toward her van when she heard something

in the distance. She stopped, turned toward the house, hand up to shield her eyes from the late afternoon sun.

She saw a flash of something, then heard a distant crash, as if boulders rolled down a cliff like an avalanche.

Then . . . nothing . . . but she knew what was going to come.

One.

Two.

Three.

Boom!

An explosion shook the ground beneath her. A fireball exploded where the house had been.

She sneered. Served them right thinking they could *cheat* the game. No one cheated her. She won.

I won, I won, I won!

Clara Audrey Amber Hope *Reid* always won.

She laughed and climbed back into her van.

Then she stopped laughing. There was a chance—a small chance—that the FBI agents had reached out to someone. A small chance that she might be exposed . . . She couldn't go back for Garrett. Not yet.

Soon. Maybe.

Instead of heading south toward Jacksonville, she headed north, then east, toward her family's vacation house.

She called Garrett. He answered on the first ring.

"Babe?"

"Boom."

"You're sure?"

"I saw."

"Okay. Franklin screwed us. We need to use the escape plan."

"I am."

He was silent.

"Tomorrow, slip away and join me," she said.

"That wasn't the plan."

"I'm concerned that the FBI might—*might*—be onto me. I'm not coming back."

"They're watching *me*."

"Unfortunately, the lawyer's family went *boom*, too."

Silence. And in the silence, Audrey heard weakness. She had loved Garrett because he wasn't weak. Now she didn't know what to think.

"Audrey," he said, his voice low. "You killed a kid?"

She frowned. He knew that might be a possibility, and he sounded so . . . *critical*. And worse, he knew not to say those kind of words on the phone.

"Of course not," she snapped.

He sighed. "Okay. Okay. Just—I'll find a way to leave. I'll meet you on the island. Are you sure your friends won't be there?"

"I'm sure," she said.

She loved Garrett, but she had never told him she (sort of) owned half the fucking island. It was easier to say it belonged to friends, anyone except her very, very, *very* wealthy family.

"It might be a day or two."

"Don't be followed. I love you, baby. I can't wait to see you."

"I love you, too . . . Clara."

She froze. She had never told Garrett that name. She almost forgot it was her name.

"Who's Clara?" she asked, maybe waiting a beat too long, her heart pounding.

"Why didn't you tell me?"

He knew. Who told him? How did he find out? "It was a long time ago. My parents disowned me. I didn't want the name they gave me."

"Do you remember what I told you when we first met?"

She swallowed. "Of course. No lies, no games."

"You lied to me."

"I didn't. I legally changed my name to Audrey. It's more sophisticated than *Clara*. Don't make a big deal about this."

"I'm not," he said. "I'll see you soon."

He hung up.

Dammit. She had a lot of thinking to do.

She loved Garrett, really she did, but it might be time for a divorce, of sorts.

Her instincts were sharp, and there had been just a teeny tiny hesitation in his voice. He doubted her. And she couldn't have that.

How did he find out? Had the FBI . . . had they gone through her house? Through her personal items? Those *bastards*. And they told him, which was why Garrett thought that Franklin wasn't with them. Franklin facilitated everything, the asshole. Damn him. She was glad his family was dead, he deserved to suffer.

She'd go to the island, but she wouldn't be there when Garrett arrived. If they were meant to be, he would find her.

And if they weren't meant to be? He would be dead.

36

By the time Michael and Sloane were in the helicopter halfway to the five-hundred-acre spread that Clara Dolan owned, they had far more information than they had when they left.

Sweetwater Cannery had flooded last September when Hurricane Helene swept through the coastal south. It had already been a struggling business, and the owners abandoned it. The cannery bordered Dolan's property, which had been partly flooded. The owner was a seventy-year-old man who'd lost his wife the year before, and because of the damage, he sold it cheap and moved in with his daughter in Atlanta.

Clara had bought the property in October, one month before Emily and Josh were killed.

The sheriff knew the area, and was heading there before the helicopter took off. He would arrive before them, but they wouldn't be far behind.

The cannery was nearly a three-hour drive from Clara's house in Flagler County. Her house was twenty minutes north of the resort, and they knew she'd stopped home because she left her car there. That meant that she could already be at the cannery by now.

And when she found that Matt and Kara were gone, her next stop would be the farmhouse. Michael hoped the sheriff got there first.

The pilot said into the headset, "Agent Harris, there's a call coming in from the sheriff's department on the ground."

"Okay, thanks, please put him through."

The pilot pressed a couple buttons, and said, "Deputy Aberdeen? You're on with the FBI."

"Agent Harris?"

"Yes, sir, have you found them?"

"We're ten minutes out and just got a call about an explosion in that area. Fire and ambulance have been dispatched. I see smoke in the distance."

Michael's fists clenched. He said to the pilot, "ETA?"

"Seventeen minutes, sir."

"We'll meet you there, Deputy," Michael said, fearing they were too late.

Catherine had found Franklin in the bar sitting alone with a glass of water untouched in front of him. She told him that her agent had found his wife and son and they were, for now, safe.

"Thank God. Thank you." Tears leaked from his eyes.

"I'm going to talk to Reid with or without you, Mr. Graves."

"I need to talk to my wife."

"We're not in communication with them yet. Two of my agents are en route now." She nodded to Ryder, who showed Franklin the message.

He read it slowly, or multiple times, Catherine wasn't certain.

"Okay. Good. Thank you, really." He took a deep breath. "If you talk to Reid without me, you're going to jeopardize your case," he said. "He may get away with everything."

"Not everything, but yeah, it creates problems. But he has information I need."

"If I was doing due diligence, I would tell him not to speak to you. There is no evidence of his involvement with this woman's schemes—except for my knowledge." He paused. "They were going to kill me, weren't they?"

"Most likely."

"I'll join you."

"He has information about the whereabouts of Clara Dolan, and I need it. I can't offer a legal deal, but my word is good—I will help him get a reduced sentence if we find her before anyone else dies. We'll find evidence at the cannery, and we'll have the statements of your wife, son, and our team members. Reid won't walk on murder, I'll make that clear, but we can make it easier for him. Plus, Ryder has information about his old girlfriend that may help him make the right decision."

"Alright. Let's go."

37

Matt had no time to think.

Lily slipped through the floor and he leapt toward her. He couldn't see her—dust and smoke swirled around him. He reached blindly and managed to grasp her limp wrist and pull her from the growing hole in the floor.

The house shook and rumbled as the two stories began to cave into the basement. Only with sheer adrenaline was he able to pull the woman from the depths of the collapsing structure.

Through it all, he heard Kara calling for him.

Stay out! Stay out! He wanted to scream but dust filled his lungs and he was coughing. He collapsed, Lily next to him. His side ached from where the table hit him. He crawled, dragging the unconscious woman with him. He wasn't going to make it.

Kara was in the doorway, trying to keep her balance as the house shook like an earthquake. She looked angelic, the sun glowing behind her. And Matt feared he was already dead and this was the last vision he'd have.

"Go!" She ran to them. "Go, I have her. Get out!"

She sounded angry and scared at the same time. Matt couldn't gain his balance, and half crawled to the door. Kara grabbed Lily under the arms and dragged her out. At the threshold, he pulled himself up, then picked up Lily and they stumbled down the stairs and away from the house.

The explosion pushed them all to the ground, but they were far enough away that they weren't sucked into the smoldering pit.

Nathan was crying. "Mom? Mom!"

Matt couldn't see much, his eyes blurry from the gas and dust. "Kara—is she—?" He prayed she wasn't dead. She couldn't be dead. The poor woman didn't deserve that fate.

"She has a pulse. She's unconscious, and she's bleeding. So are you."

"The windows exploded."

Kara rolled Lily on her back, and Nathan put his mom's head in his lap. Tears streamed down his face. "Mom, please be okay."

"She's breathing," Kara said. "That's a good sign."

The house was on fire, and it was hot. "We need to get to the clearing," Kara said. "If these trees catch fire, we're screwed. Can you make it?"

Matt nodded. "I'll get her." He motioned to Lily.

"Like hell you will. Nathan, you pick up her legs, I'll pick up her shoulders, and we'll carry her to that willow tree on the edge of the field, okay? It's about fifty yards—can you make it?"

Nathan wiped the tears from his face and nodded.

Matt followed Kara and Nathan as they carried Lily. It had been close, too close.

But they were all alive. They were going to make it.

Lily moaned, but didn't fully regain consciousness. Nathan held her hand as they sat on the ground. Matt leaned against the tree, and Kara finally sat, put her head on his shoulder. "Dammit, Matt, that was too close. I'm not going to lose you because of some fucking psycho."

"You didn't." He kissed the top of her head and winced as

his side burned with pain. "Don't let Catherine hear you talk that way."

"I want that woman's head on a platter."

"We'll find her."

"I hear sirens," Nathan said. He started to get up, but Matt motioned for him to stay put.

"Let's see who comes before we make ourselves known."

They heard the sirens, but it was several minutes before they saw lights. Then Kara said, "I hear a helicopter."

Matt heard it, too. He started to get up, but Kara said, "I think you have a broken rib."

"I doubt it," he lied. "Just bruises, I'm sure."

She glared at him, then kissed him. "I don't believe you. Just sit."

Kara got up and limped over to where a fire truck and police car pulled up side by side. There was another sheriff's car behind them, two more fire trucks, and a paramedic. She held her hands up and said, "I'm Kara Quinn, FBI." Technically, she was still LAPD, but figured saying that would elicit too many questions. "We need paramedics over here STAT. A woman, thirties, unconscious. My boss is injured, likely a broken rib, and he's bleeding."

The deputy was on his radio, and as he spoke to someone, Kara watched a helicopter land in the field next to them.

Michael climbed out of it.

"Michael," she said though no one could hear her over the sirens and rotor blades.

She started crying. Damn, she never cried. But the tears came and wouldn't stop as she limped toward him.

Michael ran to her, picked her up and squeezed.

"Kara." He kissed the top of her head and put her down, gently held her face between his large hands. Stared at her as if he thought she might be a ghost. "Are you okay? My God, you're here. You're alive."

She nodded because she was unable to speak. She hugged him again. His hug hurt her multitude of bruises, but she didn't want to let go.

"Is Matt—is he okay?" Michael whispered.

She nodded into Michael's chest. "It was too close, Michael. Too close."

He held her tight. She was so damn happy that Michael was here. He wrapped his arm around her waist, and she led him to the tree where Matt was sitting. Three paramedics were there, two working on Lily and one checking Matt.

"Ma'am, you're bleeding," the paramedic who was checking Matt's vitals said.

She looked at her leg. The bandage that Lily had put on was red again. The cut had broken open.

"He's worse," she said.

"Kara," Michael said, and urged her to sit next to Matt. "Just humor me and let them check you out."

Kara agreed, but looked over at Lily and Nathan. "How is she?" Kara asked.

"She's coming around, but has a serious concussion and a deep wound in her side. A lifeline chopper has already been called in. ETA is ten minutes."

"Can't you get her to a hospital faster?"

"Closest trauma center is an hour away."

"She needs to be in protective custody, both her and her son," Kara said.

A deputy walked over. "Hello, folks. I'm Deputy Aberdeen."

Michael said, "Agent Michael Harris. We spoke on the phone."

"Yes, and I also spoke to your boss, Assistant Director Greer. He filled me in on what's been going on with y'all. But he didn't know where you two have been for the last what, fifty-some hours?"

"How about if we write it in a report?" Kara said.

Matt grimaced as the paramedic inspected his ribs.

"Broken?" Kara asked.

"I'd need an X-ray to confirm, and we need to make sure there's no internal bleeding. You should both be checked out at the hospital."

"Did I understand correctly," Aberdeen said, "that you two were held captive in the Sweetwater?" He gestured with his thumb across the field toward the cannery.

"Yes," Matt said. "And no one goes in."

"Excuse me?" He sounded irritated, as if Matt was giving him an order.

"There are booby traps and dangers all over the place. A net of bowling balls is secured over the main set of doors. If you go in that way, they'll fall on you. And that's just one of many potential dangers."

Aberdeen nodded and stepped away, already talking rapidly over his radio.

"Damn, there's already cops over there," Kara said. "I hope they're okay."

Matt took her hand and said, "You're bleeding again."

"So I've been told."

"Let me just finish here, then I'll check your wound," the paramedic said.

"It's just a cut," Kara said.

"You need stitches and antibiotics," Matt said.

"Michael, what's happening on your end?" Kara asked.

"When Matt didn't show up for his meeting with Tony Monday morning, Ryder figured out pretty quickly that something happened to you both at the resort. We flew down within hours. Reid was released on bail Monday afternoon, and since then we've learned quite a bit about Reid and his partner, Clara Dolan. She has many names, and legally her name is now Audrey Reid."

"Reid?"

"She is in fact legally married to Garrett. She also went by the name Hope Davidson."

Matt said, "Davidson works at the resort. In the gym."

"Yes, sir," Michael said. "In a nutshell, while Garrett Reid was a willing and able partner, Clara Dolan was the instigator. The first victim—Emily Masters Henderson—used to work with Clara and married, then divorced, Clara's ex-boyfriend. I honestly don't understand why she was so offended by Masters. And she has control of a multi-million-dollar trust fund. That's how we found you. One of her LLCs owns this property, and Jim matched forensics with this area, which helped us narrow it down. And then Ryder got your message."

Michael relayed what they'd done over the last twenty-four hours, and how they were clued in to Hope Davidson as Garrett's partner.

"Damn, I should have seen that," Kara said.

"Why?"

"Because she was too attentive at the gym. Asked questions that were all small talk—where are you from, oh you're newlyweds, how cute, things like that. I mean, some people are just chatty, but in hindsight, I don't know. It seemed off, but I didn't register that she was involved."

"Because we weren't thinking he had a partner," Michael said.

"I see it now."

"So you didn't see her when she grabbed you?" Michael said with a frown.

"Nope," Kara said. The paramedic told Matt to stay still, and moved over to Kara. She winced as he removed the bandage on her leg. "I sensed that someone was watching me, but as I was about to check it out, we both felt sick and then she hit us with tranquilizer darts. I remember nothing after that until we woke up in the factory twenty hours later."

Another helicopter was landing, this one red with a white cross underneath. Conversation was impossible, but Kara shouted to Michael, "They both need protection. We don't know where Hope, Clara, Audrey, whoever she is, is going next."

Matt said, "Nathan can identify her. He saw her before she put on a disguise and kidnapped him and his mother."

Michael nodded, went over to where Sloane was talking to the deputies, spoke to the group, then pulled out his phone and walked away from the noise.

Lily had regained consciousness once, then went out again. Kara said to Nathan, "She's going to make it."

"Promise?"

What should she say? She couldn't promise—she had no idea what her injuries were. She didn't want to give false hope, but she needed to give him hope.

"She was talking there a minute, right?" Kara said. "That's a good sign. And honestly, we didn't make it out of that house to have her do anything but make a full recovery."

"Are you coming with us?"

"I don't know," Kara said. She didn't want to go to the hospital, but she knew that someone would make her, and she also knew she needed to get stitches. Her leg was mostly numb now, with periodic sharp stabs of pain. She hoped she could walk on it soon. "There isn't enough room in the helicopter, but I'll see you soon. That I promise."

Nathan nodded. The paramedics were ready to transport her, and Sloane came over to Nathan. "I'm FBI Special Agent Sloane Wagner, you can call me Sloane. I work with Matt and Kara, and I'm going with you and a deputy to the hospital where we'll meet your mom, okay? She'll get there faster and get the medical attention she needs, but it won't take us long."

Nathan glanced at Kara as if looking for permission.

"Sloane is the best," Kara said. "She'll make sure nothing happens to you or your mom."

Matt said, "Nathan, you saw the woman. If you see her again, tell Sloane immediately, okay?"

Nathan gave Kara a hug, then hugged Matt. "Thank you both. If I was still in that cage . . ."

Matt glanced at Kara and she could read a lifetime in his eyes. It had been *way* too close, for all of them.

Nathan left with Sloane. The paramedic said, "You definitely need stitches and maybe surgery."

Kara groaned.

"I can't say for sure, but it's a deep cut. The doctor may be able to wash it out and stitch it, but it'll hurt. You'll want pain killers. And antibiotics, considering you've been walking around with an open wound for who knows how long."

"About seven or eight hours," Kara said.

Michael came over and pocketed his phone. "That was Catherine."

"Good news?" Kara said hopefully.

"Garrett Reid isn't talking, and he left the hotel."

"Is he in the wind?" Matt asked.

"No, the deputy following him says it appears he's heading to his apartment."

"Why didn't Catherine arrest him?" Matt demanded.

"She thinks he'll lead us to Clara Dolan. Now she wants to know if Kara feels up to talking to him."

"She wants me? She never wants me to talk to suspects."

Michael showed them a photo of a pretty young blonde. "Who's that?" Matt asked.

"Becca McCarthy. Garrett's high school girlfriend. Catherine believes that Garrett and Becca were getting back together seven and a half years ago when Clara killed her. Becca has been missing since then, and Garrett has an ironclad alibi for her disappearance."

"So that doesn't tell me why Catherine wants me to take a stab at Reid."

"Because you look just like her," Matt said.

Kara didn't see it. Becca looked . . . sweet. Innocent. Big smile, bright eyes.

"On the surface, but—"

"You do. And things are beginning to make sense. But you need to be checked out first."

"We're going to lose her, aren't we? She's nowhere. You," Kara gestured to Michael, "said she'd gone to her house and was heading up here. When she sees all these cops she's going to drive on by."

"If Garrett Reid attempts to flee, Flagler County Sheriff's will arrest him," Michael said. "Anson, the DA, isn't happy about it because the case is a mess, but we're not going to let him get away. If we have to, we'll take him into federal custody as a material witness."

"Do you think Reid knows where Clara went?" Matt asked.

"Yes," Michael said. "Catherine believes they had an escape plan, and that Clara had no intention of returning for Garrett. But that won't upset him, according to Catherine. He might have even told her to leave and protect herself. But Catherine is positive that if we can convince him that Clara killed Becca, he'll talk."

"You'll have to fill me in on all the details," Kara said, "if I'm going to have a chance to turn Reid against his partner." It felt really weird for her to think that they were married.

The paramedic interjected, "And she needs stitches. The longer she delays in getting medical care, the more complications. It's pretty serious."

Matt looked from Kara to Michael. "We'll fly back on that chopper of yours, go straight to the hospital in Jacksonville. Then talk to Reid."

"I have an idea," the paramedic said. "As long as you sign a consent form, I can work on your leg in the ambulance and drive you down there. It's a couple hours, and my boss will have my hide, but if it'll help you get the woman who put that boy in a cage, it's worth it."

Kara frowned. "How did you—?"

"I listen," he said. "Y'all've been very chatty."

"What's your name?" she asked.

"Billy."

Kara looked at Matt. She saw what she wanted in his eyes. Love, determination, and most importantly, complete trust.

She nodded. "Okay, Billy, let's do it."

38

Seven and a Half Years Ago

Garrett followed Becca upstairs to her childhood bedroom that looked and smelled like they were still in high school. She turned, closed the door behind him, and smiled. Was she thinking what he was thinking? That they'd both lost their virginity here, in her bed, on Becca's sixteenth birthday?

All these feelings were filling him, feelings he only had when he was with Becca.

All the other women he had been with were games. Fun, satisfying, interesting . . . but he didn't feel this wonderful and terrifying pressure in his chest when he was alone with them. He didn't feel hot and cold and happy and sad all at the same time.

Becca sat at the end of her bed and patted the space next to her. He dutifully sat down, then took her hand because he needed to touch her.

"I've missed you," he said. It was the last thing he planned to say. "Dinner was nice."

"I've missed you, too."

He touched her face, pushed her soft, wavy blond hair behind her ear. "Do you think . . . has too much happened?"

"I think we should take it slow."

He nodded. "Slow. But moving forward."

She smiled, kissed him lightly. "I've never stopped loving you, Garrett. I just didn't know it when we were nineteen."

"I hurt you."

"We hurt each other."

Garrett remembered their fight. Rather, Becca's fight. He stood there and listened to every complaint she had about him, things he said and did and didn't do, and he took it. Then he'd said, "If you don't love me, just go." And she left.

That was when everything changed for him. When he no longer cared about what other people thought. Becca didn't love him, so nothing else mattered. He had fun. He did whatever he wanted. His moral compass—the love of his life—didn't love him. He had no moral compass of his own.

"We're different people," Becca said. "That's why it worked so well, but I didn't see it until I no longer had it. Seeing you again after four years? Wow. Everything came back. Every feeling, every dream. Back then, I guess I wanted you to fight for me. Which was dumb. We had everything, and I thought you didn't care enough. That if you cared, you would have fought back, in some twisted belief that your willingness to argue would prove your love."

"If you didn't love me, what would be the point? What would I be fighting for?" Garrett said. "I don't show my feelings because I really don't have the . . . well, intensity that other people have. But I love you. I have always loved you. You make me feel things I don't feel with anyone else."

"We go slow. I'll visit you in February like we talked about, then I graduate in May. If nothing has changed, if we still feel the same, then we can talk about the future."

Garrett grinned. It felt dopey on his face, the genuine joy that wanted to burst out of him. He liked to have a plan, a schedule, something to look forward to. "Okay." He kissed her. It was old and new, familiar lips he hadn't touched with his in four years. "I want to make love to you," he whispered in her ear, then nibbled on it.

"Me, too," she said with a breathy sigh. "But my parents are downstairs. Anticipation is half the fun, right? When I come out in February, it'll be like the first time."

He hugged her. Garrett wasn't into spontaneous bursts of affection, but with Becca, it felt right.

Garrett was packed and ready to leave the next day. He didn't have many things—he didn't really care about stuff. He liked nice things; he liked living well and having a state-of-the-art gym to work out in, good food and drink, nice clothes. But he didn't need any of it, and wouldn't miss it when it was gone.

Audrey came over. He had been dreading this, because he liked Audrey and the last two months had been a lot of fun. More fun than he'd had in a long time. Maybe ever. Audrey was fire and heat and together they were combustible. The sex was honestly the best he'd ever had. He would never tell Becca that, but that was okay. Because with Becca it was more than sex.

Garrett explained that he wanted to check out Scottsdale alone, see if he even liked the job. Then maybe she could come out and visit in a few months.

It wouldn't happen. While he didn't come out and tell her he was breaking it off, she had to have known.

"I understand, baby," she said. "I have some projects to wrap up, anyway. Call me when you get settled?"

"I will," he said, knowing he wouldn't.

She walked over to him as she pulled her dress over her head. She was completely naked underneath and he immediately became horny. Audrey did that to him. Every single time.

"To hold you over until I can make it out to Arizona." She put her perfectly manicured hands on his chest and pushed him down to his bed.

She didn't have to know this was the last time, he thought.

He rolled her over so he was on top. "How much time do you have?" he asked with a low growl and a smile.

"I have until dawn. And I don't need much sleep."

"I have to be at the airport at seven in the morning."

"Want a ride?" she asked suggestively and bucked her hips.

"You drive me wild," he said, and meant it.

He barely got his cock out of his jeans before he plunged into her.

By dawn, they were both exhausted and completely satiated.

By the time he landed at Sky Harbor Airport in Arizona, he was only thinking about Becca.

A week later, he learned that Becca had gone missing while driving back to college after Christmas break. He was shattered, as if he had been made of glass and someone dropped him.

Two months later, Audrey came back into his life. He was still broken, feeling a pain deep inside unlike anything that he had felt before. Audrey fixed him. She gave him what he needed—sex, fun, games. He told her he loved her. And he did, in his way.

But no one could replace Becca.

39

Present Day

Kara told Matt he needed to get an X-ray to confirm that his
ribs weren't broken and he wasn't bleeding internally. Matt didn't
want her to talk to Garrett Reid without him, but Michael assured them both that Kara wasn't leaving his sight. So Matt let
Billy the paramedic take him to the hospital; Ryder joined him.

Kara got into a sedan with Catherine and Michael. Detective Fuentes and a deputy followed them. Catherine said, "Kara,
I'm staying in the car."

"Why?"

"He didn't respond well to me. He will to you."

"Because I look like his dead girlfriend," she said bluntly.

In the ambulance, Matt and Kara had been brought up to
speed on everything that the team had learned about Garrett
Reid and Clara Dolan. Ryder had also uncovered information
that, while Becca McCarthy's remains hadn't yet been found,
the local police were very interested in the theory that Clara

Dolan killed her and were putting the case back to the fore-front. They had boxes of potential evidence and video surveil-lance that they were going to reanalyze against Dolan's photo and social media history. Ryder had offered the FBI lab and ex-pedited facial recognition processing if they needed it—but it would still take a few days.

Jim had driven to Clinch County with the Jacksonville ERT to take point on the crime scene—both the farmhouse and the abandoned factory. Matt had given him a strict warning not to go inside the factory until it had been completely cleared, no matter how long it took.

Now they were sitting in a sedan outside Garrett Reid's apartment with Catherine insisting Kara was the only one who might get Reid to talk. Kara wasn't certain she believed Cath-erine, but she was willing to try.

"We're going to find evidence of his involvement at the fac-tory," Catherine said. "It's just a matter of time before we can charge him with federal kidnapping, torture, and homicide since they transported their victims across state lines. He'll be an ac-cessory to the kidnapping and attempted murder of Lily and Nathan Graves—Nathan is not yet twelve, so that's special cir-cumstances felony endangerment of a child. Even if he didn't know what her plan was, we can wrap him up in it. If he co-operates, and we take Clara into custody, we can charge him as an accessory. He might get out in twenty years."

"That's bullshit," Kara said. "He may not have been the in-stigator, but he participated in the murders of six people."

"Ultimately, those decisions aren't ours. We need to find this woman. She is wily and has the money to disappear."

Kara understood making deals, she just didn't like it. And Catherine was right—this wasn't their call to make.

"I'll do my best," Kara said.

"I know you will." Catherine hesitated, then said, "I'm glad that you and Matt were not seriously injured."

"Me, too," she said. Her leg was sore and still partly numb from a local anesthetic that Billy injected into her. She had declined pain meds because they messed with her head, though she might take them tonight. But Billy had done an amazing job on her leg and given her antibiotics, plus had the doctor call in a prescription that she'd pick up when she was done with Reid.

"Have you heard about Lily?" Kara asked before getting out of the car. "Is she going to be okay?"

"She regained consciousness," Catherine said, "but they're still running tests. She has internal bleeding and will likely go into surgery. However, she has a severe concussion so I don't know what their plan is at this point. Franklin, her husband, is there now."

"Good. She and Nathan are innocents. They should never have gone through that—it was pure psychological torture. But they would have died in that house because Clara sabotaged it. She didn't know when it would collapse, but she damn well knew it *would* collapse. That's all on Clara Dolan."

"Yes, it was primarily psychological torture. All of the murders were psychological as well as physical. I think that was what motivated her, twisting emotions. Setting up painful ways for her victims to die while keeping her own hands off them."

Kara glanced at Michael. "All right, let's do this. You good?"

"He makes one move toward you, I'm putting him down," Michael said.

Kara grinned. "Good to know."

Her leg felt like it had been put through a meat grinder, but she could walk slowly. Still, she accepted Michael's arm as a crutch.

Her phone vibrated. It was a text from Matt.

Nothing broken, three cracked ribs, one giant bruise. No internal bleeding. But they gave me an IV of fluids and vitamins and I feel like a half-million bucks. Come to the hospital when you're done and I'll get you one of these amazing IVs, too.

She chuckled and sent him a thumbs-up emoji. She wondered if he was on pain killers or just happy to be alive.

Michael knocked on Garrett's door. "Who is it?" Garrett said from the other side.

"LAPD Detective Kara Quinn, aka Kara Costa, who you attempted to kidnap along with my pretend husband, FBI agent Matt Costa."

The door swung open and he stared at her as if he was not only shocked that any cop would show up, but specifically surprised to see her.

"What'd you think? That your wife killed me? Nope, though it was close. May we come in?"

"You, not him."

"He's going to insist. I suppose the three of us can chat out here, but it'd be much more comfortable in your place so the neighbors don't hear our conversation."

She motioned to the apartment next to Garrett's, where a kid and his mom were looking out the blinds at them.

"Fine," Garrett said. He let them in and shut the door behind them. Michael stood like a rock next to the door, watching.

"I don't have a lawyer anymore, but I still don't have to talk to you."

"No, you don't. Would you mind if I sit down? My leg is killing me."

He stared at the bandage around her calf, then motioned for her to sit on the couch. She took the chair instead.

"How'd you get hurt?"

"Like you don't know," Kara said.

"Why don't you tell me?"

Kara weighed giving him something, and decided that building a rapport would go a long way. She didn't have to like him.

"Your wife—I still can't believe you married that woman, she is a piece of work—shot Matt and me with a tranquilizer. By the way, she left one of the darts behind, which was *really* helpful for forensics to match with the other victims. But that's neither here nor there."

"Your coffee was poisoned," Michael said from the door.

"My coffee?" Kara said. "Damn." She almost forgot that she'd felt ill before the dart hit her. "How?"

"The mugs." Michael glared at Garrett. Garrett averted his gaze back to Kara.

"Not me," Garrett said.

But he knew. He had to have known. She didn't say that. Instead, she said, "Your wife drove us across state lines to an abandoned cannery in Clinch County, Georgia—a place I had never heard of. We woke up about twenty hours later. Matt in a break room, me in an elevator. Long story short, it took us twenty-four hours to get ourselves out of the building." She motioned to her leg. "I did that running across the flooded factory floor when Matt fell from one of the sabotaged catwalks. By then, we knew that there were booby traps all over the place, so we were super observant, tripped a few on purpose, and then bypassed the net of bowling balls. Lucky there."

He didn't comment. Did he look impressed? She thought so.

"Did you know that your wife kidnapped a woman and her son in order to blackmail a lawyer into helping get you out on bail?"

"That's on her, not me," he said.

"You know what I think? I think it's *all* on her. Yes, you were a willing and able participant. But she's the psychopath."

"Audrey is not a psychopath," he said.

"She's perfectly aware that her actions are crimes and she does them anyway."

Garrett didn't comment. He also didn't turn away.

"Do I look like your ex-girlfriend Becca?"

He flinched, shrugged. "Not really."

"I don't think so either," Kara said. "Becca was very cute. Really pretty. Smart. Beyond the superficial hair and eye color, blonde and blue. Oh, and she was short, like me. She would have been thirty now, like you."

"Do you have a point?"

"Do you know what happened to her?"

"The other fed has this ridiculous theory that Audrey killed her."

"You mean Clara. Clara Dolan."

"That's what the female fed said. But I think she was pulling a name out of her ass."

"Well, actually, Dr. Jones is right about Clara. Audrey. Your lawyer knew her as Amber. She was Hope at the resort. I wonder what name she'll use next?"

"My wife is Audrey Reid. Her maiden name was Audrey Dolan. Maybe this *Clara* is her sister, or you completely made her up."

"Why weren't you living together? Why did no one at the resort know you were married?"

He didn't say anything.

"You and I both know that your life is pretty much over. You help us find your wife, you might see the outside of a prison before you're sixty."

"There is no evidence against me."

"You tried to kidnap me last Friday."

He smiled and there was humor there. "I thought you and your husband were in trouble. I was trying to help."

He knew she didn't believe him, so she laughed. "Sure. Maybe that defense will work. But can you honestly tell me there is not one cell of your DNA at the abandoned cannery?"

Again, silence.

"I don't think you would have hurt anyone if it weren't for your wife. I think you would have been fine continuing to seduce older women and living the high life as long as you could. And once you hooked up with Clara and started conning unsuspecting businessmen at resorts around the country? I think you were okay with that, too. Some of them may have even deserved it. You and Clara could have had a very nice life. But when you turned to murder, you brought a whole lot more attention on yourselves. By the way, Florida is a death penalty state."

"I didn't kill anyone."

"You simply abducted them, took them over state lines, and left them to die in a maze of deadly traps. Got it."

Kara pulled out her phone and leaned forward. "We've done our homework. Let me show you how your wife has been lying to you ever since you met her. Clara Dolan, thirty-five, born to Piper and Gerald Dolan, both college professors. Clara came into her trust fund, established by her grandparents, when she was twenty-five. Ten million dollars. Nice. She moved the bulk of her trust to three LLCs, using one of them to buy and sell property—in all the places you've lived with her. We're still going through her records, but we *will* find her. When we do, she'll put everything on you—you know that, right?"

He had a slight smirk on his face, nothing too blatant, just a little arrogant tilt of his lips.

"You've probably never had to want for anything," Kara continued. "Did you ever question where the money came from? How *Audrey* was able to buy a nice beach house? How she bought the farmland next to the cannery, where she held two people, including a child, against their will?"

"You're talking a lot, but I have nothing to say to you."

"Here." She turned her phone to show Garrett the evidence. "You need proof—I have proof."

"You'll lie about anything."

"Here's Clara's high school graduation portrait." Kara looked at it, nodded, showed it to Garrett. "She's beautiful, that's not in doubt. I mean, truly a natural beauty. Nothing fake, no fillers, no cosmetic surgery. She did lighten her hair recently, but this dark blond with all the light blond and amber highlights? Gorgeous. When did she start dyeing her hair? Before or after she found out that Becca McCarthy was a natural blonde?"

"Don't talk about Becca."

"Becca's parents liked you. They knew that Becca wanted to get back together. They were supportive. What did you tell Clara?"

"Her name is Audrey."

"That's what she told you. But she has other false identities, right?" Kara leaned forward. "Clara knew Emily Masters. She hated her because Emily married Clara's ex-boyfriend and supposedly took her job, or some such thing. But we talked to the ex. He and Clara had been split for years. And Clara was a trainer at the gym . . . Emily didn't take her job—Clara simply wasn't hired into a position that she wasn't qualified for. And for that, Clara seduced Emily's father and then exposed the affair right before the wedding." She showed him her phone again, which had a clip from an article that had a photo of Clara and Emily's father in a compromising position. "'Clara Dolan,' it says here," Kara said. "Sure looks like your wife."

"What is your point?"

"She's been playing you for over seven years, ever since she killed Becca."

Garrett scowled. "You're trying to pit my wife and me against each other. It won't work."

"The police in Ventura County, where Becca disappeared while driving back to Santa Barbara, have renewed their investigation. The FBI is assisting them with facial recognition of all the security tapes they have in evidence. There was a lot of evidence, but they didn't have a suspect. Bet you that Clara is on the cameras. Gas station. Convenience store. Red light camera. Somewhere. Bet you that she doesn't have an alibi. Yeah, sure, seven and a half years, who knows where they were? But they still have Becca's car. There is evidence in the car, and once they get a suspect they can get her DNA, her hair sample, her prints, and match it all up."

Kara didn't know what the police had or didn't have; most likely they no longer had the vehicle in storage, or if they did it had been exposed to the elements. Seven years was a long time, and once they'd gone through it they may have given it back to the family. They would have collected evidence, but what they had, Kara simply speculated.

But Garrett didn't know that.

"Did you love her?"

"Of course I love my wife. You can't make me talk about her."

"I meant, did you love Becca?"

"That was a long time ago."

"Was it a lie that her parents supported the relationship? That she was going to visit you in Scottsdale? That she still loved you?"

"I'm not talking about Becca."

For the first time, she saw something other than disinterest, annoyance, or arrogance. She saw . . . pain.

"If I can prove that your wife killed Becca, would you tell us where she is?"

"She didn't even know Becca."

"If you think that, I can't help you." Kara stood. "We're going to find evidence in the cannery. You know we are. We have a team going through Clara's beach house. Do you think she left nothing behind that incriminates her . . . or you? Unless you help us, there's nothing I can do for you."

She walked to the door.

Garrett said, "I need to find a new lawyer. He'll work out a deal."

"Okay," she said, looked him in the eye. "When?"

"Tomorrow morning. He'll call you."

"He should call the DA of Flagler."

"I want your number."

"Then I want yours." They already had his cell phone number, but this was a test.

Garrett rattled it off and Kara sent him a text message. Michael cleared his throat, but didn't say anything.

"I'm an early riser," Kara said. "If you want to talk, I'll answer."

Outside, Michael said, "What was that all about?"

"He's going to lead us right to her," Kara said.

"He knows we're watching him."

"He's going to try to slip away. We need to be prepared."

She slid into the sedan where Catherine was waiting. "We need to sit on him. He's going to go after her. I think he'll kill her."

"He believed you about Becca McCarthy?" Catherine asked.

"Not at first, but I think he believed *you* when you told him his wife was Clara Dolan. I don't think he knew that, and because she lied to him, it makes him suspicious. He's going to think things through, put together past events, and when he has convinced himself that she killed Becca, he'll leave."

"Interesting," Catherine said. She called Detective Fuentes, relayed Kara's theory. "Put your best people on him, but pull back a little so he doesn't see them. When he leaves the property, follow but be discreet and let me know." She ended the call and said to Kara, "I talked to Matt when you were inside. He made me promise to take you to the hospital."

"That's fine with me," she said. "Do you think I could get my own clothes?"

"Already waiting for you."

WEDNESDAY

40

It was after midnight by the time Michael brought Kara to the hospital to be checked out and given an IV.

Kara didn't care for needles, but she was still dehydrated and agreed to stay until dawn. She needed the rest. She'd dozed on and off driving back from Georgia, but she could sleep for an entire day and still need more downtime.

Matt sat with her. He had showered and put on slacks and a polo shirt. "I still don't feel clean," he told her.

"Did you sleep any?"

"I crashed for two hours while getting the infusion."

"When this is over, do you think Tony will give us a day or two off to soak in my hot tub?"

One of the best things about owning her own house was that she had a private hot tub. She used it often.

"You can't soak in water with those stitches," Matt said. "And you're going to be on desk duty until you get a doctor's clearance."

She frowned and glared at him. "What about you?"

"Me, too. We're probably going to be out of commission for at least a week, probably longer."

She groaned. "I hate sitting at a desk."

"I'll get you a standing desk."

She rolled her eyes and he laughed, took her hand, kissed it. "While the doc was checking you out, Michael told me about your conversation with Reid. You gave him your number."

"Yes, I needed to—it was a test on his part, and I want him to reach out to me. He will either call me, or he'll leave to meet up with Clara, so he can kill her."

"That's what Michael said you thought. Why?"

"Something Catherine said when she was debriefing me. Catherine is convinced that Clara killed Becca to clear the way for her to keep Garrett. Maybe that was why she did it, or she just couldn't stand someone smart like Becca winning back her boyfriend. Whatever." Kara rolled her eyes. The drama of the situation was just too much for her. "Anyway, Catherine told me if Garrett believes it, he'll help us. Maybe. But if Catherine is right that Becca was Garrett's first and only true love—and I think she is, because Becca's parents believed it—then Garrett is going to want to kill Clara. Garrett isn't stupid. He's well-educated, he's sharp, he'll see exactly how Clara manipulated him—and he'll be angry."

"Why would he kill her? Maybe he doesn't care that his first girlfriend is dead," Matt said, playing devil's advocate.

"Clara is extreme. She falls, falls hard. She wasn't going to allow Garrett to leave her for anyone, especially a cute, successful, college-educated ex-girlfriend. The older women he dated were no threat to her . . . Becca was a threat. So she took her off the game board. Becca was a threat because Garrett loved her."

Matt nodded as Kara spoke, then said, "You're beginning to sound like a shrink."

"Bite your tongue," she said. "All cops have to be part psychologist. We have to be able to read people. And Garrett is going to avenge Becca." She sighed, leaned back. "You're right, this IV is amazing. I almost feel human again."

Her cell phone rang. It was Garrett Reid.

"I guess he wants to talk."

"Answer it," Matt said.

She did, put it on speaker and motioned for Matt to keep an eye on the door and make sure no one came in. "Hello, Garrett. It's Kara."

"She called me this afternoon," Garrett said. "But you probably already know that, if you have my phone records."

"What did she say?"

He didn't answer the question. "I knew she wasn't coming back. I thought about what that other fed, Jones, said. That her name was Clara Dolan and she had a trust fund. When I called her Clara, she denied it at first, but then gave it up. Said her parents disowned her and she hated the name. She legally changed her name to Audrey."

"She may have done just that," Kara said.

"I told her when we first met, no lies."

"She didn't legally change her name to Audrey until after she left LA."

"She told me that even though you were a cop, that you and that other agent were an item. Showed me a photo of you two outside a restaurant, said that you were staying together at the resort even after I was arrested. Is that true?"

"Yes," Kara said. Matt winced. They were never supposed to give personal information to suspects. But in this case, Kara had to maintain the rapport she'd built with Garrett earlier. His whole world was crashing down around him, and he knew it was just a matter of time before he was back in jail, this time for decades. And if he didn't help them, Clara would remain free while he paid the price.

"Do you love him?"

"Yes," she said without hesitation.

"I loved Becca. It feels different. It's . . . hot and cold, exciting and scary, and I would have spent the rest of my life with her. I would have married her, we would have had kids, we would have been happy. I never really felt anything until I met Becca."

"What happened, Garrett?" She left the question open-ended, not sure where his head was at.

"We went to different colleges. She came to visit and we got into an argument. It was stupid. She wanted me to fight for her, but I told her if she didn't love me to leave. She left, so I assumed she didn't love me. It gutted me. But I wasn't going to chase her if she wanted to be free."

"Because you loved her," Kara said.

"Exactly."

"Did Audrey know about Becca?" Kara used the name Garrett was comfortable with, her voice calm, no accusation.

"I never thought about it. Until now."

"And?"

"She stole the only person from me that I have ever loved, the only person who was so good, deep down in her soul good, who made *me* good."

"Where is Audrey right now?"

"She will soon be in hell, where that fucking bitch belongs."

He ended the call.

"Well, shit," Kara said. "Get the nurse, get this thing out of me, he's going to do something stupid."

"The sheriff's department has a team on his apartment," Matt said. "And Zack is wired on energy drinks pouring over all her financial statements. We have every ID we know about flagged and she's not flying out or crossing the border. We'll find her."

"She could have identities we don't know about. Get the nurse, please? It's almost done anyway, and I need to be prepared."

"Neither of us should be in the field right now."

"We can observe, can't we? I can't lie around here and do nothing when he is going to kill her."

Matt reluctantly left the room.

Kara tried calling Garrett back. It went to voicemail.

"Garrett, it's Kara. If you tell us where she is, we can appre-hend her and tell the court you cooperated. That'll help you in the long run. But if you do anything rash, if you go after her your-self, you're only going to be putting the final nail in your coffin. What would Becca want you to do? Call me. We'll talk again."

She hung up, tense and agitated.

A text message came through a minute later.

Becca was a saint. I am not.

She tried calling him back. She got a call center recording.

"The number you are trying to reach is unavailable . . ."

She ended the call mid-recording, swung her legs around to sit up, and was about to take the IV out herself when the nurse came in. Maybe it was the look on Kara's face, or Matt had said something to her, but she didn't argue about taking out the IV.

"I need to make note that you're both leaving against doc-tor's orders," she said.

"We're fine," Matt told her.

"Get Zack on the phone," Kara said. "I have some ideas about how he can narrow the search."

"You're amazing, Kara," Zack said when he came onto the video chat screen.

"Yep, I know. What did you find?" She was too tired for Zack's long-winded explanations right now.

They were back at Sapphire Shoals in the conference room where Ryder and the team had been working.

It was after three in the morning and all Kara wanted was four hours of uninterrupted sleep. Or longer. Maybe a day. Maybe being forced to take time off wouldn't be a bad thing.

They were all there, except Jim who was still in Georgia and

Sloane who was with the Graves family at the hospital. Detective Bianca Fuentes had also joined them, though she looked like she hadn't slept much, either.

"Kara said to focus on properties within a half-day drive of the cannery on the coast, not only those owned by the LLC or Clara Dolan or any of her aliases, but property owned by her parents or grandparents."

"I hadn't thought to look at her family," Catherine said. "Her mother essentially disowned her."

"She would probably get great satisfaction using one of her mother's homes," Kara said. "A big fat middle finger from afar."

"Why the coast?" Michael asked.

"Because of the victims. They were dumped in the ocean, which tells me she has access to a boat. Probably owns one. And if she has access to a boat, she would have a place where she could dock."

"There are two properties," Zack said. "Both owned by the Wilmington Family Trust. Wilmington is Piper Dolan's maiden name. They're originally from Georgia, but I haven't been able to track down any relatives still in the area."

"You said two properties," Matt said, refocusing Zack, who often went off on many tangents before getting to the point.

"Yes. One in Savannah, which isn't on the coast, but the property abuts a river with access to the ocean. Moreover, there's a dock attached to the property and no current residents. It was used as a second residence for Gerald Dolan when he taught an annual seminar at a college in Savannah."

"So Clara would have been familiar with the property," Catherine surmised.

"It's been in the family for more than fifty years. The second property is a two-acre spread on Kiawah Island, purchased by the family trust as a vacation home sixteen years ago. There's a dock, and aerial photos show a boathouse."

"Do you have visuals?" Kara asked.

Zack typed on his keyboard. The first property that popped up on screen was in Savannah. The satellite image showed a boat at the dock and easy access to the river from the house. Moreover, it was three hours from Clinch County, and accessible to Flagler Beach by waterways.

He clicked again and highlighted the Kiawah Island property. It had privacy, and Kara would bet her pension that's where Clara was.

"There," she said.

"Savannah is closer," Catherine pointed out.

"There are neighbors close to the Savannah house, and if her dad lived there on and off, they might know her. She won't risk it. She may have used the place at some point, but if she's regrouping before she disappears, she's going to Kiawah Island."

Matt said, "Bianca, can you contact Savannah police and have them check out that property? We'll fly to the closest airport to Kiawah Island, contact local law enforcement on our way, but I don't want anyone tipping her off. She can leave by land or sea, and if it's by sea she's going to be that much more difficult to catch."

"Not if we call in the Coast Guard," Michael said.

"Do it," Matt said. "I should have thought of it."

"You're on leave," Catherine pointed out.

"Not today," Matt said with a glance at Kara.

"When that bitch is in custody, I'll take all the time you force on me," Kara said. "Until then, I'm all in."

"You're both impossible," Catherine muttered, but she was smiling.

Garrett destroyed his phone after he called Kara Quinn. He liked her. She was direct. She didn't break eye contact. She was pretty.

She wasn't Becca. But Becca would have grown into a pretty, confident woman, just like Kara.

She didn't have the opportunity to do so because Audrey had killed her.

Garrett no longer doubted that Audrey wasn't even her name. He didn't doubt that she killed Becca. When he realized she had lied to him for nearly eight years about something as simple as her *name*, he knew she could have lied to him about anything.

He'd always known she had money, but thought it was from her honey traps. He had no idea she was a trust fund baby, given everything on a silver platter. She'd never told him. She'd told him *nothing* about herself, or she'd lied.

She had lied about everything.

They'd had fun, a good seven years, but through it all, she had kept secrets that could have made a difference in their lives.

If she could lie to him so easily and for so long, there was no way she respected him. She had never intended to protect him when things got too hot. Which meant she'd never planned to bring him along, give him a new identity, create a new life.

Not that he would have gone with her. Not after learning she had killed Becca.

His anger was a slow-burning ember. Audrey was fanning the flames with each lie he uncovered.

She was playing a very dangerous game.

41

Two hours later, Kara and the team were at the staging area near Clara's family property on Kiawah Island, along with Detective Fuentes and local law enforcement. Dawn was just starting to creep over the ocean, promising a beautiful morning, though the humidity was quickly rising.

Catherine and Bianca Fuentes were talking to the people in charge outside the tactical van, and Michael stood with Matt and Kara. Bianca had informed them before they left Florida that Garrett had slipped his tail. It made Kara angry—she'd warned them to be on high alert—but either Garrett was that good, or the cops Bianca had assigned were that bad.

"You both promise that you'll take direction from me," Michael said. "Neither of you should be here—you're tired, injured, dehydrated."

"Anything you say, Michael," Kara said.

"You're enjoying this, aren't you?" Matt asked him.

Michael cracked a smile. "Sure am, boss."

Catherine returned. "The officers all have a photo of Garrett Reid, so if he shows up he'll be arrested."

"What's the status of the Coast Guard?" Michael asked.

"Standing by," Catherine said. "If she manages to escape by boat, they will take the lead. The property has a dock and boathouse near where the Kiawah River merges with the Atlantic. They are stationed offshore, out of sight of the property but close enough to apprehend her in minutes.

"The local police confirmed through digital surveillance," Catherine continued, "that a white van using a code at the guard gate assigned to the property drove onto the island at 8:30 p.m. last night and has not left."

"She could have left by another vehicle," Matt said.

"They have a dedicated team reviewing all security feeds looking for any lone female driver who left the island. However, they did a quick assessment of the property and have good reason to believe that someone is in the house. They can't approach because of the security system. The property is owned by a trust and they reached out to the trustee to get the security codes, but we also have to take the risk that someone who manages the property will contact the house itself, which could alert Dolan to our presence. Still, getting the codes will make it much easier for everyone so we can approach without Clara being forewarned."

"Do we know if there is anyone else in the house? A potential hostage?" Michael asked.

"Negative," Catherine said. "The house is not listed on any short-term rental sites, and the sheriff knows the family who owns it. The Wilmingtons—Clara Dolan's maternal grandparents. Everyone in their extended family has access to the property, including Clara, who is on the list maintained by the homeowners association. While the gate logs every code, there are other ways to access the property, so there's no guarantee that someone else isn't there."

"So she could have a hostage," Matt guessed. "She could have even picked up a stranger in the van."

"Yes. The sheriff sent a deputy to talk to the closest neighbor, who lives on the island full-time. That neighbor will have more information about the comings and goings. We're going to wait for answers before we proceed. And, hopefully, have information about the security system, so we can bypass it."

More waiting, Kara thought. She normally didn't mind waiting, but she was antsy. Clara Dolan had slipped through their net more than once. Kara couldn't help but think she had a plan that would not only get more people killed, but would also allow her to escape. And if she escaped, it would take that much longer to track her down because of her financial resources.

Fifteen minutes later the edge of the sun was visible on the water, and Detective Bianca Fuentes came over to them. "Neighbors say that no one has been here since April. The wife said she saw a woman on the dock last night, and house lights on up until midnight. She wasn't concerned because there is a security system and the house is used often by friends and family of the owners."

"There's one boat visible in the boathouse," Michael said. "Is that the only one with the property?"

"It is," Bianca confirmed.

"She could have been checking it out, planning to leave by water," Kara said. "Maybe we should take her there. Is there a way to get into the boathouse undetected?"

"Only if we can bypass the security system," Bianca said. "There are cameras on the dock, and sensors on the land. She's going to be on high alert, so anything that sets it off could put her on the defensive, and we don't want to risk anyone's lives."

"What if," Catherine said, "she's planning to meet Garrett out at sea? We have the specs on the boat here, but if he has access to another boat, he could pick her up and they'd disappear. We wouldn't know what to look for."

"If he picks her up," Kara said, "he'll kill her."

"You can't be certain of that."

"He knows she killed the love of his life. It might have taken a while to sink in, but he didn't slip the tail because he wants to get away. He slipped it so that he could find Clara and punish her."

Catherine obviously didn't agree, but didn't comment further. That was fine with Kara. They didn't have to agree all the time, and she appreciated that Catherine no longer rudely shut down her theories.

Kara had sensed a shift in Garrett's attitude when she talked to him earlier, which was why she shared her phone number. She knew he would call—she had hoped he would give her information about Clara, but she wasn't surprised that he planned on killing her. Clara had used him, but worse, she had been playing games with him—a game he didn't even know he was playing.

The sheriff came over. "Good news. We spoke to the trustee who manages the property. They have given us permission to take down their security system, which can be done remotely through their contracted company. We also asked that they not alert the owners in case someone in the family is still on good terms with Dolan. How do you want to do this?"

They discussed the options, and in short order decided to put together three teams of six: team A on the main entrance; team B on the beach; and team C on the water. When everyone was in place, the security company would take down the system and teams A and B would breach the house front and back. Team C would keep line of sight on the dock in case she eluded them and reached the boathouse.

"She is armed and dangerous," Catherine reminded everyone. "She is wanted for seven murders and four attempted murders, including that of two law enforcement officers. She is known to use any means at her disposal and may have set up deadly traps, so be extremely observant of your surroundings. Look up and down. Be ready for anything."

Clara only had one night to prepare the house and grounds, unless she'd been there earlier, Kara thought. But she wouldn't know when her extended family was using the place, or when they would return, so the chances were this was just a way-station for her, and she planned to leave this morning. She thought ahead—she might know that the FBI could find her LLC and properties.

Or, she could be like half the criminals Kara had encountered in her career: she thought she was smarter than everyone, and tripped herself up.

Michael ordered Matt and Kara to remain at the staging area. Catherine was staying as well, helping to coordinate with the Coast Guard and sheriff's department. Michael and Bianca joined one of the six-man teams.

"He's really enjoying giving me orders," Matt said.

"Let him have his moment," Kara said.

"We were all worried," Catherine said quietly. "The entire team thought we wouldn't find you in time."

"You did," Matt said.

"You saved yourselves," Catherine said. "I expected no less," she added with a slight smile.

"Let's hope we apprehend Dolan without any casualties," Matt said.

Kara looked down at her phone when it vibrated in her hand. She read it, then showed the text message to Matt. "This is from Garrett, but not the number I have for him."

Audrey joined me in Scottsdale two months after Becca disappeared. She said she'd gone camping along Sespe Creek to "find herself" and that's when she decided to find me.

Catherine said, "I'll have Ryder work on tracing this other number ASAP, and get the information to law enforcement in California."

It was dawn when Garrett called Audrey over video chat. He could almost see the island from the wheelhouse of their boat.

Four hours ago, he'd slipped the cops watching him and headed straight to the docks. They'd kept the boat in plain sight at a private pier near the resort. Taking it out at two in the morning wasn't difficult; by the time anyone figured out that he and Audrey owned it, he'd be long gone.

He believed every word Kara Quinn told him. Audrey wasn't who he thought she was. He had loved a fantasy, a mirage.

She used him. Manipulated him.

She had no respect for him, and certainly didn't love him.

That's why she planned to kill him. He now knew all of her secrets.

"Garrett," she answered on the third ring. She was dressed, her long beautiful hair pulled back into a high, tight ponytail. Her face completely devoid of makeup, she was still the most beautiful creature on the planet. "Darling, where are you?"

"On my way to the rendezvous. Just as we always planned."

A flicker in her eyes, then, "Well, baby, plans change. You won't be here in time."

If Audrey had her way, he wouldn't make it at all.

But he knew her tricks. She wasn't as smart as she thought she was.

"I'm already near the buoy."

She raised an eyebrow. "You are?"

"Right. The bomb was supposed to explode when I reached thirty miles per hour. You would rather kill me than trust me."

"I've always trusted you, Garrett. You're my one true love."

He laughed. "I believed that for a long time, sweetheart."

She pouted. It wasn't going to work on him anymore. It had taken him far too long to see the truth.

"Baby, I need to go. I'll find you."

"You failed, Audrey."

She tensed; her eyes flared. "I don't know why you're being so mean."

"They didn't die in the cannery, and they didn't die in the farmhouse. Everyone lived. And they're coming for you."

"What do you know? You can't possibly know that!"

"I know more than you think. You put a bomb on our boat. You think I didn't find it?"

She stared at him, then a slow smile came across her face. "A bomb? Never underestimate me, Garrett. Everyone has *always* underestimated me."

For a second he wondered if he missed something.

"You killed Becca. For what?"

"I don't know what you're talking about," she said in a lofty tone that convinced him that the feds were right; his gut was right.

"You'll pay for that."

"What time is it, Garrett?" she asked, sounding innocent.

His heart pounded in his chest. Dammit, she had something up her sleeve.

"Six in the morning."

"Is it really?"

It was 5:57.

"Game over," she said. "I won."

An explosion far out in the ocean made Kara jump. "What was that?"

"A distraction?" Matt said. He pulled out his phone, started texting people on the team.

"Garrett," she muttered. "Dammit, it had to have been Garrett coming for her. Zack found that she owned two boats, right? Want to bet that she sabotaged the one Garrett had access to?"

"I won't take that bet," Matt muttered, waiting for answers.

Catherine said, "Security system is completely down, teams A and B are going in."

Michael heard the explosion, glanced out at the horizon. Smoke rose at least a mile out. Was that Clara Dolan? Had she slipped through their net again?

Or was that Garrett Reid coming to meet her?

Michael had moved seamlessly with the SWAT team that had been put together. He'd been a part of FBI SWAT in Detroit before Matt recruited him to the Mobile Response Team. He missed it.

The FBI was team B, coming from the beach. The local sheriff's was team A, and the sheriff's water patrol was team C, monitoring activity in the boathouse.

The Coast Guard was holding with two boats; one was now being sent to investigate the explosion.

"System down, on three," the team leader, Grant Cole, said. *Three. Two. One.*

Michael followed the leader's signal and moved with the group toward the rear of the house.

The property was a nightmare with too many exits. His team split into three pairs to cover each one. Michael was with Cole.

The garage door opened to a narrow side path, shielded by thick ivy and shoulder-high hedges. Movement—quick, almost imperceptible—flashed through the green. Michael and Cole froze a moment to assess, then moved in.

No one was there. But the door hung open, swaying slightly.

Cole pointed toward a dark trail that wound through neatly trimmed man-sized hedges. Michael saw a figure darting out of sight through the foliage. Female, agile. They were in pursuit.

Cole whispered into the comm. "We've got an unidentified suspect, likely Dolan, fleeing through the garden between the house and boathouse. Pursuing on foot."

The distance between the house and boathouse was at least a hundred yards, but it wasn't a straight shot as decorative hedges, flowering bushes, and trees filled the area.

Michael ran just behind Cole. They glimpsed her again—black clothes, but the telltale blond hair bounced behind her like a flag.

She was fast, running parallel to the boathouse. Where the hell was she going?

Cole updated the team. In Michael's earpiece, chatter crackled: the sheriff's men had breached the main house and were clearing rooms.

Please don't let her have rigged it, Michael thought. Clara Dolan was smart enough to turn the whole place into a deadly trap.

Then team C reported, "Boat motor just engaged."

"Negative," Cole snapped. "We've got eyes on the suspect—she's not near the boathouse. I repeat, she's running southeast of the boathouse."

"We're checking it out," team C leader replied.

"Use extreme caution," Cole warned. "She may have an accomplice."

They pressed forward through the hedges. The faint light from the rising sun and tall hedges made visibility poor, making every step a risk. Ten minutes from now they'd be able to see better; they didn't have ten minutes.

A metallic *clank*.

Then Cole screamed and went down.

"Man down! Man down!" Michael shouted into the comm. He dropped to his knees beside him. "Are you shot? Where are you hit?"

"My foot," Cole growled, jaw clenched.

Michael looked and nearly recoiled from the sight. A steel

trap had snapped around Cole's ankle just above the top of his boots, blood darkening the fabric of his khakis.

"Don't move," Michael ordered. Into the comm he said, "Man down, I need a medic at my location. Roughly fifty yards southeast of the house. Watch your step, there are ground traps. I repeat: watch the ground."

"Medic en route," came the reply.

"Go," Cole gasped. "Go get her."

"I'm not leaving you."

"She's escaping. Go! My men are on their way."

Michael hesitated, then ran. Cole was right—the traps were cover for her escape.

"Boathouse clear," team C reported. "Boat was started by remote."

"She's using it as a distraction," Michael replied. "Maintain distance. It could be rigged, or she could attempt to circle back to access it."

He slowed, wary now. Another animal trap nearly caught him—he sprang it with a stick so no one else would get hurt. *Too close.*

Ahead, the path curved toward the river. Multiple boats lined the water—not just Dolan's. He hadn't regained visual after Cole had been hurt, and he wondered if she'd changed direction.

He felt helpless, chasing echoes.

A whisper of movement caught his attention.

Instinct kicked in—he dropped just as a thick tree branch whipped through the air where his head had been. A cut rope swung beside it.

It had been meant to knock me out.

Then he heard running, fast, through the bushes. She was close.

"Suspect heading toward the waterway behind address 11250," a deputy called out. "Two boats docked. Multiple escape routes."

Michael had studied the maps and knew that property. Big lot, access to the channel that led to the ocean, just like this one.

"I'm in pursuit," he said. Team C confirmed backup was on the way.

"Extreme caution," he warned them.

Through the trees, he saw Clara sprinting toward the dock.

"Clara Dolan!" he shouted. "FBI! Freeze! Hands where I can see them!"

She didn't stop.

Michael sprinted after her. Two deputies were cutting across from the east. Clara veered left, raced down the dock, and dove cleanly into the river.

"Shit," Michael muttered. "Suspect in the water," he told the team. "Visibility low."

He dropped his gear with a quick release of his tactical belt. One deputy shouted, "Harris, wait!"

No time. Clara was almost gone. He saw her surface—then slip back under.

Big mistake, Clara. Michael was a former Navy SEAL. The water was his domain.

"I'm going in," he said. He yanked out his earpiece and dove.

Silence enveloped him. He swam hard, reading the current, feeling for movement, sensing her trail.

She surfaced—and he was right there.

She screamed. "Agent Harris? Oh my God—someone was chasing me! I think Garrett's trying to kill me!"

"Save it," he snapped, grabbing her arm.

She kicked out, aiming for his groin. He twisted just in time to avoid the worst of the pain, but her heel hit the sensitive area between his groin and leg. Pain flared, but he grunted and held tight.

She struggled like a wildcat, trying to break free while also trying to drag him under. "You're drowning me!" she shrieked. "Let me go!"

He held fast, even as she dove again, slippery and vicious. Her nails raked his face, then his shoulder, her hands pushing him down with surprising strength.

He broke the surface, gasping.

Then—she went limp. A dead weight.

It was almost comical. Like a toddler pretending to faint to avoid bedtime.

She was easier to tow that way. He hauled her onto the bank, soaked and silent. The two deputies arrived just as he dropped her onto the grass.

She lay still, eyes closed.

"No one believes the act, Clara," Michael said. "You're under arrest."

She bolted up and tried to dive back into the channel.

Michael lunged, caught her mid-motion. The deputies handcuffed her as she screamed, "I want a lawyer! You can't do this! I want a lawyer!"

Michael stared at her, wet, bleeding, and breathing hard. He felt a grim sense of satisfaction knowing the killer was finally in custody. But beneath that, anger simmered, a deep ache for the lives she had taken.

He read Clara Dolan her rights.

SATURDAY

42

Kara rarely slept in, but the sun was already streaming through her blinds and the smell of coffee filled her small house when she woke up Saturday morning.

Coffee. Someone had made her coffee.

She climbed out of bed and pulled on her pajama bottoms that were tangled in the bedsheets. Her leg itched and there was still lingering pain, but she walked almost without a limp. She'd have a nasty scar, but Kara honestly didn't care. It wouldn't be the first scar on her body.

She brushed her teeth, then followed her nose all the way to the kitchen, where Matt handed her a steaming cup of rich-smelling coffee.

"Yum," she said and sipped. "The first sip is always the best."

He leaned over and kissed her. "I would have made break-fast, but you have no food."

"When did I have time to shop?"

"We'll fix that today."

They'd returned to Virginia Thursday morning, leaving the

team split between South Carolina and Florida to deal with the paperwork and the jurisdictional nightmare that the case had become. Yesterday they both had follow-ups with their respective doctors and were told light duty for two weeks, then another checkup before they were cleared. Kara surprisingly wasn't all that angry about being sidelined. She needed the break.

Then the debrief with Tony Greer yesterday, which went better than she expected. There hadn't been much they'd done wrong—being shot with tranquilizer darts took decision-making out of their hands—though he was displeased that they'd joined the team on the raid in South Carolina when they hadn't been cleared by medical. And he wasn't happy that the FBI was getting a bill from an ambulance company for a three-hour ride.

By the time they returned to Kara's house in Alexandria, they were exhausted, ordered pizza delivery, and collapsed into bed.

Now, Matt said, "Catherine and Chris are on their way over."

Surprisingly, that thought didn't fill Kara with dread. She glanced at the clock and realized it was after nine. She *never* slept in until nine. She couldn't remember the last time she'd slept past six.

"They have a housewarming present, and Catherine will fill us in on what's been going on with the case."

Thirty minutes later, Catherine and Chris arrived with their twelve-year-old daughter, Lizzy. They chatted for a few minutes, eating donuts that the Jones family brought, while Matt brewed a fresh pot of coffee. Then Chris took Lizzy for a walk along the river to give the team time to talk in private. Kara had lucked out. The park across the street was protected, so her front yard had an (almost) unobstructed view of the Potomac. Her lot was unusually large and odd-shaped for the neighborhood, and one of the few houses that wasn't a townhouse. And because of a historical designation on the location (not the house, which had burned down a hundred years ago and been rebuilt), no one could develop it into townhomes. She'd been very lucky that her condo in Santa Monica had appreciated nicely before she sold it so that she could afford this special place.

The house needed a lot of work, but it had a solid foundation and privacy while also being in the middle of town. It was exactly what Kara wanted.

They sat at her kitchen table—one of the few pieces of furniture she had other than her bed—drank coffee, and ate a second donut, this time a bear claw.

"A lot of people want to prosecute Clara," Catherine said. "We're taking the first crack, however. Kidnapping and murder across state lines gives us jurisdiction, and the AUSA is eager. She's been working closely with DA Anson in Flagler, so I think it'll work out between the two jurisdictions."

"She's not going to get off on a technicality, is she?" Kara asked.

"Anything can happen," Catherine said, "but Nathan Graves positively identified her as the woman who kidnapped him and his mother, and Franklin Graves gave a statement about the blackmail. The kidnapping of a minor child alone is plenty to keep her locked up, but the fact that she has the resources to disappear and had, in fact, been planning to do so, which we can prove, will likely keep her behind bars without bail."

"Lily's going to be okay, right?" Matt asked.

"Yes. She should be released tomorrow or Monday at the latest. She said you saved her life."

"We both did," Matt said, looking at Kara.

"Did Jim find anything to tie Clara or the victims to the factory?" Kara asked Catherine.

"She actually owned it through her LLC, but that alone won't convict her. He confirmed other DNA present, but is still awaiting tests to match physical evidence to each of the victims," Catherine said. "The biggest find was her phone—she didn't wipe it. She had an outside server that linked to her phone, which still had recordings from the factory and the farmhouse on it, including a recording of one of the victims who fell to his death. There is also blood evidence on two different boats that Clara had access to—the one at the house on Kiawah Island, and the one at the house in Savannah. The blood is also being tested against the victims. Ryder is working with other jurisdictions from California to Florida putting together other possible victims, but those might be harder to prove. What won't be hard to prove is her honey trap scheme. Zack found evidence that multiple married men have been paying into one of her LLCs going back ten years, the one called SmartGirl Business."

"She has more than one?" Kara asked.

"At least three."

"Ten years—that's before she left Los Angeles," Matt said.

"She's extorted millions from at least nineteen men."

"Are any of them going to testify?" Matt said.

Kara snorted. "They paid to hide an affair from their wives. Why come forward now?"

"We know their identities based on the wire transfers," Catherine said, "so they'll be contacted as they may become part of the record. I don't know whether they will be asked to testify or be subpoenaed. That's way down the road. And they would be considered victims of extortion, so the court may determine that their identities can remain hidden from the public."

"Were they drugged?" Kara thought about what Franklin had said. That he didn't drink alcohol and didn't succumb to Clara's seduction, but he saw her put something in his soda water. She didn't know if she believed him, but Lily had.

"I don't know. Clara was a beautiful, manipulative seductress."

"Do you think Franklin was lying? That he really did sleep with her, and then she blackmailed him to not tell his wife? Because why would Clara wait years before reaching out to him?"

Catherine thought about it, then shook her head. "I think he was telling the truth. The reason Clara targeted him was because he rejected her. She is not used to rejection, doesn't expect it. When I spoke to him yesterday on the phone, we went over everything again, and he said that he had threatened to report her for drugging his drink. So it was rejection coupled with a threat that I think made him a target. She would have gotten her revenge one way or the other."

"Still, nearly eight years . . . that's a long time to hold a grudge."

"Not for Clara Dolan," Catherine said.

"Did they find Garrett's body?" Matt asked.

Catherine shook her head.

"Maybe he planned the whole thing," Kara said. "And is now on a beach in the Caribbean drinking mai tais."

"He's listed as missing and presumed dead, but if they don't find his remains, they'll change it to missing and he might make the Top Ten Wanted list," Catherine said.

"Was the information he shared helpful in finding Becca's body?" Kara asked.

"I haven't heard back from Ventura County yet," Catherine said. "Ryder would know more, since he's been coordinating with law enforcement from other jurisdictions."

Catherine rose, said, "I like your house. It has a lot of potential."

"Thank you," Kara said. "It's going to be a work in progress, but being chained to the desk for a week or two means I can spend some time figuring out what to do first. And thanks for the dishes. I really like them."

"Matt said you were eating on paper plates. You can trade the plates in for any of the colors they have, the gift receipt is in the box."

"I like the white. It'll go with whatever color I decide to paint the kitchen." The kitchen had god-awful wallpaper and while Kara didn't cook much, she liked to eat, so wanted her kitchen to be comfortable.

Chris and Lizzy were coming up the walk, so Catherine hugged Matt, then Kara. "This could have been so much worse."

"We know," Matt said. "But it wasn't." He took Kara's hand.

An hour later they were showered, dressed, and about to head to the grocery store when Jim, Michael, and Ryder showed up together in two cars.

"Sloane wished she could be here," Michael said, "but she flew out early this morning for Montana. Her parents' fortieth wedding anniversary party is tonight."

"I completely forgot," Matt said.

"It's not like you had anything else on your mind," Jim said. He hugged Kara. "It's so good to see you, kid."

They hadn't actually seen each other after the rescue. Jim had stayed in Georgia to help process the factory and only returned late last night.

"I don't have a lot of furniture yet," Kara said.

"You don't have any furniture," Michael muttered.

"Hey, I literally moved in one week before we went on assignment in Florida. Cut me some slack. I have a table and a bed. All I do is eat and sleep here anyway."

She gave Matt a sly glance. They did a lot more than sleep last night in the bed.

She led them to her large ugly kitchen, where they sat at the country table that had been left with the house. It had been built for the space, and the previous owner had asked if Kara wanted it. Big yes, since as Michael said she had no furniture.

Michael looked around. "I can help with any DIY projects."

"I'm holding you to that," Kara said. "The floors are in great shape, but need refinishing. The walls are yuck, so that's probably my first thing. The kitchen needs updating, but I saw something on this home and garden show where you can refinish cabinets pretty easily and fairly cheap."

Matt offered coffee. Jim and Michael accepted. Jim took one of the last donuts from Catherine's box.

"You actually watched an episode of home and garden?" Michael said with a smirk.

She stuck her tongue out at him.

"I have some news," Ryder said. "Ventura County Sheriff's Department found female remains in the area Garrett indicated. They're exhuming them now and we should have a definitive answer in a few days."

"At least her family can have closure," Kara said.

"Los Angeles FBI spoke to the Masters family. We're having local offices reach out to all the victims' families to give them a status report on the investigation."

"Has any other motive been uncovered?" Matt asked. "She targeted Emily Masters Henderson because she knew her, but what about the other two couples?"

"None have surfaced. They don't appear to have ever met," Ryder said. "But we're continuing to look. Catherine believes that the other couples were targeted partly to mask her motive for killing Emily, but also because the women reminded Clara of Emily and her success, or because the women reminded Clara of Becca. Clara hasn't talked. Catherine is going to have a sit-down with her on Monday. I'm sure you can observe," Ryder added.

Kara shrugged. "I don't care why. I never want to see that woman again."

"Catherine also said they both likely enjoyed setting up the abandoned factory and creating elaborate and deadly traps, but for Garrett with his mechanical background it was a challenge, and for Clara it was more likely to watch her victims' psychological torment."

"Sick," she muttered.

"Speaking of the factory," Matt said, turning to Jim. "Catherine said you uncovered forensic evidence."

Jim nodded. "Quite a bit. Enough to keep her in prison. They had to have spent days—maybe weeks—setting up the traps. Some were ingenious, some were basic but effective. It's in line with Garrett's background. He had been an engineering student at one point, and everything we've learned about him is that he has above average mechanical skills. Most of the traps we believe he created, but Catherine thinks they were Clara's ideas. The Jacksonville ERT unit is staying on site to assist the sheriff's department, and we brought in a local contractor with heavy equipment. It's going to take another week, at least."

"How did she make the house explode?" Kara asked. "Lily and Nathan were there for days before it went boom."

"Arson investigators are still going over the wreckage, but from what they could determine, she had a chemical time bomb."

"Which is—?" Kara asked.

"A plastic bottle with a tiny hole that slowly dripped out a lye solution into one of the main support beams in the basement. The lye eroded the beam, but it takes time—anywhere from three to ten days."

"And then it explodes?"

"No, that didn't cause the explosion. When the kitchen floor collapsed and the stove was ripped out of the wall, a spark caused the gas to ignite. There was a propane tank too close to the house—it was old and not up to code. You have a guardian angel on your shoulder, Matt."

Kara shook her head. "She told Lily she would let them go. That lying bitch."

Matt took her hand and squeezed it. "So there's enough evidence to keep her behind bars?" he said.

"Oh, yeah. And Zack is still going over her finances—did Catherine tell you about the extortion?"

Matt nodded. "Good work," he said. "Great work. You all came through during a difficult time. Tony wants a meeting with our legal rep on Wednesday. We're going to be talking about probable cause and procedures and it's going to be a slap that we don't deserve. But everyone needs to be there."

"Sloane will be back Tuesday morning," Ryder said.

"I'm heading to Dallas," Jim said as he got up. "Ryder was kind enough to offer to take me to the airport. I'll be back Tuesday night. After a week like this, I need to see my family."

The three men left, and Matt put his arm around Kara. "This case is going to weigh on all of us for a long time."

"We'll bounce back," Kara said. "The team really went above and beyond." She kissed him, then made a move to grab her keys. He pulled her back to him.

"I thought we were going to the grocery store?" Kara said.

He kissed her. "We will." He kissed her again and backed her down the hall into her bedroom. "In an hour. Or two."

MONDAY

43

Catherine sat across from Clara Dolan in the federal detention center. She had been denied bail this morning, and was now in a sour mood. Her lawyer sat next to her, a young private practice junior partner who worked for a big Florida firm. Catherine suspected they would stay with Clara as long as she could pay them; she had plenty of money, but may go through her entire trust. Already, she'd put her properties on the market. One of the LLCs—the one that had multiple men paying into it after Clara blackmailed them—had been frozen because of the extortion, but the AUSA couldn't make the case for the other LLCs because Clara's trust fund had been lawful.

"I don't have to talk to you," Clara snapped, the chains at her wrists rattling.

Clara did not look good in orange. Somehow, that pleased Catherine.

"No, you don't," Catherine agreed. "But I'm the forensic psychiatrist who will be an expert witness for the prosecution at your trial. The more I know about you, the more I can determine if you're mentally diminished or fully responsible for your crimes."

"I'm not stupid," Clara said.

"No, you're not."

Catherine waited.

Her lawyer said, "You can go back to your cell if you wish. You don't have to speak with her."

Clara blanched at the mention of her cell. Catherine had suspected that taking away her freedom would be a devastating blow to the woman. She expected to always do what she wanted, when she wanted.

Catherine really wanted to know why. What was the trigger? The cons, the honey traps, even killing Becca McCarthy, Catherine understood. But why Emily Masters and the others?

But to get her to talk, Catherine needed to be sneaky. She needed to appeal to Clara's vanity and her deep need to be seen as intelligent—then tell her that she wasn't.

"For more than seven years you held a grudge against Emily Masters. You must have planned this for a long time. And if you'd ended with her and her husband, walked away, I don't think we would have ever caught you. Another unsolved murder. But then you targeted the Blairs. The Avilas. And the FBI is really good at catching serial killers who are so obvious with their victim choices."

Clara snorted, didn't speak.

"Taking two federal agents was really not very smart," Catherine said.

Clara reddened, remained silent.

"Do you want to go?" the lawyer asked. The firm should have sent a senior partner, someone who would have shut this down and walked Clara out of the interview room.

"No," she said, then turned to Catherine. "Hypothetically, because I'm not admitting to anything."

"Hypothetically," Catherine agreed.

"Emily had always been a stuck-up snob who thought she was better than me—I mean, better than everyone. Is it any surprise that when she bragged about bagging some rich dufus and moving to Florida that someone might take offense?"

"So you stalked her, found out where she was going on her honeymoon, and set up the factory just for her."

"Nope," Clara said, gloating. "Not going there."

"No, it wasn't the factory, not at first," Catherine said. She'd read Matt and Kara's reports multiple times. "You brought her to the farmhouse. Which I bet you bought because of that cage in the basement."

Clara grinned, but didn't speak.

"We found her wedding ring outside the house," Catherine said. "Tying Emily to the farmhouse."

Clara shrugged.

"So you convinced Garrett to set up the factory. Because we both know you didn't have the brains to set up those elaborate traps and pitfalls."

"I'm smart enough to do anything!" she snapped. "Garrett had no imagination, he just—" She stopped talking.

"He had fun with it," Catherine said. "Maybe got into it because you convinced him that Emily had hurt you, that she was your arch enemy. And when they died, you thought oh, maybe someone will know that you knew her, so you targeted another, similar couple. I don't even think you knew you were targeting women who looked like Becca McCarthy." The realization hit Catherine just then. Each woman looked more and more like Becca, until Kara, who could have been her sister. They had thought "blonde, blue" but it was more than that.

Clara hated the women because she thought they might remind *Garrett* of Becca, so she wanted to not only kill them, but have Garrett participate in their murders as a form of subtle manipulation. If Garrett killed women who looked like Becca, she could imagine that he was with her when she killed Becca all those years ago. She could convince herself that he *would* have killed her.

"I don't even know who you're talking about," Clara said. She tried to cross her arms in front of her, but her wrists were chained to the ring on the table.

"Ventura County Sheriff's Department found Becca McCarthy's body near Sespe Creek. They're running tests, but so far everything matches Becca."

Clara's lips twitched into a smile, but she didn't say a word. She was pleased with herself. No remorse for her actions.

"Lily and her son will make a full recovery," Catherine said. "You're really lucky there. My team was skeptical about my analysis. Some of them thought Franklin had slept with you and you blackmailed him to help Garrett, but no. You'd always planned on killing him and his family for the crime of rejecting you."

Clara suddenly slammed her fists down on the table. "*No one* has ever rejected me."

"That's not true. Your mother. Your father. They didn't know what to do with you because you were so different from them."

"Arrogant jerks. Both of them. Mother's probably hiding in her big house not wanting to face anyone. *Oh, your daughter was arrested! Oh, you poor dear.*" Clara laughed. Then she couldn't stop.

The lawyer looked worried.

When Clara's laughter turned to giggles, Catherine said, "If you make a full confession, from Becca McCarthy to the present, I'll talk to the AUSA about not charging the death penalty. You'll get life in prison."

"I'm not going to prison," Clara said with a smirk. "Garrett did everything. I was forced to help."

"No jury will believe that."

Suddenly, Clara looked panicked, her eyes wide, and the tears came, almost on cue. "He, he would hurt me. I loved him—I just wanted to make him happy! I'm so sorry, I'm so sorry, I would never have done anything like this. It's awful!"

Then, as quickly as the tears came, they were gone.

Now Catherine laughed. "We have evidence, Clara. Your games won't work here. You have federal charges. If you slip away? Florida. Then multiple states will get a shot at prosecuting you for nearly two dozen criminal blackmail schemes. A wrongful death charge in Scottsdale—yeah, you think you got away scot-free there? Think again. And there are a few other suspicious deaths at resorts while you worked there. DNA was collected, and we now have yours." Catherine rose. "And then you'll face the case of killing Becca McCarthy. So even if you get off on all these cases, it'll take years. So don't be so smug, because my guess? The federal jury is going to convict you on all counts."

She walked out. She'd had enough. She wished she never had to see Clara Dolan again. At least, not until her trial.

She could rot in prison for all Catherine cared.

EPILOGUE

Garrett had followed the legal case of Clara Dolan for the past four months. He wasn't going to get another chance.

He'd considered disappearing. That would be the smart thing to do. The unemotional thing to do. The police thought he was dead . . . or they didn't. He didn't know; he didn't care.

But Becca deserved justice.

It was nearly time.

No one really saw the homeless, so he lay on a bench, face unshaven, hat pulled low, layers of dirty old clothing. And he waited.

He knew the police in Ventura County had found Becca's remains. Her family would have closure, a body to bury. At least he had done one good thing before he finished it.

He had a prepaid cell phone with one number he'd put in it. He dialed it now.

"Quinn," the female voice answered.

"Hello, Kara."

A long silence. Then: "Garrett?"

"She was going to kill me. The boat was rigged to explode when it reached a certain speed—she knew I would come by water—so I disabled it. But she had a backup plan, so I bailed."

"You need to turn yourself in."

"I am."

"Good."

"But first things first. Thank you for following up and finding Becca's body."

"That was the local police."

"They listened to you."

"It was a good lead."

"Are you still with that fed?"

"I am."

"Good." He paused, saw the van pull up to the side entrance.

"What are you planning, Garrett?"

"Take care of yourself, Kara."

"Gar—"

He ended the call and tossed the phone into the trash can. He rose, shuffled along the pathway, head down, hand clutched around the gun in the paper bag.

People saw what they wanted to see. They saw a drunk bum, or they looked right through him.

The side of the van opened.

He continued to shuffle forward. Slowly. Don't attract attention.

Two corrections officers escorted Audrey from the van to the side entrance of the courthouse. They barely noticed him.

"Audrey," he said, not raising his voice.

She heard him. Recognized him.

He fired three bullets at her, making sure one hit her in the head. In case she was wearing a vest.

He dropped the gun and fell to his knees, hands up before the officers had unholstered their weapons. Audrey lay bleeding only feet from him. Half her beautiful face was gone, showing the ugly underneath the surface.

He smiled.

Game over, Audrey.

I won.

★ ★ ★ ★ ★

ACKNOWLEDGMENTS

I am always grateful for everyone who helps me research for my books. Sometimes, my questions are so bizarre that I worry they think I'm losing my mind, but I still get answers I need!

As always, if I get something wrong, it's not their fault. Either I misinterpreted their answer or changed it for story purposes. While I always strive to be as authentic as possible, I write fiction and my goal is first to entertain.

Crime Scene Writers has been my go-to group for so many law enforcement, legal, and forensic questions. Who knew there were so many experts out there willing to help writers? In particular, Wally Lind, Wesley Harris, John Robinson, and Brooke Terpening were super helpful in their areas of expertise, mostly related to criminal law. Thank you so much—I hope I make you all proud! And if not . . . I'll do better next time!

Retired ATF Agent Rick McMahon has always answered my myriad explosive questions through the years, and this time he really saved my bacon when I ran through a couple scenarios in my story and none of them would have worked. In writing, sometimes, less is more . . . and sometimes a bomb is not actually a bomb. Thank you for being such a great sounding board.

Historically, after more than fifty books, if I get something really wrong it's medical. It's always my fault—trust me on that! But I do endeavor to get these things right, and Dr. Doug Lyle, fellow author and all-around great guy, helps me work through my medical problems with the patience of a saint.

I'm also lucky to have a cousin by marriage who is an emergency room nurse! DeeDee Gifford has helped me get the details right in many of my books, even when I give her an impossible situation . . . like I did with this book. Thank you so much!

But you know who really shined helping me this time around? My husband. I am not a mechanically inclined individual, and Dan can fix anything. I literally make shit up for a living, and my experts help me make it realistic. I ran through all my wild ideas for the deadly escape factory with my husband, and he helped me weed through the ideas that just wouldn't work at all . . . and those that were plausible. He also explained how and why they would work (or not work), but I ignored most of that. Because sometimes, less is more.

I am very proud of this book. We're not supposed to have favorites, but this is one of my favorites. Thank you to my editors April Osborn and Dina Davis—especially Dina, who pushes me to be the best writer and storyteller I can be. Thank you to the art department for the amazing covers in the Quinn & Costa series—again, you knocked it out of the park. Thank you to Justine Sha for helping to get the word out for my books, and the entire team at HarperCollins and Hanover Square Press.

And always, I thank my agent Dan Conaway, who is my anchor in the storm of publishing; his assistant, Sydnee Harlan, who hit the ground running last year and hasn't slowed down; and everyone at Writers House who helps us authors navigate through good times and bad. Fifteen years down . . . here's a toast to at least fifteen more.